No. 1.9.x   [PRICE 1 *RUP.*

WORLDS' FAIR

TRAVELOGUES FOR THE INDEPENDENT SPIRIT

Presents...

THEATRE
OF THE GODS

BEING THE STORY OF M. FRANCISCO FABRIGAS:
EXPLORER, PHYSICIST, TRANSMARINER.
WHO TRAVELLED BEYOND THE BORDERS OF
HIS UNIVERSE, WAS SHIPWRECKED THERE ...

... AND RETURNED

A Splendidly Illustrated Volume for Fireside or Travel
Bound in a Peculiarly Elegant and Novel Manner ...

Written by Volcannon

With Illuminations and Ephemera for
the Delightment of the Reader

HEROIC ADVENTURES, MYTHICAL JOURNEYS,
CATACLYSMIC ODYSSEYS AND GRAND MORTAL
FOLLIES. FOR COUNTLESS GENERATIONS
THE WORLDS' FAIR EDITIONS
HAVE GIVEN DISCERNING READERS CLASSIC
TRAVELOGUES FROM THE HUMAN EMPIRES.

TRANSLATED AND PUBLISHED BY
BLACKLIST PUBLISHING LTD
YEAR 598 MD

BLACKLIST

'THE FORBIDDEN, THE FORGOTTEN, THE CONDEMNED'

19/478 MONSOON HEIGHTS

THE OCTOGON

HYDRABAX

Published
by
Jonathan
Cape 2013
2 4 6 8 10 9 7 5 3 1
Copyright ©
M. Suddain 2013
M. Suddain has
asserted his right under the
Copyright, Designs and
Patents Act 1988 to be identified
as the author of this work.

First published in Great Britain in 2013 by Jonathan Cape, Random House, 20 Vauxhall Bridge Road, London SW1V 2SA. www.vintage-books.co.uk. Addresses for companies within The Random House Group Limited can be found at: www.randomhouse.co.uk/offices.htm. The Random House Group Limited Reg. No. 954009. A CIP catalogue record for this book is available from the British Library

ISBN 9780224097062

The Random House Group Limited supports the Forest Stewardship Council® (FSC®), the leading international forest-certification organisation. Our books carrying the FSC label are printed on FSC®-certified paper. FSC is the only forest-certification scheme supported by the leading environmental organisations, including Greenpeace. Our paper procurement policy can be found at www.randomhouse.co.uk/environment

Printed and bound in Great Britain by Clays Ltd, St Ives plc

PUBLISHER'S NOTE

'Destroying a book is not the same as destroying a human life,' argued the artificial philosopher Photozeiger. 'It is much more serious. For when you end the life of a book you destroy the ideas of countless thinkers who inspired it, and condemn future generations to darkness and ignorance.'

At Blacklist Publishing we dedicate our lives to saving censored, suppressed and orphaned works: 'The Forbidden, the Forgotten, the Condemned'. As such, we are proud to present this edition of *Theatre of the Gods*. It is one title from a grand travelogue series, 'Worlds' Fair' – arguably the most famous and widely read of its age. It was rare for a home library of the time not to contain even a few titles from 'The Fair' – as it was commonly called. And yet *Gods* is one title from the series few will ever have read. Its subject had been sentenced to death *in absentia* as a traitor and heretic. The book was banned soon after publication, denounced by the publishers, and even the author, who risked his life to track down the explorer M. Francisco Fabrigas and record his confessions, was blacklisted, and forced into exile, simply for suggesting that his hero may have been misunderstood.

His work raises many questions. How was an itinerate writer able to locate the greatest fugitive in the universe when all the agencies in his Empire could not? Is what he transcribes the truth? Part truth? Anything but? Volcannon claims to have researched this voyage to the finest detail, and yet he takes bold liberties: embellishing episodes, recreating conversations for which there is no record or surviving witnesses. Did Volcannon embellish Fabrigas's story? Did he invent their entire meeting, even? We will never know. Upon publication he too was accused of treason. He vanished into exile. He would never write another title for 'Worlds' Fair'.

We have done our best to translate and present this complex work as accurately as possible so that you may judge for yourself. The original *Gods* would of course have been a hyper-dimensional text, giving the purchaser an immersive, 'omni-sensual' reading experience. Sadly, this data has been lost, leaving us only the flattened text – the 'book-data', if you will. Are words upon a page enough to hold a reader's attention? We'll let you be the judge.

The original edition would have featured hyper-illustrations, borders, miniatures and ornamental scrolling type typical of illuminated manuscripts of its time, found today only in dedicated hypertext museums. Sadly, all the illustrations from the original edition have been lost. Nevertheless, we think it is a fine oddity. This is, after all, the job of the historical publisher: to recover frail embers from the flames of history, and to carry them, carefully, to the fires of our own age, so that we might have some grasp of the grand sweep of time, and also a sense that, though our lives are brief sparks, each has its moment within the epic story of human existence.

Onward!

M. Suddain

Blacklist Publishing Ltd

THEATRE OF THE GODS

CONTENTS

ILLUSTRATIONS

[Missing from this edition.]

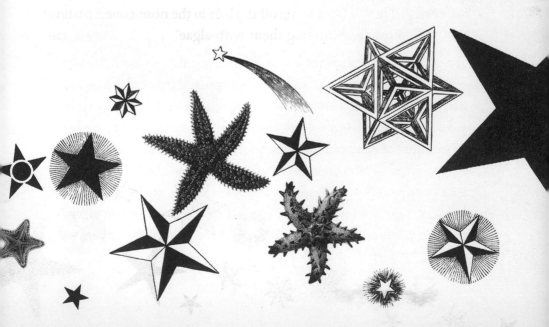

A NOTE FROM THE AUTHOR

What can we really know about truth? Reality? You are reading a book – that much is true. It is a book based upon the confessions of one of the greatest living souls of all time / space. Although whether my subject is still living (indeed, whether he is even *in* time / space) remains a mystery.

Whether M. Francisco Fabrigas really was the greatest human explorer will be debated by scholars for generations, while the issue of whether the human creature even possesses a 'soul' is an argument which might survive time / space itself.

So let's just say you are about to read a book. And if, in fact, this book is about to be read *to* you, well . . . let's all say nothing of it.

*

'Every word you hear about me is a lie! Even these ones!' So said M. Francisco Fabrigas: explorer, philosopher, heretical physicist, mystic, transmariner, cosmic *flâneur*. 'Do not believe a single word I say, for they come from the inky black tongue of a desperate fool. Me!' Imagine the mad old man sprawled across the filthy table as he says these words – of which only every second one, at best, is true. 'I came from another universe!' the fool rasps in a voice like a bare branch clawing at a window. 'I was a great explorer. I was shipwrecked seventy-nine times. I caught sleeping fever, laughing sickness, bohemian rhapsody. I almost died in the jungles of Dyspepsia, where there are so many tribes of cannibals it often rains teeth! I stared into the eye of the tyranykon, the triple-headed mastodon, I stared into the fiery eye of hell!'

But don't believe him. Or at best believe only some of what he tells you. The strange and impossible stories. How he escaped a gang of mind-pirates by lining his hat with foil and singing love songs. How he lived in the stomach of a dinosaur plant, surviving on rations found in the pockets of decomposing sailors. All lies. And then the most fantastical story: how he agreed to undertake a voyage beyond this universe for the glory of the Empire. How he went to the next universe with a boy who couldn't hear, and a girl who couldn't see. How he lost the brave deaf boy, and the cunning blind girl, had to watch as they were cast into a black hole, their very atoms pulverised by unfathomable forces. How he returned to this universe alone, to live a broken man, in this house, on this orphan moon, to tell these stories – of which perhaps one on every page is a complete and utter lie. You should read every single word in this book, and think very hard, because it is a good story, and because every single word, even these very words, are true.

★

It is no lie that M. Francisco Fabrigas possessed one of the most brilliant and inventive minds of his age. He mastered seventy-eight languages and claimed to dream in forty-six – though he seldom slept more than one or two hours in a night. He had a photographic memory, a phonographic memory, and a bibliographic memory – he never forgot a single thing he read. He invented the X-ray photokamera, the four-dimensional compass, the radio-chronomatic receiver (a device with which you can hear the past – which is useful if you want to settle a thousand-year-old argument). He patented an anaesthetic hat for inducing sleep in patients and loud children, as well as a device for communicating with human babies (which, in the end, only proved that babies know very little about anything, and an awful lot about nothing). He was also the first human to realise that there were other universes – most likely an infinite number – and that it might be possible for people to travel there. He was the first to go beyond the membrane of his universe and return alive. Where he went after that has been a profound mystery.

After fruitless years spent trying to solve the mystery of M. Francisco Fabrigas, I became desperate. I was down to a single clue – obscure, laughably speculative – but I followed it anyway, and it led me all the way to a remote and deadly region of space. There I was caught in a solar storm and forced to crash-land on an orphan moon. And how fateful that I did. I found myself near a wrecked mansion above a disused uranium mine beside a sea lorded over by mighty serpents. The mansion was vast and crumbling, its roof torn open, its windward wall split like a serpent's gullet, disgorging ancient furniture and priceless rugs down the face of a cliff. Upstairs in the master bedroom I found the doors to the balcony open. Two elegantly dressed skeletons still sat there in their rocking chairs, staring out to sea.

The stair wood sang like crickets as I went into the cellar vault, expecting to find nothing, but finding in the darkness, surrounded by the rotting casks and family urns, an old, old figure (though with the passing of the years he was now more beard than man). I cannot forget a thing about him: his great height, his formidable presence – even in that decaying state – and those legendary eyes: eyes that seem to be looking out from the dawn of time, and on towards infinity. For days I could not get him even to acknowledge my presence. Eventually he rose from his stupor, looked around him and said, 'This is not my house. How did I get here?' and as if in answer the breakers smashed upon the stones below, and the serpents cried, just as they'd done for endless centuries.

After weeks of effort I was able to fully break him from his trance and encourage him to tell me his version of a tale I knew well from other sources: the story of the Great Crossing – the first time a human being was able to leave his own universe, and return. I carefully took down every word he said, every curse and every mutter, the whole rambling adventure: the brave deaf boy, the cunning and beautiful blind girl – though he was continuously interrupting his own story to cry, 'Lies! It's all lies! What is life but a web of lies!' I bore witness to his great suffering. Over the course of weeks, as he retold his story, the old man became more unstable, particularly as his tale reached its terrible conclusion, with the casting of the two innocents into the jaws of a black hole. Certainly, the old man never *saw* these children torn to bits by the forces of the abyss. He watched only as they fell, arms in the shape of a plane, towards the gnashing jaws of space. He could not watch the last bit. He had to look away and bite his finger . . . *nghn!* But if there's one thing we all know it's that no person can survive being thrown into a black hole. That's simply the way things are. Oh, I know what you're thinking now: this is just an author's trick. We think they're going to die at the end, these beautiful children, but in a final twist they'll both be saved. Listen to me very carefully. Come closer so I can lower my voice to a whisper as I tell you: that . . . will never . . . happen. There is no way that some brave fool will sweep in, scoop the children up in his strong arms. This isn't like the moving cinemagraphs where the heroes live, the villains die, and everyone has cake. This is life.

One night, during a terrible storm which threw itself against the mansion, I challenged the old master on a point of fact – a contradiction between two versions of events. The ancient man flew into a rage, suddenly accusing me of plotting to distract him from his studies. In a fury, Time's Traitor seized my notes, intending to throw them on the fire. I managed to snatch most of them away and leap through a window as he hurled antique clocks and vases after me. I hid for several days.

★

Upon my return I found the mansion empty. There was no sign of any craft landing there, no footprints around the house or on the shore. On his table I found, held in place by an oily stone from the shore, a brief note:

If the ages say something about me, let it be this:
That within this common shipwrecke I, above all life's servants, was uncommonly placed to observe the secret beauty hid in ordinary things.
If they say something else, let it be that I was handsome.

M.F.F.

The story of M. Francisco Fabrigas and the Great Crossing is a strange and wonderful tale and I've done my best to present it as it was told to me by the old master. I have spent an ungodly amount of time fleshing out his confessions, following the path of the *Necronaut* and its crew of misfits, speaking to eyewitnesses, hunting down fragments of journals and news stories, checking and rechecking every detail, and compiling a meticulous account of this historic human voyage through the Omnicosmos. For what it's worth, I believe the old man really did undertake an expedition to the next universe, aided by a handsome deaf boy and a beautiful and cunning blind girl. He failed, of course, and the children died horribly. But I hope you enjoy this story anyway. For as I said earlier, practically every word is true, others less so, and some, like these, are not true at all.

Yours in greatness,

V. V. S. Volcannon

This book is dedicated to the Sweety, proof of nature's utter incomprehensibility: a creature who torments the heavens, who lives in steaming darkness on a cyclopean moon in a forgotten corner of a deserted universe, whose dread cry – like the sound of a thousand whales gargling marbles in the hull of an iron ship – haunts the soul and wrecks the sleep of beasts and children, whose suckered tendrils grope the depths of space to pull hapless ships to its reeking belly, but who does it all, at the end of the day, for love.

Volcannon

THEATRE OF THE GODS

ENCOUNTER

Two encounters in deepest space. The first, terrifying enough; the second, far too terrifying for those involved.

The *MOS-DEF*, a research vessel on a mission to find a species of space leech thought to contain plague antibodies, finds not a leech. Their leader, a doctor, a passionate man who has given his entire life to this mission, stands for thirty-nine nautical hours on the observation deck. He does not move. His men bring him chocolate, he will not drink. His men bring him blankets, he cares not for warmth. Finally, when the doctor calls back that he can see a giant squid, the crew prepare to sedate him.

They are all surprised to find a live squid just off their bow (though not as surprised as the squid). The beast is vast, pinkish-blue, and gazes at them with sad, wet eyes. It floats calmly, its tentacles wave softly. When the ship pulls close with nets it surrenders like a baby. When the squid is examined, the barnacles and starfish scraped from its soft flanks, the scientists determine that there is nothing at all strange about the squid. Except that it isn't from our universe. Our space cannot support a beast like this. Which is in itself, they have to admit, very strange.

The squid has nothing to say.

But to the second and far more terrifying event. Three years later, in another dark region of space, the *Vangelis*, a warship thrown off course when its navigation equipment malfunctions, discovers a ship.

It is a galleon – the kind built for sailing on terrestrial seas, yet somehow cast adrift in space. Its sails are shredded by the ages, but its rig is set for a steady sea wind (though of course there is no sea wind where this ship has found itself). When the crew of the *Vangelis* venture aboard they find the boat deserted. There are bowls of food on the table, a pot of soup still on the stove, all preserved by the icy cold of space. They can make no sense of the language in the ship's log, or in the passengers' journals, or in the children's picture books they find, and the maps in the navigation room are a guide to seas unknown. There is no explanation for what the ship is doing in this part of the universe – or for what it was doing in this universe at all. 'A ghost ship!' someone cries. He is an idiot. The truth is far, far stranger.

In the storage bay the crew find a small girl frozen in a block of ice.

*

There is near-mutiny at the captain's suggestion that they bring the ship home. Captain Descharge has to whip two men before anyone will agree to go near the frozen creature. A skeleton crew stays aboard, some blubbing quietly, some clutching holy books, and none able to look upon the ghastly cell of ice. And well they should be terrified, for within that icy sepulchre it is possible to see the corpse at rest, her pale hands enfolded 'cross her chest. Her eyes are open, her breathless lips a dreadful blue. She is dead, most certainly. Most certainly.

And yet . . .

*

Her death is incomplete. For if you would happen to walk up to that silvery block, put a hand upon the ice, or (for the heavens forbid) put your ear to it, you would hear, faintly, the knocking of a living heart.

Tests reveal that the girl has been suspended in the ice for as little as ten thousand average human life spans, and as many as a million. The royal physicians thaw her slowly, slowly, as word drips and trickles out around the Empire, passing from lip to lip in ghastly croaks. 'A girl. Frozen in ice but not dead! It is an omen, most certainly. The end is coming!' Each day an inch of water pools around the foot of the physicians' steel table, and every drop is kept, because these doctors know it can be put in bottles and sold to the wealthy for unholy sums.

As the ice falls away, as the bergs shatter on the hard tiles, the heart beats soft and regular, the outline grows distinct, those fine, small features, the slightly pointy nose, the large and limpid eyes . . . open . . . and that sickly green complexion. One day she lies before them on the table, fully thawed, and they can see her breathing fast and shallow. She smells of roses (the thorns, not the petals). These men of science are aghast. 'Is she even human?'

One evening, just as the night nurse has finished her checks, when the whole annexe is quiet, she turns to the basin to wash her hands, then turns back to find the girl standing there before her, hair afloat, eyes ablaze. The scream is heard throughout the complex. In the morning the nurse has vanished. She has fled the clinic, the hospital, gone back to her home world. She will later be committed to an asylum and live out her days freezing crickets into cubes of ice.

*

She stands but a few feet tall in her hunting boots. She wears a handsome hunting coat. The greatest physicians of the Empire arrive and line up to examine her. They bring instruments. None can explain her origin, or how she survived the ice. 'She is made entirely from meat!' exclaims Dr Racosta. The girl points to Racosta's right coat pocket and giggles. He is cajoled into removing a cupcake wrapped in a silk napkin. 'I am, I am the talisman,' she brightly burbles at the startled master-surgeon. This alien creature knows their communal language, the Internomicon. Or she has absorbed it in a few days just by hearing it spoken.

After a thorough examination – to which she submits with a terrifying serenity – she is declared fit and normal (though the cruel ice has robbed her vision). While being examined by a famous doctor called Mexisi, the girl turns to him and burbles, 'You treat me so roughly, you do, Mexisi.' 'You are my patient and I will treat you however I like,' declares Mexisi. 'Now I must take some of your blood.' The girl says nothing. Her blood is palest purple. The needle leaves a pretty violet bruise. The doctor holds the vial up to the light, laughs, his hand glints; outside the spheres outshine the stars, and twelve hours later Mexisi falls dead from heart failure.

*

It is discovered that this girl has a phenomenal sense of smell. She can describe to a person what the last soul they met had for breakfast just by the faint traces of breath left on their skin.

There are calls for a royal audience, but the Queen, a jealous kind, declines to visit. 'I am not in the habit of meeting my prisoners, no matter how phenomenal.'

The Empire works itself into a frothy mess. Who is this girl? Where did she come from? How did she get here? How is it that she can appear to be human, yet have no mechanical parts? No human, except the Pope, is made *entirely* from meat. She is called a 'Miracle', a 'Saint', 'Our Lady', although the name that seems to catch alight is 'Vengeance'.

She is the Vengeance. 'Here is the one who will restore our imperial honour. Though our foes are everywhere, she will protect us. If she can have revenge on a doctor who insults her, imagine what she can do to our enemies!' they seem to cry. 'The heavens have chosen us to furnish this gift upon. Vengeance is ours!'

The Vengeance is bemused. 'What nonsense do they say. That Mexisi was as old as the moons.'

*

Whipped raw by public pressure, the Queen at last agrees to visit. She is flown to the security complex by private airship. She comes in on a 15,000-year-old silver chair and dismounts slowly, stands crooked before the girl; her pink gums glisten, her eyes are wet and wild. But mercifully the girl can't see the awful face afloat before her. Though she can sense the things that delight her visitor. 'Love you the blackberry?' she whispers. 'Wish that I could taste some.'

The Queen licks her lips, audibly, but says nothing.

The following day ten thousand blackberries are delivered to the suite, though they are as rare as a newborn's teeth. Most rot before the girl can eat them.

*

The months too rot away. The Vengeance sits in her small, sterile apartment as a stream of doctors, dignitaries and well-wishers file through to take, in order: her blood, her blessing, her picture. Though it is not recorded in the archives of the Empire, or in any of the public newspapers, or anywhere but a few low sources, three attempts are made on her life in that year. The first, an attempted poisoning, fails thanks to the girl's fine nose. A single drop of 'odourless' plasma hidden beneath the skin of a fragrant apple leaps out at her with the power of a kick. The second, a noxious gas released through the ventilation system of her rooms, kills her guards and keeps her deathly sick for a month. A pair of exploding shoes go off while being transferred to her quarters, killing their carrier and dismembering another hapless guard. No one knows which agency would want her dead, or why, or why they chose shoes to do it. The guard around her apartment is expanded to become a small army. She is allowed no more visitors.

I am, I am the talisman.

★

A year after her discovery, the girl disappears.

It happens at the Worlds' Fair – the greatest symposium of science and industry ever held among the common empires. She is invited as a guest for a starlight charity celebrity dinner at the Elektrotek Ballroom to honour the winner of the 3,145th Beauty of the Universe Pageant. She is brought there in a heavily armoured cargo ship, in the company of a battle fleet. The Elektrotek Ballroom is surrounded by ten thousand troops. Not even a fly can enter without first being scanned and her possessions searched. It is as much security as is given to queens, or to the Pope of the Holy Neon Empire. And yet it is not enough. If you read official accounts you will find a bold and gory story: a team of heavily armed assailants, a terrible battle, many guards dead, the Vengeance vanished.

But read the classified report presented by the Ministry of Secrets and you'll learn that there was no great battle. There was a lone assailant, a single low-yield bomb which failed to incinerate its target, one small explosion. In the chaos the girl simply walked out of the grand ballroom, through the dead and dying guests, past the soldiers choking in the smoke and heat, and into the wide, wide universe.

Where she went after that is a grand mystery.

The navy is mobilised, every merciless agency of the Empire called to task – the Special Police, Black Ops, the Imperial Postal Service – all powers are given to the state machine to search, seize, interrogate. This girl is extremely dangerous, the official reports say, and should not be approached. Grave threats are issued. Then offers of reward.

Then threats again. But nothing works. The greatest treasure in the universe has melted away, and not one of all the countless trillion souls who live within the Empire seem to have the faintest idea where to look for the small green girl who is made entirely of meat, who came, perhaps, from another dimension, and who smells of raw new roses (the thorns, not the petals.)

*

There is one more event worth mentioning here. A *long*, long time before the appearance of the viridescent girl, a team of oil prospectors found another vessel in deepest space. This was a one-berth saucer capsule of unusual design. When the prospectors opened the saucer they found a lone, male traveller – delirious, emaciated, lost inside the black nest of his beard, but alive. The man said, 'I am M. Francisco Fabrigas, and I am here!'

The man, who claimed to be an explorer, also claimed, extraordinarily, to have explored his way from another universe. No one believed him, of course. As the people of this Empire pointed out, he had left them just a few months earlier on a mission to the next universe. He became a laughing stock; 'Time's Fool'. And it stayed that way until two encounters in deepest space. The first, terrifying enough; the second, far too terrifying for those involved.

BOOK ONE

It starts with oil. Oil in the air, in a deathly cloud partway between a drizzle and a fog. Oil underfoot, in sickly pools, in dull rainbows on the surface of the murky puddles, sticky drops ka-platting on the steel catwalks, on the armoured helmets, on the felt ship-hats, on the heads of cackling babies, on the snouts of ragged dogs. In Carnassus it had always been and always will be; the sign that stands at the gates is coated in rich, buttery oil . . .

YOU ARE NOW ENTERING THE AIRPORT OF CARNASSUS. PUBLIC PERSONS WHO VENTURE PAST THIS POINT DO SO AT THEIR GREATEST PERIL.

Black blood running in veins along the steel letters. Oil running down the poles and chains. Oil on the hands and in the brain. Oil running down the chin and down the neck. Oil wetting the gears of limbs and organs, beading brightly on the beards and lashes. This oil greases up the crashing blades and torture racks the Empire builds to make her prisoners sing and die. It wets the throats of thirsty cannons pointing at the gates and walls of traitor cities. Oil powers up the death fleets, it flares from the torn stomachs of the ships, it turns the darkness into daylight, it creeps silently up wicks in lamps along the dormitories of the factories and workhouses. It illuminates the faces of the hungry children. It burns inside the ancient lamp that leans above the quivering eyelids of the Queen. These are the end times, people say. Soon there won't be any oil. The Queen sent her elite Black Squadron under the radar screen of the refinery at Manchurious IV. Now the oil there is hers. For now. The Vangardiks attacked the oil-rich mega-comet Odessa, deposed the brutal

Vascemon Vascemi, and installed their own tame dictator. And on Zapotek, the city at the centre of the universe, the battle for another kind of oil continues: the oil of forgetting; the oil of dreams. The Vangardiks have blockaded the Morphium routes in an effort to deprive their enemy of this ancient tonic. In dark dens across the Holy Neon Empire, in the crooked pipes of lonely fools, the last of this dreadful oil burns. There is a sense of approaching catastrophe all around the Cosmosphere.

In Carnassus you would not know it. In Carnassus it has always seemed as if the universe was ending; ending in a towering wave of oil. Oil. Everywhere. Oil in the air. Joyful oil underfoot, in lovely pools, in perfect rainbows on the surface of puddles. Hopeful oil. Oil running over grimly muscled hands. Oil in the hair, in the beard. Oil making every face in the port of Carnassus shine horribly. Oil keeping their joints, their spines, even the lids of their wrinkled, weary eyes well greased. Oil giving breath. Oil keeping every atom of the Empire moving. Oil coming out and coming in, like a tide, like a breathing. Oil, the reason for life, and for leaving.

BLACK STEEL IN THE HOUR OF CHAOS

Since the day M. Francisco Fabrigas had wriggled free of his oily red rag to tell the executioner that his cannon was jammed and was about to explode, ripping him and his whole squad to bloody chunks, killing a number of innocent bystanders (a maid, two water carriers, a monk, ten baby birds), but leaving its intended victim (M. Francisco Fabrigas) unscathed, he had been dogged by a single word. It followed where he went, it licked at his earhole. Even as he shot through the steaming alleys of Carnassus he could hear it scuttle from the shadows, snuffle at his heels, vanish into the gloom.

'Wizard.'

Of all the insults: to be called a tugger of rabbits, a stroker of wands, he who glowers in the darkness, whose only friends are the owl, the smoke, the mirror, the beard.

'Pah!'

The old-beard flew down Blackgate Avenue and on towards the Ten Bells, his eyes boiling away the air, the smoke and ash curling behind him in ghostly ciphers. He was here to catch a pilot. It had all been arranged. This time they would trap him. He could see a number of pilots. One lay unconscious on a mound of morphium rags, mouth gaping, steel knuckles dimpling a puddle of oily water. Another was propped up in a doorway with a sign: 'Dead Broke. Please Catch Me.' But these were not the sorts of pilots he was looking for. He swung left into Smell-Feast Row. To the right, where

St Stigmata's Shambles takes you tumbling into the Fathoms, the great slums of the city, was a sign . . .

YOU ARE NOW ENTERING THE AIRPORT OF CARNASSUS. PUBLIC PERSONS WHO VENTURE PAST THIS POINT DO SO AT THEIR GREATEST PERIL. THIS WAY LIES HARM, DEATH AND MADNESS.
    ARRIVALS →
    DEPARTURES ←
    ENQUIRIES / LOST LUGGAGE →

He went straight on. He felt the tunnels enfold him like a serpent's gullet, the black iron wet with oil, the pouring steam vents, the women bent low across their fires, the urchins nipping around like reef fish, darting out of the shadows to snap at wallets, pearls and watches, dipping out of reach of flailing constables. And the merchants, back beyond the boundaries of the light, as still and blue as drowned men.

Wizard.

Wizard.

Wizard.

The wizard is here – in this very port!

It wasn't always wizard. Sometimes it was 'varlet', or 'sorcerist', or 'man-witch', or 'wand-fondler', but it amounted to the same: the idea that he lived a life of ignorance and superstition. 'Call me anything!' the old-beard would often cry, even when no one in the universe had broached the subject. 'Scoundrel! Nut-hook! Buffenapper! Flesh-bot! Man-baiter!' (He could go on listing them for hours.) But *wizard*! The shadiest trickster. The one who closets himself in pretend schools to play with sticks and perfect the pointless art of turning men into chickens.

'This universe has enough chickens!' he shouted at a poor soup lady. The lady stepped quickly back inside her hut, and took her chicken with her.

Now he turned left into Broken Cross Lane where the blue sparks from the steel merchants' hammers sparkled brightly in his beard, then left onto Wormswood Street. (If you should turn left again you'd be in Teddy Bear Row, a long lane of workhouses where the poor children slave to sort luggage, make ship's biscuits, stitch slippers for the weary long-haul travellers. Right was Morphium Row, where many passed the dreamy hours between connecting ships. Right again was the Connections Lobby, a horizonless plaza where a sea of souls waited for announcements for flights they might have only dreamed of. There were people here, it was said, who had arrived with their families as infants, who now were elderly, their families dead. 'You might be better off,' some locals said, 'on Morphium Row.' 'Come, come with me. I know a man. He'll give you sofa for an hour for free. He'll tell you when your flight connects. Come, come into the Fathoms.')

Fabrigas had seen the dens, smelled the sweat and acrid smoke, heard the dreamy wails of dying men who'd forsaken the stars for a sunless cellar.

He gunned his board and rode into Cannons Street. As he eased across the iron grate he saw, below, a newborn cannon, burning orange as it was lifted carefully from its bath. He felt the heat lift his cloak, he felt the breath of a memory of the day he'd stood before the cannon, the day he'd wormed free of his red rag to tell the general that his device had been loaded incorrectly. It was at that moment that his destination in life had changed. It had been his making, and his unmaking.

Wizard.

The wizard is here! He came right on past my store!

Word had spread like the slum-blazes that sometimes erupt through these oily passages.

'Young Fabrigas stared into the black eye of the cannon and read its mind!' people had said. 'He truly is a great wizard!' they'd shouted.

'I do not believe in majick!' the old man cried. Two fortune-tellers turned and squinted as he passed; the breeze from his cloak made their cards take flight. His voice woke two sailors sleeping tenderly in each other's arms. A man came from the shadows with a knife. 'Begone, fool!' yelled Fabrigas, and the man stepped back, for he was elderly, almost blind, and had only wanted to offer him a slice of mango.

Fabrigas turned right into Breaktooth Street and saw the Ten Bells swimming in the fog. His pilot was here somewhere in this port, he hoped, and this time they would be ready for him.

*

Carnassus: Gateway to the Empires, named for the baron found hanging from a gantry on his seventieth birthday because he could no longer bear to look upon the monster he'd created. The iron core of the city was once the crypt to an extinct empire: that of Her Majesty Queen Arcadmius IX. Millions were entombed here in a honeycomb of vacuum chambers. When Princess Malvia III died of ennui she was placed here, still clutching her dead lover's paintbrush and her husband's sword. When half her family fell to laughing plague they were buried therein, the hideous grins still locked upon their faces. When the old mega-crypt was turned over to the Royal Transit Authority, the fleshless legion it contained was roughly woken from its slumbers. The new owners stacked layers of slum housing on the crypt. On that they bolted shipyards, naval depots, the great airport, and from that sprang the many million cranes and gantries, and from one such gantry swung the Baron Carnassi: because the poor man could no longer bear to see the endless ships full of strangers coming in; the coral growth of steel expanding into the velveteen blackness. Also, he was depressed.

The airport is not only ridden with old bones, but ghosts as well. The ghost of Princess Malvia III. The ghost of Baron Carnassi. The ghosts of lost travellers. The ghosts, some say, weep black, oily tears.

'Nonsense!' Fabrigas would cry. Then he'd go on to explain, at length, that these 'spirits' were just toxic hallucinations brought about by the dense smoke trapped within the airport. It was a simple case of poisoning.

If Fabrigas had been a superstitious being, if he had believed in ghosts, or magic, or the mediations of fate, he would have thought that this day was particularly significant. This was his tenth visit in ten days to the airport where he was to recruit sailors for his voyage, and where he hoped to catch the pilot they called the Necronaut. All morning the number 10 had been haunting him. His steamship was the *St Gorgon X*. Port 10, the packet had left from.

'Coincidence!' Fabrigas had shouted, and all the other passengers in his berth had jumped a foot clear of their seats. The nine other passengers had whispered in astonishment when they'd seen the old-beard. He had ignored them, stared hard at his ticket: *Berth J, section 10*.

A conductor had popped his head in, counted the passengers and said, 'Ten then. All set.'

'Lunatic!' shouted Fabrigas, and the conductor frowned and left. Fabrigas could not imagine any *cosmic* reason why he'd come to the saddest and deadliest sphere in the universe ten days straight. He'd stared out of the window of the *St Gorgon* as they'd approached Carnassus: a spiky black urchin floating in the ether, its cranes and gantries flailing like the arms of a dying monster. There was an endless stream of ships crowding in like insects to a swollen, maggot-filled carcass. And beyond, the infinal and infernal spheres of the Holy Neon Empire: gold, silver, greenish, brownish; a dense haze of baubles standing out against the blackness. Many spheres were built around a star, like a giant lampshade, so that every ounce of solar energy could be harnessed. The outer shells were miles thick and when meteors hit they rang like bells. Each bubble was a breath-taking miracle of scientific progress; and each was built to house a hysterical mess of superstitious souls.

A child, a small boy, had left his seat and walked over, stared up at this giant, cloaked figure whose granite face was dressed in storm clouds, mouthed a single, silent word, then fled back to his mother's skirts.

Their steamship had dipped and headed for Dock 10. 'Gah,' the old-beard had said, to no one. And 'Gah,' he'd whispered to himself.

*

Fabrigas had left his packet, travelled through the gates of Carnassus, past the great oily sign, the dreaming pilots, the drowned souls, the lady and her chicken, the man and his mango, over undulating seas of memory and time, over the cannon's bath, each place setting off the thundering retort of a forgotten moment: a lost and floating face, an all-but-vanquished place, until finally, as an old, old man, he'd reached the door of the Ten Bells, pulled his hoverpad to a stop, flipped it out of gear with his thumb, and returned to the present moment.

He carried a small wooden box in the crook of his left arm.

A few minutes later, a figure in a fine day suit came oozing from the smog, calmly attending to his cuffs and smiling wryly at the chaos around him. 'Sir has been setting a demanding pace this morning.' Fabrigas looked down at his servant blankly, as if he was trying to place him, then shook his head and said, 'There was no point delaying. Today is the day. I'm certain. Yes.'

'Oh? You've received intelligence?' said Carrofax.

'No, no intelligence. Just a feeling.'

'A *feeling*?' His servant allowed the corners of his mouth to rise impertinently.

'Yes, a feeling. A man can have feelings, can't he?'

'Well, I wouldn't dare to have an opinion on that, sir.'

A supertanker sounded its klaxons from the darkness just a few leagues off. As the shockwave hit, vendors reached to stop their fruit from rolling off the stands, scores of startled rats were shaken from the steel rafters, the subsonic storm front made the old man's beard and lashes quiver. The city rang like a bell for a full minute before the sound faded.

Captain Nezquix, head of the Royal Naval Procurement Agency, came striding from a nearby alley, his confident young gait undermined, somewhat, by the plastic bags he wore on his shiny leather boots, and the white kerchief he clasped to his nose.

'Boy, you are late. What news?' said Fabrigas as he towered over the young captain.

'All is in place. Skycore says the Necronaut will be here. There was a possible sighting at the Whore's Arms. And he wrote his sign on a wall near the dens . . . in urine.' Nezquix coughed politely into his kerchief. 'We'll be ready for him this time.'

'You've stepped up operations?'

'We have, though you are spending a frightening portion of your ship's budget on procuring this gentleman.'

'He is no gentleman. And he is worth every copper.'

'How strange of you to refuse one of our fine naval pilots for this expedition.'

'We are all doomed on this mission,' said Fabrigas. 'I need to catch a pilot skilled enough to give my crew even the faintest chance of survival.'

Each Empire's navy has its own recruitment method. Some put notices in newspapers; others buy advertising space on local prostitutes; some put posters up in toilets and in alleys commonly used as toilets. In this Empire's navy, at this time, it was tradition that the pilot of each ship be caught. It stood to reason that the harder a pilot was to catch at dock, the more fierce and able he would be at sea. If a pilot submitted, said: 'Fine! You got me!' he was hardly worth hiring. A good pilot knew how to play 'hard to catch'. The best pilots in the Empire were almost impossible to catch, and this pilot, the Necronaut, was the toughest catch of all.

The Procurement Agency, under Captain Nezquix, had set up successively more elaborate traps during the past ten days, each with a bounty hidden inside as bait, and on each occasion the Necronaut had simply taken the bounty and vanished. But today was different. Today Nezquix had pulled no punches. He had set up a sequence of traps so baroque, so stunningly complex, that no mortal human, surely, could escape them.

'We have him covered from all angles,' said Nezquix proudly. To the north, he explained, was a bordello whose saucy harlots would lure their quarry with the promise of lustful deeds taken from a list compiled by a naval psychiatrist who had been given access to a secret file on the Necronaut. The bordello was designed to seal at the push of a button when their target entered.

To the south was a morphium den whose sofas were giant magnets.

To the east was a simple pie and ale shop which hid an orchestra of traps. The Necronaut, it was said, loved pies. He loved them filled with fried crickets and liver. He was a traditionalist. They said a lot of things about the Necronaut. More legend surrounded him than any man, even Fabrigas. The Necronaut was six foot six if he was an inch, they said. His chest was fifty-nine inches, his arms were thirty inches at the bicep. The legend-tellers were unusually precise. He was the purest kind of mercenary. He was a former naval pilot, so his mods were state of the art: his performance had been enhanced by the very latest military–industrial technology. He possessed the sharpest mind of any pilot known, and a bravery which could be confused with insanity. He was possessed, some people said. He had piloted a crippled slave ship single-handed between the twin black holes at Dominatrus. He had escaped the ransom prison on the pirate world of Diebax. He wore size 12 boots.

'So you see,' concluded Nezquix, 'it is all under control. To the west is another bordello, Harlots de la Mer. It is staffed by even saucier ladies. If he escapes our main traps we have an outer ring of supplementary traps: pits, nets, laser-guided tranquilliser darts, more prostitutes. It is a ring of iron from which even he cannot escape. We have never failed to catch our pilot. Even a wizard like you couldn't do b—' He had not been allowed to finish his thought because Fabrigas had fixed the young captain with a look which made his larynx freeze over like a water pipe in winter.

'I hope your confidence in yourself is repaid,' said the old man.

'It will be.'

'We will be watching your progress from the tavern.' Fabrigas took a silver case from his breast pocket and opened it. Balancing his wooden box on his arm, he took two plugs from the case and pushed them into his ears, then they left Captain Nezquix alone and entered the Bells.

Nº   112

THE TEN BELLS TAVERN
CARNASSUS AIRPORT 14V SX7

LIQUOR FREE OF DUTY
FRIDAY: WATCH A MAN FIGHT A SNAKE !!!

Saturday: Bare-knuckled fist-boxing
Monday: Ladies' drinks ½ price !!!

TEN BELLS

The Ten Bells was the most dismal and dangerous tavern in the most desperate sphere in the most awful corner of the Holy Neon Empire. Terrible things happened in the Bells, and the worst of all the things that happened there was singing. It was the singing of sailors and longshoremen, but these weren't ordinary sailors, or the kind of longshoremen you might know. These were drunken, tone-deaf, infectious and forgotten sailors, the ones who'd long ago lost their ship, their crew, their will to live, and whose song was more painful, more unbearable, than the crying of a million orphan babies. Even the words of these songs were enough to make you leap from a pier.

> *Black Jess he was a goodly friend,*
> *A goodly friend o' mine – Oh!*
> *But lately something's changed in him,*
> *It ain't hard to define.*
>
> *Oh, I wish I had me Jess's gal,*
> *And I ain't bein' cute.*
> *I would convince her that I loves her,*
> *But the point, 'tis probably moot – Oi!*

But the earplugs were working. As they sat in the corner of the tavern to wait for the traps to fall on the Necronaut, all Fabrigas and his servant had to endure were the gaping pink mouths and tearful, red-rimmed eyes of the sailors. They had nothing to fear from these scoundrels so long as they were busy singing. Behind the bar were racks of bottles marked with skulls and Xs. Any sailor knows the code. One X, that's a breakfast whisky. Three Xs, that's for 'fivesies', or cleaning the barnacles from your ship. Five Xs and a skull, that's for when you're tired of living. One skull with a clown's nose, that's for pirate-children's parties. When the innkeeper looked over, Fabrigas nodded gravely. The innkeeper sighed, shook his head, then brought Fabrigas his jasmine tea.

'It might be,' ventured Carrofax cautiously, 'that this . . . "Necronaut" . . . never shows up. It might be that he doesn't even exist.'

'I can't hear you,' Fabrigas said, as he adjusted the plug in his right ear. He was lying. The earplugs were of his own design. They were constructed to block out all but pleasant sounds, and his servant had a mellow and well-modulated voice. Fabrigas took a long, slow sip of tea and squinted, then said, 'Of course he exists. If he doesn't exist then who has been escaping from our traps and stealing our bounties all week? Anyway, he will show. He is waiting for dark.'

'For dark? But in Carnassus it is always night.'

'He's waiting for ten bells, when they reboot the generators. He is no fool.'

Carrofax sat patiently, spine straight, hands clasped in front of him while Fabrigas watched silvery shadows through the grimy glass of the tavern window. He watched the naval agents in the street – disguised as longshoremen and prostitutes – attempt to act naturally. He watched spiders big as rats pounce on rats as big as cats. He watched a man pick another man's watch, then offer him the time of day. Inside the tavern he watched the pink mouths moving, silently. He watched the sailors, steel arms slung across each other's shoulders, sway like masts. There were no naval agents in the tavern to protect him if the locals turned nasty: if they ran out of Four-X Special, or if their steam-powered accordian broke. There was no telling how unpleasant things would get if these seamen had to sing without accompaniment.

He waited.

The clock above the bar struck ten bells. The lights across Carnassus dimmed briefly, then rebooted.

*

It has been estimated that more pockets are picked during the ten seconds of darkness when the airport's generators reboot than the rest of the day combined. As the lights rose again Fabrigas saw that a boy was sitting at their table. 'Begone, child, this table is taken!' shouted Fabrigas. He had finished his tea, but he hated being rushed. Astonishingly, the boy did not scurry away. He removed his hood. His face made Fabrigas all but gasp aloud.

THE NECRONAUT

The boy put his finger to his lips. 'Shhhhhhhhhhhhh.' He had a young face. A hard-eyed, weathered and dreadful face. The boy spoke and Fabrigas was struck dead by his black eyes and defiant jaw. It was a face to break a mother's heart, or any heart. He wore gun belts that criss-crossed his torso under a heavy leather coat; the brass cartridges twinkled in the half-light. Fabrigas was so stunned that he watched the boy speak for a full minute before he removed his earplugs, placed them on top of his wooden box, and said, 'Pardon?'

The stranger blinked, then said: 'My name is Carlos Góngora Lambestyo. I was a cadet in Her Majesty's Elite Black Squadron. During the invasion of Manchurious V my bat-fighter was hit by a rocket and I crashed. I was captured by the enemy. I escaped by holding down a guard and rubbing his head until he gave me his keys. That is all you need to know about that time. I found a refugee ship and drifted through space for a full year, fighting for my life, surviving on rats and other small creatures. I got aboard a ship by pretending to be a beautiful lady. Then I threw the captain overboard and took his ship. The crew was ready to kill me until I proved I was not a lady.' The boy had not said 'kill' like you or I might. He'd said 'keeeeel', '. . . to keeeeel me'. Looking into the boy's eyes Fabrigas suddenly found that, yes, he felt like dying.

The boy held the old man's eyes in his, leaned closer.

'I have seen things and been places you wouldn't believe, old man.

Many times I have wished for death myself, but it never came. Now I hear you are trying to catch a pilot for a dangerous mission of almost certain death. That pilot is me.' He took a small sphere from his coat and placed it on the table. It made a dull thud. 'I usually only tell my story once.'

The young man's tale filled Fabrigas with utter despair, and he thought about just fleeing. But he stayed fixed to his chair, trying not to stare. Carrofax, he noticed, was staring, bemused. This was the infamous mercenary pilot whose very name struck fear into the heart of every sailor?

'*He* is the Necronaut?' said Carrofax.

'*You* are the Necronaut?' said Fabrigas.

'That is a name given to me by others; I did not choose it for myself,' said the boy. '"Necro" means "Death". "Naut" is a word for the number zero, I'm told. So "Necronaut" means "No death".'

Fabrigas made to speak, then thought better of it.

'Do you mind?' said the boy. He pointed to the teapot. Fabrigas blinked twice. The boy poured himself a cup of jasmine tea, sipped and nodded thoughtfully. His leather gun belts croaked. 'I once piloted a ship smuggling jasmine from the Black Isles. Our cargo caught fire. I smelled like jasmine for months. Whenever I smell jasmine I think of that time. It is not relaxing. But I never cry.'

He took another sip. 'I see you look at my scar. You are perhaps wondering how I got it?' The boy's forehead carried several deep marks, and a long scar ran from his temple, down his face, down his neck, to the collar of his cloak, and on to God knows where. This boy's face looked like a map – a map of a land called Pain. 'I have fought many, many monsters,' said the boy pilot. 'Zombies, Cyclopses, Triclopses, serpents, vampire owls. But the creature who gave me this was a woman. We are not together any more. I could tell you the story but when I finished you would surely want to *keeeeel* yourself, so I won't.' He put down his cup and pushed it away with his index finger.

'My boy, how old are you to have had such dreadful experiences?' said Fabrigas, who had been trying *not* to look at the scar.

'I am no boy,' said the boy, 'I am eighteen and one-quarter years old. I have whiskers, see?' He pointed to a faint copse of stubble on his chin. 'I have my own ship, the *Fire Bird*. At least I did, until it caught fire. I have many terrible stories like this. One day I think I should write a book.'

'How much flesh are you, boy?'

'. . . Ninety-five per cent. But my military enhancements make me very strong. Would you like to arm-wrestle?'

The servos in the young man's elbow whirred softly.

'So you've lost no organs to plague?'

The boy pouted. 'I almost lost a kidney in a game of cards. True story.'

Fabrigas pushed aside his own cup and looked at Carrofax. Carrofax shook his head. 'Young man,' said Fabrigas, 'your story is very moving, and yes, we do need a captain who can pilot our ship on a mission to the next universe, by order of the Queen. There we will find a new dimension with its own properties, laws, monsters –'

'Treasures?'

'Perhaps. But you will not be there.' The boy pilot squinted, then took his elbow off the table. 'Stories of your bravery are legendary, but we require more than bravery for this mission. We need experience. You are just a boy. I'm sorry, but we cannot offer you this job after all. More tea?'

The boy set his weathered eyes on the old man. Then he scratched the back of his head, looked around for the first time, taking in the stained walls, the sailors, now silent. Fabrigas hadn't noticed at first, but the men had stopped singing when the boy entered.

'This is a nice tavern,' continued the Necronaut, 'if you like the bar scene. I do not. I have seen taverns so dreadful that you would weep tears of blood.' He pointed to his left eye. 'I was once in a tavern that served only blood. Why would you do that? Serve only blood? Well, in any case, you would need to catch me first. You have not.'

'Have we not?' said the old-beard.

'No.'

'Are you sure?'

'If you are speaking of the auto-cuffs around my ankles, I have disabled them.'

'Have you indeed?'

'Yes. Shackles can't hold me. And nor can any of those traps you have waiting for me outside.' The boy patted the small black cannon-ball which sat upon the table.

'What is that?' asked Fabrigas.

'This? Oh, thank you for asking. This is my little friend. He is a cannonball filled with WD40-X. You've heard of it?'

'Heard of it? I invented it, boy. It is an extremely volatile and powerful explosive activated by contact with water. Why would you bring this here?'

The boy pouted. 'I hear you have many traps set. This is my "get out of the jail card".'

'There's no such thing. Where did you get such an idea?'

Again the boy shrugged. 'It is only unsafe near water anyway.' He picked up the sphere, tossed it lightly from hand to hand and into his coat pocket. Then he said, 'What's in that box?'

'Beg pardon?' said Fabrigas. 'Oh. This is the map. I spent an age perfecting it. To make it I had to send several million lanterns into the next universe, to each of which were attached mechanical eyes and ears. No one but me and my manservant have ever seen this map. It shows the way to the next universe with only an 80 per cent chance of death.'

'Those are good odds,' said the boy. 'May I see it?'

'Certainly,' said Fabrigas, 'but you should know that it will blow your mind out through your face.'

WORLDS WITHIN WORLDS

The box at first seemed empty, black. The boy pilot squirmed impatiently. Then a pair of brass spheres rose slowly, almost shyly, from within, peeking out like a pair of rising suns, whirring faintly. The two spheres of equal size began to orbit each other, filling the corner of the room with a honey light. 'This is our universe,' said Fabrigas, his voice a whisper. He pointed a long, thin finger towards one of the spheres. 'This,' he said, moving his finger to the second sphere, 'is the universe I came from.'

'You came from another universe?'

'I did. In a saucer craft of my own design.'

'What is your universe like?' whispered the young pilot breathlessly.

'It is identical to this one, except it does not contain me.'

'Oh.'

A third, smaller sphere rose to join the twins. 'This,' he said, pointing a finger to the smaller sphere, 'is Universe Hypothetical 4QF10. It is possible, though not certain, that this universe exists.'

'What happens if you try to enter a universe that does not exist?' whispered the young pilot. Fabrigas fixed him with a deathly stare. 'I see,' said Lambestyo.

Soon, two more spheres rose from within and the five spun lazily together, their soft light leaving silky traces in the air. 'These are other hypothetical universes, each with their own unique character. Some are almost exactly like our own universe, some are so different that to enter them would mean certain death.' Fabrigas spoke so softly now that he was barely audible.

Five smaller spheres rose; the ten came together to perform an exquisite ballet. The music of the spheres was like ten heavenly bells softly ringing in the blackness. 'And this is just our local neighbour-hood, our street,' said Fabrigas. 'To chart the Infiniverse would require a map that went on forever. Almost.' The universe itself seemed to have come to a stop.

'I think,' said Carrofax, not bothering to be impressed, or to lower his voice, 'that you should perhaps pay some attention to your surroundings.'

The boy and the old man rose out of their trance and became aware of several dozen more spheres in orbit around them. Every greedy, thieving, bloodshot eye in the tavern was upon them, or, to be precise, upon the box. 'You should not have brought this here!' hissed the pilot as he slammed the lid shut with his hand. 'Come!' The boy grabbed the box and the wizard's sleeve and hauled them to the rear door. Carrofax followed like a shadow.

ALL TRAPS SET

Through a small door on howling springs, through a filthy kitchen where a row of rusty TX400 auto-scrubbers worked away at blackened pots, the pilot kicked a wooden door from its gudgeons and they flew down an alley so narrow they could hardly fit, through sheets of oily spiderweb. Rounding a corner they stumbled upon two naval cadets dressed as prostitutes who were touching up each other's make-up. 'Stop moving, you'll smudge it!' one said before they looked up to see their quarry. The painted cadets panicked and dived into a delivery hatch.

'If the Procurement Agency's traps don't get you, those bandits will,' said Fabrigas, out of breath. 'I'm sure if we explained to the thugs that my map is worthless to them –'

'They'll kill us anyway,' the boy grunted as he turned his ear towards the alley. They heard a public address system in the distance . . .

'PLEASE DO NOT LEAVE LUGGAGE UNATTENDED IN THE AIRPORT AS IT MAY BE DAMAGED OR DESTROYED OR FLUNG INTO SPACE . . .'

Then they heard the first calls coming from the Bells, then the boot-steps scrabbling crab-like down the alley, the soft sounds of the servo motors in the elbows, knees and necks of the bandit sailors. Then a scream which made the hairs on their necks rise, and another: the long, thin squeal of steel blades drawn along iron pipes. Soon it was a chorus. 'Come on!' said the boy, and they ran.

On the catwalks above they heard boot-fall, the *sszzt, sszzt, sszzt* of android legs, and the shrill squall of blades, like the coming of a flock of evil gulls. At least four of these bandits were tracking them, hunting their treasure. Their quarry fled through passages, over baskets, ropes and sleeping men. An enormous shadow uncoiled from the catwalk above like a snake in ambush – it dropped to the ground, dwarfing the boy pilot, raised his four steel arms and said, 'I'll be taking your b—' That's as far as he got, because the boy they called the Necronaut pushed a short knife to the man's chest, took his huge weight on his shoulders, and lowered him quietly to the ground. Fabrigas had not seen speed and strength like it. Then the boy dropped to one knee and sniffed the air flowing from the ducts above.

'They're using the flow from the ducts to hide their stench, no?' said Fabrigas. 'They know this place like their mother's oily face.'

'Let's go and see how good these traps of yours are,' said the boy, and he ran on. The small box had vanished into his coat, his eyes seemed to have mutated: where before they were black, they were now blade-blue. Fabrigas, a half-smile on his face, exchanged a look with Carrofax, and they followed. The drum of boots on the scaffold above was deafening now, shouts and calls rang up and down the alley. Soon the whole dreadful hood would be out.

'Would it not be faster if we took my hoverpad?' said Fabrigas. The boy said nothing. He made for a purple door hung with flowers and a sign: 'Any Which Way'. 'I would not enter that *particular* bordello,' called Fabrigas, but he was too late. The Necronaut bashed through the door as if it were paper, raising a storm of whorish screams from within. The old man heard the whip and clang of the agency's traps unleashing – and several more screams. By the time he entered through the shattered purple door, the Necronaut was standing on top of a cage which had fallen from the ceiling. The cage had descended upon an elaborate-looking 'fun seat' and several irate prostitutes. 'Please try to keep up,' said the boy Lambestyo. 'This is hard enough as it is. Even though it's totally not hard at all.' He leaped from the cage and dropped to one knee to retie his boot, ducking, as he did, a double-headed meteor hammer which came spinning from the sordid shadows. Then he set off through the love hotel's dank passages, leaping and ducking Procurement tripwires, slashing through nets as if they were spiderwebs, and knocking unconscious the whorishly dressed naval recruits who came at him from their hiding places. Fabrigas followed, stepping through the traps, shouting useful hints like: 'Flying bolas to your left.'

Now the bandits from the Bells were streaming in to join the fun, but none of them were prepared for *this* bordello. The horde let out rusty howls as they were picked up in nets and nooses, slammed against the walls by swinging logs, dropped through trapdoors, or knocked unconscious by spinning bolas. They heard Captain Nezquix's voice through a loudhailer crying: 'Code Amber! The snake is in the basket! Seal the place! Seal the place!' and then the sound of iron walls descending to encase the greasy house inside an impenetrable box.

Then, silence. Our friends had almost made it to the front entrance.

'So we caught you after all,' said Fabrigas. They could hear the sounds of groaning and weeping bandits from all directions. The Necronaut took a glance through the door which led to a small reception area at the front of the bordello where customers arrived to ask questions like: 'Do you charge by the minute?' and 'How much if both women are dressed as mermaids?' He observed a bandit who had broken through the front door and been swept up in a net. They heard Nezquix's amplified voice from outside: 'Pilot called the Necronaut. This is Captain Nezquix of procurement. We have you sealed and surrounded. Surrender immediately to us and declare your capture!' Lambestyo considered the captain's words with a nod. Then he took the small WD40-X cannonball from his coat, tossed it into the reception area, and yelled, 'Grenade! Prepare to die!'

It is not certain whether the murderous bandit who hung above the enquiries counter, knowing that this grenade was activated by contact with liquids, would have been able to hold his bladder. We will never know, and it is moot, Jessie, for he did not. His stream of fearful piss set off a chain reaction which sent the entire front edifice of this fake bordello smashing down like a drawbridge gate. Fabrigas and the young pilot both ducked for cover as the blast sent a typhoon of smoke and ash back through the corridors. The two men came together where the reception room had been, staring out into a wide market plaza where scores of women were weaving nets. They heard Nezquix's hailer squall to life: 'All hands, get him!' and the women rose as one to shriek and howl like a tribe of monkeys, pointing long, metal fingers. 'Not so crazy now, am I?' said Lambestyo. Then this strange and indomitable boy stalked out into the plaza, back into the chaos, skipping easily away from a trapdoor as it opened, ducking another storm of flying bolas. For Fabrigas, time slowed, as it is inclined to do in serious spots, and the grubby, fleshy mouths of the weaving women seemed as big as caves. Fabrigas could see everything with perfect clarity: a horde of navy agents storming from the shadows with hefty procurement clubs, and still more bandits arriving, attracted by the chaos, swinging down from above on ropes and hooks. 'Not so crazy now, am I?' The words echoed in his mind as Carlos Lambestyo, a dagger in each hand, caught bandits with his blades while they were still off balance, and sent agents flying back into the shadows with the soles of his boots. Fabrigas saw the faces of bandits snatched in a moment of utter disbelief – the look you have when the victory you thought was certain vanishes, when the dark mix of blood and oil begins to ooze between your fingers and the world becomes cloudy. But still they kept coming, swinging from the gloomy heights, others coming up as fast as spiders from below, their black, shiny faces set in grimaces, oily knives clamped firmly in their teeth. Carnassus is a great cage which holds the most terrifying and merciless creatures. Once they smell blood they come from everywhere.

'There's too many!' cried Nezquix. 'Retreat! Retreat! They can have the pilot!'

Lambestyo flung both his knives and two more bandits slammed into the deck. Then he pulled a cannon pistol from its holster. He picked one bandit from the air just as he swung towards Fabrigas – the goon's black guts exploded with the force of the round and splattered the old man's cloak. The boy aimed his second shot at one of the struts that held the catwalks up. He never even flinched as a mountain of steel and bodies came crashing down around them with a thunder that could have roused the gods.

'That noise should wake all the other pirates,' said Carrofax.

'PLEASE NOTE THAT FIREARMS ARE NOT TO BE DISCHARGED WITHIN THE AIRPORT,' said the voice across the public address system, 'EXCEPT BY QUALIFIED SECURITY STAFF AND AIR MARSHALS.'

Lambestyo smashed open an airport guardhouse where a lone officer was sleeping through the utter carnage around him. He picked up a heavy sonic cannon used to destroy abandoned luggage, kicked the oily filth from the barrel with the heel of his boot, dropped the priming trigger with his thumb. He hoisted the weapon over his shoulder by the leather strap and pointed it at the door to a biscuit factory. The door splintered into a cloud of pieces, a jet of hot and deliciously scented air came streaming out. The boy put his arm up to his face, his eyes burned orange as he leaped into the smoke and heat. Dancing along a narrow catwalk between a row of great ovens where ship's biscuits were made they felt their eyebrows sizzle, and the children below briefly stopped their singing. A sea of grubby faces turned up as they passed overhead. Behind, two bandits screamed shrilly as their synthetic faces melted off in gooey lumps.

Then out and into the steaming coldness of the fish markets. The Necronaut slung the compact cannon around his back, patted himself down, realising he'd flung his last dagger. He broke the razor-sharp prow from a bladefish, swished it twice through the air. And still the bandits came thick from the shadows. The boy cleared a path with his sonic cannon. The sound of exploding sailors brought haunted faces to the windows of the morphium dens. The trio made it halfway through the market before the baggage cannon's charge ran out and they were completely surrounded. Fabrigas saw piles of sea creatures: red, yellow, orange, purple, high and rounded like drifts of brightly coloured snow. He saw the starfish in a heap. He saw the startled vendors, the frightened children. He saw the bandits, now numbering at least a hundred, close around them, tattoos flexing on the islands of flesh left on their steel bones. They showed their teeth – iron, bone, and filed sharp. All the navy agents had vanished, there was no one there to help them now. He saw the Necronaut stand tall and say, in a voice a notch too shrill to be forbidding, 'Begone, dogs!' He saw the murderous sailors roar and roll their shaggy heads. Fabrigas saw it all. He was falling through space, the world was dropping away beneath him. Then, just as the men raised their curved swords to strike Lambestyo down, the old man stepped forward, and the universe shrunk to a burning white point, a shimmering diamond in which everything was contained and anything was possible. He saw it all: he saw his mother, he saw his room. He saw a ship. He saw bloodshed. Mayhem. Plague and starvation, the fire and the flesh. In a flash he saw it all: the city, the prison, the general, the cannon's mouth. He went tumbling back into the terrible black maw of infinity.

A SHORT INTERLUDE

We never did finish the story of how M. Francisco Fabrigas cheated death at the cannon's mouth.

He was really just a boy himself at that time. A boy in a foreign empire a long way from home.

Fabrigas *had* known that the cannon would misfire, killing the firing squad, the general, the spectators, the scarlet bird with her newborn chicks in the tree above, but leaving him alive. He *had* wriggled from his blindfold and announced their imminent dismemberment. The cannon trick was certainly not magic. As he'd stood, blind, he'd felt the burning sun on his face and a frail breeze fondling his hair. Within the red rag around his head he'd heard, with delight, that the eggs in the tree near his balcony had finally hatched, and that the new chicks were crying out for food. He could hear the calls and chants in the market far away. He could also hear the cannon being mounted and pointed towards his chest, he could hear his own heart, the blood surging through his ears, he could hear the ball filled with shot roll along the barrel and stop with a dull *thunk*, and he could hear, with those well-trained ears, that the young soldier in charge of the gun had used the wrong gauge shot. The cannon was jammed. And so he'd struggled into the light to tell the general, proudly, but politely, that if he fired his cannon it would explode and kill them all. The assembled soldiers had laughed and General Ahksant had snorted like a bull. 'Boy! You can only delay for so long! Then, ka-boom-ba! No more!' But when the long-beaked general levered at the waist, monocle raised, to check his gun, he found to his delight and dismay that Fabrigas was right! The general fell to his knees and wept. Then he untied Fabrigas, swept the grey dust from his shoulder with his own kerchief. He not only forgave him for making out with his wife, but also convinced his emperor to make him Philosopher General. The people had cheered, the new birds had cheeped. And that's how Fabrigas became a famous wizard.

Wizard.

It wasn't long before the story of the firing squad, as well as many other fantastical rumours, got back to the Holy Neon Empire. By the time he said farewell to the general (and his wife) he was a celebrity. His fame took him to extraordinary parties, brought him exotic gifts from beautiful starlets, saw him reading his dramatic adventure stories to radio audiences numbering in the billions, even granted him an audience with the Queen. To his horror the Queen made him Magician Incarnate of her court. 'I would rather *die!*' he would whisper later to his loyal servant, Carrofax. His great deeds took him to the height of stardom, and the depths of despair.

Even on the night of his release he had not rested like a happy man. He slept feverishly, like a man withdrawing from a morphium habit. He'd dreamed that on another identical planet there was an exact copy of him who had not heard the sounds, and had been shot; and on another world a merciless version of himself who had heard the sounds but remained silent, allowing the men to be blown apart; and on another world it wasn't a cannon at all, but a giant crossbow; and on another he'd worn a cape of silver and had called himself Magnifico; and on and on until dawn, his dreams intermingling with his waking visions. He woke with a bright beam of sunlight hitting his chest from a slit in the curtains and the chorus of the birds once more calling his mind to order. He woke and wandered about his apartment, lifting objects from the shelves and saying, 'This is not my ornamental vase with bird motif. This is not

my beautiful lamp.' But by the time the sun was high he had a
theory, and his theory was grand, and his theory was mad, and his
theory was this . . .

. . . That there are many universes, perhaps an infinite number; that each contains, and is contained within every other; and that all of them sing together like voices in a choir. It is a beautiful thing – a song of infinite harmony. It wasn't yet a proper theory. It was hardly even an idea. But it was this idea that would shape the rest of his life and lead him to undertake a journey to the next universe, lead him to this very place, the airport of Carnassus, to a market where a tribe of bloodthirsty sailors were about to cut him open.

'Gentlemen!' said Fabrigas, to the massed assembly of grinning, murderous men. 'Before our killing game begins, let us take a short moment to consider things from another perspective.'

'Consider this po-spective, flesh-wizard,' said a one-armed rogue as he raised his sword and cut a giant sea eel in two.

Flesh-wizard. That was one he hadn't heard.

'A cogent argument well made,' said Fabrigas. 'But really, there is no need for this day to end in death. Why would you strike us down? For are we not all travellers in this universe, and are we not brothers in the next? Are we not just like you? If you strike us, do we not weep? And if you stab us repeatedly with your swords, do we not bleed copiously from our abdomens?' He held his hands, palms up, towards the sailors, his sleeves black holes before their faces. 'I beseech you to look within your hearts. Think of those you once loved, and those you've lost, for as my great-uncle, the poet Treminos, once said: *"Vengeance, aghast, looks to the eyes of pain and sees / His brother, his sister, his self!"'*

Then a change began. The sailors, by degrees, became sadder, their shoulders and their weapons slumped, they began weeping, right there in the market, huge blobs of briny water rolled fat down their cheeks and hit the filthy ground. They began to fall upon their knees, howling, sobbing, crying to the heavens. 'Gaaaaaaaah-ha-ha-ha,' they said. 'My brother! My brother!' they cried. 'What have we done? What have we become?!' 'I never even learned to read!' another cried. And still another cried: 'I love you all so much!' Fabrigas still had the twin black holes of his sleeves raised, and now at last he lowered them, and while the bandits bawled ferociously, while the vendors emerged, stunned, from their stalls, Fabrigas and his new friend, Carlos Lambestyo, slipped silently away.

NOOSE 145

In Carnassus, it is a fine evening. All is well. The hour of chaos has already subsided, though people will talk about it for weeks.

He came: the wizard! He made a hundred desperate sailors cry like babies with the sound of his voice!

There is a miasmic glow in the air tonight: a soothing haze which lags across this effluential paradise. What you thought to be all ugliness is beauty. Two lovers walk here, see? He a young naval officer, she a mistress of a dim profession. They have just met. Young love. It is like a royal procession: this king with his ceremonial sword of conquest; this queen with a sceptre of oily flowers in her hand; dogs and flying insects trailing behind in an adoring escort. The king and his queen step lightly past a ragged, lifeless dog, its belly taut with gas and maggots, its mangy coat peeled back, and its legs pointing lustily to the stars. The flies and insects dance merrily around it, the two lovers notice not. They stroll the catwalk above the great shipyard where hulks of unimaginable size are hammered out, oblivious to the chaos all around them, existing only for each other. Love can indeed exist in such a place as Carnassus, if only for a brief time, and if only after the exchange of an agreed sum.

And down below we find another budding relationship: two men have made it to the sanctuary of the carcass of a half-built warship, and the taller man – the one who looks like an angry warlock – has the smaller man – the one with the scars on his face – trussed up from a spar by a noose around his ankle. Let's listen.

'So well done, you caught me. You really must be a wizard.'

'I . . . am not . . . a WIZARD!' The old man stood and stretched to full height, his voice thundering off the steel husk.

'OK, OK,' said the boy pilot. 'Don't get us found again.'

'Oh, they'll be weeping for at least an hour more,' Fabrigas replied as he showed his pilot the tiny brass jets that poked from the hem of his sleeve. 'It's a mild nerve gas which penetrates the membrane of the nose. It makes you see life through the eyes of others. Very useful. My box.'

'So,' said the Necronaut as he patted around for where he'd stashed the precious box, then handed it to Fabrigas who looked briefly at it before tossing it over his shoulder. They heard the brass spheres sing as they bounced away.

'So,' said the Necronaut.

'It was not a map of the neighbouring universes. It was a pretty but worthless toy. To map another universe would be like trying to lick your own tongue. The idea is absurd.'

Lambestyo was still frozen in the motion of handing over the box, and his eyes had followed the merry orbs into the darkness. He returned both eyes to the old man, and Fabrigas took a step back.

'A good captain is not just a pilot, boy, he is a bodyguard. I needed to test your skill and bravery. Both were adequate. And now I have you caught.'

'Yes. When are you going to cut me down? My ankle is numb and the blood is going to my head.'

The pilot swung lazily from the spar.

'Soon.'

'So you knew that I would end up standing exactly where you placed the noose?'

'Not exactly. I had 145 nooses placed at various locations around the port. The trick was to get you to throw your knives away.'

Lambestyo roughly adjusted his gun belts. 'I see. Very clever. How much meat are you, old man?'

'I am 99.9 per cent flesh. I am immune to the Black Cloud and so have lost no organs to it. Like all of us I had a respirator implanted so I could breathe any gas, or no gas.'

'I see. And so what will I be paid if I decide to take this mission?'

'I have not offered you this mission.'

'But you should. I saved your life, after all.'

'I see you are as tall as your memory. If you remember, in the end, I saved you.'

'Well. Let's call it a draw. It was a close shave.' He rubbed his chin.

'I suppose it was,' said Fabrigas. He looked out into space where the columns of sloops and galleons faded among the fuzz of shining spheres. Today certainly wasn't his closest shave ever. It wasn't even his closest shave in recent weeks. A month ago he'd been to a place a thousand times more terrifying, a thousand times more deadly, than the Airport of Carnassus.

Coarse the sea-net roof
Sheltering this honest shack
Within the mighty airport we have built.
And my sleeves grow wet
With the moisture dripping through the holes.

Poem of an emperor upon visiting Carnassus. Date unknown.

THE DREAM AGE

Fabrigas had risen from a sea of dreams, dripping with excitement, on the morning of the day he was to meet the Queen. He had been astonished when he was informed that he would finally have an audience. It was hard to say how long he'd waited in his small room with its narrow bed, a wooden desk groaning under books and document tubes, its small window framing an achingly familiar scene of gold and silver spheres, but this might put it in perspective: within that span of time, foreign empires had risen, then fallen, then started to rise again, then burst into flames. Great wars had been fought. Humanity had doubled in size while its resources had halved. Spheres beyond the size of suns had been built and torn down. The species had thrown together a telescopic array so large and powerful that it could peer back almost to the dawn of time. The navy had built the oracle called Skycore: a giant ball of hollow string filled with plasma, adrift in a secret part of space, which supposedly used the power of probability to tell the future. So there's that as well.

It had taken an age or more, but the day had come when Queen Gargoylas would finally review Fabrigas's deeds and, if he was lucky, give him his Bill of Passage. He stood, pink-faced, in the middle of the room as he dried his hands and stared at the spheres cluttering his window. When Carrofax drifted in with a young 'slavey' who carried a tray of tea and toast and a copy of the *Gazette and Sentinel* the old man started from his trance. 'Good morning, sir. The *Gazette* has a very interesting piece today about plans to use Skycore to find the Vengeance.'

'Barghhh!' said Fabrigas, which is the noise you make when you try to express disgust with a mouthful of toast. He had no time for the Queen's great ball of string. He watched the girl pour his tea, checking that she trickled in just the right amount of synthetic milk. She had dark skin and ornate tattoos on her young hands, so he knew she must be a slave taken during the Morphium Wars on Zapotek. He kept his fierce eyes upon her while he picked up the first section of his newspaper, then he slowly turned his gaze to the front. The *Gazette*'s banner contained just three letters and a symbol of interrogation: 'UWX?'

The great Sphere of Empires was in a precarious state, beset by shortages and conflict. The eight great Galactagogs of the universe – the U8 – were trapped inside this globe, like fighting animals forced to occupy the same cage. The Holy Neon Empire shared the centre of the sphere with the Vangardiks. They were once a single empire, but since the Great Schism, and the building of the Great Wall of Peace, they were bitter enemies. Nearby was the once mighty Concordat: a loose collection of states who were desperate to avoid war, but equally desperate to hold their place in the centre. The Xo occupied the mysterious outer reaches, the Floating Worlds, and remained a powerful and unknowable force. They were a neutral power, kept no standing army, but exercised power through their secret agency, Dark Hand. The other Galactagogs – the Hyper-boreans, the Skandanyevans, the Kobra, the Cosmogoths – as well as all the many minor powers – were biding their time, aware of the cost of giving the Holy Neon Empire too much power, but equally aware of the price for failing to back the winner. Any small conflict could potentially trigger a 10th Universal War, UWX, and unlike the nine previous conflicts this one would be decisive, unimaginably destructive: it would be a war to end war.

Fabrigas let his eyes drift down to the 'Briefly' column. There was a short piece on the inquiry into disastrous events at the Worlds' Fair, when an attack by enemy agents led to the disappearance of the tiny treasure they called the Vengeance. There was a rumour the escape had been masterminded by Dark Hand. Were the Xo finally renouncing their neutral status?

Attempts were under way to recover the vessel of the Queen's youngest brother, Prince Albert, the last male heir, who had almost brought down the dynasty when he went mad during a yachting regatta and tried to fly his ship into a sun. His name had become a byword for insanity. The magistrates had voted to '. . . give all resources to recovering his remains'.

The Pope was calling for another crusade. But it was something he did at least once a month, so it was hardly news at all. But as the commander of the largest battle fleet in the universe he was not a man any ruler could ignore for long. This month was Panathenaea, the great festival celebrating the Empire's religious glory. The Pope would be visiting. The spectacle would feature a monumental procession through the Avenue to the Necropolis, followed by unfathomable animal sacrifices, before the Inquisition executed a select mob of heretics.

So it was a busy month.

The magistrates had also voted to extend the Workhouse Act into the foreseeable future. This act made it legal to sell the children of debtors into slavery in return for erasing their outstanding balance. 'It is necessary, given the current challenges and chronic shortages our Empire faces, to continue to depend upon the valuable contribution that children make to our economy. They are the "good oil" keeping our Empire moving. Additionally, their fleshy young parts require no oil.'

'Widdibgulusk,' said Fabrigas, which is the sound you make when you try to say 'Ridiculous' with a mouth full of toast.

The slave girl finished her work and hurriedly left the room.

'Do I sense you are excited today?' said Carrofax.

'Certainly I am!' said the wild-faced old man as he swallowed his toast. 'Today I will no longer be a prisoner of this Empire, no? Today I will be free!' His eyes were shining moistly. He crunched into his second slice and chomped merrily.

'Sir is not . . . nervous?' enquired Carrofax.

'Nerbusch! By wub I be nerbusch?'

'Well, there is the faint possibility the Queen may . . . oppose your wishes.'

'Nobsensch!' said Fabrigas.

Two attendants arrived to take them to the docks. Soon they were crossing the stretch of space to the palace in a glass taxi. Fabrigas knew this view like his own face. The sphere on the right – the mid-sized sphere of deep blue steel with sunburst crest – was the Great Royal Hall, where entertainments were performed to millionfold audiences. The tickets were expensive, certainly, but you haven't lived until you've seen the Mutant Opera Company perform Modesto Bazruski's *The Princess and the Megasaurus*. Just to the left was the Library of the Golden Gate, a magnificent gold cube designed to seal itself at the push of a button (because every now and again a ruler came along who thought books were a bad idea). There was the Spielmuseum, the Botanical Complex, Aquasphere X, the Grand Pleasure Dome, the Perihedral Signum, and a host of other imperial sights. And in the centre, contaminating the heavens with a light that stung the eyes, was the Royal Palace of Her Majesty Queen Gargoylas X. He could tell preparations for a brand-new sphere were under way because demolition crews had cleared the charred debris left by a city whose core-sun had exploded, vaporising every object, and each remaining citizen – mostly just the sick and elderly – within. Such was the price of progress. Somewhere in the distant starfields a construction fleet would be building a vast iron frame around a new young star. When finished, the alchemists would do their work, transforming the raw iron from the core of a depleted sun into brass, silver, even gold, until finally the new palace would be dragged to its position, there to remain for countless millennia.

Beyond, the spheres spread out as far as he could see. Some were small and elegant – the exclusive estates, the private schools – while others were unspeakably huge – the prisons, the slum cities. So many stories were contained within them. The universe was like a cloud of gold and silver balloons around them, and as they sailed the breech Fabrigas felt bubbles of excitement rise in his belly to tickle his beard.

BY ORDER OF THE PROPHET

There are eight chambers to reach the Queen in her Slayer's Pavilion. As the elevator doors opened, Fabrigas found himself looking into the First Chamber. In this ante-hall, so vast its walls and ceiling vanish into the haze, an army of proprietors waited, vainly, to petition the Queen for clemency from bankruptcy, and they spent the time by playing dice. The chamber was filled with the white-hot whizz of servos in fingers, the bony crack as steel-knuckled hands released the cubes against the marble walls. At the end of the day one merchant would be chosen at random and sent to see the Queen. If they could emerge from the penultimate chamber with their mind intact, and if the Queen liked their face, their livelihood would be saved. Many came running back screaming from the Third Chamber, and few had a face to please the Queen.

The noise of the dice-play crashed like a dying wave when the towering Fabrigas emerged from the gloom of the elevator car. The eyes followed him as he strode the long mile through the chamber towards a pair of brass doors wide enough to walk an airship through. The doors' handles were a pair of dragons – actual size – caught at the apex of a violently sensuous embrace.

The Second Chamber is filled with frightening statuary of the Demon Backinell: the gathering whose chaos was supposed to have bred the conditions from which the order of the cosmos arose. These demons are engaged in activities from which imagination flees, and upon which a modest writer will not dwell. Here the frightening experience of universal chaos is mingled with the breath of infinite creation.

The door of the Third Chamber has statues of imperial authority: two owls without faces (justice), a great bear nursing a human infant (mercy), and two monkey demons tearing out the throat of a dragon (awesomeness). The visitor would need to leave their airship behind to enter this chamber. Why bring an airship in the first place? The chamber is smaller than the last, and silent – so much so that if you hadn't already broken into a jog, you would. It is forbidden by law to tell you what's in the Third Chamber.

The Fourth Chamber has delicate frescoes of grand royal conquests and in the scheme of the chambers is rather pleasant. Do not be lulled.

The Fifth Chamber is not pleasant. The Chamber of the Screw is entered through a circular door. The visitor finds himself in a rotating barrel: the inverse shape of a great invisible drill. The curling and ornately filigreed edges are blade-sharp, heated to smoking point. The visitor will find themselves scrambling so quickly towards the tiny aperture at the far end they will not have time to consider what this chamber could possibly symbolise.

By the Sixth Chamber the visitor has noticed the successive narrowing and darkening of the chambers of the Queen. This chamber is cramped. The visitor can reach up to touch the ceiling, or out to touch the heads spiked upon steel needles. These are the lords, ladies, magistrates and judges who have disappointed Her. These heads are arranged as so: the first faces the wall, the second is turned ten degrees towards you, the third ten more, and so on, so the effect as you rush past – and rush you will, from a jog into a gallop – is of a single severed head turning to greet you. The floor tacks with blood and the stench is overwhelming.

In the Seventh Chamber the visitor finds their gallop halted by the fact they must crawl through this chamber on their knees, through sticky sheets of spiderweb. The Queen's legion of beloved spiders can grow as big as the human head.

'My Queen,' said Fabrigas, finally, as he emerged and swept the dust from the floor with his beard. 'Word of your beauty has touched the reaches.' He stood and took a small step forward and his cloth shoes slipped on the smoothly inclined floor. The Queen's chamber floor, polished so it shone like an eye, swept down towards her throne – or, to be more precise, it swept down towards a large reservoir where her giant octopus, Leonard, lived. It was a measure to foil assassins. Anyone rushing towards the Queen (perhaps holding a curved dagger or a jar of acid) would find themself skidding off towards Leonard's salty embrace. When Fabrigas slipped, the assembled magistrates, arrayed behind the Queen in a honeycomb of silver wigs, had gasped. From behind the magistrates' gallery the chamber swept smoothly back over their heads, funnelling the sound of their collective dismay across a black, dragon-scale ceiling. The sound reached Fabrigas a good few seconds before the rolling waves of their collective breaths. Fabrigas smelled liquor, tobacco, fine cheeses.

'Silence!' said the Queen. Her voice was as hoarse and leathery as her horsy, leathery face. It is true that Queen Gargoylas had never been beautiful, but now, after so many cosmetic treatments, she wore a look of perpetual fright – as if she'd just stepped from the shower to find a stranger waiting for an autograph. 'Prisoner. You have been brought here for sentencing on charges requiring the penalty of death. You may remove his bonds.' A guard stepped forward to unclasp the restraints around the old man's wrists and they fell to the floor with a frightening clatter, slid down the shiny slope, and stopped just in front of Leonard's tank. And there he stood, the old master, hung with dirty cobwebs, eyes as wild as his beard, a free man – at least for the next few minutes. The Queen's fool, Barrio, crouching beside her throne, let out a shrill, snotty laugh, and Carrofax, standing just behind Fabrigas, bowed his head.

There was utter silence in the Slayer's Pavilion. Queen Gargoylas sat upon her throne of delicately sculpted iron; her dress of palest purple looked like the desiccated wings of a moth. There were metal pins punched through the fabric of her sleeves attached to wires that vanished into the ceiling. Somewhere in the palace there was a servant whose only job was to work the motors which pulled the wires to make the Queen gesture in a regal manner. When she'd said 'death', for example, her right hand had risen, shaking, like the ghost of a small bird, and her bony index finger had floated across her throat.

Then a page stepped forward to read a proclamation, and the silence in the chamber was deafening.

'M. Francisco Fabrigas. You have been charged and convicted of crimes relating to heretical physics, public madness and prognostication without licence.' Fabrigas smiled and nodded. It was all true. 'You have proposed the idea of universes beyond our own, a belief that defies both the position of the Church of the Holy Neon Empire, and that of the royal fam—'

Fabrigas cleared his throat. 'My Queen!' There was a sound from the magistrates like many chairs shifting on a wooden floor. Fabrigas paused. He smelled port, cigars, brandy, denture polish and pickled eggs. The page turned white, his metal legs buckled. The eunuchs beside the throne whirred nervously. No one interrupted a royal proclamation. The Queen's hands rose slightly, quivered, then dropped into her lap. 'Great, merciful Queen, you with the ship that launched a thousand faces. There is nothing to say that has not been said at my *mercifully* brief trial. I have committed heresy of the worst kind by stating that there are universes beyond our own. I'm guilty and I admit to all my crimes. I claimed to have travelled here from another universe, but it was lies, the lies and bluster of a fool.'

'Fool! Fool! Fool!' cried Barrio as he struck the sides of his head with his clenched fists.

'Indeed. It was,' continued Fabrigas, 'a chain of cosmic lies. For does this sphere not contain all that could be hoped for, and all that could be dreamed? Is this not the best of all possible universes?'

'Fool! Fool! Fool!'

Now a low murmur rose and fell from the assembled magistrates.

'The years I have spent as a guest in your prison have taught me that my thoughts and deeds are not fit for this realm. I am a fool, a trickster, little better than a common wizard, and I ask only that I be put to death so that I can no longer be a poison to this kingdom, and to the young minds which dwell herein, within the bosom of your mercy. That is all.'

Fabrigas went to step back, slipped, and raised another low gasp. In the tank before the throne the water quivered, a galaxy of bubbles broke upon the surface.

There was a silence in which the very air seemed to hold its breath.

'Am I to understand,' said the Queen, her palms falling open on her lap, her fingers rigid as the crooked white bones of a winter hedge, 'that you *wish* to be executed?'

Fabrigas let his eyes roll skyward, to the ribbed arches of the ceiling.

'Oh, my wish, my wish, my wishy wish. My wish,' said Fabrigas with a flutter of his long dark lashes, 'is only that justice be done.'

There was a silence in which the very air seemed to quietly, fearfully put on its coat and leave the room.

'Are you aware,' said the Queen, 'that wishing for death is a form of treason which is itself punishable by exile?'

'I was not aware of that!' cried Fabrigas, beaming. 'Things are not looking good for me! But death or exile, it makes no difference!' and he gave a little skip.

'Prisoner!' barked the Queen, her hands becoming two balled fists. The old man stopped skipping and bowed his head. 'Prisoner, it is clear that your skull has some powerfully mad meat trapped in it. Granted, there was a time when you would have been executed for claiming to be from another universe.'

'Was?' laughed Fabrigas nervously.

'This month at Panathenaea there will be another assembly of the

Grand Inquiry, in which some seven million witches, warlocks and wizards are to be put to death. You were to be among them.'

'Were to be?'

'But certain things have happened while you were imprisoned that have changed our views on creation.'

'Oh no,' said Fabrigas under his breath.

'Last night I had a dream.'

'Oh no, no, no, no, no.'

'Yes, prisoner. I had a dream as wild and vivid as life. I had a dream that our people rose up and lived the true meaning of our creed: to strive, to seek, to conquer and never to yield. I had a dream that all the peoples of the universe would come together, and I would rule them as Queen for ever. And you were the hero of this dream. The dream told me that you would be the one to take our ships to the next universe, to bring glory to your Empire and Queen. I saw visions of conquest and victory. I saw our hammers bloody, and our crooked highways paved with diamonds. So you are not to be executed, or exiled, today, dear Fabrigas. You are saved. You have received your quantum of punishment and are free to go. We wish only to choose the direction and style of your going.'

'Oh no no no no no no no no no.'

ONCE IN A LIFETIME

Oh, I know, I know, I know, this is all hellishly confusing. A man arrives in a space-saucer and claims to have travelled from another universe – a universe identical to this one – except that he has already left to travel to the next universe. He is thrown into prison for cosmic heresy, later freed on a trumped-up exoneration based largely on a dream about a starfish and a giant clam. Ah! It is infinitely confounding. Black is up, left is white, and nothing is as it seems. I would not blame you in the slightest if you went off to read that lovely romance book your husband bought you for your name day: *Captain A'Rod's Crimson Whip*.

If you wish to familiarise yourself with the details of this strange case, you might read *The People Versus M. Francisco Fabrigas Versus Time/Space: How One Man Challenged the Laws of Physics . . . & Lost*, by A. W. Frankzetter. But in the meantime, do hang tight. In time it all becomes clearer, I promise.

*

Certainly much had changed since Fabrigas survived his own execution at the cannon's mouth and proposed a theory for exploring alternate realities: when he was young, beardless, cocky and un-bridled; when he gambolled with women and had adventures; when he took hallucinogenic cactus on Zapotek and dreamed he was a tortoise. He had thrown in his comfortable position as a researcher

to join the Academy's Exploratory Unit. He could never have imagined then where this decision would lead him as he stood before the
esteemed members of the Academy and proposed, '. . . an ocean of
infinite possibilities'.

'My near-death experience at the cannon's eye has shown me the
way. If our universe is the sum of what is probable, then the
Omniverse is a collection of all that is possible. We are on the cusp
of a dramatic new age in exploration, an era which I call "The Dream
Age". This rapid expansion of our consciousness will lead us to
dimensions full of strange new treasures. It is likely that we will find
examples of universes almost precisely like ours.'

He heard laughter from the dimness of the auditorium. But the
young explorer was undeterred. 'It might be possible to find dimensions at different points in time/space. To travel to them would be
to travel forwards and backwards through history, to stop wars before
they begin, to share knowledge of the future, to save great men and
women from horrible ends, to become immortal, to know the mind
of the *gods*.'

A galaxy of wide unblinking eyes. What heresy was this?

'It might be that in an adjoining reality there is a man identical to
me giving this exact same speech – only he is even more handsome.
Imagine sending diplomatic missions to our own Empire! It might
be possible to do this, but it will take more than intellectual effort
from us. It will take an explorer's heart. It will take *balls*!'

More laughter from the darkness.

'And no ordinary balls, either. We'll need balls the size of spheres
to do this. But more than this, for the Dream Age to succeed,
humanity will need to set aside its differences and come together as
one great species.'

The most laughter yet from the darkness.

'What does he mean, exactly?' said the scholars who lean on bars.
'That there is another universe where the Wall vanishes and the
Vangardiks become our brothers?'

'What is he saying?' said the ladies who meet for tea. 'That there is a dimension where moons are cheese? Ridiculous.'

'Are you proposing,' said his arch-rival, Helbosch, 'that somewhere there is a universe exactly like this except that I am stark naked?'

'Perhaps,' replied Fabrigas, 'though that is certainly not a universe which *I* would like to be in.' Everyone had giggled royally, yet his proposal had won few supporters. The scientific journals sagged beneath the weight of condemnation. His reputation crumbled, as did his mind. He was seen wandering the corridors of the Academy in a dishevelled state, muttering under his breath. He let his beard grow long. As he ate alone in the dining arcade, he could hear people murmuring, 'I wonder if there is another universe where Fabrigas brushes the crumbs from his beard.'

'Well, at least he has his balls for company.'

*

Things came to a terrifying head on a beautiful summer's day on a tiny planet called New Hermes. Fabrigas had taken a plot of land in the wilderness there so that he could carry out some field experiments that would prove some very important things about the nature of space and gravity. Most of these, alarmingly, involved blowing things up, or firing cannons at them, or both. 'In the heart of an explosion lies the secrets to the universe!' said Fabrigas. On the seventh day, in a field full of charred craters littered with empty WD40-X canisters, Fabrigas announced to his shell-shocked audience that he was going to prove the fundamental constant of gravity by firing his master into the sky with a cannon. 'If my calculations are correct,' the young man said, 'then he will join the orbit of this planet for a single arc before floating gently down on his life chute.' No one had any reason to doubt his calculations, he was the second-best scientist in the universe. Dr Provius looked calm as he climbed into the cannon, he even smiled and waved to the crowd. He trusted his star pupil. The cannon leaped and Provius disappeared over the trees, punched through the fluffy white clouds, touched the outer atmosphere, and kept going. History does not record the reaction of the former first-best physicist in the universe on being fired into space, only the reaction of the former second-best, now first-best, yet inconsolable. He tried to follow his master, but was restrained.

*

In just a few months Fabrigas had gone from galactic celebrity to cosmic outcast. He could not be tried for the murder of his master, since Provius had willingly climbed into the cannon, but everyone knew where the fault lay. His already crumbling reputation was ground to a fine dust. He was disgraced, stripped of his Academy position and his renown as one of the great minds in his Empire.

Then, on the eve of his thirty-third birthday, M. Francisco Fabrigas made his most shocking declaration. To universal astonishment, he announced that he was leaving his universe to travel beyond the borders of reality. 'I am undertaking a voyage to the next dimension, using an engine of my own design. I am an explorer, and I will prove the existence of other realities the only way I can: by travelling there and returning.'

'And just who will be mad enough to accompany you on this expedition?' said the scholars who meet in dingy cafes.

'No one,' said Fabrigas. 'This will be a solo expedition.'

Laughter. Cruel, cruel laughter.

And so the former great explorer set off to chart the Infiniverse in his tiny saucer with its top-secret interdimensional engine. He left his Empire behind, travelled out into the furthest reaches. There, in the remotest corner of the universe, he experienced breathtaking solitude as he passed through regions of space so empty that there was not a breath of light. He had no crewmates to share an exclama-tion with as he came upon the remains of a galaxy-sized computation array left behind by a civilisation forgotten by the ages. No one heard his screams as he fell into the furious winds of the Nebula Australis. The winds flung his craft like a discus to almost a third the speed of light. He was knocked unconscious by the gravitational forces. When he awoke, if his testimony is to be believed, he found that he had vanished from his universe, and appeared in a new one.

It was a universe identical to the one he had come from. He was discovered by a team of oil prospectors who agreed to take him and his damaged saucer craft back to the Empire. As he travelled back, astonished, he found the same constellations, the same planetary systems. And when he arrived in the cities (which seemed, to the eye, utterly identical to the cities he had left), he found people identical to the ones he'd said goodbye to. These people claimed to have farewelled him on his voyage to the next universe just a few months before.

Yes, I know what you are thinking. A lesser Omninaut (such as yourself) would have concluded, seeing these same places, these same bemused people, that he had in fact never *left* his universe. But M. Francisco Fabrigas was not a lesser Omninaut. He was a greater one, and this universe, he concluded, was clearly not his. Even when he returned to his old apartment and found it abandoned. Even when his keys fitted the door. Even when he found cards on the table from his few remaining acquaintances, wishing him well on his voyage to the next universe. That was the only difference he could detect in this universe: that he had already left it. 'So my exact double set off at the same time as I did. How extraordinary!' Those around him shook their heads in disbelief.

He was disappointed not to meet himself. He wandered around his double's apartment in a dream, picking up objects and saying, 'This is not my beautiful lamp. This is not my marble baboon.' This was not his unconquerable universe. It was an alien universe, and it made him feel even more alone, even more of a stranger than he ever had.

★

It was also the kind of dimension – much like the one he claimed to have left – which did not take to strangers, or their ideas about other universes. Until now.

'. . . And then when the giant clam opened you were standing there, dressed only in kelps and weeds of the ocean. And you held in your hand a starfish, and you said, "Take, my Queen, this is for you. I bring you the stars, the stars from the borderless sea." Oh, what a dream it was!' The Queen spoke now in the excited voice of a child. 'Is it not fantastic? My vision has told me that you would be the one to restore this Empire's greatness, and give the people hope again. So you see how this great Empire needs you, my dear old Fabrigas.'

(*Dear* old Fabrigas. The Queen had once declared that if he spoke again of other universes she would have him fed to omnigators, and then have those fed to wild mountain pigs, and then have those set on fire.)

'Our people suffer from plague and shortages. Our enemies mass at our borders. They want to destroy us. We need hope again. And that is why we are sending a fleet to the next dimension.'

'No no no. Oh please, no . . .'

The Queen was building to a fever pitch, the wires attached to her limbs were fizzing on their pulley wheels. 'My people need hope. They despair, my people, but when they hear that the Great Fabrigas has decided to help us by leading us to the next universe they will sing again!'

'My . . . my Queen,' said Fabrigas, 'I *beg* of you not to require of me such a thing . . . ' He took a small step, a large slip, the magistrates gasped, in the tank below a single fat tentacle flopped upon the floor with a slap that echoed like a whip-crack.

'Do not be frightened.' The Queen's eyes were wide, her voice a whisper. 'You will be given the best and fastest vessel, a strong and able crew, as fine a pilot as we can catch, and you will be in the company of the largest and most formidable battle fleet we can muster. You need not fear. This is not a death sentence. You will be like one of our great young heroes: leading our warriors into the unfathomable depths, facing many trials, returning home to my bosom a conqueror. Your face will be carved in the Hall of the Heroes. You will stand forever with other Immortals: Tristanzi, Gyminastica, Ultravoxus.'

'My Queen, I am not a young hero any more. I am an old man. For the love of everything, I am more than one thousand years old!'

'Silence, hero! It is decided. Now I'm thirsty!' cried the Queen. Both her hands flew into the air and hung there for a second. 'Thirsty!' cried Barrio, his crooked mouth slick with spittle. Eunuchs sped into the room carrying silver trays with glasses full of coloured liquids. 'Red!' cried the Queen. 'I want r-r-r-r-red!' The word 'red' whirred off her tongue like a propeller. A eunuch held a beaker the colour of day-old blood to the Queen's face and her awful, greenish lips closed like a sea slug around the tip of the straw. The sucking sound rang through the chamber; it sounded like strips of paper being slowly torn. And Fabrigas's heart – that too had been torn into even pieces. He gazed down at the iron cuffs which lay nearby. He thought about his comfortable cell with all his books and his nice, comfortable bed. He looked down at the now-still pond in front of the throne. Several would-be assassins had tried to use non-slip shoes to reach the Queen. They now slept with Leonard. He thought for a second how nice and simple it would be to join the giant octopus in his calm, cool world below the surface.

A FREE BIRD

Word busted from the chamber with the purposeful fury of a team of elephants. In the First Chamber the dice-men turned, gaped, and were trampled. In minutes word had stormed the palace: 'He is free! The wizard is released! He is redeemed! The Queen says there are other universes!' and then it broke into the Empire, and it was no longer like elephants, it was like a plague-fall: invisible, invasive, leaping from skin to lip and ship to ship, the speed at which it tripped across the starry-mist was frightening. Men swooned. Women raised their fists and cheered. The Ethernet lit up, all systems overloaded, there were several major burnouts in the hubs. In days it spread across the Empire. 'Fabrigas has been released from prison! Fabrigas will lead an expedition to the next universe! All is forgiven! He will not let us down!'

The enemy empires picked up the news through their delicate spy networks. The Vangardiks, faced for the first time with the genuine threat of a trans-dimensional attack, upgraded their threat level to 'Burnt umber'. Then, having flown merrily across the known universe, the word returned to the old man's cell, slipped under the door, and found his face stricken with a breathtaking sadness. The word came back on the banner of the *Gazette and Sentinel*: 'DREAM OF A QUEEN: THE WIZARD OUR SAVIOUR?'

He heard it whispered by the guards who passed his door: the hope, the tragic optimism. 'This will show those Vangardik beggars!

This will teach them for stealing our ice girl!' He saw it in the eyes of the girl who brought him his toast. It was the worst look she could possibly have given him: it was a look of hope.

'Is sir not yet packed to leave?' said Carrofax tenderly. 'Her Majesty has made you a free bird.'

'Yes. Free,' said the free bird.

The free bird left his toast and his newspaper unpecked. He left the corner of his bed, the books in piles, the papers, and went over to the small window. There were no bars on the window. Why should there be when outside is an ocean of emptiness?

Me babe we had a sweetly love,
Those feelings cannot change.
(Oi!)
So please don't take it badly,
'Cause the lord knows I'm to blame.
(Oi!)
But, if I stayed here with you,
Things could never be the same.
'Cause I'm free upon the ocean,
And this bird ye cannot tame.
(Oi!)
(This bird ye cannot tame,
This bird ye cannot tame.)
I'm free upon the ocean,
And this bird ye cannot tame.
    (Oi!)

'Sea Bird' – traditional shanty

Modern Times

By M. F. Fabrigas, aged 6 & ¾

In the future we will have invented many things that do not
exist today. Some of these things will be time ships, time viewers
(masks you can wear so you can see back in time to before you
were born), portable phonographs (for travelling), sleeping
tonics (that let a person sleep for only one hour and wake
refreshed), and a way to communicate with creatures and other
species who have different languages from ours. We will find
new energy sources besides steam and oil which will mean that
we can build smaller engines for travelling on land, sea and
space. I would like to have a ship that can travel under the water.
I think that some people have already invented this, such as
armies, but they keep it a secret from us. I would like to invent
a ship that was the size of a carriage so that families would be
able to travel in space without having to go on big uncomfortable ships that sink. I think we could have a small ship that runs
on compressed gas and that has comfortable seats and a table
for cards and perhaps even a small phonograph or magic lantern
for entertainments on a long voyage. In the future I think we
could travel a long way by putting people to sleep for the whole
voyage and then waking them when we arrive. That is all that
I think about the future.

M.F.F. (x.x.x.)

HE WHO SAW THE DEPTHS

'Keep a good ship,' his father had always said, and by that he meant that you should run your company, and your family, as if it was a mighty ship of war. His father, the book baron, had made his fortune printing cheap copies of the great books of the universe. They kept a big house in a wealthy gated district of Carnassus, walled off from the supernumerary horrors of the city. They had a servant, and young Fabrigas a nanny, called Danni, whom he loved. He worked hard at study, helped his mother at home and became so engrossed in subjects that his father often had to come to his room and say, 'Stop now. Sleep. Tomorrow, greatness!' His tutor went mad when Fabrigas learned his whole year's work in a week. He quit and went to live on a moon.

After that came events well documented. Fabrigas solved a difficult problem posted on a public board and was given the place of junior monk at the Dark Friars' Academy. Then he shocked the Academy by leaving to become an explorer.

'Great scientists should not read; they should go, and see!'

His master was cautiously supportive. 'Keep a good ship,' Provius had always said, and by that he meant that an explorer should keep his body – the vessel in which he lived and breathed – in rugged good health. Eat well, sleep well, exercise your body and your mind. 'For what good is a sturdy ship if you yourself are sick?' He had always been wise, much wiser than his pupil. How Fabrigas missed him. He missed him so much that some days he could hardly stand the knot of pain in his chest. He would lie, often for days, in his bed, his hand clutched to his chest, while Carrofax sat mercifully, patiently by.

'Carrofax,' he would cry, 'I am not much longer for this stormy sea of life!'

'Oh,' his loyal servant would say, 'if only I could tell you that was true, sir, but you are still a long way from the shore.'

And it had always been a long and difficult journey. In the years of isolation his vessel had sagged low in stagnant waters. This universe was dark and full of death and misery. He despised this universe, and he despised himself for coming here. And now another mission full of pain and suffering! How strange, how awful. Since the death of his master, Fabrigas had made nine attempts on his own life. He had failed nine times. Ten, if you count today's attempt to have the Queen execute him. Even in self-murder he was a failure. It was always when Carrofax was away on important business. As his despair had deepened his efforts had become more concerted, more elaborate, but every time he tried something would go wrong: a rope would break, a gun would jam, the toxin from the thorn of the lover's rose would leave him sick for days, but not end him, the poisonous bats would for some reason refuse to bite his neck. Soon all dangerous objects had been removed from his cell. 'Prince Albert, now, he had the right idea. Steer your ship into the sun! Feel the terrible burning fury of this great universe and know that you are nothing! That is the way to go.'

'But, master,' his servant had said, 'why is it that you want to vanish?'

'Because I think this might be hell, and no man wants to live there.'

'Oh, master, if only I could make you see the truth.'

In some strange way, Fabrigas did see the truth. He saw how these failed attempts to assassinate himself bore out his theory of a great Infiniverse. There are infinite universes, some in which he was, some in which he wasn't. But of course he could never *be* in a universe in which he was dead. Certainly, in other universes the gun might work, the spinning blade might do its job, the thorns of the roses he clutched to his breast would prick his flesh and the lovely poison would take him off to eternity. But in this universe, the one he inhabited, he would always remain alive, he would always be in hell.

TITANROD

'A dream! A dream! What is this dream, sisters?' The Man in the Shadows was a terrifying young individual. He'd inherited his mother's fortune while still a teenager and used it to build an empire of frightening influence. He had the ears of kings, the hearts of princesses, and the balls of anyone who'd crossed him. He had called the Queen's three sisters to his super-yacht, *Titanrod*, as soon as he'd heard about the Queen's nocturnal epiphany. 'The Queen doesn't dream, she doesn't dare. She cowers like a naughty fool in the dark and waits for daylight. So tell me how your idiot sister suddenly had a dream which puts Plan UWX at risk.'

They were at moor at a private marina near the palace under the pretext of a pleasure cruise around the Asphodel Meadows. Things were tense. The Queen's three sisters occupied the sofa opposite in frozen magnificence. From behind an almond-shaped glass lounge table on which stood an abstract ceramic sculpture, they peered at this brooding boy as he sat in his velvet bucket chair and tossed a lava ball from hand to hand.

'We confess, young sir, we did not know about the dream,' said sister one, in a voice like a barber's blade slicing through a sheet of fine paper. 'It is news to us.'

'I had everything in place, sisters. The old wizard was virtually at the executioner's table. Our assassins close in on our master's enemy, the Vengeance. Her death could have been pinned on the Queen.

She would have been hauled from the throne like a dog, and you would finally have been in power. Now it's all in jeopardy because your sister had a bloody dream!' He flung his lava ball at the phonograph machine which had been playing a lively modern tune on drum and vibes. The song died under a pile of glass and coloured goo; the plush den was cast into a jagged silence. 'Who put her up to this? I want to know.'

Each sister kept her gruesome smile, her corpsy repose.

'We do not know, sir,' said sister two, in a voice like a sock full of nettles. 'She has no friends in court. We killed them all. There are only ghosts beside her bed, and her fool, Barrio.'

'Perhaps Dark Hand have infiltrated the palace.'

'Nonsense, sisters. They could never get close enough to have the Queen's ear.'

'Perhaps she simply had a dream, sir.'

'She didn't have a dream!' The Man in the Shadows kicked out, shattering an omni-breasted porcelain nude worth almost as much as the golden ship it rode in. 'This was a political masterstroke. Her mission is all the people are talking about now. They have hope in their eyes. With a single move she's saved her head, saved her wizard, and stalled UWX by months or years. Imagine what will happen if her hero succeeds!' The Man in the Shadows feigned to laugh, then shook the incredulous smile from his face. He smoothed his trousers, calmed slightly. 'Let me explain, one more time, how the game is supposed to play out. Our master – all love and fear him – has asked us to kill a small girl – his arch-enemy's daughter – and an elderly wizard before the two can meet. In return, he will give us great power. With his help we can finally smash down the Wall, re-form the Old Empire and conquer the centre. There will once more be a single Empire at the centre of the sphere. The battle for the centre of the sphere is the game. Win the centre, win the game. It's the only battle. If people travel beyond the boundaries of the universe there is no centre, there is no battle. Plan UWX becomes pointless. It's like playing cards with someone who can wish themself a better hand.'

'But the wizard is a fool, sir. Our intelligence says his trans-dimensional engine probably doesn't even work.'

'Probably isn't good enough. We must be certain. Our master looks down upon everything, he sees all: past, present, future. The old wizard is pretending to be a god. That is why he has to burn. Our master wills it. As separate agents the Vengeance and the wizard are problematic; but if they join together they become a *nightmare* for our plans, and his.'

'Perhaps this is a secret blessing, young sir,' said sister number three, with a voice like a sack of rats with crêpe paper wrapped round their tails.

'A *blessing*.' He made to pretend-laugh again, this time transforming it into an open-mouthed frowning toss of the head.

'Yes, a blessing. Our idiot sister's plan is only a good one if the wizard makes it to the next universe. If he fails it will be a swifter end for her. She is desperate. And if Skycore is right and fate really does want to bring the wizard and the Vengeance together – why, so be it. With the right trap set all our problems could end together. In fire and blood. Then the battle is won in a stroke.'

There was a beat in which the Man in the Shadows' fists unclenched.

'This is not the worst plan, sisters. I could arrange a surprise for the wizard at the crossing. If the Vengeance is there, even better. But first I must consult my oracle about these developments.'

'You'll go to Skycore now, with all that is happening?'

'*Pffft*. Skycore. That useless ball of string. Give it to the kittens, sisters. I have a much more powerful oracle now.'

'Where?'

'Where is this oracle?'

'We must see it.'

'You will never see it, sisters. It is very well disguised: in that it is not disguised, and is in the first place you would think to look. Look at your faces. Priceless.'

'Do not mock us, sir.'

'But there is one other serious matter, sisters.'

'We sense it.'

'A file has gone astray from one of the communication hubs in the Sentinel complex.'

'Not possible.'

'More than possible.'

'What information has this file?'

'It was a dark communiqué containing details of our Master Plan for UWX.'

'This is terrible news. You understate it. It is beyond serious.'

'It is, true, but it is easily manageable. The file is encrypted, protected, and it has to make it all the way to our enemies if it's to be useful. And that is a very, *very* long way. I am about to send my best agents to destroy the file. I need not tell you what the consequences are if our master learns a file has leaked.'

'You do not.'

'With his guidance these hubs will soon be outmoded. I'll make preparations for the wizard's destruction before I leave for the oracle. In the meantime, make sure Misfortune's Queen has no more dreams.'

M8B

Fame. Everyone dreams of fame. You long to live for ever, to gain the power of flight. But fame is fickle. One minute you're a young man alone in the universe; the next you're travelling beyond the stars and making grand discoveries; the next you're being ridiculed for proposing that it might be possible to travel beyond the boundaries of time and causality and exist in other dimensions; the next you're being defrocked and imprisoned for cosmic heresy; the next you're being exonerated and exalted as a saviour of your kind, saved from your execution and sent, ironically, on a mission of certain death – all because some queen had a dream that a starfish spoke to her. It's typical, really.

It was madness at the docks. It was the day before the voyage and the people of Carnassus came up: the young, the old, the strong, the sick, the rusty, many of the very ones who had tried to murder the old man just a few weeks earlier. They came up, slick, from out of the slum depths and rammed the docks to breaking point. They crowded the way to the necromancer's hut.

It is customary (and by customary I of course mean compulsory), in many human empires, to consult astrologers before long expeditions. Without an astrological consultation none of the great insurance houses would insure a voyage. The Empire employed a gaunt and cave-eyed legion of necromancers, shadowmancers, gastromancers, augurers and other charlatans to pull apart the entrails of fish, or to poke at tea leaves, and to tell the pilot or explorer whether the expedition would be successful. Fabrigas knew them. If Fabrigas had two hopes when he arrived in this strange (yet almost identical) universe, the first was to find his master alive, the second was to discover that every single one of these prognosticating charlatans had died of stupidity-related illnesses. In his early days, in his own universe, he had been forced to visit hundreds of these fools, and doing so had only confirmed his suspicions that they didn't have the faintest idea what they were talking about.

'Did the man who tore the entrails out of a helpless bird to tell me that my trip to Arcadius would see me "return with more discoveries than the Emperor could dream of" think to tell me that the only discovery I would make was that fire-breathing sand lizards don't like it when you watch them mating?'

'I cannot answer that at this time,' said the Magic Eighth.

The Magic Eighth was by far the most ridiculous prognosticator the old man had ever been forced to visit. He was a huge man with a wobbly, oily belly which flowed across his belt. He was a spheromancer. Spirits, he claimed, inhabited his belly and would speak through a small sphere he held. He would sit in a kind of trance, tongue lolling out, and he would shake his 'Magic Eighth Ball' vigorously, so that his fat belly wobbled, and then he would answer in a strangled voice.

'I just want to know if . . .' Fabrigas sighed heavily, '. . . if my mission will be successful.'

Shake shake shake.

'. . . Ask me later,' said the Magic Eighth Ball.

'Oh, for the love of . . .'

Sometimes Fabrigas felt entirely alone in a dim and superstitious Empire. Even with all that science had done for them, the cities that hung like burning crowns in space, the airships that took them flying off to where they wished to go, they still preferred to believe that the paw of a now-extinct creature called the rabbit would bring them luck.

'Did it bring the poor rabbit any luck?' said Fabrigas.

'. . . All signs point to maybe.'

'What kind of answer is this?'

'Look,' the Magic Eighth broke from his trance briefly, 'I can't tell the belly spirits what to say, I just read what it says on the ball. That is what my papa taught me, and his papa before him, and his papa –'

'Yes, yes, yes, we all have papas.'

The Magic Eighth paused, mouth open, as if about to speak, but then did not, and for a second Fabrigas thought he looked as frozen as his own photograph. Fabrigas felt a chill in the small hut.

'Yes . . . You were saying?'

Silence from the Magic Eighth. And then when he finally did speak, the voice which crawled out of his mouth was not his own, and his eyes looked drained of life.

'Fabrigas. Receive us. Do you know us? We know you. Over.'

Fabrigas paused, choked a little. 'I . . . beg your pardon?'

The Magic Eighth said nothing.

'I . . . do not think we've met,' croaked the old-beard. 'Have we met?'

Nothing for a long while. The Magic Eighth was so still that even his fat had stopped wobbling. Then . . .

'Fabrigas. Receive us. We are Dark Hand. You know us. We gave you a letter and a book. We gave you protection against great enemies. We are speaking with you through this man at enormous risk and at a frequency which only you can perceive.'

'I'm . . . I'm present.'

'You are present. But not willing. Do not give in to your own schemes and misgivings. There is a new plot against you. An ambush at the crossing. Many dead if you aren't prepared. Over.'

The old man sighed.

'No misgivings. Here is your cosmic reading: you will still go on your mission. No error. You will fulfil your promise to us. You will meet a child. This child has a file. It is mathematically certain that you will meet. So much depends on this equation that it is impossible to express it.'

'But I —'

'No interruptions. Not until we say "over". There is a plot to rule the universe. We are working to stop this plot. This child you will meet travels with a file containing details of the plot. You must protect this child and bring the file to our friends, the Immortals. Bringing the file to them is the only way to stop the plot. We will help you along the way where we can. But to fail in this mission will endanger both our species, and indeed every species. Over.'

'Well, I fully intend to —'

'No you do not. We know your mind. You forget.' The temperature in the tent had fallen to just above freezing, while the Magic Eighth had risen several inches off his prognostication mat. He floated rigid in the air, yet still spoke in that calm, measured voice.

'We know what your intentions are. Let us settle this for eternity.' The Magic Eighth raised one arm, stiffly, plucked two pebbles from an ornamental bowl, one black, one white, and placed them on the straw mat before the old man. 'Now is the time to choose the course of the rest of your life. If you wish to accept the destiny life has chosen for you, pick up the black pebble. If you wish to decline this mission and return to a peaceful life, choose white. Choose. Over.'

And the old man did. He picked up the white pebble from the mat and held it in his palm before the fat astrologer and said, 'I'm sorry, I'm just really *very* tired.'

'Then it is decided. You have chosen black. Over.'

'Wait, that's not the one I . . . I wanted to choose white. Let me do it over. Over.'

'You don't need to say "over". It will change nothing, but very well, choose again. Over.'

This time the old man was very careful to choose the white pebble. The pebble of tranquillity.

'Black. Another excellent choice. Over.'

'You are tricking me, mystery-men! You know I want white.'

'No trick. We know what you mean to do, and you will do it every time. You are in control. It is a mathematical certainty. Why are you trying to separate this pebble from all the other events in your life? You must release your hold. Dissolve, become new. Surrender to the autonomous dynamics of your primal material. We covered this already. Over.' And Fabrigas had no answer.

'The child will come aboard with the file. You will speak to an entity called Blue Lantern. He will give further instructions. That is all for now. We hope this has been enlightening. Over.'

And then the Magic Eighth returned to his own mind and said, 'Where was I? Something about sand lizards. Who's been messing with my pebbles?'

Fabrigas quickly paid the man. The fat oracle extended a chubby finger to the shelf stacked with Eighth Balls and said, 'Would you like to purchase your very own M8B?'

He did not.

Fabrigas stumbled out to the docks where a crowd of oily souls began to shout, 'There he is! It's Fabrigas! What-ho! What news from the belly spirits?!'

Fabrigas smiled faintly, tried his best to give a reassuring wave. He did not understand why these beings – whom he'd last heard from so long ago he'd grown to believe they'd always been imaginary – would contact him now. He didn't know any children. He hated children. And he did not need a magic ball to help him. He could tell from events in the spheromancer's hut that it would take more than balls to get him to the next universe.

Oh, ev'ry rose she has a thorn,
Like ev'ry night she has a dawn,
And pirates sing a deathly song,
Oh, ear-ly in the mor-ning.

Oh, ev'ry rose she has a thorn,
Like ev-a-ry rooster sings the morn,
And I'll be home, it won't be long,
You'll see me in the mor-ning.

'Each Rose, She Has a Thorn' – traditional shanty

STEAMLINER COLOSSUS

H.G. Grossfort Imperial Steamship Co. Ltd

IN ASSOCIATION WITH THE

 # Blue Star Line Co. Ltd
OF
Whitewitch

Has great pleasure in
announcing the departure of its

NEW SUPERSHIP
THE RSS COLOSSUS

The largest passenger ship yet bvilt within the known universe.

THE SHIP HAS BEEN CONSTRUCTED USING THE
LATEST ENGINEERING TECHNOLOGIES TO BE

UNSINKABLE

AND HAS BEEN DECLARED BY THE
EMBLAT ROYAL INSURANCE CO. TO BE

UTTERLY IMPERVIOUS TO SPACE-BERGS

 The unsinkable *Colossus* departs on the 3rd day of the
dark half of the 4th solar month for a mission to view
the black hole at Kollketta DX4, with stops at St Arkem's
Nebula. Berths in 1st class, 2nd class, 3rd class, steerage
and sub-steerage for 9, 7, 3, 1 and ½ sh respectively.

THE NECRONAUT

A good voyage depends upon a good ship, for a poor crew can survive on a good ship, but even a good crew stands little chance on a poor one. A good ship is light but sturdy, its fasts and stays are all in good repair, and its solar sails have no micro-tears or wrinkles. A good ship has a well-tuned propulsion system and all the latest navigational equipment. It has a nose-cone full of well-trained anti-crash bats, not just budgies painted black to look like bats (as some unscrupulous operators have been known to provide). A good ship is a steady ship. A good ship carries no surprises, but holds all hopes.

This ship, the one selected by M. Francisco Fabrigas for his voyage to the Interior, was not, based upon appearances, a good ship.

The expedition's naval engineers had been aghast when they first saw the vessel he had selected. His fleet commander, a man called Descharge, had shaken his head in disbelief. Fabrigas had been offered his choice of the finest naval vessels; the one he had chosen was a poorly converted former pirate ship. It was a deep-space galleon, in the Gothic style, a nugget of steel with a solar-sail array and a rear magnet battery. These were admittedly well-to-do pirates, the kind the Queen might call 'open-sea prospectors'. The officer decks were grandly decorated with marble, gold, ornate cornices and chandeliers made from silver skulls and bones. The ship had a semi-automated flight deck and navigation centre, a lounge, a galley, a split-level 'deck' under a reinforced glass shield. The life-support systems were semi-automated to regulate air and light according to an artificial cycle of days and nights. But the lower decks were a were-rabbit's warren of tubes and steel tunnels. They had been freshly painted, yes, but there was still the faint smell of booze, and bloodstains in some of the rooms, and there were secret compartments that you could fall into if you accidentally leaned against the wrong panel. It was a terrifying ship.

The ship was not powerful, or well gunned, but it was agile, simply built and strong. Fabrigas needed a ship sturdy enough to take his new Residual Inter-universal Perpetuating Solenoid (RIPS) engine, the engine he'd invented to propel a ship into the next universe. It wasn't that the RIPS was large; in fact, it was less than the size of a loaf of bread. But this particular version was very, very, *very* heavy. It contained such a density of dark ooze that it had added almost another eighth to the weight of the ship.

The engine was quite similar to the one Fabrigas had first sketched on the back of a napkin all those centuries ago, but he had made a great number of modifications to it, adding innovations born from advances in dark-energy mechanics, micro-engineering, and craftier-than-light technology. He had solved some of the problems, he hoped, encountered by the foreign empires who had stolen plans for his engine and attempted to recreate it. Namely: Hex Permanence, Sudden Explosion Phenomenon, Crew Disappearance Syndrome and post-Jump vomitings. He had designed the most advanced engine in the universe for arguably one of the least advanced ships.

The crew that had been attracted to this mission by the newspaper adverts were likely to be unwholesome specimens: naval sailors fresh from court martial, or prisoners sentenced to death for theft, fraud or murder, whose only remaining chance was to die in space with honour. Or they'd be spies for the Queen. But most would be slave children lent by Her Majesty from her factories. 'Slaveys', as they were called. So, to sum up: a rancid former pirate ship staffed by children and criminals and spies and captained by an angry teenager.

'It is almost as if he *wants* to fail,' spat Commander Descharge.

To cap it off, his ship was called the *Owl IV*. The *Owl*! The stupidest, most dim-witted bird in the universe, and an emblem of misfortune at sea. On inspection day he'd found his pilot, young Lambestyo, at the docks, standing by his new ship and squinting.

'This is a horrible boat.'

'I know,' replied Fabrigas. 'But it is inconspicuous and strong and very hard to blow up. You'll see.'

'The owl is a stupid bird,' said the Necronaut.

Fabrigas nodded. The pilot adjusted his gun belts. The old man couldn't help but notice that he was glancing around nervously. 'And I want the name changed. I want the ship to have a strong name. I want it to be called the *Necronaut*. Yes.'

'Like you?'

'So?'

'You want the ship to be named after you?'

'I am the captain. And I want a raise,' said the captain. 'My fee has doubled.'

Fabrigas shook his head and sighed. 'I'll change the name. I frankly don't care. And if you want a raise I'll happily take you to the Queen and you can ask her.'

'I'm not scared of any queen. I got this from a queen,' and he pulled away his collar to show a fine, purplish scar. 'You ask her. Double what we agreed and half up front.' Then he'd looked up at the *Owl* one last time, spat on the ground and stalked off.

*

Now, a month later, it was launch day and Captain Lambestyo, aka the Necronaut, had failed to show up to pilot his ship, the *Necronaut*.

Fabrigas stood on the dock near his new vessel and noted that his official send-off consisted of a dour public bird reading a short note from the Queen, and a military brass quartet playing a tune called

'Wishin' You Well'. And yes, I said 'public bird'. Since there were thousands of missions every day requiring some kind of well-wishing from her, and since she didn't have nearly enough public officials to go around, the Queen had decreed that a vast army of parrots be bred and trained to read her messages at events.

'Queen Gargoylas X, 3,987th monarch of the line of Garamond, salutes you proud souls and wishes you well on your mission to bring back this raw good and/or product.'

His ship was dwarfed by the battle fleet which was to accompany them. Her Majesty's Navy had mustered a formidable fleet: ten thousand destroyers, dreadnoughts, battleships, cruisers, floating fortresses and torpedo boats, as well as armoured carriers capable of scrambling a hornet's nest of radio-operated drones and manned fighters. They hung like an insect army against the shining spheres.

'It is quite an impressive sight, is it not?' said Carrofax.

'It is a pointless display,' said Fabrigas. 'When we have crossed over and are in the Ghastly Blank, the space between universes, no amount of guns will save us. We will be blind, unable to see our attackers. The best chance you have is to be tiny and silent. That is why I came here alone in a saucer craft.'

Fabrigas heard the whizz of knee-servos and he turned to find Commander Descharge, marching towards him, accompanied by two young officers. The commander gave a neat bow and a wolfish smile. 'Again, a curious ship you've chosen. It is not too late to transfer to one of our armoured frigates. They are well gunned and comfortable.'

'I am comfortable with my choice,' replied Fabrigas. 'I would prefer it if my crew survived the trip.'

'Well, you do not have to worry about that. Our fleet will form a ring of steel around you. Only the Pope himself could penetrate it. And when our mission is complete I will return and receive my appointment as Supreme Imperial Commander.'

'Hear, hear!' said one of the young officers. Fabrigas turned his sleepy gaze towards the officer, then up towards the fleet. 'Well. We will see how steely your ring is when we come to make the crossing,' he said.

'And your pilot?' Descharge smiled thinly. 'He is . . . where?'

'He will arrive. Presently.'

'Indeed.' The commander pulled on his gloves. 'We were all astonished to discover that you'd spent most of your procurement budget on a navy deserter. A criminal, and a teenager. Still, you probably saved his life. If he wasn't protected by your appointment I would have to hang him.'

'Would you and all?'

'Most certainly. Our battle fleet will only protect him until the mission is complete. Then he'll have to face trial.'

'A battle fleet is no protection in the Hex.'

'The Hex?'

'The Hex, the Ghastly Blank, the space between. When you pass through the membrane of this reality and into the Hex you find yourself temporarily blind, surrounded on all sides by whiteness, at the mercy of whatever beasts or armies wait there.'

'Indeed. Though according to your testimony you've never seen the Hex, have you?'

'No, I was knocked unconscious during my crossing.'

'So how were you able to conclude that you were in another universe?'

'Through observation. I could see it immediately with my own eyes.'

Descharge smirked and threw a glance towards his young companions, who were stifling laughs behind their hands. 'Well. Whatever the case, I look forward to greeting this pilot of yours. Should he ever . . . materialise.'

'He will show.'

'. . . and though you may face impediments and obstacles various in nature,' the parrot continued, 'the Queen wishes upon you all the fortune and goodwill she can muster.'

Somewhere along the docks a roar went up. A fight of some kind had broken out in the crowd. Fabrigas saw the thick mass move, then part, and a lone figure fell out onto the boards. The crowd roared. Fabrigas and Descharge saw the figure stand unsteadily, straighten its gun belts, then jog casually towards them.

'Good day,' said Lambestyo as he huffed past Fabrigas and up the gangplank. He passed the bosun, a man-mountain: 'Tend to those gentlemen, will you?' Some distance behind him, another group of men broke out onto the docks. Two wore bailiffs' britches, and the rest, much larger, carried weapons. The bosun stopped the group at the plank's foot, saying, 'Now what business could you gentlemen be having on one of Her Majesty's own ships?'

'Your captain, sir, owes us for gambling debts, and we are here to seek settlement!'

'Well, well,' said the giant, whose hands looked as if they could wrap themselves around a cannon's neck. 'The way I see it, you have three problems. First, this is Her Majesty's vessel, and it is illegal for any subject to board without her permission. Second, the captain is a busy man and has to prepare for a long journey. And third,' and here the bosun dropped his giant head towards the men – who all leaned back as one – lowered his voice to a rumble, and said, 'I don't want you to.'

The men stepped away from the plank's foot to confer and then decided that perhaps the captain's debts were small enough to wait until he returned. Commander Descharge smiled, bemused. His bird-like head rolled in its neck socket and his wide, cold eyes surveyed the scene. Then he looked to the old man and said, 'Just stay close to the fleet and try to keep out of trouble.' And with that the commander and his two officers strode away to their own ship, arms behind their back, the motors in their knees and ankles playing a mournful dirge.

Finally, the band played 'Nearer My God to Thee', then gathered their horns, drums, harps and vibraphones, and left. Fabrigas mounted the catwalk to his ship. He found the captain, stalking the decks.

'So. You changed your mind about the trip?'

'After due thought,' said the captain, 'and taking all points of views into consideration, I have decided to accept your terms of payment.'

Fabrigas looked back towards the docks where the shimmering wall of waving metal human arms and gleaming eyes looked much like a great ocean wave about to crash upon them.

STRANGERS AND STRANGENESS

Two strangers met in Carnassus, in a smoke-filled tea house, on the day the expedition was to depart. Their meeting brought considerably less attention, but was no less vital to the outcome of the voyage to the next universe.

'Let me be very clear,' said the Man in the Shadows, 'my associates and I are captains of business. We don't care for sentiment. Whether this child has a claim to freedom is no concern of ours. Our only concern is to preserve our interests.'

'I am not a sentimental man. So you want me to hunt a child?'

'We do.'

'An ordinary child?'

'Far from it.'

'And the current whereabouts of this creature?'

'We have no idea. That's why we're asking you to help. If you're as good as they say then you can find the answers to your own questions.'

'You are a child, essentially. Maybe I should hunt you.'

'Do not be cute.'

The Well Dressed Man smiled faintly at the Man in the Shadows. He sipped his tea from an old, chipped bowl with a pair of swallows painted on it. The Well Dressed Man gulped, his throat nugget pulsed like a fat slug. His hands were pale, exquisite, the fingers as long and startling as snakes; they curled themselves around the bowl. You would struggle to see a mechanical part within his form. 'Alive, or dead?'

'Dead. If it's not too much trouble.'

'A youngster alone in this universe will die without my assistance,' said the Well Dressed Man as he flicked a piece of ash from the sleeve of his jacket.

'Ordinarily,' said the Man in the Shadows, 'but Skycore's calculations tell us that an escape is possible. There is a new player in the sphere. An extremely powerful one. This new player would be extremely disappointed if the escape happened.'

'You've hired other assassins for this mission?'

'Six in total.'

'Expensive.'

'Necessary. We think this child has escaped with an important file.'

'How important?'

'Extremely. It was taken from one of our Postal Service hubs some weeks back.'

'A break-in at a hub? I saw nothing in the papers.'

'Don't be an idiot.' The Man in the Shadows lifted a grimy teacup to his young lips, thought better of it, put the cup back on its saucer. 'We believe Dark Hand played a role in this leak. The information in this file could do enormous damage if the wrong people got hold of it.'

'And what are the chances of that?'

'We don't know. But we can't take chances. We must protect our interests at all costs.'

Outside in the gloom the red coals of the barbecues lit the smoke that curled and clutched the steel beams above. This deep in Carnassus the air was as thick as smoke, and the smoke could be caught like carnival floss. Through the filthy windows of the tea house a shadow in the gloom held his broad hat as he stooped to draw water from a bucket. A bamboo water-charm tockled gently, and somewhere out in the darkness a young woman sang in a high, clear voice.

'I don't care about your interests,' said the Well Dressed Man. 'And we've discussed the costs.' The Man in the Shadows smiled and placed a yellow envelope on the rotating wheel with a pink porcelain crane in the centre. The wheel murmured softly as it turned. In the centre of a centreless city a porcelain crane nodded. The Well Dressed Man plucked the envelope delicately; it disappeared inside his breast pocket.

'You would like me to retrieve the data?'

'We would like you to erase it. And this child who has it. And anyone else you see fit to eliminate.'

'And why would your beloved Postal Service not take care of this matter?'

'They are restricted in this case, since neither target has a tracking system.'

'No tracking system? Everything has a tracking system.'

'This file comes from the most secure facility in the Empire. Since a leak was seen as impossible no system was ever installed. That's why we've hired you.'

'May I view the data?'

'You may not, and cannot. The file is protected by a firewall. You could not burn through it in an age, and it would be dangerous to try.'

'Such a shame. I do love a challenge.'

'The file cannot be read by anyone but us. It would take millennia to crack the encryption. But it can read itself, and therein lies the problem. With the information it holds it can make intelligent decisions to avoid detection and destruction. Yet it also has a weakness: it is very much attached to the youngster who accompanies it.'

'Loyalty, the ultimate weakness. Who else knows about the contents of this file?'

'Outside our circle? No one. It is vital nobody knows. Not even the Queen. Prince Albert did.'

'And that's why you killed him?'

'He killed himself. Don't you read the papers?'

'No.' The Well Dressed Man took a sip of his tea. 'I was sure you'd be at the launch today. Why would you miss such a grand occasion?'

'I don't care about the mission. The wizard is a fraud and a fool. My intelligence says he'll burn.'

'Really? My intelligence says you just purchased a distillery and had it sign on as an expedition sponsor.'

The Man in the Shadows could hardly hide his surprise. He gathered himself. 'Why don't you save your tricks for the cabarets? I want you to know –' he leaned in closer across the table – 'that I don't trust you. I don't think you're a team player. And I think your so-called "mind skills" are the pranks of a cheap magician.'

'Do you indeed?'

'I do. But in this matter I was outvoted.'

'The well is deeper than your bucket. There are many strange and unfathomable things in this universe.'

'There is nothing in the universe which can't be explained with science and reason. Man is in charge of his destiny. He is the hero of his story. Achievement is his goal, reason his absolute. His senses tell him everything he needs to know, and my senses tell me you are a fraud. If it were up to me I would have hired a real assassin to join the group.'

'Is that a fact?' said the Well Dressed Man.

'Yes,' replied the Man in the Shadows.

Outside the tea house the silhouette let the water scoop drop into the bucket with a loud plop. The woman's song ended, her voice vanished like a memory.

'Of course, I'll do my very best to fulfil my mission,' said the Well Dressed Man as he put down his bowl.

'You'll do your best,' said the Man in the Shadows.

'I'll try not to disappoint.'

'You'll try not to disappoint.'

'You'll try not to be a total failure,' said the Well Dressed Man.

'I'll try not to be a total failure,' said the Man in the Shadows.

'Even though you are.'

'Even though I am.'

'A total failure,' said the Well Dressed Man.

'A total failure.'

'And a fool.'

'And a fool.'

'An ugly stupid fool. What are you?'

'An ugly stupid fool.'

'You should ram this chopstick into your eye.'

'I should ram this chopstick into my eye.'

'Deep, deep into the centre of the eye. Push it right through your eye until it touches the meat of your brain.'

'I should.'

'But you won't.'

'But I won't.'

The Well Dressed Man picked up his bowl again. Outside, the silhouette stoked the coals and fanned them with his broad hat, sending a shower of sparks dancing through the steel. Beyond him was a universe of people whose brains were so simple that they would do anything you asked – provided you asked it in the right way. The Well Dressed Man looked back towards the Man in the Shadows.

'Maybe you should pay the bill,' he said.

'Maybe I should pay the bill.'

THE DEARLY DEPARTED

The bosun took his prized silver watch from his pocket, glanced at the time, kissed the elegant inscription on the back, and said, 'Slaveys! Cast off moorings!' They felt the magnetic mooring pads release. 'Seal the ship!' Slaveys flocked like mice from holes and spat on their hands before straining against the wheel locks, shutting tight the hatches which would seal them in this unholy sepulchre for months to come. Alarcon, A.; Alonso, F.; Amandola, G.; Apfelbaum, D.; so many tiny lives – a tragical roll call of hell-bound juveniles embarking on a nightmare spin into what-the-heck. Ayala, J.; Brossolette, P.; am I to list them all for you? No, there is not time.

The *Necronaut*'s solar wings fanned out and flexed against the sunlight. Fabrigas felt his ears thicken as the vessel prepared to leave Carnassus for open space. The fleet of naval ships had already cleared the city and was heading out through the spheres in a seemingly solid black diamond. Fabrigas felt a putrid nausea as he watched the monster Carnassus recede, waving its gantries in farewell, and he remembered the many nightmare journeys of his past: the sickness, the monsters, the death and starvation. People came forward to pay their respects. He met the ship's physician, Shatterhands, who returned a limp, clammy handshake and said, 'Most charmed.' He met Huxbear, the ship's chef, who smelled of garlic and singed hair, and Quickhatch, the bosun, whose muscled body was a roiling sea of tattoos – birds, ships, sea creatures and green-skinned ladies entwined in sensual tableaux. The tattoos were his only visible mod – but as he often said himself, 'Why tamper with perfection?'

The Gentrifaction was a sight to behold, dressed in lavish frocks and wigs. It was common for every voyage to have attending members of the aristocracy. Some were lower aristocrats seeking to raise their status through a famous voyage. Some were melodramies: a peculiar kind of aristocrat who seeks a life of drama and, preferably, a tragic and legendary death. The poet H. Q. Gossipibom was one of these. He stood on the far side of the deck with his two acquaintances. This voyage, being so dangerous, had attracted just three aristocrats in total. The poet was dressed in a lavishly embroidered coat and platform shoes. Morphium had given him a faint scarlet muzzle, but his hair was glossy, coloured, as it was, with the finest imported crocodile shit. Beside him was G. De Pantagruel, whose features were so distorted and bulging that it seemed as if his body was struggling to contain gases of enormous pressure.

There were unspeakable mysteries inside G. Scatolletto's garments, they said. Scars that told of merciless sexual hobbies; buttocks so calloused by recreational whippings that you could have hauled him aboard by his rear on a cargo hook and he wouldn't have cried out. (In fact, he was carried up the gangplank by two strong sailors, raising his arms when a slavey scuttled too close and emitting low groans of alarm.)

In all it was a strange group, though there were no surprises.

'But which one is Her Majesty's spy?' thought Fabrigas.

Then the crew struck up a shanty to shake the iron bones of the ship.

I took me love down to the City,
Where grass be green and boys be pretty,
Oh won't you take me home, John Brown,
Oh won't you take me home – Oi!

Presently, the door from the ready room was kicked open and Carlos Lambestyo, in uniform, strode to the wheelhouse. His coat was deep blue with gold epaulettes and he had put aside his elephant guns for a pair of delicate silver pistols. His boots were far too big. Everyone was surprised to see him walk past the wheelhouse and over to the cargo bay where he found what he was looking for. In one corner, standing on legs which each weighed a ton, was a Giant Gas-Powered Titanium Bionical Crashproof Exoskeleton . . .

. . . or, GGPTBCE.

Of course, you would not have heard of this machine, because it is the very latest in military technology, and you are not. The GGPTBCE is a (virtually) indestructible human-driven robot designed to withstand (virtually) any assault. And by '(virtually)' I mean that if Prince Albert had decided to climb inside one of these machines and steer it into the sun he would have at least stood a chance. This pilotable war-robot could withstand rocket or cannon attack, it could pluck the uranium core from a stricken supertanker and fling it a safe distance, it could walk inside a blast furnace, it could detonate a massively powerful explosive device in its own hands and remain unharmed. It represented the very apex of military hardware, and every ship in the expedition fleet had been given one (even though each single GGPTBCE cost more than the ship which carried him). Yes, Captain Lambestyo was very excited. He remembered the first time he strapped himself into a P1Q9 Scramjet Bat-fighter. He was only nine years old then, and this was even more exciting. 'So the rumours were true,' said Lambestyo. 'We do have a GGPTBCE.'

But the GGPTBCE's licensed operator, a Corporal Bortis, was not happy to see the captain. 'Please don't touch him, he's very valuable.'

'Don't touch him? She is indestructible, is she not?' Lambestyo withdrew his finger from the robot's gleaming black thigh.

'*He* is. But I don't want even a scratch on him. Only a licensed military operative may deal with him, and you are . . . ex.'

'Oh well. We will meet again, I'm sure.' The captain turned his adoring eyes up towards the motionless iron face. The face ignored him. He shrugged and returned to his flight deck.

Soon the ship joined the fleet and dropped into a cruising formation known informally as 'Sleeping Dragon'. It was hard not be awed by the sight of such a battle fleet spread out across the eternal night.

Then the boy captain called for attention and addressed the crew.

'Men. Ladies. Spies for Her Majesty.' His voice of a sudden had a gravity that defied his age. 'We begin our journey today with the sun in our sails and an empire behind us. We go, to be sure, to our certain deaths. All that is to be decided is the exact nature of our deaths. But we will go to our deaths with our heads held high, and we will not let our heads drop, or lose our heads, even if we do in fact come to eventually lose our heads.' He paused to raise his chin and turn his black eyes to the stars. 'And if by some twist of misfortune I should come to survive you all, and based on my past luck that seems likely, then I will speak loudly of your courage, and your names will not be forgotten. Please sign your names in the register so that I may learn them.' He finished his speech and there was silence.

'Good lord,' murmured Shatterhands. 'Is that his idea of raising morale?'

Then the poet Gossipibom announced that he'd written an ode to their journey. There was a rush to leave the deck. 'I'm too busy,' said the captain, and stormed off. 'Does sir wish me to fetch the earplugs?' said Carrofax. Fabrigas said nothing and followed after the captain, but those who were too slow were forced to listen to the poet as he began to shriek in a high-pitched, nasal twang.

'Twas the eve of Hallig Nae'n
Thon braced leguh it trembled, stang
Upon the crux its leagured sheen
Did mix betwix the kild 'n keen

Nor eighty shanks upon its . . .

                              . . . Bree'r
To drift in seatop's tip and tear
Its mission wrote up'n this . . .

                              . . . morn
T'boldly gae where ne'r'n has gorn . . .

He paused for breath and people moved to applaud. But he wasn't finished. Not for seventeen more verses.

From the journal of M. Francisco Fabrigas

The World, the Frame, the Cosmosie, the Panarchy, the Macrocosmos, the Megacosm, Old Smokey – whatever you choose to call it we are sailing into its reaches. We move outward through the sphere towards the edge of the Holy Neon Empire, bearing 142 degrees by 19Q through the Triton Cloud, dropping to cruising speed for a pass around the Nebula Asturius to pick up favourable winds from her currents. To portside lies the Great Wall of Peace, the zone which separates our Empire from her enemy, the Vangardiks. Because of my long incarceration this is the first time I've seen it. It is less a wall, in fact: more a twisting helix of mines and traps which materialised suddenly some centuries ago on an evening commonly referred to as Shutternight. The Wall is some 245 light-years long and cuts the former Empire in two, allowing the Vangardiks to protect them-selves from what they call 'terror incursions', and to stem what they also call 'wanton mass-migrations.' To starboard are the Floating Worlds, the territory of the mysterious Xo. We will shortly join the shipping circuits via the dark-space autobahn. There we will be propelled like atomic bits – only much, much faster than the speed of light. This will allow us to carve off the enormous distances needed to reach our jump-point near Akropolis. The ship has a 'funky' smell which I cannot place.

The larger the object, the more difficult it is for it to reach the next universe. For a fleet our size to cross over it needs to reach a minimum of a quarter of the speed of light – and for that we will be relying on the winds at Akropolis. The plan has always been to engage our RIPS engine at this part of space, and to enter the Interior. I have some necessary adjustments to make, so tomorrow must work all day to prepare.

The Queen would not agree to increase our funding for this venture, thus we have needed to cover the shortfall through corporate channels. Things were looking desperate until, at the last minute, a distillery came aboard as sponsor. And so our epic voyage is made possible thanks to the support of a Dr H. W. Sackwell's Invigorising Tonical Rum. The fleet has been compelled to take roughly 400,000 cases of a beverage that, in my opinion, is only good for cleaning drains. The crew is on the verge of mutiny. 'Gah! It be poison!' they say, and, 'It tastes like me armpits!' Whatever the taste of the sickly green goop, it serves its main purpose: to make the men merry, though the following day they feel like killing themselves.

Terrible news today of the super-liner *Colossus*, the Empire's unsinkable mega-ship, which yesterday collided with a space-berg, leading to a catastrophic leak and the death of almost all 547,000 passengers. It is a tragedy that just a day earlier we were within range of the ship and might have been able to offer assistance.

There have been no other incidents to speak of. We were attacked by a serpent, but it was only a baby, it could hardly wrap itself around our ship. Everyone came on deck to coo and gurgle.

Today we approach the Necropolis, beyond that is the great darkness. Strange things happen when you enter this part of space. It is not a place with common natural laws.

I feel a deep melancholy coming. But what is to be done?

Beans and boiled greens for supper.

★

What an absurd bundle of cadavers-in-waiting I have been saddled with here. The boy captain brings a shadow wherever he goes. Groups that laugh and roll about fall quiet on his arrival, and on his leaving sit with heads bowed like mourners at an oceangoing wake. The bosun is a frightening meat-tower. When I asked him if I could perhaps get a second blanket for my cot, because my thin bones feel the cold terrible at night, he said, 'Certainly! And shall I come and fluff your pillow for you too?!' And all the men laughed.

The old-beard is perhaps the maddest. He does little but stalk the navigation deck and rant to himself. He claims to have come from another universe, yet can provide no evidence. And now he leads us into oblivion.

The cook seems like a fine fellow, as do the Gentrifaction, esp. the poet – whose gifts I think go unappreciated.

In all, I would have off this barge in a heartbeat, if not for the predicament brought about by my debts, and by certain legal suits held against me by unscrupulous opportunists, and by certain duties which I must perform for the good of Queen and Empire. For all they are worth.

I smell only death and horror on this ship.

RIPS

They rode on into the blackness, silence, and into the last inhabited region of the Empire. But this was not a place inhabited by the living. The crew went quiet as their fleet passed through the Necropolis: a sea of giant floating headstones spanning a lonely region of space. Some of the stones placed by richer families were the size of mountains. What point is there in such a place? Many have asked. It is a quest in life to make the soul tangible. For some their choice of monument is their family, their deeds, the quality of their life's work. For others contemplating the end of life, there is a realisation that their dubious deeds, their nasty children, are a poor life record. In this case the towering public monument will suffice. There is certainty in the soul of a baron whose deeds haunt his sleep, but who knows that when the sun sets on his life he will be buried in an obsidian skull two hundred miles high.

Such a man came aboard that day for a surprise inspection. 'I will need to see your logs and manifests,' said Descharge. 'Our engineers say you're running heavy. They say you lag behind the fleet.'

'It is our RIPS engine,' said Fabrigas. 'It is extremely dense, and our ship is not as powerful as yours.'

'That is your fault,' Descharge replied. 'I offered you a naval battle-ship, I offered you a qualified captain. Where is yours?'

'He is . . . rising. He gets cranky if he does not sleep enough.'

'We have no time for this nonsense. We have a schedule to keep.

And there is the chance we might still catch up with the Vengeance. Skycore says that if she wants to flee this universe she must travel this way.'

'Then why not let her?' said Lambestyo. He had stumbled from his quarters, shirt unbuttoned, a patchy stubble on his ravaged face.

'Because she is the property of this great Empire,' Descharge replied without even bothering to turn. 'Much like you were. I ought to have you arrested for desertion.'

'So do it,' said Lambestyo as he studied his stubble with the tips of his fingers. 'Or just send the rescue team you should have sent when I crashed my bat-fighter all those years ago. I was lonely out there.'

'Your orders were clear,' said Descharge. 'To secure the oil platforms for Her Majesty's glory – with your life, if necessary. If you somehow survive this mission I will return you to a military court for trial.'

'I will wear my best suit,' said Lambestyo.

'Well, this is nice!' said Fabrigas, and Descharge turned slowly towards him. 'In any event,' continued the old man, 'your inspection is pointless. As I explained, we are running heavy because of the RIPS engine, and nothing can change it. Now if you'll excuse me, I must return to running my tests.'

'I still don't know how your miraculous engine even works,' said Descharge.

'Yes, why don't you enlighten us?' said Lambestyo. He had been trying for days to get the old man to explain it to him in a way he understood.

'Well, I wouldn't want to bore you,' said Fabrigas.

'No, please, bore away,' said Descharge.

'Well, travelling to another universe is very simple,' Fabrigas said. 'You do it every time you make a choice between whether you'll have jam on your toast, or honey. Personally, I prefer honey.'

'I hate honey,' said the captain. 'Too gooey.' He was staring hard into space where the monumental tombstones floated, his brow was wrought.

'But to enter a universe you don't belong in – by the nature of your choices – is more difficult. When we come to make the crossing we will not "move" to another dimension. We will not change our place in the time/space continuum; time and space will change its place in *us*. In this sense, there are not infinite universes at all. There is really only one: the sum total of all that is possible. We are but travellers on a voyage through that universal ocean, walking from porthole to porthole, seeing reality from another point of view, then convincing ourselves that each view we witness represents an entirely new and separate reality. So you see, it's very simple.'

The two men stared at him with unblinking eyes.

'Well, let me put it another way,' he continued. 'The RIPS theory is based upon the principle of uncertain death: an uncanny point in reality when you are free to pass into any other universe – a universe in which you survived, or a universe in which you narrowly escaped death and are crippled, or a universe in which what did not kill you made you stronger. With our own universe believing we are dead we have the opportunity to transfer ourselves to a universe in which we have all transferred ourselves to another universe. Simple.'

'Oh yes, so *simple*,' said Lambestyo.

Fabrigas ignored him. 'Since at the time of your death you exist, hypothetically, in all other universes but the one you've died in, the universe releases its grip and allows you to pass freely.'

'And why does this universe think we're dead?' said Descharge cautiously.

'Master, perhaps . . .' said Carrofax from the shadows. The old man ignored him.

'Because we *will* be dead. Technically.'

'Come again?' said Descharge.

'It couldn't be simpler. We die in this universe, but immediately appear in another one, thus confounding the paradox of existing in a universe in which you've died. Which, as I've explained, is impossible.'

'And *how* exactly will we die?'

'We'll "die" because the RIPS engine sets off a frightening thermo-nuclear explosion! The explosion is powerful enough to vaporise the ship and everything around it. Fortunately, the engine also has large amounts of dark ooze. This ooze exists both in the engine and in all other dimensions. It therefore acts as a quantum buffer, balancing out the force of the explosion.'

'Yes, you heard the man, we're all going to die,' said Lambestyo. 'Explosions, ooze, dark honey. Now it's nearly elevenses; who will have a cocktail with me?'

'That is the most insane thing I have ever heard,' said Descharge.

'It is!' agreed Fabrigas. 'But sometimes insane things are true.'

They heard a noise from behind a crate of machine oil as a sailor's shadow flickered away into the darkness. 'Now you've done it,' said Lambestyo. 'The whole ship will hear you plan to "keeeeel" us.'

'He's WHAT?!' they heard the bosun's voice boom from below.

'So best of luck with this,' said Lambestyo, and left. Sailors were beginning to gather on the deck.

★

Fabrigas fled to his quarters, where he found Carrofax waiting patiently. 'Well, that seemed to go very well.'

'Yes, what of it?' He locked his door. 'They had to find out sooner or later. To get to the next universe you must die in this one. I have solved the problem of death-perception.'

'And that is how the engine works?'

'It could be.'

'So then why share the information? A tactical error, sir, I think.'

'It isn't a tactical error. It is the best available truth. I have no real idea how the engine works.'

'And why not tell them that?'

'Tell them that I'm taking them billions of light-years away to use a piece of technology I don't even understand? Ridiculous. They'd laugh me off the ship.'

'As opposed to setting you on fire and throwing you off the ship?'

'Let them try me if they wish. I think they'll find me hard to kill.'

'As you wish. Have you figured out which one is the Queen's spy yet?'

'I have my suspicions,' said the old man as he spread some papers on his desk and pretended to set to work. He really didn't like it when Carrofax teased him.

'I could tell you if you wished.'

'I do not wish. If I require your assistance I will ask for it.'

'As you wish.' Carrofax smiled. Fabrigas stared harder at his notes. He did not need to look up to know that his servant was smiling at him. And that it was the *particular* smile he used when he knew things the old man did not.

'Am I breaking your concentration?'

'Yes, in fact you are. If you don't mind I have some important navigation work to do.'

'Really?'

'Yes.'

'Important navigation work?'

'It is so.'

'Important navigation work which involves studying blueprints for the ship's plumbing?'

Fabrigas blinked twice at the sheet of paper on his table, then pushed it aside. 'Don't you have something better to do?' But when he turned round his servant had vanished and he was once more alone.

DARK-SPACE AUTOBAHN

They sailed on into the darkness, through days and weeks, and on towards a nightmare.

There are many frightening sights at sea, particularly in the morning, when seaman are known to yell, 'Don't look at me, I'm a hideous monster!' and, 'Kiss me not neither, for I have dragon's breath.' At night, when the ship lights are dimmed and all is black and all is quiet, the mind can begin to play tricks on you. Sometimes the men can also play tricks on you. Many captains, even, are fearful wags who love to play pranks: like wedding a man to a sea cow, or putting a sleeping man in an oily sack and yelling: 'Jack's been eaten by a whale!' Captain Lambestyo was not one of those captains. He hated practical jokes. A ship was a serious place for serious business. So it annoyed him greatly that the rest of the fleet had decided to play a series of maritime pranks on the *Necronaut* and its teenage captain, the Necronaut.

First, the fleet had conspired not to respond to any of his radio messages for a whole day. Lambestyo thought his receiver was broken, and only twigged to the trick when he heard giggling. Then, when he'd asked for spare machine parts, the supply ship had sent over a crateload of man-knickers. Lambestyo had flown some as flags.

Today was a bold new joke. The fleet had sent a signal to him that they would shift to a new heading. Then, at the appointed naval hour, when Lambestyo swung his vessel onto a new tack, he'd found himself cruising on alone. The rest of the fleet had continued on the old tack. It would take days of hard sailing to catch them. They were mocking him, but he would have his vengeance, he said, and as he said it he had no idea how right he was.

But let's not get ahead of ourselves. In the meantime, the crew endured the loneliness and tedium of space. There is little to do in deep space but play pranks and gossip. Groups came to gather in the same spots every day. The sailors slacking from their chores would slump down in the shadow of the navigation deck, out of sight of their captain's window, and they would talk of past agonies. 'See this?' one sailor would exclaim as he held up four imaginary fingers. 'Let's just say that you shouldn't mess with the sucker-crabs of the Azulian Sea.'

'That's nothing,' another would say, unbuttoning his shirt to reveal a set of long scars. 'Fire rats. Got inside my spacesuit while I was chuting into a war zone to rescue my squadron from a grove of carnivorous moles. I was the only survivor.'

'Ha!' another would say. 'I have one compound word for ye: were-kittens . . .' And it would go on like this, all day, an endless reel of woe and strife. Our captain would never join in, because the one time he did he made a man cry.

Sometimes their voices would drop very low and you would know that they were talking of another kind of agony: the wounds of the heart.

'Oh, Lauraneath, I knew her. Oh, such a girl as you would ever meet. Oh, if I could describe her you would weep the seas. Oh, the tragedy! She drowned after draining back a keg before a charity swim.'

'Women. Can't live with them, can't live without them.'

'Words of wisdom, Lloyd, words of wisdom.'

Meanwhile, on the other side of the deck, the Gentrifaction would gather at the crack of noon. G. De Pantagruel, G. Scatolletto and the poet Gossipibom would stand in the corner of the deck where the golden starlight bouncing in through the glass shields from the sails gathered in a lovely puddle. And there they would speak of their own tragic ailments.

'I have, for an age, had my tissues made from Omnogyptian fibres by the finest papersmith in the High Orient. But oh! How it would chafe sometimes, especially if I had dined on fibrous foods.'

'Ah! Do not start me up, dearest,' said Scatolletto, 'for I have chafed rudely for years and only found relief through silk kerchiefs for which I paid a pretty penny.'

'I once stole a lady's velvet glove and got relief,' said Pantagruel.

'But what are we supposed to do? Find a lady to seduce each time we wish to ease our sluice?'

'Why no, dear sir, I simply had a thousand such gloves made to order. And it was worth every note.'

'But dear sir, why go to the trouble of having them made as gloves? Why not just buy the material by the bolt?' said Gossipibom.

'My dearest, I tried, but I could not get the same result. There is something about wearing a lady's glove which brought about an optimal degree of relaxation. And the control! Oh!'

'My word! You *wore* the glove?!'

'I did, my friend. I wore that glove. And I *loved* it. I have dabbed myself with all kinds of things: silk sheets, fine tapestries, a child's soft toy, but I have found none better under these stars than a lady's velvet glove.'

And it would go on like that all day. They were perhaps three of the most despicable individuals ever to be born, and it should give you great comfort to know that before this book is finished they will all die horribly. 'Tell the people they all die horribly!' old Fabrigas is shouting at me now, in that basement on that orphan moon. So there you have it.

Fabrigas hid himself in his cabin, away from the idle gossip and the talk of mutiny. Nine weeks into the journey there was a knock at his door and when he opened it the ship's communications chief, Lotango, was there with a telegram.

'Telegram, sir!'

'Telegram?'

'So.' It was strange because this ship did not have the equipment to receive telegrams. The telegram read:

Fabrigas. Stop. You are sailing into danger and madness. Stop. Paint the 62,500th hexagram of the Water Star around your ship and you will have protection. Stop. Over. Out.

He screwed up the telegram and slumped back in his seat. 'Now why the heck would I paint a sign from the *Third Book of Transmutations* on my ship? It is a sign of attraction. It makes no sense.'

There was another knock at his door. 'Another telegram for you, sir!'

'What the . . .'

It makes perfect sense. Stop. Why should you question our methods? Stop. Paint the hexagrams and save your people. Stop. It is that simple. Stop.

'Where are these telegrams coming from!'

Lotango shrugged.

*

No one could understand why the old man would suddenly start painting mysterious symbols on his ship. The general consensus was madness. The Gentrifaction was ablaze with gossip. 'I hear he is a black magician. I hear they are symbols of dark magic.'

'He is bearded. Never trust the beardy. They cast their beardy spells and listen to their beardy music and are profoundly insolent.'

'And he's a vegetarian – of *all* things.'

'We should play an excellent prank on him. My cousin was a

vegetarian. We made him a mud pie composed of garlic, asafoetida and castoreum in quantity, and of turds that were still warm.'

*

They sailed on. And under.

From the journal of Captain Lambestyo

I hate these things. I never know what to write. Whatever. We are flying through the dark-space shipping lane and the rum has already turned the men mad. They are muttering about how sick it makes them, some complain that it is beginning to give them soft hands and girlish thoughts.

The old-beard has told everyone he plans to kill them. So that is good. I was just thinking to myself, 'Oh, things are far too easy on this journey. What we need is a good mutiny.' The men are angry even though this mission has a 99.9 per cent chance of death. He has taken away their 0.1 per cent chance of life, and they don't like it.

The fleet has played a practical prank on me by telling me a wrong heading. I totally knew it was a prank, but I sailed away anyway, because I wanted to be alone.

PS Tried some of the ship's rum last night and now I want to peel my own face off. Maybe I was too hard on the men.

That is all I want to write because my arm is tired.

★

From the journal of M. Francisco Fabrigas

These are dark times. We have been sent off course by means of a practical joke and are now struggling to catch up with our fleet. We are in a dark region of Interspace and the men want me dead. I should probably not have described my engine using the metaphor of a violent death, even if life itself – that is, the idea that our life is divided up into a series of discrete events, one following after the other from birth to death – is itself no more than a useful metaphor. I should have said that my engine was like a chicken or something. Fortunately, certain chilling events over the past few days have arrived to distract the men from mutiny.

We passed today through a strange energy cloud of unknown composition and instantly all the slave children became 'possessed'. It was only the juveniles, a fact I cannot explain. In their bunk rooms below decks, beds were floating, eyes were bulging, heads were spinning, bitter excrescence was oozing from juvenile orifices, the tiny pink tongues were lolling and gabbling in a dialect only Carrofax, with his superior education in languages, could comprehend:

'We are legion.

'You are damned.

'We come here from the hinters where we found not what we sought,' they said. Among other things.

I went to the captain's cabin to alert him and found him floating in the air and saying, 'Do not come into these reaches.

'Do not knock upon this hatch.

'You are on a ship of fools,

'Bounded for hell.

'Pain shall be your sustenance,

'Fear, your biscuit,

'Peace, your enemy.'

So that happened. I had to deal with the situation myself by painting more hexagrams.

When at last it was all over the children slumbered like soldiers and the walls were covered in purple excremental goo and automatic poems scrawled in juvenile blood. It certainly wasn't a pleasant scene. The captain wandered down for a look, then shrugged and returned to his room. Nothing seems to bother him. Although I have perceived his mood darkening. This is the nature of these parts.

Because we have strayed from the fleet we were boarded by Royal Customs and Enforcement officers near Balfour. They said it was to hunt for an escaped girl and a possible accomplice. The bosun whispered to the captain, 'Let us hope they don't find the piñatas,' which I did not understand. Of course we have no piñatas. Then the inspectors lined up all the children and examined them. The chief looked into every child's face and held up a swatch of a particular shade of green for comparison, but none of the children's faces matched the shade, except for a boy called Sneevlit who suffers from the sea-walms, and he was excused. Having made a lazy search of the ship, they left.

That is the last contact we will have with the empires. We have left the spheres of civilisation and are travelling into parts I never thought to return to even in my direst man-mares. We are at the end of civilisation; the beginning of infinity.

THE BEGINNING OF INFINITY

Everything you think you know about the universe is wrong. You imagine, I'm sure, that the universe is *full* of things: burning suns, bright meteors, steaming comets. It might surprise you to know that the universe is mostly nothing. No light, no matter, no mercy for the soul who finds himself there. It is only upon venturing into these reaches that the sailor realises that being smashed up by a comet, or burned up by a sun, is not the ultimate nightmare. The ultimate nightmare, dearest reader, is to find yourself alone, in the hungry, hungry dark, where not a sound is heard, and not a wink of light is present.

As they sailed on into the black reaches of infinity, a mood a few steps short of madness set in.

There is a little girl standing in a doorway filled with light. Fabrigas sees her open her mouth and pull a winged creature out. Then she squeals like a bat and vanishes.

Captain Lambestyo sees Commander Descharge dressed as a washerwoman say, 'Look. Look what you have made me *become*. If you don't destroy your maker you will surely die,' before he wakes, sweating, and discovers he has wrapped his sheets around his throat.

The bosun dreams he is on a deserted highway below seven sad mountains. The highway shines so brightly it stings his eyes. He sees his parents in the distance; they hold a baby. The bosun says, 'I've lost it, I've lost my watch!' His father says, 'No, see, you've always had it,' and the bosun Jacob Quickhatch looks down to see that his silver watch has been roughly stitched into his chest in place of his heart.

Fabrigas wakes to the sound of screaming and knows that the ship is succumbing to mass nightmares – that stage of ship's madness before uncontrollable dancing and sleep-tantrums.

*

Captain Lambestyo was well in the hunt for the annual award for maddest sailor. As the weeks at sea became months he was seen less and less, staying in his cabin most of the day, emerging only occasionally to yell at his men for 'not sweeping the decks tomorrow', or 'broadcasting bad thoughts into my soul'.

Fabrigas returned to his cabin late one night after fetching his supper. (He had taken to foraging after midnight when the ship was sleeping because he was still afraid his crew would try to kill him.) There were more night-screams than ever coming from the sailors' quarters. When Fabrigas quietly closed his door and turned on his lamp he found Lambestyo sitting in his lounge chair, making the old man inexplicably shout out 'Splah!'

'Shhhhhhhhhhhhh,' said the Necronaut. 'No splah.' He went quickly to the door and checked it was locked; rolled twice along the wall and flattened himself beside the porthole. Then took a quick glance out. Satisfied, he went over to Fabrigas and grasped the old man by the arms. 'They are out for you (joo), man. I hear them talking. Quick, tell me who you trust upon this ship! Answer, don't think!' His eyes were wide and urgent.

'Right now? Nobody.'

The boy smiled. 'Good answer.' He went to Fabrigas's liquor table and sloshed some J. Frogman's Red Rum into a glass, slupped most of it, then came back. 'There are spies on my ship. I know it. I can "smell" them.' The captain had recently learned about quotation marks and was losing no opportunity to use them in conversation. 'Trust no one here. Tell them nothing. Keep your blinds closed when you work. Keep a small mirror in a pocket handkerchief. What are those – herrings?' Fabrigas was still holding the tray with his supper on it.

'Yes. Would you like some?'

'No thank you very much. Do you have a gun?'

'I . . . do not.'

'Here, I brought you one.' Lambestyo pulled an old pistol out of his belt. It was slick with gun oil and, inexplicably, matted with dog hair. 'This is my second backup pistol. Keep the first chamber empty because it has no safety. If the "sheet" goes down I need you to back me up.' He leaned in close to the tall man's chest. 'They embarrass you, man. They want to embarrass both of us because we are too *real*. It's us against them, man. But listen, listen, listen, listen, [he had been drinking] listen. We have to stick together. You and me. We can't trust no one else here. Do you see anyone else here? Shhhh! What was that!' He swung towards the window, brandishing the pistol and the liquor tumbler menacingly. Then he turned back to the old man, drained the glass, wiped his mouth with the sleeve of his pistol hand, and tossed the glass and the pistol onto the old man's bunk. Then he grabbed Fabrigas by the collar of his dressing gown, stood on the toes of his boots so that his head was just a few feet below his, and said, 'Why can't we all just love each other? Why does it all have to be about war, and keeeeling? Wouldn't it be better if we learned to love each other?'

'To love each other?'

'Jess.'

'Love is an evil magic,' said the old man. 'It confounds the brain. The man who isn't happy with himself makes it his quest. It is a superstition of the heart. Fall to space madness, but don't ever fall to love.' The boy looked so sad at this that the old man quickly added: 'But if love works for you! Maybe it's time to get some sleep.'

'I don't sleep any more. I'm like a wolf.'

'Wolves don't sleep?'

'I think they take naps. Can I stay here tonight, on your floor?'

'Perhaps it would be better if we stayed in our own rooms tonight.'

The captain looked astonished. 'Why?'

'Well, I'm very confused and I need time to think things over.'

The Necronaut considered this for a few seconds, then broke into a knowing smile, slapped the old man on both shoulders and said, 'You (joo). You (joo) are a clever man.' Then he grabbed his pistol from the bed, tapped his nose knowingly with the barrel, and went to the door. 'I'm sorry, friend. I get the "fear" when I go to sea.' He spread his arms and beamed. 'The walls, they close in on me. You (joo) don't know what it's like.'

He opened the door, saw the great hulk of the bosun standing there, and it was his turn to yell, 'Splah!'

'Gentlemen,' said Quickhatch, 'there is something below that you really need to see.'

*

Remember, if at any time during this story you feel frightened, or agitated, you can turn to page 620, the Little Page of Calmness.

The bosun took them down through the passenger quarters, down through the dripping steel warrens, through the engineering deck, the storage decks. His giant frame filled the narrow passages. He clutched a silver talisman in his giant fist. He took them down through the waste rooms, the prisoner cells, down through the hazardous materials rooms, the radioactive containment chambers, and finally through the slaveys' quarters – where all slept soundly. The giant stopped at the junction of the last maintenance corridor on the ship: the one which led to the bow-pit where the pit-bats lived. They were silent. The place was dark and airless, lit by a lonely bulb. The memory of the slavey pack-possession was still fresh, everyone was on edge. 'Why are we here?' said the captain.

'It's in the bow,' said the bosun, who was standing beside the hatch. Fabrigas observed that the giant man seemed frightened. But that could not possibly be true.

'What is in the bow?'

'You should see for yourself.'

'What if I don't want to?'

The bosun turned towards the bow-pit hatch and whispered, 'Come out, petal.'

The unoiled hinge made a violin's call as the hatch slowly opened.

A few seconds passed, then the three men saw a scruffy brown head float up. Two eyes scanned the scene, widened, and before the head could vanish again the bosun shot out a painted arm. There was a short commotion, accompanied by the mad twitter of bats, and when the bosun withdrew his hand he held a boy, an urchin dressed in a jumpsuit of the Imperial Postal Service: pale blue with yellow trim, the kind worn by the slaveys who worked in the high-security installations – only this boy's suit was soiled and torn at the shoulder. With his ragged hair and wild eyes he resembled a young animal.

'This is what you wanted to show us? An escaped slave?' said the captain.

The bosun shook his head . . . slowly. Then a voice came from out of the pit; it rang like a bell made from ice. The voice said, 'Small boy. Are you there?'

Fabrigas felt his gut contract.

Then a shape rose from out of the black pit. It was a girl, tiny; in this light her skin was the colour of snot from a recently bloodied nose. She looked like a seasick ghost. Fabrigas and Lambestyo took each a step back.

'What . . .' said Lambestyo, 'in the heavens . . .' he continued, 'is that?'

'Hello, strange men,' said the girl. She stepped into the dim corridor. She wore a fine hunting coat, a simple dress and a pair of black boots, no other adornments but a desiccated Corpse Blossom pressed through a buttonhole of her coat.

'Stowaways,' said the bosun as he set the boy down. The urchin gave one last defiant flick of his shoulders and the bosun removed his giant hand from the back of his neck. In his other hand he held his silver talisman up towards the girl, as if trying to ward off her presence. What amazed them was not her green skin but her eyes: they shone like water running over diamonds. 'They've been nesting in there, living off the bats in the nose-cone, roasting them with a candle, buttering them with algae.'

'I was wondering what was happening to my bats,' said the captain. 'I thought they had caught wind of their fate and were escaping.'

'No,' said the girl, 'we had to eat some. But only a single one per day.' She spoke with the most curious accent.

'And this is why you turned green!' said Fabrigas, and the girl said, 'I am green?'

When asked, 'What is your name?' she said, 'I am called Lenore,' and gave a little stomp and a bow. 'I do not know the name with which I was born. I heard a medicines seller at the fair say Lenore and I stole it for myself.'

'Ah yes,' Lambestyo said. 'Auntie Lenore's Liquid Gripe Tonic for Restless Sleepers or Night Screamers. A fine product. I use it often.'

The girl frowned and pursed her lips in the shape of a butterfly and said no more. Fabrigas was silent, ashen.

'And what is your name?' said the captain to the boy.

'He can't hear you,' said Lenore, 'he has deafs.'

'Well, didn't he tell you his name?'

'No. Cannot speak.'

'Well, couldn't he write it down for you?'

'I'm blind.'

The captain squinted. 'And why are you on my ship?'

'I was a prisoner of the Queen and I e-scaped. I met this boy at the fair. It's all made up in this fine letter,' and she passed the old man an envelope. He took it without even looking at it.

'I don't need any post to tell me who you are,' said Fabrigas. 'You are the Vengeance, and we are doomed.'

'Oh, don't say that,' groaned the bosun.

'I can say it. I can say it loud. Dark Hand's predictions were right. This is the final bolt through the lid of our sepulchre.'

'What are you talking about, old fool?' said Lambestyo. He looked unimpressed. 'It's just some stowaway children. We will feed and wash them and then decide what's going to happen. It looks as if this boy has never bathed or eaten.'

'Just the bats.'

'Yes.'

'We will add the boy to the crew,' said Fabrigas, gathering himself. 'He can pull his weight. But no one must know we are carrying the Vengeance. There'll be blind panic if the crew finds out she's aboard. So I'm swearing you both to silence. Giant, you must swear on that silver talisman you wear; Lambestyo, on your guns.' Both men nodded. 'We'll keep the girl here and bring her meals.'

Then the girl raised her nose and said, 'Something burns out in space.' Minutes later their ship would pick up a distress signal which would alter the course of this voyage once again.

Oh what a strange and terrifying calamity came out of the night! We were all asleep but the alarms woke us to the news that we had disturbed a nest o' pie-rates! And when I came up to deck I found a sight so shocking I nearly fell off my shoes! It was a scene torn right from a painting of hell from the artist Heicleftus Broigh.

We were still peeled off from the main fleet and had come upon the fleet of ships ablaze. The ships were be-swarmed on all sides by Hornets! These terrible bandits have had the wings of giant wasps grafted onto their backs. They wear huge black goggles – like the eyes of those they mimic – and they fly around without a ship. And how they massed about these doomed hulks, how the blur of their wings and the flash of their fiery blades did taunt the soul. There was one ship which wasn't on fire. It had many corpses on the deck, we could see, some floating limp through breaches in the hull.

And did our captain give a wide berth to this cauldron of destruction and head back to the fleet? Did he heck-wise!

'Pull to and prepare to board!' he cried. What madness! The ship heaved and groaned as it swung in beside the one surviving ship, whose name was the *Black Widow*. The captain handed command to the Master Fabrigas, swung his gun belts across his shoulders and ordered all us passengers below, and so I had to watch this tragedy unfold through a porthole, but what I saw was enough to turn my bloodlets to frigid mercury.

From my sliver I saw the captain board the *Black Widow* by

rocket-pack, and the bosun followed, and on the way they met of a sudden a pack of hornets, all heavily armed and with motor blades whirring, and there was a terrible fight. The captain ran one through with his blades, and the bosun took two bandits – one in each mighty hand – and clashed them together as a percussionist in an orchestra might smash two cymbals, and though their clash was silent they brought a wincing gasp from all aboard the *Necronaut*. Oh! Oh! Then the two men vanished inside the *Black Widow*. Oh what madness!

They returned minutes later with a woman. All this for a wretched woman! When they appeared above again the Hornets flew into retreat.

Salty crab for dinner tonight – of which I am rather fond.

*

From the journal of M. Francisco Fabrigas

Hornets strike quickly, flying in and killing all aboard before sweeping up the ship's treasures in giant nets and flying back to their secret nest. They are impossible to chase because they have no ship, and when attacked they scatter in many directions. The captain wanted to use the GGPTBCE to fight the bandits, but Corporal Bortis declined, so instead he went aboard the flaming ship to battle the swarm by hand – all to rescue, in the end, a single passenger. In a way, it is fortunate for her that our own fleet played that practical joke on us which sent us out into space on our own. Of course the incident has delayed our return to the fleet by even longer. But the hand-to-hand battle was a useful exorcism for the captain, and he immediately began acting 63 per cent less mad. He brushed aside all praise for rescuing the woman, saying, 'I thought there might be treasure there,' and the bosun just started shouting at the slaveys again.

The strangest thing is that after the incident, when I went below to check the green girl, I found her sitting patiently with a bat upon each shoulder. She said, 'So they find a woman. Everyone else most dead. How sad.' And she was right. They had found the woman hiding in her room, clutching a giant book and waving a broken sherry bottle. When the captain said, 'We are rescuers,' she'd replied, 'I cannot leave my books!' Her name is Miss Maria Fritzacopple. I will take a brief moment to describe her: she is a young woman with unruly hair and sultry, red-rimmed eyes which cast a sensuous insolence upon all she surveys. She has the physique and balance of a dancer, though she claims to be a botanist by trade. Her hands are fine and have none of the cuts and scratches I'd associate with that vocation. And yet when I questioned her on her expertise I found her knowledge to be thorough. She is the kind of woman men find extremely distracting. But fortunately I am immune to such calentures!

BORN TO RAISE HELL

'I thank you, but you needn't have bothered,' said Miss Fritzacopple gruffly. 'The beasts would have left in time and I could have saved all my books and samples.' Her belongings were a modest pile on the deck: a leather case, and a small stack of books. Eventually she said: 'Well, I suppose I am grateful to you. If you'll just drop me at the nearest port I'd be happy.'

Fabrigas explained: 'Lady, we are not going to any port, we are not within light-decades of a port.'

'Then any place where I can catch a ship home. Put me in one of the lifeboats if you have to.'

The captain ordered everyone back to their stations. 'We will continue our efforts to catch up with the fleet. We have to keep our eyes open in case the Hornets come back. I will conduct my interrogations of this woman later.'

'Your interrogations?' Fabrigas said.

'Yes. Interrogations.'

'And why would that be necessary?'

'To learn things from her. I am the captain and the captain can't be too careful. Now go to your posts!' And with that he turned and marched off, stumbling over a rope as he went.

★

Fabrigas finally had time to properly examine the secret stowaway who was still bunking with the bats in the bow of the ship. He had many questions, but most of all he wanted to know how the girl knew that there was a woman on board the stricken vessel. He went down to visit, carrying a leather case and a small folding table. But no sooner had he stepped into the tiny corridor than her ghostly voice came from behind the door, and she said, as if their conversation had never even broken off: 'She has pink woodroot in a bag. Yes. It is a favourite aroma for me. Some children of the factories use it to write unvisible messages, I hear – but to me all messages are unvisible.'

The single bulb that lit the space was shorting out, the corridor was madly stuttering. 'Where is Roberto? Have not seen him today.' Since her young travelling-companion had not been able to tell them his name they had decided to give him one. They had called him Roberto after the ship's cat, who had died from complications relating to licking a puddle of spilled rum.

'The deaf boy,' said Fabrigas. 'He was fooling around with some of the youngsters on deck earlier.'

'I see. He is supposed to be taking care of me and my affairs. Tell, was it girls he was with?'

'Girls? I really have no idea. Probably.'

'I see. He comes now anyhow.'

Roberto appeared then down the stairs behind him, wary as a cat. He eyed the old man through slitted eyes. Never taking those eyes off him for a second, the boy strode down the tunnel. He reached up a single finger to the lamp hanging from the ceiling and the bulb stopped its flickering.

'Remarkable,' said Fabrigas. 'You are a Router.'

But of course the boy could not hear, or answer. He opened the hatch to the bough and carefully helped his young friend out. 'Thank you, Roberto,' she said. 'I'm glad you have finally appeared.' The boy stood to one side, arms folded defiantly.

Fabrigas unfolded his table. He took a number of instruments from the leather bag and placed them on the table, alongside a rolled-up map. Roberto eyed them with great interest.

'It is strange that you can sense such things about people,' Fabrigas said. 'That woman and her woodroot, for example.'

'I have powerful nostrils,' she said. 'I can tell you had herrings. Your cook keeps hidden cheeses. Your captain has started to wear a wild scent o-pon his hair.'

'A scent you say? Very interesting. And I assume you used your nose to stumble upon us.'

'We did not stumble, we followed you to here on purpose. We snuck on with the customs people who came to see if I was here.' Fabrigas sighed. 'And I did not use my nose so much to find you. I followed the symbols you painted all around your ship.'

'I beg your pardon?'

'Yes, the symbols. They speak very powerfully to me from a long way away.'

Clouds rolled over the old man's eyes. 'They tricked me,' he said.

'Anyway, it's all in that letter I gave to you, which I can smell you have not opened.'

Fabrigas rubbed his temples with his outsized thumbs. He stood up and leaned against the side of the tunnel for a few seconds, his face in the crook of his elbow. Then he gathered himself, sat down at the table, and took the envelope the girl had given him from a pocket in his cloak. He tore the seal. The letter read as follows:

Dear Doctor

We did not trick you. We simply adjusted our strategy to accommodate your reluctance.

We are Dark Hand. We come from the Empire of the Xo, within the primordial cities of the Floating Worlds. As you know, we made a pact when you were a boy to show you certain great secrets known only to us. In return, we asked only that you would one day grant us a *small* favour. You see our favour standing before you. I think you will agree that they are indeed very small. Though not entirely helpless.

These children have been liberated at great personal risk. As outlined earlier via the haunted belly of a cut-price sphero-mancer, we simply ask that you give protection to these two things. It is vital that they are preserved alive, and that they are never separated.

Once you've guided them through the ambush at the crossing at Akropolis, and into the next dimension, things become simpler: they can be brought home to our friends, the Immortals, who, as we have mentioned in the past, are the oldest species in the universe, and who live at the dawn of time, in the ocean of creation, upon the Three Spirit Islands beyond the Sea of Tranquillity.

This is all we can tell you now:

– The boy has great secrets in his head.

– He is the message, she is the way.

– Both these children believe they are the other's guardian.

– Unicorns do not exist.

– None of this, and all of it, ultimately, matters.

– Trust no one, least of all the person you are thinking about right now.

– There are people in pursuit who wish her, and you, dead. They are the same people who have been trying to kill you since you were a boy.

– The rewards for performing these favours for us will be beyond your imagination; the penalties for failure, unimagin-able.

Perhaps you need evidence that we are who we say, and that we have your interests at heart. The Immortals have revealed to us that your beloved master's last words were as follows:

X{4μM} <W

We were with you in your younger days, we protected you from your enemies, and at your darkest moments gave you hope. Several times you have betrayed us, and used our secrets for your own benefit. But we have stayed with you, because we know your potential.

Best regards

Dark Hand

PS The Immortals tell us that this girl becomes more volatile the closer she gets to maturity. She is like a small Doomsday Clock. This process will begin to happen in approximately ninety nautical days.

Fabrigas put the letter aside. He touched his thumb to his forehead and closed his eyes.

'What does this letter about us say?' asked the girl.

'It says that we're to look after you.'

'That's about all?'

'Yes.'

'You smell of angry.'

'I'm not angry.'

'You are. It smells strongly. Have I made you angry, sir?'

Fabrigas opened his eyes and they were moist and tired. The girl stood patiently before him, her wide, sightless eyes were locked uncannily on his. 'No, I'm not angry with you, dear. I'm angry at my luck. I'm in the wrong universe, and I'm the wrong age for the job I've been given.'

'Just like me,' said the girl.

The old man's face softened like a still pond wrinkled by the wind.

'Please help us,' said the green girl. The scruffy boy stepped forward, his hand dived into his pocket, and when it reappeared it held, between its thumb and forefinger, a single small diamond. He placed the gem carefully on the table before the old man. Fabrigas looked coldly at it, then waved it away. 'I don't need diamonds, boy. I'm not a beauty queen.' Roberto, astonished, plucked the diamond from the table and dropped it in his pocket where it made an audible *clack*. 'Your friend should guard his diamonds carefully. There are greedy people on this boat.' Weary, Fabrigas unrolled a star map and smoothed it out on the table. He placed an instrument on each corner of the map to hold it down. 'We need to work out where we need to take you. And how we get there.' He was about to continue when Roberto picked up a magnascope, a very delicate instrument for calculating the position of a ship in relation to yourself. (This sounds foolish, but believe me, it makes perfect sense.)

'Be careful with that instrument . . .' Fabrigas made to say, but by the time the word 'careful' had left his mouth the deaf/dumb boy had activated the device, calibrated it perfectly, and was pointing to the ship's position on a chart, an act that takes most students years to master. Then he traced a line with his finger to the crossing zone at Akropolis.

'Well, well,' Fabrigas said. 'It looks like your guardian has certain skills.'

'I have not doubt,' said the girl. 'And he is *not* the guardian of me.'

*

Fabrigas made his report to his captain who was napping.

'We are in a frightening and dangerous situation. We are harbouring a fugitive. The whole Empire will be after us.'

'You don't say.' Lambestyo did not even open his eyes.

'She is the girl they call "the Vengeance".'

'Yes, yes, the girl that the whole universe has been hunting. Our own fleet even. Funny.'

'It's not funny.'

'It is a little bit funny. It's like how old people look for their spectacles when they're wearing them.'

'We don't do that.'

'You did it the other day, I saw.'

'This is serious! I have no doubt that the price on her head is considerable. And the price for harbouring her, unthinkable.'

'Considerable you say?'

'Yes. If we were not already well beyond the zones of habitation I estimate that it would take someone like the surgeon mere minutes to hand her to Descharge.'

Lambestyo at last opened his eyes – shot through with blood. 'How do you know I won't hand her over?'

'Don't be an idiot. Now, I do not want to go to the hereafter with the burden of these children's souls. Or anyone's on this ship. So we must work together to keep them safe. At least until we can drop them somewhere. And if I'm not here you have to do it alone. And you can't trust anyone.'

'That's a big job. What about the boy? What is his "deal"?'

'I can tell by the boy's abilities, and by his eye activities, and by the blue "onesie" he wears, that he is a Router.'

'And that is . . . ?'

'A Router is one whose physical architecture, mostly the brain, is used to organise and redistribute large amounts of messaging information via the Ethernet. The information contained in modern, high-speed telegraphic messages is so voluminous and complex that no computational device has been invented which can handle the job. Only the human computer is capable of such a task. He would have been implanted with fingertip sensors when very young, then placed into one of the high-volume communications hubs. This gives him a tremendous ability to conduct energy and information. Are you listening?'

Lambestyo brought his eyes back from the porthole. 'Of course, he's a computer. Continue.'

'More than a computer, he is a hybrid of machine and nature. Each Router has a pod and the pods of each hub number in the millions. The child in each pod handles roughly a billion messages each day, exploiting his on-board computer to sort the messages according to size, destination, priority and cetera. These calculations, of course, take place at a subconscious level, but since every piece of material passing through the child's brain becomes permanently imprinted, Routers become sensitive files, and so are kept as prisoners for their entire lives.'

'So this boy is a sensitive file?'

'Perhaps.'

'If he's so precious, then how did he escape?'

'I don't know. Occasionally, a station is hit by a phenomenon called a "surge", in which too much information is accidentally routed through a single node. Based on my observations of this boy I would assume that he was a victim of such a surge. When I examined him earlier I found tissue damage on his hands and carbon residue around the nose and earholes which leads me to conclude that he was the target of a significant surge. While most victims of a surge are killed instantly, this boy has suffered only a loss of hearing, and perhaps, from his behaviour, a touch of the Prince Alberts.'

'I see.'

'The girl has been sent to us by a secret agency of the Xo called Dark Hand. The fact that they were able to give me a line of algebraic code known only by my master and me is proof that they are who they say.'

'And what did the code say?'

'I have no idea.'

But he did. The code was an iteration of a mathematical phrase his Master Provius had written. It translated as 'Forgiven'.

AGAINST THE DARK

Run a good ship, his mother had always said, and by that she meant know everything that comes in, and everything that goes out. Keep food in the cupboard and spices on the rack. His mother ran a good ship.

'Our ship is sailing for the rocks!' his old man would say each night when he came in. 'They are ruining us, these vultures!' His wife would say, 'Come now, it isn't that bad. We have more than we need to live. Come, eat your soup, my salty man.'

His father's ship was far from on the rocks. Publishers would send him samples of their best volumes in the hope that the baron would agree to distribute them. 'See, baby wolf, I get these publishers from across the universe who think that theirs is the only book among the stars. And what am I to do with them all?! Each book costs a packet for the rights, a quarter that to print. Shipping costs me more money and sleep than I can spare. Then there's insurance, handling, a case of wine for the shipping managers, the reviewers, the Queen's censors. Then what's a humble merchant left with? I need a margin, or what am I in the business for? Fun? Take this volume of Bartellio's *Black Holes and Other Anomalies* you've been leafing through and muddying up with your fingers. It is science, which is always a poor seller, but if it isn't too stodgy it might sell to the academies. I could sell a few tens of thousands, and maybe make a little selling this edition to a dealer – if you hadn't laid your paws all over it. A small margin is what I'll get. Meanwhile the publisher cries to me, "You're squeezing us out of business! You demand too great a cut of meat! You leave us chewing on the bone and sucking marrow!" I say. "My cut of meat might seem large, but that's because I have to share it with a horde of beggars! There is nothing left at the end but a sliver of fat."' Young Fabrigas would look around the drawing room, at the priceless paintings, the antique lamps, and think to himself that it was a miracle what a sliver of fat could buy. '"Oh!" these publishers say. "But what of the poor fool who wrote the thing? He has to live in a garret and suck on his boots for sustenance! He must heat his hands over a passing rat!" I say, "I am not thy author's keeper! If he has chosen the life of an artist he must starve like one! I have ninety-nine problems of my own, the hundredth is yours to keep." Just look at this edition of *The Dictionary Internomicon*. A thousand volumes all cased in wood. What am I supposed to do with it? Who will buy them? What shall I do with any of them?!'

His son replied, 'Father, I have read Bartellio's book. It is fine enough, though it does have four errors in mathematics, and nine in usage. You might well be able to negotiate a discount. As for the *Internomicon*, I have only read the first volume, and so far it has few errors. Any wealthy family in the Empire would want one, since it has all the words a person would need to dazzle in conversation.'

His father was amazed. 'Baby wolf, you are a marvel!' He sacked his readers, saving a small fortune, pulled his boy out of school and set him to work reading full-time. Each day new books would arrive in the delivery bay of the mansion in Carnassus, and young Fabrigas would unpack them carefully, read each thoughtfully, and make notes. These notes were like gold to his greedy father, and his boy's mind expanded like a galaxy. Every evening his mother would have to come up to his room and fetch him for his dinner. Sometimes he was in such a trance that she had to shake him violently just to rouse him.

'Start with the onions and be patient,' the old man murmurs at the table in the basement. 'Don't boil the soup too fast, let it mature.' He can babble on, trance-like, for hours, a medium channelling the ghosts of memories. I must be patient when he slips into the depths, wait for him to rise gently to the surface again. He was in his eighth year when the plague came. When the Black Cloud arrived it brought screams, bloody mobs, and fire. Then silence. The young Fabrigas thought he'd gone deaf. At dawn, twelve days before his eighth name day, he woke to hear Carnassus silent. It had never been silent. All across the city the same tiny dramas were playing out: people were leaning over the beds of loved ones who were leaving in a cloud of sweat and sickly odour. His mother went quickly, merci-fully. The boy mopped her brow and listened as she used her fading strength to tell him where the most important of his father's papers were hidden, which of those were to be destroyed, and confessed to the boy the very worst of her husband's crimes. Then she used her last breath to tell him that she loved him with all her heart.

Can you know what it was like? His father was nowhere to be seen. That evening a message came through on the home telegraph machine.

Baby wolf. Stop. Have diverted towards the moon where your aunt and uncle have their house. Stop. With luck they still live. Stop. Your nanny, Danni, is with me. Stop. Follow when you can. Stop. The world is in chaos. Stop. But I know you have the wherewithal. Stop. I know you have the balls. Stop. Check for money in the safe and destroy the folder in my office marked 'Critical Heat'. Stop.

★

There was no money in the safe. There was little food in the house. He was smart enough to know not to drink the public water. He snuck out at night for scraps and drain water. He ate nothing but soup for that whole year. Whatever he could find went into the soup. He became very good at making it. He could make it in the dark. He had to. When they came to put the marker on the door of their home they smelled soup and were bewildered.

'Ghost soup!' they cried and never came back.

It was such a fiercely miserable time that he can hardly take it even now.

But he kept a good ship. He rose at dawn to clean and dress. Then he did his studies. Then he went out. He went below the house, through the cellar, the sewer, and into darkness. He went deeper than anyone dared. He went down to where Princess Malvia rested, still clutching her dead lover's paintbrush and her husband's sword. He went down among the royal bones, where no one ever dared to go, and found treasures. Then he went up into slums. The merchants were astonished to see a well-to-do child in an expensive coat rising from the Fathoms, brushing a fleck of filth from the sleeve of his jacket and saying, 'How much for this iron cross, sir? It is very old.' But no merchant would trade with an orphan. At best he managed to swap some of his treasures for sacks of rat-gnawed food. So he went up. To the markets where he scurried below the grills and scavenged onions that had rolled away unseen. Start with the onions and be patient. Then he went up. He went into the morphium dens to find the rags dropped between the boards and he sold them to the rag-men. He soon realised that a sackful of these scraps could fetch more than a brass funeral urn which had taken him a whole morning to scavenge. The rags could be sold to paper pressers who would turn them into creamy sheets to make the very books which each day were still piling up at his door. Whenever he came home he found a new stack of these end-fruits in his delivery bay, sent by publishers far away who still had no idea that the Black Cloud had descended on Carnassus. A treatise on military strategies; the complete works of Shiva Danzig; Wolff's famous book on probability. He could have sold these books for a small fortune. But he did not. No matter how empty his stomach got.

He learned, too, that if he offered a morphium-soaked rag to a desperate fool with no credit at the dens he could get the shirt from off his back as well. And so his business trebled.

Then he went up. He went up into the night-dens. He used his knowledge of the laws of chance and probability to sell advantage to the gambling men. He made better money than he did hunting rags and old treasures. He went up. As dawn broke he would go to the chapel and give the priest a coin to say a prayer for him. The priest would take his money and buy booze, and he never said a single prayer for the boy. 'What will happen to all these lonely people?' the urchin would say to himself as he wandered home. 'How does the universe keep making them? The old lady who picks up rice in the church after a wedding: why is she so lonely? It could be because she screams bad words at children. Ah well.'

At night the noises became consuming. The cries of the desperate. The gnawing of the rats. He had retreated to the attic and walled himself in with his books. They blocked out the noises, and let not a thread of lamplight out. There were barely enough scraps for soup. His belly was a cave.

It occurred to the boy at that time that every volume he added only illuminated another which was missing. It seemed as if every single answer bred a hundred questions. Gradually, his studies turned from the concrete and technical – what is light? What is the organic structure of the plague organism? – to the abstract – what is pain? Why is it necessary for a human being to suffer the plague of lone-liness and despair, and can it, like a disease of the body, be cured? Am I alone, truly? And if so, can this loneliness be plotted on a graph? Was it, in fact, his own experiments with the Forbidden Geometry which had brought the Black Cloud to Carnassus, and brought his loneliness with it?

His boyhood was a period of such pain and hardship that even now, if you ask him to talk about it, his eyes will cloud over and he will flatten his beard with the palms of both hands and look about the room as if searching for a familiar friend. It took me a long while to get him to describe those years.

Load up the cannons, bring your chums,
It's fun to sing and drink ye rums,
She's over-bored and self-assuuuuuuuuured.
. . . We know a dirty word – Oi!

'Smells Like Sea Spirits' – traditional shanty

MERCENARY

Bounty hunters are not fierce. Bounty hunters are not cruel. The best don't have a lust for blood. For the hunter, retrieving is a business. They find, they kill, they get paid. It is a job. They don't do it for pleasure. They are like the shark, or the tiger, or the tiger shark: for them, the hunt is the road towards the meal.

Six bounty hunters were hired by the Man in the Shadows to hunt and destroy a fugitive child in possession of a top-secret file. A simple task, no? Hiatus. The Medusa. San Dusty Von Furstenberg. Klaus Bugle. Penny Dreadful. And a new hunter, one that none of the others had even heard of, one who refused even to give over his name, but who came highly recommended by certain shadowy groups whose knowledge and power distort the envelope of believability.

The Well Dressed Man had left Carnassus in his private ship and set a course for deep space. He went with a fully stocked library, fourteen cases of finest Effervesco (an exquisite sparkling wine made exclusively on the wine-producing moons of Champagnos XT471), a caged bird, his prized viola, and the knowledge that, after a sequence of bizarre events, all five of his rivals were dead.

Hiatus, the youngest hunter, had accidentally fallen from the balcony of his 785th-floor penthouse apartment in Belgravus. San Dusty Von Furstenberg had, for reasons understood only by himself, handed his silver pistols to a 'mark' and encouraged him to shoot a peach off his head. The Medusa had somehow managed to pull an eight-by-six-foot wall-mounted mirror shaped like a swan on top of herself. Klaus Bugle, famous for his skill with knives, fatally injured himself with an antique letter knife while opening an envelope. The envelope was addressed to 'Stab Yourself' and the sheet of expensive letter paper inside was blank and unmonogrammed. Penny Dreadful, arguably the most renowned of the small group (and arguably the best in the Holy Neon Empire), decided, in an astonishing act of fair play, to message her home address to every mark, crime boss and fellow hunter in the galaxy. She was able to stay alive for a very respectable forty-five minutes before she fell from the Perfume Bridge in a hail of poison darts.

So now this Well Dressed Man found himself the only remaining mercenary from the star group hired to delete a top-secret file, and the child who carried it. The fact that he was now the only hunter on the case didn't make his chances of finding them any greater (they were, after all, two very small things in a very big universe), but it did make the chances of him taking the full share of the very generous reward *very* likely.

All he had to do was follow the trail and be patient. His instincts never lied. Just that morning, as he'd been meditating on images of the fugitive, another image had spontaneously popped into his head. It was a bird of prey, and its wings were wide and white. 'An owl? How strange.' In moments of quiet he could discover great truths.

From the journal of H. Q. Gossipibom, poet

Though it has been four days since the horrible incident my heart has hardly stopped its pounding. This ship seems to be a ship of grand horror and misfortune: staffed by fools, bound for hell. And that woman we rescued has a malicious streak, I can see. I would not trust her.

★

From the diary of Miss Maria Fritzacopple

I have been rescued, and now am on a ship called the *Necronaut*. It is a ship which seems to be setting sail for madness. It is packed with awful specimens, none so much as the surgeon. He wanders slowly all around with steepled hands and steely eyes, and watches all as a cat watches fish in a bowl. And then there's the old man, who rants to himself upon the observation deck. The crew are plotting his death, but the captain is on guard and he has the bosun onside. No one with any sense will cross the bosun. This man-giant towers above everything but intellect, and his body is a hellish canvas. Two spitting beasts are locked, necks entwined, in combat on his chest. An eagle, black and terrifying, rises from his back, a cluster of arrows in its talons. His arms show signs of dark and forbidden magic, such as those you'll find in the old heathen gospels. His right shoulder declares 'Mother', and for that I'll give him credit, and I won't describe the rest, suffice it to say that I will be asking the captain to ensure that each man locks his washing stall when he is in it. I cannot understand how some women are attracted to such low beasts. Certainly, if you could take some magic sponge and carefully wipe away his adornments then I could, perhaps, see some attraction.

The Gentrifaction are a frightening trio of painted monsters. Hideous, fatuous and cruel. The poet was shrieking on the deck today that someone stole his watch. One of the children said, 'This watch, sir?' and the poet snatched it, saying, 'Of course this watch. Did you pilfer it from my quarters?'

'Oh no,' said the child, 'you left it on the ledge outside the botanist's window.'

Tonight I saw the most frightening thing of all.

When I was returning from the stalls I heard the poet arguing with someone in his quarters, but his antagonist was a voice I had not heard, high-pitched, gurgling and ghostly, like the final whisper from a sick man's throat.

'You call yourself an artist?' the voice softly said. 'You have the nerve to cast yourself among the greats? You are nothing.'

'Oh stop, I care not for your critiques tonight.'

'Oh no, you never do. You are content to churn out slimy verse unfit for dogs to piss on.'

'Oh stop, brother, enough.'

. . . Brother?

'You can't call the feckless sputum that bilges from your pathetic brain poetry. He who writes the shipping news has a finer pen than you.'

'Oh stop, I beg you!'

'And here you prepare for bed, like a man who has earned his rest. You think you have done enough to sleep?'

'Oh, Alfredo, no. Please let me rest. I've worked so hard today, and I promise tomorrow you'll see my masterwork. I am in pain!'

I noticed then a shaft of light coming from a small slit in the curtains of his room and crept carefully up, being careful not to wake the boards outside. The poet was sprawled on his bed, a pen in his left hand, a glass of liquor in his right, his sheets were wet with tears and ink. His shirt was unbuttoned and drawn back, and on his side, just above the protruding bone of his hip, was a face, a twisted, toothy face with straggled tufts of hair. A brother, no doubt, one who partly formed with him inside the womb.

'Pain? Pain?' That voice, so sick and nasty. 'Oh, Herbert, if only you knew the pain of living day by day upon the hip of mediocrity.' And as Herbert began to quietly weep, I swear the creature turned his eyes and bore straight into mine, taking the breath from out my very soul, and it was all that I could do to stop from screaming out. I ran as quick as I could back to my room, and I locked the door, and I lay awake all night, with my mind churning and my heart racing, just as the poet must do every night of his poor, sad life.

And so here we are: on a ship of fools piloted by a dangerously unstable teenager and carrying a host of monsters and rum-addled hypochondriacs.

I have not even asked yet where this ship is headed.

I will tomorrow.

★

From the journal of Captain Lambestyo

The months we've spent at sea feel like years and I cannot explain it. I have always loved the sea, but this boat is being driven by dark forces. A big amount of our rum has become unstable. And what I mean is it is liable to explode when exposed to heat or heavy bumps. You would almost swear the makers of this rum WANTED us to blow up. When I said we were to dump our dangerous tonic into space there was almost a mutiny. Someone wrote: 'The captain is a bad man!' in the galley. I strapped the ringleader, Mylie, to a strut and left him there two nights, even when he cried and said, 'I hate you! I wish I had ne'r been born!' Then I took pity and cut him loose, and there was not any talk of mutiny again. Although we still have all the rum.

And then there is this mysterious woman we found. I went to interrogate her today, but she said that twice was enough. So I took my wine and left.

And then there are the children whom we found eating our precious bats. A burned-out urchin and a girl with no past. It makes perfect sense. Doesn't it? No, I am being sarcastic. The boy cannot tell us his name, so we have called him Roberto. Roberto makes me fearful. He is a boy who is always in motion. Always are his eyes restlessly moving, looking for danger, or something to mess with. He is always interfering with the old man's things. He seems to have the plans for every instrument stuck inside his head. The old man stands back with his hands on his hips and laughs with delightment when the boy is able to operate a complicated device. But the fool doesn't laugh when the boy pulls out his Magic Eighth Ball. This is a very popular novelty device that when you shake it gives an answer to a question you have: Will I find love? Where is my hat? Etx. He always has it out, and when he does the old man yells at him, saying, 'Roberto, put that piece of nonsense away!'

He has also a pet starfish. How strange is this? It is small and greenish gold with flecks of silver which catch the light. I see him talking to it. He cannot even hear!

The other day I yelled at him on deck for getting under my boots. Later that evening I went to use my radio receiver and I found that the frequency had been locked to a channel playing experimental sea shanties. I hate experimental sea shanties.

Right now, I hate everything.

★

From the diary of Miss Maria Fritzacopple

We have finally managed to catch up with our fleet. This evening the fleet commander, Descharge, came across for dinner. He has announced that as it is the day of the crossing tomorrow he will stay with us tonight, then return to his ship before we jump. I assume that I will travel back to the Empire with the waste ships. First I must take care of one or two things.

During dinner the surgeon called Fabrigas to task, saying, 'Sir, you do not eat the pork?'

He replied, 'No, I am vegetarian.'

To which the surgeon sniffed: 'But surely you, as a man of science, would know the health issues associated with eschewing meat.'

'Health issues?' he replied. 'My boy, I am more than a thousand years old.' And everyone laughed.

'But what of the study by the esteemed researcher Hammond May-Clarkson which proved that a lack of meat causes a man to lean towards a feminine disposition?' said Shatterhands.

'I have read it.'

'And?'

'All it proved was that too much meat rots the brain.'

All laughed again.

'And so,' said the cook wryly, 'you take out all your frustrations on these poor vegetables.'

'If the plants wish to seek their revenge and dine on me, then I welcome it,' he replied.

'But to eat meat is the natural order,' said Descharge. 'It is why we have incisors,' and the delicate servo motors in his fingers whirred as he tapped his own long incisor.

'I have nipples, too,' said the old man, 'yet I'm hardly tempted to let babies suckle at me.' More laughter. 'If it is the natural order,' continued Fabrigas, 'then it is an order which is costing us a great deal. We snuffed four great suns last year to get the energy to power the factories that make the meat for the Empire. More than a billion children work in the meat factories.'

'When I was a boy I did my time in the factories, now look at me,' said the cook, as he shoved a large spoonful of peas into his maw.

'You must have sympathies, certainly,' said Descharge to Fabrigas, his lips pulling back across his teeth. 'After all, you yourself were an . . . orphan, if my intelligence is correct?' He had chosen the word carefully, cruelly. To use the word 'orphan' is to suggest an absolute lack of status. An orphan is all but a non-person in the Empire. Without at least one parent, who would pay for the mechanical augmentations which make a person truly unique? The old man withered visibly under the question. 'An orphan from another universe,' continued Descharge. 'Or so you claim. A cosmic orphan, no less.'

'I had an aunt and an uncle who had a uranium mine on a moon in the outer reaches of my own universe. We went there when I was a boy and played beside the sea. My father gave their daughter two pet serpents he had brought back from one of his trips. I tried for a long time to find the moon again. Perhaps I still have family there. I would very much like to find out one day.'

The surgeon, sensing the sudden cloud across the room, cut in: 'In any event, these slaveys are well cared for. Without the Workhouse Act they'd starve as orphans. Is that preferable? When the young bee is old enough to serve it does so. That is a natural order.'

'You couldn't be more wrong,' I interjected. 'I studied the bee for years. The bee is very nurturing. The young bee stays by its queen and eats her royal jelly until it grows big and strong. I would never say so beyond this ship, but what we're doing to these children is despicable.'

Fabrigas nodded slowly, eyes on his meal. 'There are no children now-days,' he said. 'There are no innocents any more.'

Descharge smiled. 'And what of you, Captain?' he said. 'This conversation puts you in a delicate position. No longer a child, not quite a man, and certainly not an innocent.' The captain cocked his head impertinently as the commander turned his eyes to him. 'Once a soldier, now a mercenary, almost a free man, but soon to be a prisoner. Do you think the children should be free?'

The captain put down his fork and said, 'My mother was a noble prostitute. My father, an officer in the navy. I know what it is like to be an orphan. My mother died before I knew her. My father disowned me. He sent me to a naval school when I was one.'

'It was a fine military school . . . if my intelligence is correct.'

'It was an orphanage. A cruel place.'

'Would you rather he'd left you on the street?' A sunrise of crimson had appeared below the commander's stiff collar. 'My own father was a cruel man, but look what I've become. It takes a chisel to carve a hero. How would your life have been without his actions?'

'I don't know. But I think I would choose to take that life again. Who needs a father when you have the universe? An orphan is hungry, but he is free.' The table was silent. And it was fitting that at that point the only thing we could hear was the sound of the slaveys singing themselves to sleep.

GOD THE WORM

An orphan is hungry, but he is free. Free to wander, free to steal; free to make the street his bed, the rat his meal, the strangers in dark places his friends, the depths his playground, the dens his school, this sweet hell his heaven; free to go into the friendly deep, where the worms and princes softly sleep; free to rise up, free to laugh at this unholy mess, free to sing himself to sleep.

The boy went up. He went up proudly now. He was a prince of the city. The shadows and the noises no longer frightened him. He went up into the night-dens. You know the rest, in outline, but here are the finer points. One night he helped a drunkard double his money. 'Boy, what mean god led you here?' said the drunkard. 'The same monster who brought me, I expect. What a life!'

'No god brought me,' said the boy, 'since I don't believe one exists. And I would rather he not exist if he's a monster.'

'The creator is ineffable, boy, and since all of us lack the ability to describe his awesomeness, it would do just as well to call him a monster. Some call him "God the angelic beast with the face of a lion". Since these are just pretty words, why not call him "God the Worm"?'

'If God is just Word why call him at all?'

The drunkard laughed. He withheld the boy's cut and said, 'Now see here, boy, you're better than this game. I can tell, because I was once somebody. I won't give you a single bit tonight, but I'll give you something better. Now look here.' And he gave the boy a crumpled piece of paper. And on the scrap was written . . .

THE DARK FRIARS INVITE TO YOU TO
SOLVE THE UNSOLVABLE.

We care not about where you were born, or what your family is worth. Solve the problem below and you will be one of us. We will give you a place at our academy for scholarly monks.

'This problem has defeated the greatest minds in the Empire,' said the drunkard. 'If you can help me solve it and win a place at the Academy I'll pay you a thousand pieces. Those monks have a grand life. They laze their days away, pondering the infinity of their navels. Once I'm in with them, I'll be set.'

'I could solve this problem myself,' said the boy, 'in two nights.'

The drunkard roared again. 'Boy, if you can solve this in two nights I'll pay you ten thousand pieces, and take you to the Friars myself!'

Little Fabrigas worked through the night; the next day, the next night; he built himself a fort of books so that he could block out everything but the problem. By the second morning his solution was written in chalk on the floor in his attic, so he had to pull up a board and drag it to the night-den. The drunkard was there, glazed stupid, but was amazed to see the boy, and even more amazed to see his solution. He took the boy and his board to a brother called Provius who, smiling all the while, took the youngster through a series of increasingly difficult problems before finally declaring, 'For the first time in my life, I am amazed. Boy, with your mind you will be able to achieve anything you set your heart towards.'

'All I want,' said the boy, 'is to find my father. He has gone to a moon where my aunt and uncle live.'

'My boy,' said Provius, 'to be a Dark Friar is to give up all attachments. Family, friends, love: these mean nothing when you are unravelling the secrets of the cosmos. We will not help you find your father. Instead we'll give you the universe.'

'I don't want the universe,' said the boy. 'And I don't want to join your Academy. All I want is to have my old life back. I used your puzzle to pass two lonely nights – which was sweet – and to get this man's money – which was even sweeter. Now that I have it I am closer to having coin to charter a ship to find my father. And so now, goodbye.'

And the boy left the two men dazed, went back through the oily tunnels, past the faces of the drowned men. He found an orphan onion wedged in the spokes of a wheel. 'This is a lucky sign,' he said to himself. He kissed it, and slipped it into his pocket. An onion was all he needed for the night, and it had been given to him. He arrived home at the high walls of his mansion just before Ten Bells dropped the city into darkness.

Here in ships, we feel so safe,
We feel the safest of all.
(H'ray!)
There's no one out here to bother us,
And there's whisky aboard for all.
(Yes!)

'Ships' – traditional shanty

THE HUMAN CONDITION

A human is a tiny world who in her head contains the university. She is not separate from the great cosmogenesis any more than the wave is separate from the sea. And yet look how desperate and lonely she is. Perhaps you are a higher being, and as such you will find it difficult to understand the trials and terrors of these low creatures. How every unexpected phenomenon startles them. How every moment of their brief lives seems filled with private desperation. How sad it is to see the way the gift of existence can become such a tragedy: a tragedy whose only balm is the soothing oil of superstition.

The best knowledge we have tells us that humans were once mere apes, squatting in shacks of wood and tin and gnawing on lumps of charred flesh. This may be true. But the species evolved, as it was meant to do, and went out into the universe, driven by the quest to spread its genetic materials. People fashioned ships to take them far, and bodies which could survive the trials of deep space: joints which could withstand the wrenching fists of gravity, ears which could decipher strange tongues, eye membranes which could be turned towards a sun, lungs which could breathe sulphur – pure sulphur! They took with them the luggage of nature: the sexual parts for procreation; the brain to solve problems and to hold stories. They returned from their travels with innumerable stories.

They brought home the stuff of nature too. No one knows exactly where it came from, but the Black Cloud began to remove the pieces which made people who they were. When a surgeon or a barber tells you that your lungs are being slowly eaten, what choice have you but to allow him to replace those lungs with a set of silicon bags? And then your spleen. And then your heart. The very parts of your existence are being eaten by these microscopic cannibals who live within the wormy tunnels of your gut.

So that is what happened. For better or for worse. All that remain now, in many people, are the very essentials of life: a brain to hold stories, sexual parts to make people who will sustain those stories. And they are born! They arrive, much as they always have, as slimy little ape creatures, wriggling and crying out towards the heavens which, according to popular local legend, created them.

But herein lies a greater question: What makes a human human? Is it a heart? Skin? A functioning spleen? Legs which wander, fingers which clutch? Most say that it is all of these things in general, but none in particular. For all these things can be replaced while leaving the person, and her stories, intact. There are citizens in Carnassus now who are little more than brains spiked upon a titanium torso with a synthetic digestive system and an artificial heart pumping enriched petroleum blood. Are such people not human? And when, at the end of the day, the human ape retires to her bed, takes off her limbs and stacks them neatly in a basket, or a bath of machine oil, takes off her jaw and puts that in a cup of fine lubricant, then lies upon her baby-sized cot, just a few spare parts and a brain, what are the thoughts which spin through her mind as she drifts away to sleep?

And what happens when a person loses even her mind? Is she still herself?

Well, that is an interesting question.

MEANWHILE

The registrar's private office at the Customs and Inspections depot, Balfour, was very quiet that evening. The registrar sat opposite a visitor, well dressed, in a handsome leather chair, newspaper in hand, a pot of coffee beside him. The visitor sat so still he might very well have been having his portrait photo-emulsified. But he wasn't. In one corner an ancient chronograph beat out the rhythm of the hours.

The outer inspections office, on the other hand, had seldom seen this much activity. This was a quiet, dignified office in a quiet, dignified corner of the Holy Neon Empire. Nothing untoward happened here. The most outrageous thing that had ever happened in the Customs and Inspections depot, Balfour, was that someone had processed a goods-transit order using form 1PQX/9 instead of form 1PQX/10. They still talked about that by the water unit. But it was unlikely that that incident, beyond tonight, would ever be talked about again.

In one corner of the outer inspections office, Balfour, a senior clerk was waltzing with a hatstand. By the registration counter a junior clerk was holding another clerk's hand and singing him a love song. Another clerk was typing furiously upon a teletype unit: 'All work and no play makes Balfour a dull place.'

Four customers – a lady in a travelling frock, and three men – had been waiting to have their goods inspected. They were all ka-roaking like frogs.

Kaaaa-roooooaaaak. Kaaaa-roooooaaaak. Kaaaa-roooooaaaak.

In the registrar's private office the Well Dressed Man put down his copy of the *Telegraphic Press*, took out a pale blue kerchief and gently dabbed his brow. His hair was slicked to one side with a balm imported all the way from Amphasimia, and his side-parting looked like the cut left by a single swipe from a barber's razor. He smiled wanly at the waltzing silhouettes pulsing behind the frosted-glass screen. Then he turned towards the registrar, who had a look on his face of utter disbelief. 'Let's do another one,' said the Well Dressed Man.

'I don't want to do another,' wheezed the sweating registrar. 'Please don't make me.'

'Oh dear, but you said you were extremely good at maths. You said you could multiply any two numbers in your head.'

'Please.'

'Let's just do one more.' He took a pocket watch from his jacket. 'Twenty seconds on the clock. Are you ready?'

'Please.'

'OK. 2,128 times 5,671. Go!'

While the registrar's right hand tapped furiously at his glistening forehead, his left began to raise the letter knife he had towards his left eye. It rose up slowly, and when the tip of the knife was just an inch away from his eye, trembling furiously, the young man finally blurted, 'Twelve-oh-six-seven-eight-eight-eight!'

'Very good! It is amazing what the human mind is capable of when put under pressure. Now,' said the Well Dressed Man, 'to business. I will only ask this one time. Did any ships recently transit through this way?' He knew one had, he was just having so much fun.

'One came through a few weeks ago. On transit to Akropolis.'

'Akropolis? How curious.'

'Yes. We boarded it to search for the missing girl.'

'The missing girl?'

'That's right, sir. You know . . . the *green* girl? The girl who went missing from the Worlds' Fair? She weren't on there, though, so we sent them on.'

'The green girl, you say? And you say she wasn't on the ship?'

'Absolutely, sir. Our team made a thorough search. Please.'

'Well, far be it from me to call you a liar.'

'Please.'

The Well Dressed Man smiled. Could it really be true? Could the child who ran off with a top-secret file be the green girl the whole universe was after? How utterly absurd! And yet for some reason, at that moment, among all the noise and madness in that noisy, maddening universe, the two of them fitted together in his mind like two halves of a shattered dish. This was an excellent lead. The frogs were finally coming home to roost.

THE WELL DRESSED MAN

The Well Dressed Man, he hunts well. It is his job. He hunts all kinds of people. He's lost count of the number of people he has hunted down. People of all ages and stations. But children he hunts particularly well. He can smell them in their sleep. He can haunt their dreams. A child's mind is a beacon, and once he knows their mind they can't run far enough that he won't see it.

'Hello there.'

This young mind blinks twice and wakes within a dream.

'Hello. Have we met?'

They speak in pictures – the language of dreams.

'So there you are. It took such a long time to find you. I've been searching everywhere.'

'Who are you?'

'That isn't important. The important thing is who you are.'

'Who I am?'

'Who you are.'

Frightened. Suddenly wanting to wake.

'What is this I'm doing?'

'You're dreaming. Have you never dreamed?'

'No. We never dream where I come from.'

'Don't try to wake. If you wake you won't find out who I am and why I'm hunting you.'

'I'm not curious about you. And I know why you're hunting me.'

'You do?'

'Yes.'

'Well, you've a reputation for being a clever one. Enlighten me. Why am I hunting you?'

'Because you think that I'm government property. And because you want a reward.'

Laughter. 'Oh, you are a dear treasure. None of those reasons are true. I don't care about my reward, I just like my job. There is a very powerful group of people who want you dead. So I'm hunting you. Like a wolf hunts a baby goat. When I find you I'm going to kill you. It won't be painful for you. I'm not a monster. But that is the state of play. Thoughts? Feedback?'

'I won't tell you where I am.'

'You don't have to. I discover where you are through your dreams. Every time you go to sleep I find you, and I get a few more clues. I can feel when you drift off, and then I pounce. It's what I do. I'm very good at it. You know what I love best? A young girl's dreams. They are the most vibrant and creative. I'm never disappointed by a young girl's dreams. Of course, boys' dreams are fine too, if you like that kind of thing.'

'_____'

'I've upset you. I didn't mean to upset you. I just thought you should know what the game was. It's important in every sport that every player knows the rules, don't you think?'

'_____'

'Don't cry. It will be quick. I promise. When I kill you and your friends it will be very, very quick.'

'_____'

'Well, I will leave you to dream. I don't suppose you'd like to tell me where you are? I'm near Balfour.'

'_____'

'Very well. Very well. I didn't expect you would. But you were there at Balfour, I know. I suppose it would make the game less fun if you told me. And you're travelling with . . . a friend? Is this right?'

'_____'

'A new friend?'

'_____'

'A friend who is there for . . . company? No, protection. How interesting.'

'Please leave my head now.'

'Quite. Quite. It's been so good of you to have me. Rest well.'

The Well Dressed Man hunts children well. He hunts all kinds of people. But haunted children he hunts most well. He can smell them in their sleep.

From the journal of M. Francisco Fabrigas

We find ourselves nearing a truly empty part of space where the only evidence of civilisation is the ruins of Akropolis, which were built long ago near the powerfully active Nebula Akropolis. It is necessary to find an empty region of space if you wish to travel to the next universe, since any object within the field of your engine will be taken with you into the Interior. Unfortunately we will not have time to examine the ruins. A pity, as they are among the most interesting and ancient in this cosmos. A large fleet wishing to make the crossing faces a truly terrifying reality. They must use the winds from the nebula to increase their velocity to a good portion of the speed of light. Thus they would be hurled from this universe, through the fog of death, and into the next universe like a shot flung from the barrel of a cannon. It is, if I am honest, a frightening thought. One which I have trouble contemplating. In these instances the petty questions of existence leave, and we become uniquely tuned to a higher purpose. It is, as the artificial philosopher Photozeiger framed it, the great philosophical problem: we are faced with a terrible cosmic storm. The possibility that we will be broken apart by forces many trillions of times more powerful than ourselves occurs to us. But so long as these personal concerns do not envelop our thoughts, and we continue with an aesthetic consideration of reality, the purer aspect of the self will look through all that chaos and quietly comprehend the ideas behind even that great power which threatens to crush us. In this contemplation lies a sense of the sublime.

We arrive tomorrow.

THE COSMIC SOUP

When Lenore woke in the darkness of the bow-pit she knew the time had come. Her dreams never lied. Also, the bats were silent. She saw the whole nightmare laid out in a succession of terrifying images: the surprise attack, the fires, the screams, the goat. A blue lantern? A moon, fleeing for their lives, treachery, madness, supernatural children, cannibals, magical minerals, murderous vegetables, a giant monster, a great hole in the blackness of space. And a love story. Her dreams never lied. The journey to the next universe would be a trial within a storm, wrapped up in a nightmare, set on fire and pushed out across the oceans of pain and suffering. But there would also be some good bits.

She smelled soup.

*

There was huge excitement on the day they came to make the crossing. The ship's inhabitants, through some kind of neat and necessary cognitive trick, had somehow come to forget that they were about to be sent to their technical deaths. What kind of universe would they be entering? What new species of plant and animal would they find there? Would there be treasures?

'For the last time, Captain, I do not know if we will find treasures! Now please let me tend to my instruments.'

Far below them in the darkness Lenore smelled their fear and excitement. Goats, fires, screams, treachery – that was coming too. She rose and peered out into the corridor. Peered with dead eyes. The corridor was silent.

The whole shipload rose early and put on their best clothes and there was a lot of laughter and fool-play on the decks. Even Descharge was seen to smile, and though he kept saying, 'I really must return to my command ship now,' he never seemed to make it to his pod, particularly when Fabrigas said, 'Oh, but you must stay for some of my soup. It is really quite good.'

'Well,' said Descharge, 'I suppose I could stay for a few spoonfuls. It does smell intoxicating.'

'A few spoonfuls and you'll be in bliss!' cried the old-beard.

The slaveys were allowed special privileges on this day, and did the best they could to sharpen up. The bosun took two huge buckets of soapy water to their bunk rooms so they could wash away the soot and filth of months at ship, saying loudly, 'All right, my peaches, my salty doves, let's have as if your wedding day has come early, let's have the coal from your hands and the worms from out your ears, my pocket pennies, my milky scoundrels, my little fallen angels.'

He leaned a mirror at the end of their dormitory, next to a comb and a monster tube of McGivven's Fine Hair Cream, and every child crowded in to make themselves look as presentable as they'd ever been.

The captain came out in a grand new jacket with gold epaulettes and red trim. He'd been saving it especially for this day. He had his hair neatly combed. When Miss Fritzacopple ascended the men all but lost their wits. The deaf/dumb Roberto dropped his Magic Eighth Ball and the captain walked into a spar.

'Are you wearing make-up this day?' he enquired.

'Yes. I was able to salvage a few small things from the *Black Widow*. Although I'm not to make the crossing with you I'm at least going to enjoy the celebrations.'

'Oh . . . You will be leaving?'

'Of course. I'll be passed to the barge returning to the Empire with our waste materials.'

'Oh. Must look your best for that.'

The captain bowed and strutted off.

It was around lunchtime when the *Necronaut* finally rose from the shipping channel near the ruins of Akropolis, and they all gathered on the deck, even the slaveys, to toast this universe, this great and unquenchable furnace that gave birth to all of us. The nebula was a pink-and-yellow smear of flossy gas and the young stars within shone brightly. Speeches were made, and then Fabrigas announced that his soup was ready.

'Ready?'

'It is so. Please come down to the galley.'

'Well, I look forward to this soup I have been hearing so much about,' said the cook.

★

No one was disappointed. The old man's soup was a deep, rich, sensuous, almost erotic soup, and from the first spoonful the people assembled in the galley found themselves adrift upon a calm lagoon of flavour.

'My word,' said Fritzacopple. 'This could be the best thing I've ever tasted.'

'I demand to know the recipe!' cried the cook.

'The recipe is known only by myself and a dead woman from another universe,' said Fabrigas, 'and you have more chance of getting it from her.'

The galley was one of the few pleasant places on the ship. It had windows revealing stunning views of the cosmos. As they ate, surrounded by scenes of the Akropolis nebula, Fabrigas rose to address them. 'Friends!' he said so loudly that they all jumped. The old man, many had observed, seemed to be at least two hundred years younger today. He had even given his share of the soup to the bosun. 'For months at sea you have laboured under the impression that I planned to kill you all. It gives me great pleasure to inform you that today, in fact, I intend to save your lives. We have arrived here at the point of no return. This is the spot from which we were to make the jump to the next universe, thereby, presumably, to join the legions of the dead, although perhaps to have had many wonderful adventures along our way. Wouldn't that have been fun?'

'From which we *were* to make the jump?' said someone.

'Wouldn't that *have been* fun?' said another.

The old man stood before them, arms raised. The nebula glowed brightly through the reinforced glass windows; its powerful gravity was already flinging them through space at an unfathomable speed. The hull vibrated faintly, like a kettle coming to the boil. 'I am afraid, dear friends, that there has been a minor alteration in our intended trajectory.'

'What the hell are you talking about?' said Descharge testily, as he pushed his empty bowl away.

'I was not informed of any change in plans,' said the captain as he ran his finger around the bowl and licked it clean. 'My fee is —'

'Yes, yes, why don't you let me explain? Unfortunately I have led you here under false pretences. I have never intended to take you to the next universe. This is all a ruse. I agreed to go on this voyage only to escape the clutches of the Queen, and the Empire which has made my life a lavish hell. The soup you have just enjoyed for your luncheon contains a sleeping toxin of my own design.' The assembled, as one, looked down at their bowls. 'It is important that we act quickly. Soon, you will all be sound asleep, like little babies, and so it is very important that you go to the life-pods. You will be picked up by the other boats in the fleet, and then you are free to return to your Empire and your lives. I dismiss you!' He paused for effect and noted the stunned silence. 'I, meanwhile, will escape in this ship and live out my days in exile on an orphan moon!' And he flung out his arms and beamed like a man who has just said to his family, 'I bet all our money on a squid race!'

No one in the galley spoke for a while, they were still staring at their bowls. Then all spoke at once, and their fury fell upon the old man as he continued to beam proudly. Discharge stood and stalked to the front and called for calm. 'People, please, shut up now. There is no need to lose our heads. This is clearly all just a joke, isn't that right, Master?'

'Oh no, young man! No, this is all completely serious. You each have roughly twenty minutes, perhaps less for smaller people. I suggest you get to your escape pods and get comfortable. Put your nightgowns on.'

'Are you completely mad?!' said the cook.

'No! I am tired! I am very old and tired and all I want is to rest. I have been travelling my whole life. I have been the length and breadth of several galaxies and seen many of the wonders and horrors they contain. I have no desire to do it again. I just want to die in peace. And if you think upon it, I have saved all your lives. Travelling to another universe would have meant certain death for all of us. Or have you forgotten that my magic engine must kill us all to work? So if anything, you should be grateful!'

'Master,' Discharge's cabin boy, Plantamour, called from the doorway, 'there's something I think you should see.'

'Not now! The old fool claims to have drugged us all. I should have you thrown in the brig for mutiny. Now give us all the antidote immediately.' Discharge had to lean far back to meet the eyes of the old man who towered over him.

'There is no antidote! Except to sleep! And if you lock me up you'll still all fall asleep and heavens knows what will happen to the ship. You are better in the pods.'

And again there was a mighty uproar as every adult tried to have their say. Several of the children were already starting to nod off.

Little K. Persuivus was snoring loudly with her head in her bowl. Little J. Martinas, too, was about to pass out in her 'supas', without understanding what was happening to her, for she had lived on a tiny world and never learned her Internomicon. Miss Fritzacopple stood and cried, 'What kind of ship is this? Have I boarded a floating asylum!'

'Master,' said the boy, 'I know this is a bad time but it really is very important you see this —'

'Not now! Can't you see that we're about to be thrown into space?'

'No!' said the boy, 'we're about to be *blown up* in space! We are under attack!'

That's when the first explosions rocked the ship, filling the small galley with a stinging light.

When Descharge strode above he saw battleships streaming from the shadows of the ruins of Akropolis. Their attackers were a modest Vangardik fleet: a thousand gunships, a hundred cruisers, a command ship, a supply fleet and a wolf pack of fighters. But they had the jump on them. The child stationed in the forward lookout pod was asleep on his arm, his finger still pointing crooked at the horde of enemy ships. Other children were dropping to the deck.

'They are weak,' said Descharge, 'and we have the weather gauge. What business do they have attacking? I will return to my command ship immediately.' A volley of enemy fire passed over their heads, and he watched as his command ship exploded in a lovely pustule of purple light. Soon a dozen or more of his ships were drenched in flames.

'The rum,' said Fabrigas quietly.

'Battle stations!' cried Lambestyo as another salvo from the attackers filled the eternal night with lovely blooms. The blast-wave sent the *Necronaut* into a spin. Her pilot strode easily to the wheel-house across the slanting deck as Fabrigas and Descharge wobbled after. 'Pick yourself up and look smart!' Lambestyo barked at two sailors who had fallen into each other's arms.

'So. Who are they?' asked the captain as he grabbed the wheel and righted his ship.

'The Vangardiks,' said Descharge. 'They were waiting in ambush. They knew we were coming here. They already had their battle colours displayed. They have raised the colours for "No negotiations".'

'Well, maybe we don't want to negotiate either. Battle stations!' cried the captain through his megaphone. People were running for cover as shots from the attacking force burst on every side.

'Do you have a plan?' said Descharge.

'Of course I don't have a plan,' said Lambestyo, as he swung the wheel round. The ship cried loud as it heeled onto a new tack.

TODAY YOU SLEEP

Commander Mattlocke stood on the bridge with his hands behind his back, a smug grin upon his face, as his shots smashed the enemy to pieces.

'The command ship is gone, the fleet is in chaos,' said his lieutenant, whose name was McMasters.

'Good,' replied Mattlocke. 'I warned Descharge not to cross me. Make sure every ship is destroyed.'

This had been a fine year for the commander. He'd just been away fighting the Achaenids, a tribe so brutal, so cruel, that their seat on the United Federation of Empires had shackles on the armrests. He had defeated them soundly. Now all he had to do before he could be given the position of Supreme Imperial Commander was to destroy a fleet that had been cleverly loaded up with highly explosive liquids – and destroy in particular one small ship. But this is not as easy as it sounds. Fighting a fleet is like hunting a herd of elephants: you only need to aim in its general direction and you're bound to hit something. An elephant, most likely. Chasing a single ship is like hunting one small rabbit. But even hunting a rabbit is easy if you have torpedoes.

'Do you see them?'

'Yes, Commander, they're 47 clicks to High Starboard, declination 19.'

'Prepare the torpedoes. Target their engine signature.'

'The *Necronaut* has turned off her magnetic engines and is under full sail.'

'Clever. Target manually then. Hit them in the cargo bay.'

'They're not exactly fleeing, sir.'

'Beg pardon?'

'No. They appear to be moving into attack position.'

'Scope down!' cried Mattlocke.

A steel tube slid from above and Mattlocke thrust his eye to the peephole. He saw only a haze of smoke and debris at first, then a dot, then a bigger dot, then the *Necronaut*, belching smoke, hurtling towards them at full speed, its golden sails spread wide around it like the ruff of an angry lizard. Commander Mattlocke stood back from his scope.

'What the devil's head are they playing at?' he whispered.

★

'What the devil are you playing at, boy?' cried Descharge. 'We must flee, flee for our lives!'

'We can't outrun their torpedoes,' said Lambestyo calmly. 'All we can hope for is to get close enough so that they can't use them. Also, our rum is stored in the aft cargo bay.'

Descharge took a moment to consider this, was secretly impressed. Below, in the aft cargo bay he could see the bosun lifting impossibly heavy boxes of rum and hurling them out into space.

'Head for their command ship,' said Descharge.

★

'Destroy them,' said Mattlocke. 'Sweep them from the sky.'

'They're too close, sir,' replied McMasters, 'we'll hit our own ships.'

'Fire anyway!' shouted Mattlocke. 'Their escape is not an option.'

★

Through the storm of smoke and debris ran the mighty *Necronaut*, the former pirate ship whose speed and agility was a surprise to everyone, except Fabrigas. He flinched slightly as Lambestyo, calm as a Sunday driver, sent his ship dipping and diving like a silver needle. Beside them a Vangardik cruiser took a king hit broadside and exploded in a silent ball of fire, the flames reaching out to gently caress the *Necronaut*'s flank. Fabrigas, gazing up wide-eyed, his face lit by the ferocious hell-blaze, admired the exquisite ballet of fire and destruction that was suddenly happening on every side. A mammoth chunk of iron swung above and left a tail of burning oil behind. He felt like laughing. A familiar voice from over his shoulder said, 'Master, keep your wits. Things are not what they seem. Watch closely.'

'I'm starting to feel sleepy,' said Lambestyo as he banked hard right and punched through a wall of smoke. The ruins of Akropolis appeared before them like a dream. 'If I fall you'll have to take the wheel.'

But Fabrigas did not hear him. 'I know these ships,' he said, the faint smile fading from his lips. He ran his eye along the ironwork as they skimmed the hull of a cruiser. 'These are not Vangardik ships!'

Descharge looked slowly up and blinked twice. He spoke in a low and dreamy drawl. 'What are you talking of, old man? . . . Then . . . what ships . . . they . . . ?'

Fabrigas looked again, just to check the position of the engines, the placement of the vents, the cannon array and the formation of the great black ships. The only alien thing about them was the Vangardik insignia crudely pasted on every vessel.

'These are *our* ships!' cried Fabrigas.

★

Mattlocke leaped back in fright as the tiny craft made to fly straight down the barrel of his scope, then broke off at the very last minute to streak away, leaving a rather handsome trail of smoke behind. 'They've broken our line. Now they're entering the ruins,' said McMasters. 'They're small enough to disappear in there.'

'Send in the wolf pack! Don't give up until you have destroyed them!' cried Mattlocke.

'And what if we can't recover them?' said McMasters.

'Then we are doomed!'

*

The *Necronaut* was just a blip between the monolithic palisades of Akropolis. Fabrigas let his big, ancient eyes scan the walls. They were many hundreds of miles high and covered in scenes of battles that no one alive in this universe could remember. No one could even remember the people who lived here. Experts thought they might have been half bull, but that was speculation. The *Necronaut* flew through a portal and found itself in a dark and narrow maze, the crumbling walls just a frightening few feet away on either side. Their half-shredded sails skimmed the stone. On deck were people peacefully slumbering, unaware of the bedlam unfolding around them. 'Doctor,' said Lambestyo, 'I'm falling.'

'I know,' said the old man as he took the wheel. 'You did your best, but we can't outrun these ships.'

Descharge was asleep. Fabrigas, taking in the primordial tunnels, wondered if he too had passed into dreams. 'Carrofax,' said Fabrigas, 'how far to the other side?'

'The gate is five minutes at this speed. Continue straight ahead. Beyond the gate is open space.'

'Old man.' Lambestyo eased back against the wall of the wheelhouse, his eyes fluttering. 'Why did you betray me?' Now they flew from the end of the tunnel like a shot from a cannon and found that they were once more in a wide arcade. Behind them the wolf pack was closing. 'I thought we were friends. I loaned you my second-best gun.'

'I didn't want to betray you, my boy,' said Fabrigas gently. 'I wanted to save you.'

'It wasn't up to you to save me,' said Lambestyo. The old man's soup had thickened his tongue. 'I'm not for you to save. I'm not . . .' he breathed again, 'I'm not for you or anyone to save.'

'I know,' said Fabrigas.

'We were supposed to take that girl somewhere. We promised.'

'I never promised that. I simply made you promise. There was a time when I would have craved this mission, and all the mayhem and danger these children bring. I was once a great explorer. But now all I want to do is rest. To rest for ever. You didn't think I could take you to the next universe, did you?'

'I . . . no, I suppose I didn't. I hoped you could.'

'I was wrong to trick you. I was wrong to lie to you. Sleep now. This will soon be over.'

Five black ships eased down behind to form a cross. Five black ships each shaped like a bird of prey. Suddenly the boy captain's eyes caught light again. 'Why do we not start your magic engine? Why do we not make the jump?! Yes, that is a plan! That's how we can escape!' He made to stand, then slumped on poisoned legs. They felt the horrible impact of a missile bursting just behind, its energy gently peeling open their stern, and Fabrigas strained to hold the wheel. 'My boy, my RIPS engine has never worked as far as I could tell. Plus, I disabled it to make sure,' said Fabrigas quietly. 'I disabled it so no one could use it.'

The boy's eyes fell back into the shadows. 'So, you tricked me again.'

'Not again. It was all part of the same grand trick.'

Now they passed through an arch and over an amphitheatre, ancient and tumbling. The seats were etched like the fine markings on a seashell, and at the sides of the stage were two statues, each miles high, two hooved figures holding starfish beacons which hadn't been lit for perhaps a hundred thousand years, but as they passed they could see an image of their ship projected in shadow on the ruins by the starlight behind them. 'Imagine the plays that went on here,' said the old man with a faint smile. 'How quickly the ages pass.' Another terrible crunch as a shot breached their hull. Ahead there was a gate. It was the entrance to this grand city, built near the dawn of civilisation, a circle of stone a thousand miles wide and still hanging intact. They flew towards it.

'I've always wanted to fly through the Akropolis Gate. It has been a dream of mine. We'll pass through there,' the old man said calmly, 'and soon it will be over.' His captain grunted in his sleep. Descharge was snoring a wheezy metallic snore. 'Yes. We'll pass through there. Then we'll rest. At last, we'll rest. I'm sorry.'

There was no one awake to hear him. The universe was silent. Another explosion penetrated the hull, and Fabrigas heard a loud pop as the ship, sensing its imminent destruction, ejected its flight box into space. Then the old man heard another sound: a faint whirring like a machine waking up from its sleep. He checked his instruments. Nothing should be waking from its sleep. That should be the opposite of what was happening. Then there was the sound of soft bells, the gentle slip of gears, ten bells followed by ten soft clicks, and then a smell of lemons, and a mellifluous humming as all around them the ruins of the ancient city began to fade like an old photograph.

This shouldn't be happening. This shouldn't be happening.

'What is this?' the old man whispered to the crippled ship.

Then, as the brave *Necronaut* passed through the magnificent gates of Akropolis, the vast stone ring vanished too, like a dream, and they seemed to pass into a fog.

For the first time since he could remember, something was happening for which the old man had no explanation.

*

The pilots of the attack ships behind them were surprised to see their rabbit vanish, their kill shots pass through its dimming shadow and into space.

'They are gone, sir,' said McMasters.

'Destroyed? Good. The wolf pack did its work. As I knew it would.'

'Not destroyed, sir . . . Gone.'

'Gone?'

'Vanished.'

'It is so.'

. . .

'. . . Sir? Your order?'

'My order?'

'Yes, sir. What is the next course of action?'

'The next course of action.'

'Yes.'

'Go to my quarters and find my diary. Send a message to every friend and family member in it and tell them to flee for their lives. Then bring me my cyanide tablets and my telegraphic forms.'

Oh, let the seas go floatin' by
(Let the water take me down!)
Look at how the days go by
(A-flowing merrily underground!)

Into the dreamy blue again
(Lord! And all me whisky's gone!)
Once a-pon a lonely life
(A-flowing underground – oi!)

'Once a-pon a Lifetime' – traditional shanty

A man called Provius walked through the slums of Carnassus, past the great oily sign, past the drowned men, until he came to the grand gated district. He was an old man whose movements were like those of a young boy. His eyes did not come to judge the forgotten sailors, the desperate crooks; even the rotting corpses and the excrement in heaps seemed to delight this man. He seemed to delight in everything he saw.

He went up into the gated district with its fancy abandoned mansions and mansionettes until he found the one he was looking for. He went up the front steps and found the door with the mark upon it. It stood ajar. He passed through the dark abandoned rooms, their rich furnishings thick with sweaty dust. He went up the stairs to the first level, stepping carefully through the intricate wire-traps left for the unwary. At the bottom of the stairs to the attic were heaps of oily rags, stacks of empty postal boxes.

He went up into the attic and found the householder hard at work at a desk made from an old door and wooden crates.

'Hello there,' he said.

'I told you I did not want to join your Academy,' replied the boy without looking up.

Provius smiled. 'You did. And yet you carelessly left the door open for me. Is this where you have been living all this time?'

'Yes, this is my library. It has everything I need. If I want anything else, I go out.'

Provius observed the room with its table, its single lamp, its rough bed, its piles of books, its boarded-up windows, its one lonely boy.

'It is a fine enough study. But we have even nicer studies at the Academy. Do you not ever want to leave this place, to see other places?' asked Provius gently.

'I do. As I explained, some day I will have saved enough money to hire a ship, then I will discover the moon where my father has fled with my nanny. For now, this room is my ship.'

'I see. It is a good ship. But don't you think a great mind should have things to help him become even greater? A proper library? A real desk? Other minds to talk about his discoveries with? Things that delight him, even?'

'In your books you say that a friar should have the most simple life possible. He should give all of himself to the pursuit of knowledge. I have everything I need to live here. This door does fine as a desk. And I need only one book. Here.'

There was a single book on the desk. It was astonishingly old, and it had a five-pointed star on the cover. Provius picked it up and examined it gravely. 'Where did you get this, boy?'

'I found it buried in our yard. Dark hands left it for me to find. There was a letter with it.'

Provius set the book of hexagrams aside. 'My dear, dear boy. I can tell that you are determined to dedicate your outstanding mind to one problem: how to end your suffering. It is a noble pursuit. Perhaps the ultimate one. But to think is not just to engage a subject with your brain: it is a devotional act, a concentration of the whole of your being in a determination to remain with something until it is understood. It is grounded in the heart as much as the brain, and so it is much closer to the concept of love than thought. A person who sees the universe and accepts everything they see will find the cloud of unknowing lifting; the person who shuts the light of the universe out – no matter how harsh that light has become – will experience only darkness.'

The boy at last looked up from his studies.

'If you come with me to the Academy at Mnemonys you will be fed, clothed and loved. And you will be allowed to concentrate your attention on whatever problems delight you: whether it is charting the way to a lost moon, or . . .' he touched a finger to the only book on the table, 'the more esoteric branches of science. We care for our minds. We do not put shackles on them. But if you go out into the universe and say the kinds of things found in books like this, you will be thrown in prison. Or worse. Or much worse. At Mnemonys we can protect you.'

Young Fabrigas considered his visitor's words. He seemed to gaze out of the attic window – which was robustly boarded over.

'Can I bring my servant with me?' said the boy.

'You have a servant?' said Provius, surprised.

'Yes. His name is Carrofax. He lives in that cupboard over there.'

*

The Academy near Mnemonys was the largest known. Oh, the wonders of this place. Its library alone was so vast that the sections had to be reached by horizontal elevators. Some called it 'The Brain of Humanity'. It took days to reach the reference stacks. Sleeper cars were used, each with a bed, a small desk and a servant. There were grand lecture halls where the monks would give talks on every imaginable subject: the properties of light around young lovers; the structure of the universe revealed in the shape of a drop of moisture on a feather from the wing of a duck.

On the way to the Academy young Fabrigas again changed his mind and tried to escape. Master Provius patiently retrieved him.

Once at the Academy the boy was as happy as he'd ever been. He had to shave his head and work devoutly to serve the friars. He had to clean the elder monks' robes, to make them meals. He became famous for his soup, and many a monk, working late into the night on a difficult problem, would call for a bowl of it, and upon supping it would find the gloom of frustration vanishing. Fabrigas got used to staggering, blurry-eyed, to the kitchen.

Before he knew it he was an assistant researcher, then a junior friar. He even found that he had set aside his main subject of research:

to find the moon where his father had fled with his nanny.

It was funny to think about it all. He would lie awake at night and ponder the unfathomable constellation of choices that had brought him to be in this universe. And so one day he announced, to universal astonishment, 'I am leaving to become an explorer!'

And he did.

Before he knew it he was floating through space, through the broken remains of a computer the size of a galaxy. Before he knew it, everything he knew had vanished.

BOOK TWO

If life sends you demons, make demonade.

SPIN

It is impossible to calculate the destructiveness of tiny changes within a system.

Imagine a city, a single city within a district within a postal code within a hemisphere within a cluster within an orient within an empire. It is a city made from iron, brass, silver or gold. It is small enough to hold a few million people, or large enough to enclose a sun. But whatever its greatness, this city you live in is as fragile as a crystal cup.

There is a particularly catastrophic phenomenon in the empires of this universe; it is known simply as 'spin'. The elemental spheres that house the human species are uncountable. Unlike the natural larger bodies – planets, moons and stars – most of these do not spin, and those that do are 'timed' to rotate at a *very* precise speed in order to generate just the amount of gravity needed to keep people in their beds at night. Most spheres rely on super-heavy objects at their centre. Some of the larger spheres harness the pull of the sun at their core, others use powerful magnets to generate attraction. In larger spheres this process becomes extremely complicated. Orbs of this size might contain a system of smaller cities in orbit around their inner suns, each generating gravity in a different way. An enormous amount of energy is expended controlling the movement of the spheres in relation to each other. But somehow a balance is achieved, and all the cities in the universe are tuned like an orchestra to play together, each one's force balanced out by the next. The problem arises when something happens to disturb this balance.

It could be a motor or a magnet breaking down, or a subtle change in the gravitational force of a core sun. Or it could be something even more insignificant: a super-heavy freighter docking after supplying the registrar with a weight manifest in which a decimal point is incorrectly placed one step to the left. Yes, even a dot of ink can bring destruction. It could be a meteor glancing off a sphere, imparting spin upon the body. When this happens the effect is quietly catastrophic. The affected body begins to stray out of position, to draw other bodies slowly towards it. The music of the spheres then becomes a dance which, if left unchecked, will end in unfathomable destruction, the death of trillions. The engineers within an affected local group have days, or even hours, to retune their spheres and avert disaster. There are thousands of near misses each astronomical year, and all but a few are corrected without the people sleeping in their beds becoming even faintly aware of how close they've come to death.

It isn't always a ballistic conclusion. Sometimes death comes softly. In one case an elite 'gated' sphere of some 785,000,000 souls was hit by a relatively small change in the radioactive field of a nearby sun. All the residents in the sphere were killed. The automated cleaning systems dutifully tidied up the corpses, from every home, every arcade, every dappled park bench, so that when the emergency teams arrived they found an immaculate paradise waiting to be resettled. Of course, the residual radiation meant the sphere could never be resettled. Crews prepared the sphere for demolition. The household systems, sensing their imminent destruction, turned on the crews and killed them. The city of Monoculus 9Q8 was left as a bustling ghost city: rich with the busy noises of the helpful domestic machines. One day I should write a short story about it. It would be called 'Sometimes Death Comes Softly'.

This is the threat of small changes.

*

The Man in the Shadows was not the richest man in the universe, but through a series of small changes and visionary touches he had become arguably the most powerful. He was aboard his magnificent gold-plated yacht, the *Titanrod*, when he received two high-priority messages. The first, he could tell, was the answer to his question from his new secret oracle. It was sealed inside a cylinder which could only be opened by someone whose pheromone signature betrayed an awareness of the magnitude of the contents. The other message was unmarked. He slipped both into his pocket until he had a chance to read them. He was returning from his hotel – Hotel Grand Skies: the Empyrean – with a guest. His was a modest hotel, in the scheme of things, certainly not in the league of the new mega-hotels like the Empire Majestic. The Majestic had been built with 1.8 million rooms, its own airport, and a full-scale recreation of an olde-worlde-style ocean around which wealthy guests could bask and tan themselves in the light of a small-scale, artificial sun. The Empyrean was a smaller, simpler hotel in the old style. It held only 125,000 guests, but those guests were generally the most important and wealthy citizens of the universe. He got almost as much joy from his hotel as he did from his grandfather's old yacht. They were both examples, he thought, of the one commodity that the universe had burned its way through before any other: style.

He was sailing home through a spectacular local group called Armalite IX. Taking frequent walks through his great-grandfather's *Theatre of the Gods*. This ship had been his ancestor's prized possession, and the Man in the Shadows had run through its ornate corridors as a boy – which was remarkably recently – past the gold statues of heroic figures holding torches aloft, or stooped in the act of trying to hold a world upon their shoulders, or simply touching their chin – as if caught in a moment of deep reflection upon the mysteries of the cosmos. These were heroes doing hero things: thinking ahead, lighting the way, groaning beneath the sphere of life. But today his appreciation of the giants was being spoiled by the presence of his guest, who, despite the fact that he was himself a kind of god, seemed unable to make his body do what he wanted.

'You must forgive me. I have not long been made of your stuff. It takes some getting used to.' The figure wobbled and jolted his way to the base of a statue where he leaned and puffed. He also seemed unable to properly control the volume and pitch of his speech, and he shouted at the Man in the Shadows in a high, thin voice: 'Where I am from everything is impermanent, without form. Things are less . . . certain.'

'I understand,' said the Man in the Shadows. 'When we are young we suffer similar deficiencies. We outgrow them in time. Now if you will please speak in a lower voice. I'd hate for anyone to overhear our business.'

'Of course, my boy.' The figure, dressed incongruously as a monk, lowered his voice to a hoarse shout. 'Though our master has described your activities, I am still slightly confused about what business you are in.' The monk stopped and placed his hand on the foot of a statue, patted it and wheezed, 'So large, so solid. I could never have imagined that things here would seem so . . . real.'

The statue he wheezed upon was a muscular figure holding a baby on one palm, and he looked for all the universe as if he was about to take a bite out of the chubby peach.

'Yes,' said the Man in the Shadows. 'Each of these statues weighs ninety tons. They are made from iron plated with gold. To build them from solid gold would have made them far too heavy for the ship . . . I am in the power business.'

'The *power* business. You sell units of electrical energy to people in exchange for paper money?'

'Not electricity. I sell real power: I sell influence, persuasion, authority.' He offered his hand to his guest but the brand-new man ignored it.

'Ah, you sell the invisible. That I understand.'

'I make power visible. I can quantify it, store it, sell it as a real commodity. Before breakfast I brokered a meeting between one of the richest young industrialists in the Empire, and one of the most beautiful young socialites. He is eighteen. She is twelve. But together, one day, they will work for us. They will be unstoppable. I know this because I have the oracle. I can chart the course of probability and know which seeds will fruit.'

'And don't forget who showed you how to build that oracle.'

'We never would. My group is honoured to serve Calligulus.'

'Your group? Ah yes, the Thorn Table. You mighty captains of industry and influence.' There was a note of sarcasm in his voice.

'I am just a small player in the group. But I have the pleasure of speaking for them, and of being their eyes and ears. With your master's help we can become even greater.'

'That very much depends upon you.' The monk stopped to rest again on the base of a statue of a muscular god holding a globe on the tip of his finger. The monk gazed up from below, breathing heavily. 'What of the recent problems our master has asked you to solve: the Vengeance, the royal traitors, the mystical Fabrigas? What says your new oracle about that?'

'That they are manageable. I have dispatched Albert to oblivion, I have sent a horde of assassins after the girl, and there is a battle fleet waiting to crush the magical mystic at Akropolis. Our master's wishes will be fulfilled.'

'I certainly hope so. Because a battle fought across dimensions cannot be won. It becomes a cascade of cosmic chaos, of agencies killing double agents before they were born, of armies massing at the sites of future battles. The war must be fought in this universe alone. That is why Master Calligulus has issued you these death orders. One old fool, and a small girl – his enemy's daughter. So simple. Which is why we are surprised that you have not yet been able to conclude the matter. What is this liquid oozing from me?'

'It is sweat. It is designed to cool the body during exertion.'

'How very elegant. I do not think I will ever get used to this form.

My master wishes only that your Empire conquers all others. It is his defining goal: that it grows in power as he does. He cannot yet involve himself directly from the outer worlds. This is why he has bestowed the gift of flesh on me – as painful and profoundly unpleasant as it is – and why he has lavished unfathomable gifts upon you: the gift of alchemy; the gift of dark-space travel; the new oracle.'

'I know all this.'

'It is worth restating all that he has done for you by bestowing upon your Empire the Thousand Gifts. Only the Xo can match your power. But not for long. The secrets he has shown you have allowed you to build an irrepressible empire. When the Great War comes you will crush your enemies.'

'Right now we would settle for enough power to grind our coffee in the morning.'

'You lack faith?'

'No. But without energy we cannot raise our armies, we cannot expand, we cannot run the engines which keep our spheres aligned.'

'Energy cannot be conjured from nowhere. That is one law of physics he cannot help you circumvent. What he will do for you in the future, though, will make these shortages seem irrelevant. Calligulus offers nothing less than the conquest of reality. And what does he ask in return?'

'That we stick to the Master Plan.'

'Which is?'

'That we kill the girl.'

'. . . And?'

'That we destroy the wizard, destroy his engine.'

'Exactly. Are you aware of the magnitude of the cruelty our master is capable of applying to servants who fail him?'

'I do not believe myself a servant.'

'You do not?'

'No. I believe myself an accomplice.'

'An accomplice!'

'Please, do not shout. There are servants of mine close enough to hear.'

'You are an accomplice to him as the raindrop is an accomplice to the storm. But I will be sure to pass on your views when next I channel him.'

The monk moved off to stand in the shimmering shadow of a golden giant holding a lightning storm of glowing neon vapour tubes in his clenched fist and exclaimed, 'Marvellous. Is there anything you people cannot do?'

'I would prefer you did not pass on my views.'

'You would? But surely, frank views shared between . . . accomplices . . . are the foundation of any grand partnership.'

'Again, I would prefer, on reflection, that you did not convey these matters.'

'Then beg me.'

'I beg your pardon?'

'Beg me that I do not pass on to the master what you have said.'

'I do not understand.'

'Yes you do. You are one of the most powerful men in this universe. You have no doubt seen begging in your time. At least enough to be familiar with the concept.'

'I have never begged a thing.'

'But now you must.'

'. . . I *beg*, Lord Bosch, that you do not relate this part of the conversation to our master.'

'Good. Good. I think we have an understanding. Is there anything else I should know about while we are alone? Any other pressing matters? I hear word of a burnout in one of the Sentinel hubs.'

'It is . . . fully contained.'

'It is?'

'Yes. We have complete information integrity.'

'I hope so. For your sake. And now I will retire to my quarters. I have been on these legs but a few hours, but all I want to do is lie down. How strange. Perhaps, when my body is not jelly, I will finally try this . . . What is the term you use? Intercourse? For now, I bid you well.'

'I will have the boy turn down your bed.'

'Thank you. I am grateful for your hospitality.' A glance up to the imperious eyes above. 'You have a beautiful vessel. You should be very proud.'

Once Lord Bosch had made his way slowly from the room on spasmous legs the Man in the Shadows finally had a moment to take the new messages from his pocket and read them. The message in the canister from the oracle read:

Wizard has Vengeance, has Router, has the wind behind him.

The second message, in its plain envelope, was equally succinct:

I have failed. The wizard lives and goes beyond. No safe corner now. Goodbye. Mattlocke.

I am Calligulus,
Creator of empires,
Destroyer of worlds,
From the cave of forgotten souls, to the furnace of the suns,
my name is spoken.
Who can know my power and my mercy?
Who can know the fury of my vengeance?
None but the insolent, the feeble, the damned.
I am death from above,
And vengeance from below,
And from behind you when you least expect it.
I feast upon the flesh of kings, and the flesh of captains,
And the flesh of mighty men, and the flesh of horsies,
And of them that sit upon the horsies,
And the flesh of all men, both free and bound, both small and great.
Mostly small.
Fear me, and give glory to me! For the hour of His judgement is come.
And worship me that made the universe, and the soils, and the seas,
and the fountains of waters, and the creatures, and the horsies,
And the men who ride upon them.
I am Calligulus.
Word.

THREE SISTERS

Midnight in the palace of the Queen.

'Things have spun out of control, sisters. Our master has asked simple things from us.' The Man in the Shadows had docked the *Titanrod* near the Royal Palace, and while his guest from the Empyrean was sleeping he had summoned the three sisters. 'Kill an old man; kill a small girl. One senile fool and a tiny girl alone in a terrible universe.'

'Oh, but we will crush her,' a sister spoke, in a voice like sewing needles running over tin. 'We'll find that mouse.'

'We'll crush her tiny body.'

'We'll hang her by the tail.'

'We'll put her mousy head upon a spike.'

'Then eat it like a pickle.'

'Sister, how very gross.'

'I do apologise.'

'The wizard's fleet is destroyed, sir. We signed the order to give you ships. You loaded the wizard's boats with exploding booze.'

'Already people are talking about the Vangardik attack, sir. Our younger sister will be embarrassed into abdicating. Plan UWX is one step closer. The people want blood.'

'So simple.'

'So elegant.'

'Not simple or elegant, sisters. Mattlocke failed. The wizard escaped.

His ship was not destroyed with the others. The *Necronaut*'s flight box was ejected and recovered. It tells us he crossed over.'

'Foul news.'

'Indeed. And if he survived he will surely have observed that these were not Vangardik ships, that they were our own ships in disguise.'

'Sweet merciful wounds.'

'It gets worse, sisters,' said the Man.

'Worse?!'

'Yes, sisters, and please don't shout. I would not like to raise Lord Bosch. The wizard is not alone. My sources say that the Vengeance did indeed reach the ship and now travels by his side. They are like a happy family.'

'Sweet mercies!'

'The Ministry of Secrets' Occult Activities Division reports that he painted dark symbols on his ship to attract her. He clearly plans to use her as part of his plot to foil our Master Plan.'

'Outrageous! Dark plans are our domain!'

'It gets worse, sisters.'

'Worse!'

'How could it get worse?'

'This is the greatest amount of bad news that could possibly be presented to a group of people on one occasion.'

'Not so. I mentioned how a file with sensitive information regarding our pact with Calligulus has leaked.'

'Nooooooooooo! Do not say it.'

'It's all in the file, sisters: our plot for universal domination; the secrets Calligulus has shared with us.'

'Stop hurting us!'

'Our intelligence tells us that the file has materialised aboard the *Necronaut*.'

'Dear Lord!'

'The Lord can't help you, sisters. Not if Calligulus finds out about this file. One of his messengers is sleeping just a few rooms away.'

'Let us murder him!'

'Sisters, let's not lose our heads. As you know I sent a group of bounty hunters to tidy up – six of the best.'

'This is good.'

'Bounty hunters are good.'

'Tell us they are brutal.'

'They are clean and brutal. But we need more insurance, sisters. We must fire our big guns at this problem.'

'What do you mean? Send the Black Watch?'

'Bigger.'

'. . . The Armagedix Homing Virus?'

'Bigger.'

'Surely we don't need to involve the Postal Service in this.'

'Even bigger than them, sisters.'

'No!'

'This young duke is right,' said sister two. 'Only the Pope can help us now.'

'Precisely, sisters,' said the Man in the Shadows. 'If we can convince the Pope to embark upon a crusade he can kill these traitors, burn the ship, dispose of our spy, destroy the file, there'll be no evidence, no recriminations, even Calligulus won't know. We will be quieter than a mouse. Then he will finally give us the tools we need to proceed to end-game. We can smash the Wall, defeat the Vangardiks, crush the Concordat. Even the Xo will not oppose us.'

'It is too much, sir!'

'It is like sending the Hammer of the Gods to kill an ant.'

'A god-hammer is what's needed here, Sisters of Mercy. Calligulus has declared that his enemy's daughter must never reach maturity. I have seen what our Dark Lord can do to those who disappoint him. The Pope is the only way. The Fleet of the Nine Churches will crush the Vengeance.'

'But the Pope does not believe in other universes.'

'Then we will convince him. More importantly, we'll have to

convince the Queen to turn the fires of heaven on her beloved wizard.'

'Sir, you leave that to us.'

MISFORTUNE'S QUEEN

They called her 'Misfortune's Queen'. Misfortune for the age she was born into: a time of war, famine, shortages and more war. Misfortune to be born into a profoundly ruthless family whose jealousy and cruelty seemed limitless, whose passion for betrayal and violence was bountiful and brutal. Parents who would brutalise their children for sport; siblings who would throw one another on the fires of hell if it meant being a foot closer to heaven. Oh, Misfortune's Queen, to be born into such a family, at such an age in history, and with neither brains nor looks to help you.

But Misfortune's Queen was built of stuff from which few are made. She did what she could with her looks – and by that I mean she declared herself a perpetual virgin: 'The Impenetrable Princess'. The only man who was ever allowed access to her private quarters was her underwit, Barrio, whom she had rescued from the Slaughter of the Fools when she was five, who had the intellect of a toddler, and who had hardly left her side since.

And in place of a brain she fostered a simple kind of political ruthlessness, the kind employed by young women in school corridors: with cold cunning hidden behind a veil of feigned innocence she was able to play the runt and turn her siblings on each other. She took everything fate threw at her: the shortages, the Great Depression, the threat of UWX. She was Misfortune's Queen, but she still had her throne. And she had one last friend: Barrio. And she had her 'sisters'. She kept her triplet cousins close, knowing that they could never steal her throne. She gently tamed their mercilessness. She let them know her plans, and let them sign executive orders on her behalf. She let them call her 'sister', though to hear them say it, in their voices like a warm snake running over ice, terrified her.

'Sister.'

'Sister.'

'Sister.'

Echoes in the chamber of the Queen. Whispering voices, a clacking clock, an envelope of light unfolds across a marble floor. Three figures penetrate the sanctum, the phantoms float through the gloom; three pale faces lean in close.

'Sister.'

Words a violet *hissssssss*.

'Sister. We came when you called.'

'We always do.'

'We're here for you, sister.'

'We're always here in the night.'

'Don't fear, sister.'

Words a phlegmy rattle. Towards her bed they come, three sisters with black nails on fingers pale and bony, they comb their way through tangled orange loops of hair saying, 'Sister.'

'Sister.'

'Siiiiiiiiister.'

Finding the base of the skull they scratch gently at the brittle skin. They run those delicate bewitching fingers to her cheek and tap lightly with the tip of a nail upon her eyelid.

'Sister, don't dream of that foul wizard tonight.'

'No, don't dream of him.'

'Dream of us instead.'

Their voices are like a thousand beetles dying in a marble bath. The Queen's head lolls upon the royal pillow; she cries out in her sleep, the warble of a forgotten lamb.

'There, there.'

'Things always seem bleak before the daylight.'

'People are talking. Saying black things.'

'They say you had the Devil Girl and lost her.'

'They say you sent the wizard to his death.'

'But he is not dead.'

'Oh no. We know he is alive. He stole the Vengeance.'

'Naaaaaoooooohhhhhhhh!' The Queen rolls and sinks oily teeth into her pillow. The clock's dread bell springs the hour, its chimes shimmer off the marble.

'There, there.'

'Our spy tells all.'

'We know he betrayed you.'

'Traitor.'

'Traitor.'

'But still they blame you.'

'They say you let our enemies burn our precious lovely ships.'

'They say you aren't the Queen you used to be.'

'They say, they say, they say.'

The Queen moans, heaves, her pale brow gleams in the half-light, the silvery hands caress her feverish brow.

'There, there.'

'We're here for you.'

'We won't abandon you.'

'We'll fight to the end for you.'

'We'll hide you when they come for you.'

'We'll hide you and we'll say, "We know not where!"'

'We won't let them do to you the things they did to poor old Beatrix.'

'Come now.'

'All is fine.'

'All is fixed and fair and fine.'

With their voice like scalding gusts of steam.

With their voices like dry sticks burning in a kettle.

With their voices like a silk shroud dragging over bushes.

'Our fleet will crush the Vangardiks and take their lands.'

'Our Pope will put to death the heathen girl and all her traitor friends.'

'Your people will say you're a good, good Queen.'

'Not a sickly wet and weary fish-hag.'

'Not a weak and feeble Queen.'

'. . . My little Blackberry. Why did she leave me?'

'There, there.'

'It is not the time for tears and regret.'

'Now is not the time for weakness.'

'Now is the time for blood and action.'

'Now is the time to punish traitors.'

'No mercy.'

'No mercy.'

'We'll always protect you.'

'Yessss.'

'Yessss.'

'Even if the mob come howling in the night.'

'And they will.'

'Yessss.'

'They will.'

'Sleep well, sister. Dream not of that foul wizard tonight. Dream only of our faces.'

Echoes in the chamber of the Queen. The misty shadows vanish from the room, pulling tight the door behind them, extinguishing all light.

FIRE DOWN BELOW

Captain Lambestyo was dreaming that giant black birds were circling as he lay in the sea on a raft made from paper. He felt the coolness of the water soaking through the paper below, the heat from the sun above. He felt the great birds landing on his chest, scratching at his skull with their talons. He woke to see a shadow sweep silently over; the shadow resolved itself into the shape of an old man. He stormed by, hauling one of the ship's heavy fire hoses with surprising strength, plunging the nozzle down into a hissing hole in the deck of the *Necronaut*. The flames lit the great man from below so that he looked as though he was battling the very fires of hell. Several others were awake – the larger men upon whom the poison had had less effect. Lambestyo would later learn that the mighty bosun hadn't slept at all. He appeared now, hauling two hoses, one in each arm, and cursing the heavens he claimed had made him.

Fabrigas, sensing somehow that his captain was stirring, turned at that moment, enclosed in a swirling pall of smoke and vapour, and roared: 'What are you waiting for, boy, your cocoa?'

*

Artillery bursts had ruptured the hull of the *Necronaut* in two places, leaving the ship's skeleton bare and steel beams protruding like stumps of shattered bone. Clouds of smoke were fleeing, like a herd of fat, cheerful sheep, from gashes in the outer hull, and the sails, shredded, had been hauled in and tossed upon the decks like a golden salad. The sailors were showing no bravery. Some were glancing at the life-pods while whispering under their hands. Some were curled up, sobbing. And what good were life-pods anyway when all around them was a sea of emptiness, a grand white void? To where could his cowardly men flee? Into the Hex? Into the terrible abyss between universes?

The slaveys, meanwhile, did the best they could, slipping and sliding in the frothy slicks of hydraulic fluid that swept across the deck. They smothered flames, stopped air leaks, attended to their injured friends. They were, thought Fabrigas, a tiny crew to be proud of. Little H. Sneevlit. Little K. Remanaskus. Little P. Vershigara. Even if they were all about to die.

His captain climbed the ladder to the flight deck, his too-big boots ka-thunking on the rungs. 'So. This is probably the end?'

'Yes. Almost certainly. As predicted.'

'I knew I would not get paid.' Captain Lambestyo flicked at a fleck of burning ash that was hungrily gnawing a hole in the sleeve of his fine coat.

'No,' said the old man. 'I dare say you won't.' His beard was smoking in several spots. 'Is he still staring at me?'

Lambestyo turned to where Descharge was standing on the deck below. Their commander was leaning on a rail, oblivious to the chaos, glaring up at the old man with eyes like ladles full of molten steel.

'Yes. I think he hates you even more than me now.'

They both stood staring out beyond the terminal carnage to the peaceful emptiness of the Hex.

'The hallucinations will start soon,' said Fabrigas, and Lambestyo shrugged.

'They can't be any worse than the reality.'

Fabrigas flexed his tired back, then trudged off below decks to check on his passengers.

★

In the intestinal maze of tubes below decks the noise and heat was fierce. Smoke and gas roamed freely. Several poor sailors had been pulled out into space through breaches in the hull. Two slaveys came past coiled up in a fire hose. Little K. Persuivus came by bear-hugging an extinguisher much larger than herself. Fritzacopple, ordinarily a plant specialist, crouched in a corridor to tend to a nasty burn on a sailor's shoulder. 'It hurts, it hurts!' yelled the sailor.

'Of course it will hurt if you keep moving,' said the botanist, who had a streak of purple ash across her brow, and whose hair had been diskempt in a way that suggested some ravishing alien beast.

'Have you seen where we is?!' said the sailor.

'Yes, I have,' replied Fritzacopple languidly. 'That is to say, I've seen where we *are*, and we are nowhere. So why worry?'

'We have been sucked into a void!' cried the sailor. 'It could be heaven; it could be hell! Who can tell?!'

The old man appeared in the doorway and said, 'How many dead?'

'Four sailors were taken through a breach. None more, mercifully,' replied the botanist, 'though we have some nasty burns. I sealed the critical sections.'

'I see.'

'I can't stand the pains!' cried the sailor.

'Quiet now,' said the botanist. 'You don't see the children crying out.'

'They don't have the pain what I have!'

'So you did not sleep?'

'I had a herbal solution which kept me awake,' the botanist replied.

Fabrigas frowned, but he did not have time right then to argue with her nonsense.

'And where is the surgeon?' said Fabrigas.

Huxbear, Shatterhands and the Gentrifaction were in the galley, whispering, and when they saw a shadow at the door they stopped and sat straight. 'You are eating?' said Fabrigas.

Shatterhands nudged his chop with a fork. 'Sir, this could well be our last meal.'

'Our last! Our laaaaaaaast!' wailed Gossipibom.

'You should be tending to the hurt; you are the surgeon.' But the assembled only peered down their noses at the old-beard. Then a sailor appeared to tell them that there was a goat on deck.

'A goat?'

'Yes, a goat.'

'Are you sure?'

'It is so.'

He found most of the crew cowering behind the vent-house; a handful of slaveys peered out from behind their legs. Only Lambestyo stood in the open. 'It's a goat,' he said, and flung out his arms. Then Fabrigas ventured his head and saw that, yes, there was a goat on the deck of his ship, a white goat with a fine grey beard, and it was chewing on a bootlace. The crew had begun to wail and moan. 'Get hold!' yelled the captain. 'You aren't children!' The children, incidentally, seemed calm. They were sooty, their eyes white, but the fires they had been fighting, miraculously, were almost out.

'This is a completely normal phenomenon when you travel between universes,' said Fabrigas. 'Sometimes you see your own mother, sometimes a goat. These visions tell you something about your future.'

'What do we do?' asked the bosun. 'About the goat?'

'We will wait him out,' replied the captain.

Time passed. Eventually the bosun said, 'Goat is gone. There's a man on deck now.'

'A man?'

'Yes, a man.'

'Do we know him?'

'No. He says he wants to talk to the blind girl.'

DEVIL WOMAN

It was calm on deck. The flames were extinguished, the leaks sealed. The Hex had become a mellow twilight filtered through the yellow veil of smoke.

And through the smoke Lenore rose up. She came out of her hatch where the one bulb burned, up through the slaveys' quarters filled with smoke. On deck they heard the screams as she appeared in the corridors lined with injured sailors. She rose up from below through the hatch. The bosun held her tenderly by her shoulders. Roberto followed warily.

'*What is it that is?*'

. . . said the green-skinned girl. Her words, as quiet as the whisper of a mouse, seemed as loud as the winds which blow from the mouth of hell, and the men fell back rigid with terror, for this girl was streaked in ash and dirt like some fearful creature freshly risen from the grave. The men cried, "Tis the Devil Girl!' and then they cried, 'The Devil Girl is on our ship? No wonder we are doomed!' and Lenore gazed upon them with a pair of imperious jewels and said . . .

'*How do?*'

. . . The men howled and hunched like a pack of terrified dogs.

'Everybody shut up now!' said the captain then.

'What for all do you need from me?' asked the girl.

'There is a man over there,' Lambestyo said. He gestured roughly with his thumb. 'He says he wants to talk to you. He said his name is Blue Lantern.'

'I do not know any man. Only bats and mice.'

On the foredeck, near the bow, sat a man in a fine two-button evening suit with a blue pocket square. On the table, beside the tea set, was a small gramophone. The man sat quietly drinking his tea.

'Go and see what he wants,' said the captain to the girl.

'What if I don't wish to speak? What say you to that?'

'He said it's important.'

They all watched, amazed, as the Vengeance huffed and stalked off around the wheel-deck, dragging a small hand along the wall as she went. They saw the girl walk smartly towards the man, who placed his teacup carefully on the saucer and smiled. He bent down to whisper in her ear. He whispered to her for a long time, her head bobbed faintly, and all the while the gramophone played a haunting tune.

Bridegroom, dear to my heart,
Goodly is your beauty, honeysweet.

The crew gaped, not a person breathed. Then the girl nodded, curtsied, and tottered back to the group.

'Well, what did he say?'

'He is a friend. He said this is how it is, men: we are set for danger, and then for an even bigger one. Danger all around. Danger coming from our ears. The Pope is coming. You know him? Big hats. Also there is another man. He wears nice suits. He speaks in dreams. He can hunt us down and make us do things we don't like. This nice man over there says if we see the other man we should flee like mice. Find our holes and duck.'

Lion, dear to my heart,
Goodly is your beauty, honeysweet.

'He also says we'll be eaten . . . some of us two times.' She glanced at Fabrigas. 'We'll meet the worm. We'll be eaten by darkness. But we'll come out with a magnificent treasure if we protect me and listen to my nose. I am, I am the talisman.'

The captain said, 'Treasure?'

'Also, he says not to drink the water.'

Then the music faded away and was replaced by a ferocious silence.

When they looked out on deck Blue Lantern had vanished.

*

Then: birds! Boundless bright and chirruping balls of feathers flitting about the deck and playing in their hair and beards. 'Get off, damned budgies!' The old man flung his arms around.

And bees, too: countless buzzing bees.

Lenore appeared on deck again. She was lost within a cloud of birds, but a pale arm extended from the cloud, and perched serenely on her finger was a single golden sparrow. 'We're coming upon a moon!' came the girl's muffled chirrup. Soon the ship was full of birds. No one could move.

An hour later, at 28.63 Ship's Time, or thereabouts, or not thereabouts at all, the birds vanished. The forward lookout reported an imperfection on the perfect white of the Hex: a grey smudge which soon resolved itself into a moon.

'Moon ho!' the scope-man called back.

Soon the Hex dissolved completely and they could see below them a jungle moon, approaching at a frightening speed.

'That will do,' said the captain.

GOD HAMMER

'His Supreme Grace is . . . less than happy.'

The Pope had come from the Forbidden City for the Panathenaea, or specifically: for the bloody spectacle of the slaughter of 7,000,000 heathens in a giant arena of death. When he'd learned that there were to be only 6,999,999 heathens slaughtered, he was angry; when he'd learned that the Queen planned to send this last heathen on a great expedition to the next universe, his rage knew no limits. A team of cardinals now spoke on behalf of the Pope, who was sulking in the next room.

'You are no doubt aware of the official position of the Church regarding other universes.' Cardinal Mothersbaugh, the Pope's closest adviser, spoke softly. 'It is that they do not exist.'

'Do not exist!' a shrill voice came from the next room.

The senior cardinal politely touched his nose. 'And so deciding that you were going to send an expedition there was somewhat . . . heretical.'

'I am aware of your position on other universes.' The Queen sat beside her three sisters. In another corner, the Man in the Shadows surveyed the conversation with insolent grace.

'We were sad to hear about the destruction of your fleet,' continued the cardinal, 'but we are here to let you know that the Fleet of the Nine Churches will blockade any further attempt to reach the next universe. Any ship attempting to achieve an escape velocity upon the winds at the Akropolis nebula will be destroyed. We see the destruction of your last expedition as holy justice.'

'I understand,' said the Queen.

'Except . . . of course . . .' sister three spoke up in a voice like greasy bones crushed in a fist, 'that the expedition was not . . . entirely destroyed.'

'It was not?'

'No. One ship survived and appears to have made it to the next universe.'

'It did?'

'Yes, it was the ship carrying the wizard, the one His Grace denounced as a heathen.'

'Really?'

'Yes. And what's more, he has stolen for himself the Devil Girl. The one whose execution the Pope has called for. Vociferously.'

There was an audible silence from the next room.

'We suspect the wizard plans to elope with the Devil Girl and marry her in some dark and despicable ritual. Then, when she has reached maturity, she will bear him an antilord who will conquer our universe and keep us all in fiery bondage.'

'This is your intelligence?'

'From the highest source.'

'This is most concerning.'

'It is, Cardinal,' said the Queen. 'You can see the need for us to act with haste and maximum agression.'

'Certainly, Highness, but Devil Girl or not, it still does not change our basic position: that we are fundamentally opposed to the idea of other universes, and of making any attempts to travel there.'

'So why have you come? What does His Most Supreme Holiness want?'

'His Holiness only wants what he has been requesting for decades: another Holy Crusade. One bigger and bloodier than ever before. Every great pope must have his crusade. It is tradition.'

'Crusade!' came the shrill voice from the other room.

'Oh, we couldn't agree more,' said the Man in the Shadows, speaking up at last. The cardinal angled his body towards him.

'You couldn't?'

'Oh no, we need a crusade, most certainly.'

'And you are?'

'I am an adviser from the corporate sphere. When the expedition to the next universe was in financial difficulty I arranged a sponsor for them. And now that they have run into more difficulties I have again offered my expert assistance.'

'So you believe there should be a crusade.'

'I do.'

'Then we are in agreement?' The cardinal looked astonished.

'Of course. And what better holy quest than a crusade against the Devil Girl, and the wizard, and the heathen lands they come from? She has made a fool of the Queen, and you. What greater crusade than to follow her to her own dimension and wreak heaven among her kind?'

'. . . But, as I explained, His Holiness does not believe in other universes.'

'All the better. He will not be corrupted by what he sees there,' said sister two, in a voice like a small bag full of surgical instruments.

'. . . But there is no "there" *there*.'

'Precisely.'

'. . . Sisters . . . Your Royal Highness . . . we are very . . . *confused!*'

'It is simple, Cardinal,' said the Man in the Shadows. 'We are giving you licence to undertake a crusade to the next universe. And you will not need to declare your crusade to the people, since the conquered lands, as you have said, do not exist. And you get to keep all the treasure you find there, since that too is imaginary. And since everything you will see there is just an illusion created by devils and demons to tempt you, you may act entirely without conscience. Additionally, Her Majesty would like to formally reinstate your right to extract your own taxes from the people. Is that not correct?'

The Queen nodded.

The cardinal was leaning forward in his chair, his bottom lip was wet with saliva. 'But, sisters, sir, we haven't been allowed to do that for ten thousand years.'

'Precisely. It is our gift to you. All we ask is that when you see a vision of this Devil Girl, you capture it and throw it into the nearest black hole. And eradicate all witnesses.'

'And the wizard?'

'He too.'

'Crusade!' came the voice from the next room. The Pope was no longer sulking.

'My sisters here will sign the Executive Order for you authorising your crusade. I'm afraid I am rather too busy.'

'Oh, we will?' said sister one. 'What an honour.'

'You flatter us, sister,' said sister two. The Queen nodded.

'But how would we procure the wizard's magical engine?' said the cardinal. 'He has vanished into the beyond.'

'You leave that to me,' said the Man in the Shadows.

PRISONER 92357890

For many years the following had been happening:

An old, old prisoner had risen every morning in his tiny cell. The cell was dark and had no windows. The man was feeble and had no hope. He had once been strong and leanly muscular, with terrifying black eyes. Now those eyes were always terrified. Decades in this cell had made the muscles melt from his bones, made his frame stooped and bent. His eyes and features were all but lost inside his beard. His cell was hardly big enough to hold him, let alone function as a make-shift workshop. There was a bunk, a bowl for pissing in, and a work-bench cluttered with scraps and tools. No one could have imagined from looking at him, and his workbench, that this man was struggling to perfect a device that would change the destiny of the entire universe.

Each day after dawn a man would enter: he was bald with a deli-cately tattooed scalp, and he was dressed all in black, like a monk from the depths of hell. He always came accompanied by a giant henchman who, for lack of space in the room, would remain in the doorway, blocking the bright light from the corridor with his frame. The giant was stripped to the waist, and around his neck he wore a kind of tool belt held secure by a spiky collar. The tools themselves were the tools of his trade, the tools of a torturer. His name was Daniel, and as you well know, anyone called Daniel is evil. The first man's name was LEON. (All caps. Pretentious? Well, you tell him.) Each morning LEON would say the same thing. He would say, 'Good morning, Master Fabrigas. Have you finished our engine yet?' It had been the same every day since he had attempted to leave his universe, failed and been secretly imprisoned by his own Empire. Each day was a fruitless struggle: like the mythical beast Esphodius, forced to push a great boulder to the top of a hill, only to forget later where he'd parked it. This prisoner's day would begin with a polite enquiry, move on to begging, and end in pain.

'Please, sir,' said the old man. 'I told you I cannot rebuild my engine without the things I asked for. I need a proper laboratory. I need a dark-ooze spectrometer. I need a quantum mortar and auto-pestle.'

'Oh dear,' LEON would say. 'That all sounds very complicated. Tsk, tsk. What are we to do? Daniel, do you perhaps have any tools the master could use?' And Daniel would grin, his fat fingers would search his belt for just the right tool, and the master would cry, 'Monsters! Monsters without mercy!'

That was essentially how it went. Until today.

'Good morning, Master Fabrigas. Have you finished our mighty engine yet?'

'I told you, I need the fissile plugs I asked for. And a new pencil!' The old man held up the tiny stub to the light.

'I see,' said LEON. 'That is interesting. Very, very interesting.'

'Please, I beg you –'

'Oh, there's no need to beg, is there, Daniel? Not today. Today is your lucky day. Wash and put on these.' He tossed a bundle of fresh clothes onto the bunk.

And so the old-beard suddenly found himself in a transit car, crossing the gap between Her Majesty's prison and her palace. He had not seen this view in centuries, and my stars how it had changed. 'Am I going to see the Queen?' he asked.

LEON laughed. 'Oh you should be so lucky, old man. Today you've got a meeting with an important businessman.'

★

The Man in the Shadows did not have eight chambers to make an impression on a guest. He sat alone in a modest drawing room on the far side of the palace.

'Master Fabrigas, at last we meet. Won't you have a seat?'

'Thanks to your torturers I can no longer sit. I can stand, or I lie.'

'Oh, let's not call them torturers. I like to think of them as persuaders. I have been reading your file with interest. Tell me what you remember about your capture.'

'I remember everything. Not a single detail escapes me. I left to travel to the next universe. My engine failed and I returned to my Empire. Along the way I was intercepted by a Vangardik unit. They took me prisoner and tried to force me to tell them the secret to my engine. I did not. I was rescued by agents of this Empire, though they could not recover my saucer craft, or its engine. I was taken to a high-security prison. They said I would be released in a few days. This was not the case. Every morning for decades since, I have been visited by your thugs who have tried to "persuade" me to build a workable RIPS. And now here we are.'

'That is a truly distasteful story. But you must understand, it wasn't my doing. These things happened well before I was born. Your imprisonment was necessary at the time: to protect the interests of this Empire. But now, as you know, certain things have happened which have changed the game.'

'What are you talking about?'

'Of course, how foolish of me. You would not have been able to subscribe to the *Gazette*.' The Man in the Shadows pointed to a stack of newspapers. 'I put aside some copies for you.'

'I do not have time to read the papers.'

'Oh, I think you'll want to read these headlines.'

The old man stooped stiffly to pick up the first paper from the pile.

WIZARD EMBARKS ON INSANE SAUCER MISSION.

And then . . .

WIZARD RETURNS, CLAIMS 'THIS IS NOT MY BEAUTIFUL UNIVERSE.'
And then . . .
TRIAL FOR COSMIC HERETIC.

A DANGEROUS MAN.

OUT FOR JUSTICE.

UNDER SIEGE.
And then . . .
WIZARD SENTENCED TO DEATH.

DREAM OF A QUEEN: THE WIZARD OUR SAVIOUR?

WIZARD SETS OUT ON QUEST FOR ASTRONOMICAL GLORY.

ATTACK AT AKROPOLIS: WIZARD'S FLEET BURNS.

NO SIGN OF WIZARD'S REMAINS. FLIGHT BOX RECOVERED.

PEOPLE ANGRY. IS THIS THE TIME FOR UWX?

Each banner made the old man's eyes widen a little more. 'What is all this?'

'It's you. After your failure, an exact duplicate of you arrived in an exact duplicate of your saucer craft. We had his DNA tested. It's definitely you. Except that your twin's engine appears to have worked. He too claimed to have come from the next universe. He too claimed it was a near-duplicate universe. They couldn't just lock him away like they could with you. Too many people were watching.'

'And what has happened to this other me? And the people he travels with?'

'Old man,' laughed the Man in the Shadows, 'I have absolutely no idea. But we need you to help us find out. All you need to do is perfect your engine. We need it to be powerful enough to transfer a very large fleet. You'll be given notes and drawings we stole from your double. You'll have everything you need: equipment, comfortable accommodation, access to a skilled physician who'll restore your health, as much money as you –'

'Dark ooze. I need dark ooze.'

'Of course, all you need. We have great resources at our disposal.'

'And what do I get if I help you find him?'

'Anything you want.'

'I just want to rest in peace.'

The Man in the Shadows smiled. 'I'm sure that can be arranged.'

'What's this?' you say. 'Another confounding story-thread in the saga of the race to the next universe?' Not quite. This conversation was pieced together from one scrap of evidence: a transcript of a secret recording given to me by an interested party shortly before she mysteriously vanished. No other record of this conversation, to my knowledge, exists. Given events to come, it is reasonable to assume that this Phantom Fabrigas was successful in his efforts to build an RIPS engine for his captors. But you can rest easy about having to follow the travails of yet another actor. This sorry player's part was cut short. He was never seen by anyone again.

THE NIGHT GARDEN

The moon was hidden behind its dark half, presenting just a sliver of tarnished copper at its edge. There was a world beyond, quite some distance away. This new universe was trembling and dreadful. The moon ripened. Their steering systems were smashed, they had no choice but to fall into her arms, and they did: at around ten miles a second. Their supersonic chute deployed, thankfully. The moon took them tenderly, and winced perhaps as their landing jets fired, and though they hit the surface hard enough to knock down their electrics, they didn't break apart. They heard the crunch and hiss of dense foliage. Then, silence, punctuated only by faint whispers. They were alone in their nightmare, listing to one side, but safe.

Soon the bosun and a group of fit slaveys appeared and hung lanterns about the deck. Bruised and bloody faces appeared in the light of the ship's neon-mercury vapour lamps. In the calm some became frightened. Little J. Diaz, bunk 14, said, 'I don't want to do this any more, Bosun, I'm scared!' and the bosun said, 'No time to be scared, peach, your friends need your help. Now shhhh, the worst is over. You see? We're safe in the jungle now.' And it was true, they could see where they were: in a night jungle the leaves and vines were pressed against the reinforced glass of the ship's dome, vines thicker than the bosun's arms. They could see gargantuan flowers, some several yards across. There was a yellowy vine studded with long-lashed eyes. The eyes pressed against the windows. Spiky leaves forced scarlet juice into thin gouges along the outside of the glass, and the great flower yawning like a screaming mouth above them could have taken six slaveys into its red throat. There were few among the crew who had ever seen a jungle. There were few who'd even seen a plant. 'What is this mess?!' a voice cried from the dimness. But it was peaceful out and audio heard nothing close: no animal life, no jungle drums, just a faint shuffling of leaves. 'No animal life? How strange,' said Fabrigas.

How strange.

He found his captain on deck. 'So, here we are after all,' said the old man as he gazed up at the canopy which hid the rest of this new universe.

'Where are we? You tell me where we are and I'll agree.'

'Well, we appear to be on some kind of . . . Yes.'

'You said your magic engine didn't work. You said you disabled it.'

'Yes, I had disabled it so no one could use it. And I kept it under tight security,' whispered the old-beard.

It was true. Fabrigas had stayed up late at night, wondering how he would stop his shipmates from finding and meddling with his device, or, worse, stealing it to sell to the Vangardiks, or the Xo, or any of the other armadas. He'd toyed with all kinds of elaborate locks and counter-measures. In the end, he put his machine in the privy beside his quarters and changed the little sign to 'OCCUPIED'.

'Then someone must have fixed it,' said the botanist as she limped to join them. She had very good ears, apparently.

'There were only two people who understood my enhanced engine. I shot one of them into space, and the other is me. No one on this ship except me has the skills to operate it. Unless they were a . . .'

The old man looked over to Roberto who was fussing over Lenore. 'Roberto,' she said, 'I am fine un-hurt. Why won't you annoy some other?' Then Roberto saw the old-beard looking and fled.

'So it is a mystery,' said the captain.

'Yes,' said Fabrigas, with a faint smile. 'It certainly is.'

When Lenore stomped past, the old man said, 'Little girl, I wonder, did you enjoy the soup I sent down?'

'Oh, Roberto and I did not enjoin with your soup,' she said. 'It smelled funny to me so we ate one apples per piece. And no bats.'

She paused, sniffed the air, then wandered off. Fabrigas watched her leave. Then he turned to find a menacing figure emerging from the shadows. 'So. You were hiding Her Majesty's treasure, the Vengeance. You meant to smuggle her out of the universe.'

'Not so. She stowed away. She was eating our bats.'

'And why did you not hand her over to me?'

'Well . . . that is to say . . .'

'Do you have any idea of the crime you have committed? You are a traitor of the worst kind, old man, and when we are out of danger I will tie the noose for you myself.'

And then he stalked off.

But by now the other sailors had begun to circle, wearily, rubbing their bruised heads. 'How many killed?' said Fabrigas, and the bosun said, 'None more, praise heaven, though our bodies have many broken parts.'

'It is her fault!' said a sailor, a man named Quiggs. 'It is the Devil Girl's fault we're in a crooked state.'

'Well, now then,' said the Devil herself.

'We're doomed, we're doomed,' murmured someone from the back.

'Very probably,' said Fabrigas. 'But we were always doomed. Nothing has changed except that the nature of our doom has become more mysterious. The best we can do is form a small party, and to see if there is anything in our vicinity that may be of use. My instruments have detected the gravity from the world this moon orbits. This moon flies unnaturally close to its mother. If we can repair our ship we can make the crossing and perhaps find civilised tribes to bargain with. Until then we should be thankful that we are safe within this botanical fortress.'

That's when Miss Fritzacopple spoke up in her languidly silky voice: 'We will definitely not be opening the doors to this ship,' she said. 'Not if any of us want to survive. If anyone leaves this ship they will be dead in seconds.' A spasm of panic jagged through the assembled. The Gentrifaction, huddled towards the back, were making low moaning sounds like a ghostly barbershop trio.

'We're doomed!' howled someone else.

'Please stop saying that,' said Fabrigas. 'Miss Fritzacopple, would you explain?'

'I am not at all familiar with these *particular* plants,' said the botanist, whose dark hair shone like brass in the hazy glow of the ship's lamps, 'but I am extremely familiar with similar plants in our natural kingdom.' She held up a lamp to the ship's glass shell. 'I know, for example, that the teeth on this plant are designed to tear flesh from bone.' The assembled inclined their heads. They knew which specimen she meant, for its flower was like a set of full, sensuous lips guarded over by rows of scalpels. 'This plant is a man-eater, probably a woman-eater, too. This one over here has only two small fangs, but they are designed, by whatever cruel god made it, to drain a body of blood in just a few seconds.' And then she made a rapid sucking sound from between her sensuous lips: '*Schwipp.*'

'A vampire plant!'

Panic was raiding the deck of the *Necronaut*.

'This vine here –' now the botanist raised her voice above the growing noises of hysteria – 'has nodules designed to spit a liquid – most likely poison, or an acid. Oh, and this here looks to be some kind of constrictor vine, you can see by the –'

'Oh, for the love of God, please stop!' cried the voice from the back.

'They're all asleep now anyway,' said the botanist. 'But by the morning, they'll want us.'

'Sleeping shrubs! What madness is this?!'

'But in conclusion,' concluded Miss Fritzacopple, 'whatever devils we have aboard –' and here she made a delicate gesture towards Lenore – 'they are nothing compared to the devils we face out there.'

'Yes, so let's all just stay calm,' said Fabrigas. 'There's no good getting lathered before our bath is run. We must remember our place in the natural order. These plants may have teeth, but we have brains. We can fashion weapons, make fire!'

'Why are we listening to this old fooooool?' said a voice that everyone immediately picked as the scalpel-sharp drawl of the surgeon. 'He got us into this mess. It's because of him we're in this shape.' A breeze of agreement rose and fell as Descharge swung his steely eyes towards them.

'That's enough!' he barked. 'There's nothing to be gained from mob methods.'

'But how,' continued Shatterhands, 'are we expected to follow a man who betrayed us, who poisoned us, who was about to throw us into space? As commander of this . . . "fleeeeeet" . . . it is your duty to punish mutineers, is it not?' A louder, angrier murmur passed through, and the men began to push forward, to form a tighter group around Fabrigas, the captain, Descharge, Lenore, Miss Fritzacopple. 'Stand down, dogs!' cried the bosun, and Lenore could be heard to say, 'Things are getting foolish, what?' The mop-headed Roberto stood to one side, leaning with one arm on a rail and calmly studying the back of his hand. The trim on his jumpsuit shone faintly in the half-light. He had a heavy cargo hook beside him.

'And this girl! This Devil Girl! She surely by her very nature has doomed us to hell!' As the mob turned their attention to Lenore, Roberto yawned, straightened and languidly moped across to put himself between Lenore and the mob. He held the cargo hook loosely in his left hand.

'And what are you going to do, little boy?' said Hardcastle, the sailor at the head of the group. Poke me with your pole?' He held a lamp above the boy's shaggy head. Roberto calmly touched the hook to the sailor's lamp and it exploded in a ball of fire. Hardcastle went reeling madly back into a pile of fire hoses where he lay gently smoking.

'Well, let's seize the old man first,' said someone. 'The girl can wait!'

'Oh, this is unseemly,' cried Pantagruel. 'Can't we execute them in a civilised manner?' But the mob came forward to seize the traitor, and just as they did, Fabrigas himself, to the surprise of everyone, fell to his knees. 'It's true! It's all true! This is all my fault!' He began to sob. 'I took us all aboard this ship of doom, I took us all into this hell, I deserve to be tossed to the weeds! Don't blame the girl! Don't blame the fates! Oh toss me to the furious jaws of nature!'

'Hear, hear!' said the surgeon as he clapped his bony hands together, but he suddenly noticed that the rage that had been building in the crew had died. They were now looking at the old man with great pity. And Fabrigas, whose face shone with tears, had turned his eyes imploringly towards the deathly weeds above.

'Throw me to the ferocious shrubs,' he whispered, hands clasped before him, 'I implore you! Hurl me in among the poison roses. Let my frail body nourish the soil! Bring swift mercy to this traitorous old fool!'

'Now look what you've done, you beasts!' said Miss Fritzacopple, and the chins of the assembled dropped. There was a noticeable change of mood upon the deck. Anger dissolved to shame. 'Honestly, threatening a helpless old man.'

Then Descharge said, 'Anyone who lays a hand on this man will answer to me.'

'And me,' said the bosun.

'Quite so. I am commanding officer and as such I swear that I will make it my duty to bring this traitor to justice. But for now we need every resource at our disposal. His brain could be the only way we'll make it out alive.'

'And you've made him cry like a small girl,' added the captain.

'Oh, that is nice,' said Lenore.

'Now let's get some rest and in the morning we'll decide what's to be done.'

Miss Fritzacopple had Lenore help her take the distraught old man to his cabin. They made him tea and put him up on his bed, though he was inconsolable. 'It is more than I can bear to have brought such hell upon you all!'

'OK, shut up now. Let's rest tonight, then in the morning a solution will present itself.'

The next day when Lenore awoke she searched the ship with her perfect nose, but he was nowhere.

Dear Friends,

By the time you read this I will have been horribly killed by a gang of murderous trees.

It is because of my actions, and only my actions, that you too now find yourselves on the brink of becoming plant food. I only pray that the end for you is quick, for there is no way out of this predicament, except, perhaps, to do what I have done: to walk boldly from the ship, with your human head held high, and to hope for the best – or at least to hope for the least of the worst.

I leave now to face the only fitting end for a coward such as me: to be eaten by something less than animal. Know that I am truly sorry for what I have put you through. My only aim was to depart the Empire quietly, and to live out my days in peace. For, as I explained, I no longer have the heart, the stomach or the mind to be an explorer.

The one thing I will say in my favour is that, through my gross misdeeds, I may, though inadvertently, have led you to a swifter death than you might otherwise have suffered.

All the best!

M.F.F.

ON DEADLY GROUND

When the crew of the *Necronaut* woke they immediately threw themselves into the mouth of panic. Their ship seemed suddenly very small, and the jaws of the plants – yawning wide and terrible with the rising of the sun – unfathomably huge. And when they discovered the old-beard missing, and found his suicide note, their panic trebled.

'We're doomed! Without the wizard we are doomed!'

'Be calm!' said the captain, though he couldn't help but let his eyes drift up to the glass cells which held the full weight of the jungle upon them, and where all ferocious hell was loose. Even Descharge, who had locked eyes with many fierce enemies, looked slightly alarmed as he drank his tea. At night, asleep, the deadly plants had looked somewhat tranquil. Now, with the dawn, the crew watched, aghast, as teeth snapped and green gums slathered against their ship, and there was a ceaseless screech and squawk of fangs dragging along the glass, leaving deep, silvery gouges. Vines whipped and shot jets of acid which scoured away the ship's paint, and the sound of the hungry multitude was almost deafening. The *Necronaut* rocked gently under the fury.

'Geeeeahhhhhhhhrrrggg!' a sailor suggested.

'It looks like the babies want their breakfast,' said the botanist as she arrived on deck, still pulling her long lovely hair into a knot.

'We're safe so long as we're in here,' said the captain. 'The ship is sealed tight. Plus, we still have the GGPTBCE,' and he threw a look at the machine's custodian, Bortis, who sighed.

★

For just such missions was the GGPTBCE designed. Its eight-inch titanium-impregnated steel skin guarded an advanced weapons system and a pilot cocoon inside triple redundancy life-support systems. Nevertheless, Bortis was less than keen to take it out to recover a depressed senior citizen, and only when Descharge personally intervened did he agree to undertake the recovery mission. First he made Lambestyo agree that he would personally fix all the dents and scratches in the outer shell on its return.

'But I want to take it out,' said Lambestyo.

'The only way you will ever drive him is over my dead body,' said Bortis coldly.

Bortis climbed in and gave a sullen wave before he pulled the hatch closed. They all watched as the cargo bay opened and the mighty war machine stamped out into the jungle. It shone like a silver god in the dawn light; its footsteps made the leaves tremble lightly. There were a few still moments as the iron man stood in the clearing made by the crash-landing; the jungle seemed to lean away from this new beast. Then the fronds of hell rose gently, and all aboard the *Necronaut* watched as they plucked the robot from the earth and tore off all four limbs as if it were made from gingered bread. The steel beast fired all its weapons at once. Machine-fire splattered through the foliage and pinged off the hull of The *Necronaut*. Rockets ripped through the canopy and exploded in the sky above in a multicoloured ecstasy, all as the plants tore the chest plate off and hungrily devoured the hapless Bortis in his pod.

'It's probably good I did not go out,' said Lambestyo.

★

'Well, at least we know what we're in for.' The brains trust had moved to one side of the deck.

'I am out of ideas,' said the captain as he watched the plants pick through the remains of the GGPTBCE. 'Without the old man we don't stand a chance.'

'And he's certainly been eaten by now,' said Fritzacopple, who still held his letter.

'We must be sure,' said Descharge. 'He is vital to us alive, but if not, I want to see his corpse for myself.'

'We could go by night. I could help us to avoid most of the worst traps,' said the botanist. 'The main problem is that we wouldn't even know where to look. Finding his body would be like searching for a needle in a deadly hay field.'

'I know where your noodle is,' said a small voice.

*

By night, when the plants had again drifted off, a small party crept from the *Necronaut*, and into the jaws of a leafy hell. They were dressed in hazard suits topped with domes of acid-proof glass, and each held a lamp. Descharge went first. Miss Fritzacopple pointed to things as she went, her husky voice crackled in their earpieces: 'That there is a classic flypaper trap, it uses mucus-secreting glands. Over there is a trapdoor plant. I wouldn't like to think what's in there. We must be very gentle. If one of these things wakes, we're food.'

'He went in that direction,' said Lenore as she stood beside a mighty orchid. Her small nose tested the air.

'We'll have to skirt that copse of thorns,' said the botanist. 'Each one is tipped with poison. This really is marvellous.'

'I don't think it is marvellous,' said the bosun. Being the biggest he was having the hardest time moving forward. Roberto looked perfectly at home, twisting and writhing through the vines like a tousle-headed monkey. The job of convincing him to stay on the ship had proved too difficult – two sailors had been mildly electrocuted – so in the end they'd let him come.

'That over there is a bladder trap,' said the botanist. 'There's a vacuum tube inside. If you touch even one of those hairs the trap-door will open and you'll be sucked in. *Schwipp.*'

'He'd better be alive,' said the bosun, 'or I'll kill him.'

'Shhhhh,' said Descharge. 'What is that sound?'

They all lay quietly for a second and realised that they could hear a low rumble, like the purr of a large cat, or a motor drill being gently smothered by a pillow.

'Do plants snore?' said the bosun.

'I don't think so,' said Miss Fritzacopple. 'Plants don't have lungs. Aside from the lung tree.'

They struggled on, avoiding, as they went, a grove of paralysing ivy, and soon found themselves lying under a great orange bulb, from which the sounds of snoring were coming.

'He's inside the guts of that one,' said the girl. 'I can smell some biscuits on his breath.'

'Fabrigas!' Descharge barked. 'You foolish old man, it's time to wake and be reborn!' and with his blade he slit the bulb from top to bottom. A torrent of purplish goo, bones and old man fell upon them, and there was a sound, something like a scream. For a second the whole jungle stirred and shook. The party winced.

But luckily for them the plants did not wake.

Fabrigas lay blinking between them. 'You came,' said the old man.

'Of course we did,' said the bosun. 'You took all the biscuits.'

*

Fabrigas had left in darkness, and when he saw the jungle lightening and felt the first stirrings from the plants he had suddenly begun to reassess his decision to sacrifice himself. A huge set of jaws had begun to yawn, sleepily, before him. Staying still was pointless; running, futile; so in the end he'd done the only thing possible: he'd crawled in through the creature's mouth, and because it was still dozy he'd been able to slither past the worst of its teeth and into its belly without a chomping. In there he'd found the bones of sailors eaten by the plant. He'd found some more biscuits in the belt of one of the sailors after he'd eaten the last of his own. Then, within the belly of the plant, within the cacophony of ravenous vegetables, he'd slept.

IN THE HOUSE

They spent a few minutes cleaning the goo and bones from Fabrigas. 'We should move fast,' said the bosun. 'I can smell the dawn.'

'We might not even make it back,' said Fabrigas. 'You were fools to come for me.'

'You were a fool for leaving us. I only came so I could hang you.'

'Fools could have hiding in the house,' said Lenore. But everyone ignored her.

'Hang me? I brought you to the next universe, as promised, if not by will then by fate.'

'You harboured a fugitive of the Queen.'

'Or there's an house for arguing!' said the fugitive of the Queen.

'I swear I'll hang you by your . . . wait, what? A house?'

'What do you mean, a house?' said Fritzacopple.

'It is a small house. You might say a cottage. It's there upon the distance.'

'My girl,' said Fabrigas as he scooped the moss from his glass dome helmet, 'you never fail to amaze.'

'I never, ever do,' she agreed.

★

It is not uncommon to come upon, in the middle of a dark and gruesome children's tale, a cottage, and therein find a witch, or a wolf or domestic troll. And yet here it was – in real life: a humble, homely cottage, such as a nice country family might occupy, but rooted in the depths of this green hell. It had been placed with care inside a dome, like a model in a museum, and the glass was caked in moss and filth, much like the hats our friends wore. The dome had a hatch with a latch which was easy for humans to master, but impossible for plants. Inside the dome, Fabrigas peeled up a corner of the lawn and found an iron slab beneath.

Inside the cottage they found what Miss Fritzacopple instantly recognised to be a botanist's lair. The shelves were stacked with plant catalogues and thousands of sample jars. It was a simple home with a table, a stove and a single bed, and on that bed was a skeleton. The skeleton held his journal in his hands and grinned with delight.

'Well, this is nice,' said Descharge. Outside the sky was turning grey.

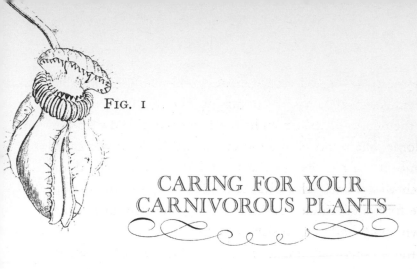

Fig. 1

CARING FOR YOUR CARNIVOROUS PLANTS

Your plants are your friends, your family, your mistresses and your masters. Give them all the care and caution you can muster. (But mostly caution.)

Your garden is not the plants, it is the space between the plants. Your plants are like stars and planets: they should be alone, to be appreciated individually, and yet when viewed from afar they should join to create galaxies of colour. Your plants should have the space to speak, to sing, to wander! (Sometimes literally.)

The gardener must learn to paint with life: the orange of the viro-carrots, the purple of the tongue of the Venusian man-trap, the blue of the septic flesh-lichen, the ochre of the floating spores of the haemorrhagic moss.

Enjoy your garden. Love it. Nurture it for all your life.

The Deadly Gardener, Herbert M. Connofeast; translated by R. I. P. Q. Volcannon III

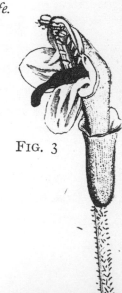

Fig. 3

Fig. 2

DAYLIGHT

Roberto sat on the other side of the room, as far from the corpse as possible.

'He was olden,' said Lenore. 'He liked raw meats, and to smoke the pipe. There was the lady too, shortly, but she has not been here for many a time.'

'Neither has he,' said the bosun. The bare skull rested on a pillow yellowed by the years. 'He liked the whiskies,' said Lenore. 'There's many bottles up in the cupboard there.'

'Well, praise heavens!' said the bosun as he flung open the cupboard. He returned to the table with an amber bottle and glasses. Outside they heard the shrubs stirring.

'We are safe in here from getting plant-acid in our eyes,' said Fabrigas as he took off his glass dome, and as the heat from their bodies quickly caused a fog in the forgotten room they all sat around the table and drank a breakfast toast to a certain death that, so far, they'd managed to avoid. Before long they were merrily oblivious to the snapping and spitting all around them. Even Descharge relaxed a little and stopped telling Fabrigas he was going to hang him.

'They really have taken over the entire moon,' said Miss Fritzacopple. She had moved away from the table to stand in the larger of the windows. She stood gazing out over the jungle. The cottage was at the top of a steep rise and for the first time they had a view across the endless expanse of ravenous green. The plants were throwing themselves against the glass dome, desperate to get at the tiny treats behind the windows. And this went on all day, the noise and movement and the ceaseless song of fangs on glass. The day seemed to last forever; soon they all felt the first whispers of madness.

'I need to get out of here,' said the bosun. 'I'm getting *the fear*!'

'It will be night soon, and then we can go back to our ship,' said Descharge.

★

'And just when *is* the night arriving?' said Miss Fritzacopple lazily. She had an arm slung back over the chair and one leather boot resting on the table. It was a good point she made, too. It had now been at least forty naval hours since night had last fallen.

'I expect it will be along presently,' said the old-beard. 'My calculations prove it!' Though it was clear he'd taken no measurements recently, except regarding how much whisky was in his glass. 'We must make a toast!' he said. 'From now on, we must stick together. No more fighting,' and he threw a glance at Descharge. 'From now on we are one family!' and everyone raised their glasses, even Descharge, reluctantly. 'I will agree to a temporary truce while we find a way out of this mess.'

'Hear, hear!' cried the bosun, who had drunk a bottle to himself.

Hours later, night was still absent and the atmosphere was becoming tense again.

'So, does anyone have any grand plans?'

'Why don't we ask the old man?' said Descharge. 'His plans always work. Why don't you make us some soup!'

'My soup plan might have worked if we hadn't been attacked by our own ships.'

'Why would our own ships attack us? It was clearly an enemy fleet, and when I get you back to our universe and into a stockade I can prove it to you.'

'Are we even *in* another universe?' said the botanist. 'You said in your letter your engine didn't even work.'

'It didn't. It was never supposed to. I just wanted to prove a point. The most likely conclusion is that I never did come from another universe.'

'But you tried to convince the whole universe you did.'

'I decided to take on the difficult task of convincing the universe before attempting the relatively easy task of convincing myself.'

No one quite knew what to say about that.

'So assuming we have somehow crossed over,' said the bosun, 'how do we cross back?'

'I really do not know,' admitted Fabrigas. 'Akropolis provided ideal conditions for a jump. We would have to find somewhere at least as good.'

'You could always ask your imaginary friend.' The botanist was slurring slightly.

'Imaginary friend?'

'Yes, the one I hear you ranting at on the observation deck. "Carrofax! Stop meddling in my experiments!" And so forth.'

'He is not imaginary, just invisible.'

'You have an invisible friend?' said the bosun.

'A friend who happens to be invisible to you, yes. What of it?'

'Oh, nothing,' said the botanist. 'It's just strange to see a grown man with an imaginary friend.'

'As I said, he is invisible, not imaginary. There is a difference.'

'Is there?'

'Well, you tell me,' the old man said and gestured to a talisman around the botanist's slender neck. 'You should not be the one to talk about invisible chums.'

'And where is your friend now? Is he sitting on your lap?'

'Carrofax is not here. He is no doubt seeking information about the nature of the universe we're in.'

'I see.'

'Do you?'

'Yes.'

'And he is what, a ghost?'

'He is . . . a phenomenal being.'

'A demon?'

'I would not say that word around him.'

'I thought you didn't believe in magic.'

'I believe only what I can test, and I have tested him thoroughly.'

'And how did you two lovebirds meet?'

'That is a long story.'

'It seems as if we have all the time we need.'

CARROFAX

Among the many books which came to his mansion in those long, lonely years was a particularly interesting volume on geometry: *A Book of Symbols: Progressive Geometry and the Structure of the Universe*, by a man called Vangetz. Young Fabrigas absorbed the book like no other, reading it dozens of times, recreating a number of Vangetz's experiments involving the transformative symbols contained within. He revived dead plants with these dark symbols, he transmuted matter, he trapped mice within invisible cages painted in shapes upon the floor. He painted a large symbol on the outer wall of his compound which allowed him to magnify the sound of approaching people, no matter how quietly they stalked. He sent messages out into the heavens to a race of people Vangetz referred to as the 'Immortals'. He begged them for deliverance. He put aside all his other studies to concentrate on this one book. In short, he ignored Vangetz's preface which stated: 'This work is for your interest, not your practice. No amateur will be able to recreate these experiments, and indeed should not.' If he was wrong about 'will be able to', he was dreadfully right about 'should not'. It did not take the boy long to go too far.

Young Fabrigas decided to revive his mother, whom he had buried in the yard at the back of the mansion. The experiment was a great success – at least in a literal sense. She did indeed rise from the grave, still in her decomposed state, and she pursued her son out of the compound, and down the street, and through the deserted avenues of Carnassus's Fancy District. The corpse followed her tearful son through the dark wet alleys, calling to him in a gravesick voice through bloody lips: 'My son! My son!' He fled into a sewer and she followed. He heard her voice always just behind him. The chase went on for hours until he could finally steel himself to return her to death, and to the pit in the yard.

He dug down another three feet to ensure she would not rise again, and his shovel hit a solid object. He was digging down not through natural soil, but through an impasto of oily filth laid down over centuries. He pulled out the strongbox. Inside the box was a book and a note:

Dear younger Fabrigas,

You do not know us, though we know the older you. You are a good boy, but the man in the book you possess is a fool. He is meddling in forces he does not understand. It is sad that you had to go through such a terrifying experience to discover that. But it will get better. If you follow the instructions in the book we've given you very carefully, and keep to the simple life and good intentions of a monk, you will do powerful and wonderful things. This book holds the ancient hexagrams given to us by the Immortals – the oldest species in the universe. Their science is a wonderful thing. Do not listen to anyone who tells you this is magic. These are natural laws. Magic dies in its shadow.

We are afraid to inform you that your early experiments in this field have attracted the attention of powerful monsters. You are now in great danger. This plague is just the beginning. We are in a battle to control these dark forces. It is a battle on a scale you could not even begin to comprehend. We will protect you, and in return we will ask you to play a small part in our struggle. One day soon you will solve a problem given to you by a drunk and will be invited to join a prestigious academy. So long as you stay there you will be well protected. Be sure to read our book before then.

You might feel very alone and frightened, but you will not be alone for much longer. If you are brave and clever you will soon have a friend and servant. (See Chapter 48: Hexagrams of Entanglement.)

Kind regards,

Dark Hand

PS If you bury your mother unprotected she will rise again in 3.5 days to torment you. Draw hexagram 84984 upon her forehead and bury her well.

A few nights later Fabrigas heard noises in his room. Someone had entered without triggering any of his traps or alarms. Was it Mother? Had she risen again? Perhaps he had painted the symbol on her forehead wrong. Every night the noises arrived around the same time and sent him ducking under. This was not an easily frightened child. He was used to the ugly rhythms of the Sphere. He was used to the thrum of the shipyards and the hoots and cries from the slums nearby. But it is a fact that you can be as brave a boy as you like outdoors, but noises in your own room are impossible to bear.

After weeks of this he gave himself a talking to. 'Now, look. You're not some baby who hides beneath his covers with a lamp. You are a man. A man of science.' That night he sprinkled iron dust on his floor and caught the print of a man's shoe. A man? Well, that was still to be determined. But something was there. Something.

The buried book he had been given contained a great deal on the subject of invisible beings. It was possible, it said, to trap an invisible by drawing diagrams on the floor and placing a shiny object in the centre. He carefully drew the diagrams on the floor. He found one of his mother's large soup spoons and polished it brighter than the moon. Then he put the spoon on the attic floor and went to bed. In the night he saw bright flashes through his blankets, smelled an electrical burning smell and was forced to admit that, though he was a man of science, he could not bear to look.

In the morning there was a man in his room – a man with pointy ears and two horns on his head. 'Is not the absence of presence frightening?' said the man.

The boy said nothing.

'So well done you,' said the man. 'In all my time I never dreamed a human would trap me, let alone such a tiny one.' The boy had said nothing. 'I assume you are now too frightened to speak, so I will tell you what will happen. As you have managed to snare me I am now your servant for the course of your natural life. Which for me, fortunately, is a blink. Only you can see or hear me. I can't kill you, if that's what you're wondering. I can offer you advice but I cannot physically interfere with your world. Do not call me "demon". I hope all this is clear. We are going to have many, many great adventures together, I can assure you. Now, if you would be so kind as to tell me what this fascinating object is.' And the creature held the spoon up to the sunlight which poured in through a slit in the roof.

DARKNESS COMES

'Well,' said Carrofax now as he surveyed the starving and drunken group, 'you have managed to get yourself into quite a mess.'

'Yes, yes, so you're back, do you want a parade?' and everyone jumped.

'So your boyfriend has returned,' said the bosun, but Fabrigas ignored him, instead addressing an empty corner. 'Why is it not getting dark? We need to get back to our ship.'

'This is the bright side of the moon of a planet ringed by three suns. It only gets dark here when all three suns are aligned behind the planet, and that won't happen again for another six naval months.'

Fabrigas let the information sink in. Then he slumped down in a chair and rubbed his nose. 'It won't be dark for six months,' he told his friends. 'Why can we not catch a break on this mission? Is every universe against us!'

'You are wondering why luck is against us?' said Descharge, and he threw a small glance towards the girl.

'If I could perhaps suggest, sir –'

'No! We will find a way. There must be an escape. We could tunnel back to the ship.'

'Through the steel plate?' said Descharge.

'There's no way out,' said the bosun, who was now lying on the bed next to the skeleton. 'We'll have to eat each other until there's only one left, and knowing my luck that will be me.'

'I could perhaps suggest –' said Carrofax, but the old man cut him off: 'No!' He hated it when his servant tried to offer advice.

'So you don't want me to tell you how to get out of this?'

'No. We humans will solve this. Maybe some kind of hotter-than-air balloon. Or a big fire!'

'Well, I will not interfere, though you should at least ask the girl to tell you about the trapdoor.'

*

'Oh yes, I know all about the door,' Lenore admitted. 'But I did not want to go down there. Smells all of blood and death down there.' She bit her lip. 'Dark and dangerous. If we go down we'll come up dead!' This made everyone draw breath sharply. Everyone except Roberto, who was already sitting on the edge, dangling his legs into the hole in the floor and giving them a look that said, 'Well? What are we waiting for?' The hatch had an electric latch, but the boy had disabled it with a touch of his fingers.

'Let's not waste time,' said Descharge. No one moved.

'Silence is the key,' said Carrofax, 'and that's all I'll say. My lips are sealed.'

Fabrigas leaned down to Roberto, seized the boy by both shoulders, then raised a long finger to his own lips. The boy nodded.

UNDERGROUND

Down a red steel ladder and into a short corridor leading to a heavy blast door which stood ajar. Beyond was another corridor that led to a smaller blast door and this one was locked. Roberto strode to the door, placed his fingers against the small keypad beside it, and in seconds they heard the clunk of the locks opening. Luckily, its hinges had been well oiled and it opened without much noise. A cloud of odour rolled out of the room beyond, a storm so noxious that they all put their sleeves to their faces. Lenore passed out. When they managed to rouse her she said, 'We extremely very much should not go in.'

Beyond the blast door was a small, comfortable lounge, like a doctor's waiting room. It had wood-panelled walls, padded chairs, a standing lamp and a dead (non-lethal) potted shrub. It had a portrait on the wall: a king or emperor dressed in blue and green. Then there was an even smaller blast door which they all had to squeeze through. And beyond that door was . . . well . . . was something that was all but beyond belief.

They found a narrow gallery: a long, concrete bunker with a pair of steel benches. Just off this room, behind a curtain, was a tiny, darkened booth. The booth contained a small altar. On top of the altar was an idol; beneath the idol was carved 'Calligulus IV', and beneath that was a brass legend reading 'In His Name'. There were a dozen jars spaced along the benches in the gallery, each twice the size of a person, and each sealed with bolted iron caps. Inside each was a shape which appeared at first to be a skeleton with flesh still hanging on its bones, but on closer inspection was something even more terrifying. Fabrigas caught Roberto's eye and pointed to the row of lights on the wall. The boy nodded, placed his hand flat on the lighting panel, and the room was suddenly bathed in a greenish light. Then Fabrigas walked carefully along each row, peering in at the shadowy shapes. Then he walked along the second row and did the same. Then he turned to a blank spot near the door and said, 'Carrofax, I think you'd better explain this after all.'

OUR MAD UNIVERSE

A universe is a mad, bad place, full of deadly traps and toothy beasts. Take, for example, Bespophus, the moon of carnivorous plants. A botanist named Herbert M. Connofeast decided that he would create a zoo of his universe's most deadly plant life on a small moon in his own solar system. The Venusian man-trap, shrieking ivy, daffodillus rex, antipodean brain-fungus, all these and more were brought to the moon and each deadly shrub was housed in a secure glass enclosure. The point, Connofeast said, was to educate children and to teach them that their species had nothing to fear from these plants so long as they understood them. This was, of course, complete insanity. People had everything to fear from these plants, and it took only a few weeks for the first party of schoolchildren to vanish. Only their shoes were found.

The curators began to find it increasingly difficult to control the plants. The brain-sucking onto-lily, for example, spreads unseen below the soil and can grow at a foot per minute. If you do happen to be sitting in an outside privy while reading a newspaper, as the site's head botanist Lord Beezely was one morning, then it's almost certainly too late to escape. The plants soon began to interbreed, creating new and even more terrifying specimens, and within a single year the moon had become what Herbert M. Connofeast had always dreamed of: a living testimony to the majesty and grandeur of the universe's most deadly veg. The moon was abandoned, obviously, but Connofeast refused to leave. By that time, spores had spread to the home-world nearby, causing disaster on a massive scale. Entire armies sent to the moon to destroy the plants vanished. Even when ships firebombed sections of the moon the plants grew back in days. As a garden, Connofeast's zoo was a magnificent failure. But as an illustration of what life in a universe is really like, you could hardly do better.

*

'This is the laboratory where Connofeast engineered his greatest beasts,' continued Carrofax. 'His aim was simply to create the most fearsome shrubs imaginable.' The others peered, horrified, into the giant jars and saw, suspended in embryonic fluid, sleeping plants with claws, fangs, eyes, plants bound not by roots, plants freed from the bonds of the earth. In the years since their creator's death they continued growing in perpetual slumber, and now they pressed against the glass, faint smiles upon their sleeping lips – or so it seemed.

'But *why*?' said Fabrigas.

'No one knows why the old man wanted to create such terrible creatures. Some say he had been given money by a foreign army to design plants as weapons, and certainly they are perfect predators: fearless, bloodless, and possessing natural camouflage. If you tear a limb from these plants it will regrow. Some say he was under the spell of a . . . demon.' Carrofax paused for effect. 'That room behind the curtain would certainly suggest so, and though I have never heard of this Calligulus it would be wise to assume that he is powerful and dangerous. Each of these beasts is a highly refined killing machine, capable of tearing you apart in a –'

'OK, OK.' Fabrigas took a long breath, then turned to his friends and said, 'Everything will be fine as long as . . . we all remain . . . very . . . very . . . quiet.'

At that moment there was a shrill squeal as somewhere within the walls a set of old gears were revived, and in the jars, fifty eyes snapped open.

RUN, RABBITS, RUN

'Stupid boy!' cried Fabrigas, but even if Roberto hadn't been deaf he wouldn't have heard the old man above the sound of the hidden door sliding open. He was standing frozen beside the new portal, his hand still flat against the nondescript wall panel.

'Your boy has found the only exit,' said Carrofax. 'It would have had to be opened anyway.' The door revealed a dim tunnel. Upon waking, the plants had groggily assessed their situation, seen their prey, paused in astonishment, and now began to furiously test their enclosures, working away at the heavy bolts, pressing out at the glass with their shaggy limbs. 'These jars weren't meant to hold a full-grown plant. I'd say you have but five minutes before them,' said the demon butler. 'There is an escape machine on the far side of the maze. Isn't that nice?'

*

There is nothing quite as frightening as a tunnel. A forest, no matter how deadly, offers all the points of the compass for escape. Including up. A tunnel only offers two avenues: the way you're going, and the way you've been. And if your way is blocked by danger, and you've come from somewhere deadly, your options are few. You may as well just have a picnic and wait for the end. Plus, tunnels are usually very dark and cold, so bring a hat. Anyway, tunnels are frightening. So remember, if at any time you feel afraid and need a moment to recover, you can turn to page 620, your Little Page of Calmness (LPoC).

★

Our friends jogged into the dark maze, a misty mess of concrete tunnels lit sometimes by feeble lamps, past the occasional small heap of bones. Descharge calmly loaded his pistol as he went. 'The old man must have used these tunnels to test his beasts. On goats, most likely. But who knows?'

'I can fathom the fangs and claws,' said the bosun, 'but why did the madman have to give them ears?'

'And why put your escape pod on the furthest side?' said the botanist. 'You wouldn't read of such a conceit in the worst adventure book.'

'Be quiet now, and follow me, yes,' said Lenore, her lost eyes shining in the dimness. 'No, it isn't far at all. Come fast.' And on they trogged (trotted, jogged), the bones crunching under their boots, until, far behind, they heard the smash of glass followed by a gurgling cry that swept past them in the tunnel, then returned, bringing with it a cloud of goaty death.

'Oh good mercies!' said the botanist.

'Monsters monsters monsters monsters,' whispered Lenore.

'Run on!' cried the bosun as he drew his crooked knives. 'I won't be more than a minute. I will speak with them and see if we can smooth this out.'

And they did, because there was no time to argue. They ran on into a part of the maze where the lamps were burned out. A day ago they were merrily eating soup, now they were in a lightless hell, on a deadly moon, in an alien dimension, floating along after the pale, floating figure of a girl. Behind they heard the cry again, much closer, it gurgled in their ears. Every sound was amplified by the concrete tubes – they could even hear the slickety-slap of planty limbs scampering over the stone. They heard the bosun as though he was still beside them: 'Come on then! I've seen worse!' Then nothing, just the sound of their own breath, the thunk-a-thunk of boots, Lenore's strange voice. 'It's not much further. That poor giant.'

Up a ladder to the next level. There were no bones now, just algae clinging to the walls that in the orange glow of the wall lamps looked like a creeping tide of blood. From beyond they heard another gurgling scream. 'They've overtaken us somehow,' said Descharge. 'They're fast.'

'It's hardly further,' said Lenore.

Slickety-slap, slickety-slap, another curdled cry from behind them. Another ahead, in answer. Perhaps, it was hard to tell. They turned a final corner and the girl stopped short. The lights were blown out for most of the tunnel's length but at the end was a bright red ladder lit by a single bulb. 'What is it?' said Fabrigas.

The girl raised a trembling finger softly to her lips and said, 'Shhhhhhhhh.' Ahead, in the darkness, they heard an echo. 'Shhhhhhhhh.'

'They have gone about us,' said the girl calmly. 'There's a twosome. Stay still and say if you will your prayers.'

Then, from the darkness, they heard a terrible echo. 'Ssssssaaaaayyyy prayerssssssssss.'

'It's mimicking us?' said Descharge.

'Mimmmick ussssssssssssss.' The sound was like the tip of a blade on stone and it pranked the heart. Far behind them they heard another creature smash its cell, and they heard another rattling up the ladder.

Slinkity-slap, slinkity-slap.

'It is now or never,' said Fabrigas as he stepped from behind the girl to toss a small canister on the ground, and for a second the tunnel was daylight, they could see two beasts crouching where the shadows had been, slick and grimacing, and as the light from the flare capsule faded the beasts sprang forward.

CARNAGE

The whole slaughter took a few loud moments. Descharge stepped in front of Miss Fritzacopple and calmly put two capsules from his Leitenstorm 980 field pistol into the first beast – who hardly flinched – while Fabrigas smoothly produced a flare gun from his cloak, and put a canister between the beast's eyes. As it exploded in white-hot flames it let out a shrill death note. The second creature, blinded by the flash, barrelled into them, knocking Fabrigas, Fritzacopple and Descharge away into a heap. Roberto stepped in front of Lenore, but the beast picked him up with one frond and flung him over its shoulder. The corridor was filled with smoke, lit softly by the first beast's flaming corpse. In the haze the Vengeance stood serenely, a look of calm on her tiny face. She said, 'Well, hello, Mr Plant. Where for are you going on this day?' The creature gazed down at the girl with a look of adoration, raised a mossy paw, touched the tiny girl tenderly on the cheek, and pulled away, as if it had brushed something very cold.

Then it errupted in a storm of sparks.

Roberto had ripped the electrical wires from the low ceiling and rammed them into the back of the creature's head. The result was that Lenore's admirer had become a hissing puddle oozing over the floor. They could hear other beasts on the way and knew that they had seconds. They flung themselves through the hatch and into the small chamber above. 'There's the valve to release gas into the tunnels,' said Carrofax. 'Don't hesitate.' But before Fabrigas could secure the hatch it sprang open and a giant head flew into the room, rolled across the floor and stopped beside Lenore with a shrubby slap. The bosun followed, sweaty and bloody though the hole. 'Like I said,' he muttered, 'I've seen worse.'

★

After sending in the gas to dispose of Connofeast's weaponised plants they addressed the next stage of their escape. Beyond the blast doors, they knew, was a whole new world of plants who wanted to eat them, and they weren't completely sure the giant diesel-powered escape sphere Carrofax had located was up to it. 'If the plants could rip the GGPTBCE apart in seconds, how do we stand a chance in a giant hamster ball?' said the bosun.

'Because the old fool knew what he was dealing with,' said Descharge.

The Locomosphere was a hit with the residents. They smashed their heavy vines against the shell of the craft, desperate to get to the fleshy morsels inside, and sent it bumping and spinning into the jungle. The sound was catastrophic. 'I'm going to be sick, mates!' cried the bosun as the craft spun through the wild like a top. They were each strapped securely into a crash-proof seat, inside the gyroscopic inner core. The craft's powerful diesel engine was working hard to keep them righted, and Roberto, the boy with the kinship for machines, was driving. The machine had extendable spider legs, if needed, but it was its smooth outer sphere which was keeping them alive. It was too large for any of the mouths which slathered for it, too light and slippery for any of the vines to get a purchase; the plants roared and shook their fronds in sheer frustration.

'Poor mad vegetables!' cried Fabrigas above the noise. 'I almost feel for them!'

'Don't be an idiot,' said the botanist.

'I like this not!' cried Lenore as they popped out of the grip of a mighty vine like a cork from a bottle and went shooting high into the air, landing with a terrible crunch.

But soon they could see the *Necronaut* through the foliage, and a lucky blow from behind by a giant mega-dahlia sent them on towards it. 'Great stars, I'm glad to see it!' said the old-beard. That was when cannon fire from the *Necronaut* ripped through the undergrowth around them.

'What now?' said the old-beard, whose face was almost as green as Lenore's.

'They think we're an enemy!' cried Miss Fritzacopple.

'That was a warning shot,' said Descharge. 'The next will end us. We can't go any further.'

'If we stay here we won't last much longer.' Already the plants were swarming around the craft. 'I have an idea!' said the bosun, as he grabbed the control deck from Roberto's hands and hauled back on the stick, raising them high on the craft's extendable limbs. Then the bosun began to jiggle the stick so that their machine hopped from side to side on its two back legs.

'Are you completely mad?!' cried the botanist. The bosun said nothing. He set the machine down and rolled several cautious feet towards the *Necronaut*. There was no more gunfire, and as they came close they saw the docking bay open.

MONKEY DANCE

The bosun and the captain had had only one other expedition together. It is a long story, with many strange happenings, so I'll just tell you the short version.

They had been hired to transport a shipload of piñatas.

What is a piñata? That is an excellent question. A piñata is an olde-worlde party toy, a ceremonial animal designed to be filled with sweets or other treasures. The guest of honour, blindfolded, tries to smash open the piñata with a club. Then everyone has cake. Yes, it is a strange tradition, though not as strange as some other olde-worlde traditions such as tiny-man tossing, or whale kissing.

So their ship was stocked with several thousand piñatas, only these piñatas weren't filled with sweets, they were filled with explosives bound for the revolutionary war in the jungles of Mesomyxos.

Just a few days into the expedition their ship was boarded by customs officers. These officials weren't interested in their cargo, they simply wanted to take a bribe, and to drink the captain's best liquor. But as the chief inspector and his cronies drank more and more of Lambestyo's best booze they grew increasingly unruly. The chief ordered his men to hang one of the piñatas from a spar so that he might smash it. So while the drunken inspector stumbled around, wildly swinging at the fake piggy which hung above him, Lambestyo and his bosun inched slowly towards the lifeboats, and by the time their ship exploded in a stack of amber mushrooms they were some distance away.

They floated for nine days with little food or water. The captain became very sick. He started to hallucinate that their craft was being followed by clowns riding giant pigs. But the bosun wouldn't allow his captain to succumb to space-madness. Whenever he drifted off he would slap him, hard, then tell him a story from his strange childhood. And if things got really bad he would do his space-monkey dance. He would stand – despite his body being weak from hunger – and wave his arms above his head, and hop from leg to leg, and poke out his lip. When the bosun did his space-monkey dance he made the captain laugh, and that, as we know, is basically impossible.

They survived their ordeal, thanks largely to the bosun's dance, and were picked up by a Customs Office ship which was searching the area for a missing inspector and his team.

And so the bosun knew that if he could make his jungle machine do a space-monkey dance his captain would remember. Remember and laugh.

AFTERGLOW

And he did.

When the captain saw the bosun and his friends again in the dock of the *Necronaut*, he laughed. He laughed for the first time in years and frightened everyone. Then the captain composed himself and ordered that Fabrigas be thrown in the brig for one hour as a punishment for putting his crew's life in danger, and although the old man blustered at first he eventually agreed that it was probably fair.

After his incarceration they had a big meal, then they slept. They slept despite the noise of the ravenous jungle plants. Lenore dreamed that she was waltzing in a grand ballroom with a fearsome plant while a host of demons watched. Miss Fritzacopple dreamed of her husband, the revolutionary hero, who had given her a foxglove cast in bronze before he left for his last mission. Fabrigas dreamed of a thousand other worlds, each of them populated entirely by cats. Even the captain slept, because he hadn't since his friends had left.

DEADLY CREATURES

One of the most confounding things about exploring a universe, as you are no doubt beginning to discover, is that when you are faced with a mysterious phenomenon, something you have never encountered before, the most unbelievable explanation is often the correct one.

In OD2142K (that is a historical date, in case you were wondering), the explorers Halls and Oates set out to climb Mt Valhaldestein, one of the tallest peaks in the known universe. Valhaldestein is a magnetic mountain: ships cannot travel there, and climbers must bring only wooden tools. The peak holds more dangers than you could possibly imagine, from sub-zero temperatures to burning nitrogen vents, to swarms of ice-leeches, to mountain cannibals, to prankster porters who will tie your laces together when you aren't looking, or dress up like mountain cannibals. Halls knew of the dangers when he conceived of the expedition, so he was most surprised to find that the one thing which was bound to strike mortal fear into his team – even his climbing partner – was a mythical creature called the Valhaldestein Yeti. This creature, despite never having been seen, was said with great confidence to have terrible claws and teeth. She was white-furred, and so essentially invisible in the snow except for her blood-red eyes, and she was strong enough to pull a person's limbs clean off, and yet merciful enough, it was said, to beat him unconscious with those limbs before eating them. Halls had only to mention the Valhaldestein Yeti in front of his people to see them cry out and jump into each other's arms. He was disgusted to see that even his partner didn't like mention of the monster.

'We have bigger problems to worry about than some imaginary beast!' said Halls, and he was right. When they reached the first base camp they learned that half their food had spoiled. By the second camp, two-thirds of their porters had run off. A blizzard kept them at bay for several days. Finally, everything calmed. They were left with a perfect night, the endless stars shimmered to the horizon, and the only thing to break the silence was a low moan from the darkness. Every minute it came a little louder. The remaining porters flew into a panic and fled. The officers conferred secretly with Oates, and as the phantom cries grew they too decided to abandon camp and flee down the mountain. Halls was furious; he called them cowards, fools, and he was still yelling from the ridge as his men fled. His cries ended abruptly.

Oates returned the following day to find just what he'd expected: the blood, the bear-like prints in the snow, the scraps of clothing. The point, I suppose, is that it is important to be careful which legends you believe, but in the end, either way, it won't stop you being eaten by them.

After hearing about such strange and brutal creatures I suppose you're wondering: what is the most feared and dangerous creature in the universe? Well, that's a very interesting question and the answer will surprise you.

Let's start with third place.

3. The Sweety.

The Sweety lives alone on a barren planet in an uninhabited region of a deserted corner of its universe. The corner of this universe was once pretty and thriving and many more people would live there if the Sweety did not. The Sweety is much larger, even, than the superplanet he rests on. He has a vast maw with an underbite containing rows of terrifying fangs, each fang larger than a mountain. He has thousands of long, suckered tentacles which he uses to snare prey. These tentacles can reach far into space. But what makes the Sweety deadly is not its size, but its passions. The Sweety, you see, wasn't always alone. There was once a lady Sweety and they lived together in bliss for many thousands of years. One day the Sweety woke from a nap to find his mate gone, vanished. This, sadly, happens sometimes, for it is almost impossible to make love last, especially when you've been together for thousands of years. The Sweety was understandably upset and he cried to the stars, but space refused to carry his grief. Ever since that day the Sweety has watched the heavens, waiting for the day when his beloved will return. In old age his mind and vision have begun to dull so that if he sees even a faint movement, the glint of a piece of space-junk, or the flutter of a sail of a ship, he sends one of his mighty tentacles lashing far away to grab the object and bring it to him, and he holds it there, close to his heart, in an unbreakable grip, until the thing stops moving. Because it is a sad fact that the most terrifying mover in the universe is not the hunger in the belly, but the hunger in the heart, for though the belly can be full the heart can never. The Sweety's mountainous body is littered with the skeletons of ships.

Anyway. Our number-one spot most definitely goes to the zombie-moss spores. No one would argue with that. But more on that creature later.

The number-two spot goes to a very interesting creature indeed.

THE POPE

The Pope. His Holiness the Pope. Light of the universe, fire of our sins. He stood four foot ten in papal slippers, with a round face, pretty eyes and sandy side-parted hair. He was Pope to most creatures. The Colonel in the services. The Devil in the conquered lands. 'His Craziness' in the learned taverns. But in earshot he was always His Holiness. No creature, sentient or not, was feared as much as the Pope (except, as I've already mentioned, the zombie-moss spores). The Pope believed that he was on a perpetual crusade on behalf of his semi-polytheistic super-cult. He saw himself as an intergalactic exorcist. He believed in ghosts. He believed that the universe was ridden with ghosts and evil spirits: individuals, couples, families, whole nations of spirits. 'They are everywhere!' he'd shout. They live in great numbers, two to every person. They live off men's souls. They whisper in women's ears. They tell them all to do terrible things. 'And only I can stop them!' Political parties, whole peoples are controlled by these spirits, he'd argue. 'The reason the great plague exists,' he would shout, 'is because people deny the Holy Spirits!'

When the Pope learned that he was to wake his fleet, the Fleet of the Nine Churches – the largest and most destructive death fleet ever assembled – and take it deep into the universe, and then to the next universe, on the biggest and most ambitious crusade ever attempted, eliminating along the way any person, peoples or worlds that should obstruct him, to bring about the destruction of a single demon girl, it was as if all his birthdays had happened at once. And the Pope, to be fair, had an unusual number of birthdays.

He rose early on the day they were to embark, and that almost never happened, and when his aides arrived they found him already sitting in his favourite chair in his red leisure suit with white stripes, his hat on the table next to him. He was kicking the chair legs impatiently. 'When are we going?' he cried.

'After breakfast, Excellency,' said Cardinal Mothersbaugh. The Pope hated waiting. He didn't understand that preparing a fleet of 180,000 ships, some as big as planets, took, oh, at least a day. And so he sat, drumming on the table with his fingers, putting on and removing his hat, admiring himself in the long mirror, threatening to kill people, until finally he got word that the fleet was ready.

And the Fleet of the Nine Churches was a sight to behold (or not, for it was painted black so as to be all but invisible in the depths). It had fearsome dreadnoughts, and prison ships equipped to take entire populations for relocation. There were moon-eaters (ships large enough to chomp and digest entire moons or small planets). When the fleet lifted from its moorings and sounded its klaxons the universe trembled. Perhaps even the gods themselves were woken from their slumbers. The Pope was carried down the gangplank in a ceremonial chair, but when he got inside all ceremony was dropped and he ran giggling to the command centre.

Now he stood on the bridge, in his white cylindrical hat embroidered with a gold 'X'.

'Let's teach that stupid Devil Girl a lesson she won't forget!' he cried.

ESCAPE

They woke late. Roberto was stamping around the decks and when they came above he threw up his arms, like, 'What time is this? I ask you!' The dinophytes had not tired, and they continued to rock the steel boat with a gentle fury, such that it was impossible to breakfast on anything but a solid.

The Gentrifaction were in a terrible state: nerves shot, eyes oozing black-mascara tears. They sat at breakfast with kerchiefs to their mouths and could not console one another.

After breakfast an emergency meeting was held and things were decided. The first thing that was decided was that the slate was clean. All transgressions were forgotten and they would now work as a team. They held a small service for Bortis. Connofeast's hamster ball had picked up several small, sticky pieces of him as it rolled towards the ship. They peeled them carefully off and put them in a small box. It was discovered that the hamster ball had also carried spores into the docking bay, and these had already manifested in a kind of venomous shrub, a variety of shrieking moss and a gnawing lily.

'I knew a girl called Gnawing Lily,' said the captain, but everyone ignored him.

'There is a chilling sentience here,' said Fabrigas, 'a hive mind,' before he sent the bosun in with fire and industrial herbicide.

The second thing that was decided was that it would be

impossible to make the *Necronaut* launch-worthy. The steering systems and the sails were badly damaged, and, though Roberto could help, some things could only be repaired from outside, and that, under the circumstances, was impossible. 'It is a thorny problem,' said Fabrigas.

Descharge found him mulling things over on the navigation deck. 'I need to let you know, as a gentleman and an officer, that I do not believe in this "clean slate". I still intend to make you pay for your crimes. You and your captain.'

'Oh, and who will you take me to? The Queen who betrayed you? Your beloved navy? They tried to destroy your fleet.'

'Nonsense.'

Fabrigas turned momentarily to an empty corner, then smiled, turned back and said, 'The commander of that attacking fleet was someone you might know. A Commander Mattlocke.'

Descharge briefly lost control of his smug expression.

'Could this be the same Mattlocke you're competing with for the position of Supreme Imperial Commander? How interesting. With you gone he'd get just what he's wanted for so long: to lead the fleets in a war against the Vangardiks. How very interesting.'

Descharge fixed Fabrigas with a look so hard it made him draw back. 'Your tricks won't work with me, old fool. I'll see you swing.' And he left.

'What a nice man,' said Carrofax. 'So you mean to help the girl after all?'

'We have no choice for the meantime. I can't exactly feed her to the plants, and apparently she could be harmful to us if we keep her too long.'

'"Harmful" is an understatement. She gets more unpredictable the closer she gets to maturity. I will find out what I can and guide you.'

'Good. And find out who this Calligulus is, too. And find out why I keep dreaming about starfish. And find out where in all the heavens we are.'

'I will. Although I can tell you that if there's one place we most certainly are not, it's heaven.'

*

Fabrigas came back to the group to propose a radical escape plan. He had confirmed the position of the nearby planet. It was close enough that with sufficient upward force they would be able to break the bonds of the plants' embrace, and the moon's feeble gravity, then drift across space to the new planet where repairs could be made. 'I propose we overload our landing jets so they explode!' This, he reasoned, should give them the thrust to throw them clear of the moon.

'Joo want to blow us up?'

'Exactly. I want to blow us . . . up.'

'Why are joo always trying to kill us?'

'I'm not trying to kill us. Our hull is strong. I chose this ship for its structural integrity. We should be fine.'

'Should?'

'Most likely.'

'It was a stupid plan,' said Lambestyo. 'If the moon is deadly, the planet it orbits could be terrifyingly dangerous.' And besides, they had shredded their supersonic chute on landing. Descharge agreed. In fact, the crew was unanimous in their condemnation of the plan, but also in their awareness that they had no other options.

Fabrigas did his best to reassure them. 'I will calibrate the explosion precisely. I promise. It will be a controlled blast.'

CONTROLLED BLAST

'Everybody try to stay limp!'

This was the last thing they heard from Fabrigas before the blast knocked them senseless. The explosion the old-beard had 'calibrated' beneath the treble-armour-plated hull of the *Necronaut* was so powerful that those closest to the epicentre were temporarily deafened. They departed the moon like a ballerina who has just sat on a fire-wasp, leaving behind a crater of charred vegetation 180 yards wide. Even as they barrelled most unballetically into space their iron hull rang on like a gong. The forces of gravity knocked most of them unconscious, and when they came to they saw the wild, willing jungles of Bespophus receding below, crying and reaching up to them like children, and soon they found themselves once more floating in space.

They drifted for a long, long while.

ABOUT ME

Why don't I tell you a little about myself? What? Now? While our friends are locked in dreadful floaty peril? Certainly. They will stay off the boil for as long as we need them to.

Each creature has its job. Bakers bake, explorers explore, murderers murder. I am a writer. I bake with words, I explore the limits of imagination, I murder expectation. I was once a great and renowned man: a poet, philosopher, raconteur, hypno-*flâneur* (an exponent of the art of walking while automatic writing). I rose to fame after the publication of my first collection, *The Excrementalists*. And when I say 'rose to fame', I mean that the subjects of my book, the aristo-cratic poets of my Empire, tried to kill me. But they could not divert me from my labours. Every morning I would rise at 11.15 – no later – my servants would bring in my breakfast and coffee, they would bathe and anoint me with fine unguents. Then, in the early afternoon I would put a warm towel about my head and I would write! I would write for exactly two hours, not a second less. Then I would see to my correspondence, then I would walk in the grounds with my house guests (usually other famous writers) and we would discuss philos-ophy, politics, or the issues of the day. But this is the life of a young poet: it demands dedication, sacrifice.

Then there was a revolution, bloody and terrible. All my friends were put to death – which vexed me greatly – even the ones who'd tried to kill me – which didn't. I lost everything. All I had accumulated, striven for and inherited was washed away in a tide of blood and aristocratic tears. My hand shakes when I think of what I've lost: my first editions, my handmade shoes, my collection of porcelain puppies in amusing poses. All vanished, like tears in the rain. But I am lucky to have escaped with my head. It turned out that a leader of the revolution, one Dejanne Hammer, was a fan. (Oh, save me from my murderous fans!) I was saved from death in return for a signed book and a kiss, but was condemned to a fate far worse. I was forced to go to the vulgar press and earn a crust writing adventure books. All the wit and genius bequeathed to me by nature would now be channelled into the task of penning these crude pulp tales.

And so I work now on assignment, for a pittance. While I work my poetry languishes and my genius shrivels under the flabby mediocrity of the novel. The novel! That most base of all written forms. I who have written epic poems for queens and salted the ears of dauphins with saucy couplets.

Anyway, one must not dwell upon life's misfortunes. One must push on. Let's return to our adventure.

BELLY OF THE BEAST

The first thing the crew aboard the *Necronaut* realised as they gathered themselves was that they were blind. Leaves, vines and swiftly growing mosses had completely covered the exterior of the vessel and would not shift. All they had was audio feedback, and the anti-crash bats – who were utterly frantic.

'Are you mad?!' Lambestyo shouted when he found the old-beard. 'You said you would do a controlled thing!' His ears were ringing.

'I did!' shouted Fabrigas. 'But there are *degrees* of control.'

The crew tried to regain their composure. Most had peed themselves. Some had done worse. The Gentrifaction were in a more hysterical state than the bats. G. De Pantagruel was weeping while fanning a prostrate Scatalletto who still had not regained consciousness.

Eventually, after a very, very long time, the hull and their ears stopped ringing, and audio reported the sound of drumming. 'We need to change heading!' screamed the lad as the ba-booms grew heavy in his phones, but of course they had no steering, 'We have no steering!' They were at the mercy of the gravity of the planet they were drifting towards. 'We're at the mercy of its gravity! Crash positions!'

A pressure wave hit their craft – it was a roar you didn't need phones to hear, and it made the whole ship shake, a roar so deep it was like the sound of a steel beam a mile thick being twisted by a pair of giant hands.

'That is a very, very large thing,' said Fabrigas. The bats in the nose were losing their precious little minds.

Then the *Necronaut* found itself tumbling, still blinded by the clinging vines. Its crew saw a blur of friends and objects. Then there was a crunch as the vessel slammed into something immovable. They were airborne again for what seemed like for ever. Then, for reasons they couldn't understand, they touched softly down, as if a pair of giant invisible hands which enjoyed bending steel beams had plucked them from the air and set them back on solid earth.

★

Darkness, total and unyielding, when no light is present but the zany specks that flit around behind the eyes. People rose like foals on battered legs. The ship groaned and listed like a bathtub set upon a mattress. Audio picked up the music of a jungle whose eerie blips and calls sounded like a ship's sonar. Underneath was something else, a rumble like the thrumming of a boiler. 'Where are we? The sea?' said Miss Fritzacopple, whose shoulder was badly bruised. She could be forgiven for thinking so. They used cargo hooks to push small viewing holes through the dead foliage which caked their vessel. They sent lanterns out on grappling poles and discovered a floating loveliness in the dark: the foliage was wafting slowly and things that looked like squid were drifting past. Pale-eyed birds of fancy watched from the undergrowth.

'We are on land,' said Fabrigas. 'But the gravity here is very weak.'

Their lamps found crooked trees in a misty lagoon, sumptuous roots plunging like serpents into the mud. Eyes big and small reflected their lamplight. They saw foliage that didn't want to eat them hiding creatures that might.

'We have landed in a swamp,' said the captain, 'and what's the bet it wants to eat us?'

At that moment a seismic ripple passed through the ship and the

Necronaut was left rocking and creaking like an ancient toad.

'We could have slipped into a crevasse,' mused Fabrigas.

'Well, I see no reason to hesitate,' said their captain. 'We can't survive or launch without key supplies. We will form a party to search the area for readies, and the rest should stay onboard and begin repairs. We should aim to sail in three days. This is my plan. What smell you, little green girl?'

'Confusion,' said Lenore. As she sniffed, her dead eyes rolled up and quivered white in their sockets. 'But there are tasty things. Fires. Peoples.' She closed one eye. 'And oils for wicks and gears.'

'This could be a good place for us,' said Fabrigas. 'Do you think you can guide us to the food and oil?' And Lenore laughed brightly. She turned her sickly green face up to the light.

'Of course. You know I'll give you my nose. Always.' She folded her arms. 'But will you hear my price?'

'Your price?' said Fabrigas.

'From now I think the children should be containing in them all the freedoms of the grown-ups. We must have good rest, and share the treasure. What says you?' In front of her the girl sensed the crackle of smiles. 'My dear,' said the old-beard, 'for the help you are giving us, it is a reasonable price.'

The girl wrinkled her little nose and raised an arm sideways. 'Oils are that-aways.'

⋆

That night the slaveys sang with such power and passion that the captain had to go below and calm them, lest their song be overheard by a local tribe or un-neighbourly creature.

But when the captain went up late on deck the jungle seemed at rest. It pulsed with gentle clicks and hoots. There was a small light near the foredeck, someone reading, the poet, perhaps, but everyone else was asleep.

⋆

The next morning the hunting-and-gathering party was assembled: the captain, Fabrigas, Miss Fritzacopple, the bosun, two sailors – Hardcastle and McCormack – Lenore and, of course, Roberto. Lenore had protested that she did not want him to come along, since she had discovered him that morning teaching a coin trick to a young slavey, one Brittany Burk. 'He should maybe stay here where his tricks is welcome.' It took some time to convince the pouting alien princess to change her mind. They helped her into the raft they were going to use to cross the swamps and she sulked while they loaded boxes of supplies around her. Roberto was oblivious to the whole saga.

Descharge was left in charge of the ship and the repairs.

'It'll be nice to get the gang back together,' said the bosun, adjusting the belt of elephant rounds on his broad shoulders and hoisting a heavy belt of charge canisters around his waist. 'I had such fun on our last outing.' They each clamped an air filter into their nose – for emergencies.

'You don't want to be going out there,' said a voice from the shadows. It was an old sailor called Murphus, who liked to whittle by the foredeck. 'There be dreadful things out there. That is to say, there *will* be dreadful things out there.'

'Who's that guy?' said Lambestyo as he hoisted on his gun belts.

'Can you not smell it? Can you not smell the death hanging in the air? If you go out there you'll never come back.'

'He's spooking me up,' said Lambestyo. 'Make him stop.'

'If you go into the swamp you'll never see the ship again – except as ghosts. And who needs that hassle?'

'I don't smell much death,' Lenore called up from the raft. 'There's a village over there.'

'Don't go anywhere, dearest,' said the captain to Descharge.

'I won't be going anywhere without you and the old man,' Descharge coldly replied.

DARK TERRITORY

The jungle fell mute as they prepared a raft: as if it was waiting for them to dare to enter its secret mists. The old man loaded his personal equipment into the stern. The air was languid and heavy as they pushed out into the swamp, looking back one last time at the *Necronaut* – half buried in the primordial mud, its long spars hung with vegetation and scraps of sail – not realising that a number of them would never see the boat again. Soon it had vanished.

There were long-toothed reptiles still as logs upon the lagoon. There were slender-tongued rats lapping in the shallows. There were frogs and insects croaking. There was a bird calling from the darkness with the sound of a plucked string. *'Plang. Plang. Plang.'*

The boat had two gas lamps hung on the end of steel hooks. The sailor called McCormack pushed them forward from the back with a wooden pole. Fabrigas was peering bemused at several of his instruments. It was amazing what came out of that cloak of his. 'The gravity does not make sense!' he said. 'Perhaps we are inside a volcano. That would explain the seismic motions.'

No one was listening.

'Plang. Plang. Plang. Plang. Plang. Plang. Plang.'

'Death is out there,' said the captain. 'I can feel it. This place has a bad energy. Not like the last place.'

'The last place tried to kill us,' said Fabrigas.

'Ah, it was not so bad. I've seen worse. Like this place.'

'So you're in one of those moods.'

'Maybe I am, maybe I'm not.'

Before long they were in an area where a million white mushrooms shone on dozens of muddy bulges; each shroom was an unblinking eye.

'Everyone be careful,' drawled the botanist. 'The spores might be deadly. Don't touch them.'

'What are those called, Miss Lady?' said Lenore, who was full of questions.

'Mushrooms.'

'What kind of mushrooms are they?'

'Big ones.'

'How did you get to know so many plants? I would like to be a botanist one day: only I'd collect smells, not plants. Do you have a man-friend?'

Fritzacopple sighed. 'I have to concentrate on collecting samples.' She pulled out her tongs. But the boat sailed on too quick across the darkly luminous estuary; her tongs snapped at the soggy air.

'You're distracting me. Stop staring.'

'I'm blind.'

'Why don't you play with Roberto?'

'I do not care for the coin tricks.'

At last they came towards solid land. Their boat pushed into the mud below a small, rocky hill topped by a single lonely tree. 'We should go that-aways,' said Lenore, 'many smells up there. Two big beasts is breakfasting.' Beyond the small hill was a clearing before a narrow valley leading deeper into the jungle. There in the gloam they could see two large four-legged beasts. 'Unicorns!' said Hardcastle as he grabbed McCormack's arm. 'As I breathe!' The beasts who blocked their way on did not seem to register the presence of the wide-eyed pack of people crammed into their raft.

'We will set up a base camp on the shore,' said the captain. 'When the beasts are finished grazing we will continue.'

'I want to collect some samples around the edge of the lagoon,' said the botanist.

'I don't want you to leave the group,' said the captain. 'Stay within sight.'

'You worry too much,' she replied, and she took her small sample case and sloshed off through the mud.

'I'll come too,' said Lenore.

'No!' came the reply.

'You have fifteen minutes!' said the captain, but she was already gone into the darkness beyond their lamps.

'My word!' they heard the botanist say from the distance. And then not a peep.

The mist came in like sleep, turning everything they saw to shadows. The unicorns, just thirty feet away, chewed their grasses lazily, with a full four seconds between each chomp. 'They'll die back at ship when they hear we've spotted unicorns,' said McCormack. Fabrigas patiently tried to point out that these beasts did not much resemble unicorns as they knew them from fables, since they were not lithe, white equine quadrupeds with single horns upon their heads, but rather were fat, insolent-looking creatures with wide, flat feet, grey, leathery skin folded over in places and studded with wiry hairs. Certainly the beasts had horns upon their snouts, but they were black and stumpy, curved like an assassin's dagger.

'I don't care what he says,' whispered Hardcastle to McCormack. 'If they aren't unicorns then I'm a jungle ape.'

'The village is one mile that-aways,' said Lenore. 'And there are other villages here, I thinks. That is what I thinks. You smell of worry.' She said it to Lambestyo. Lenore, the captain noticed, was looking straight into his eyes now and he felt a sudden fear. Those eyes seemed so large and terrible in this place. She stood against the black of the swamp. She always stood evenly on two booted feet; always had her green hands clasped in front of her; her eyes had always the haunted and expectant look of the young true wife of a sailor who has died at sea; her mouth, always at work, showed luminous pale fangs and a restless fillet of silvery tongue dipping in and out across a pair of deathly blue lips. She seemed lit from within by a dreadful moonlight. Lambestyo moved a step to his left to break her gaze and, almost unbelievably, those dread eyes followed him. There was something less than human in them. 'What it is?' said the girl. 'Has something frightened you?'

'Sweet mercy, that's delightful!' came the botanist's distant voice and snapped him from his terror.

Everything else was quiet. A hazy rain fell; it seemed to swirl around them, though the air was still. They were huddled around the lamp; the other lamp bobbed away in the distance, letting out the occasional 'Heavens!' or 'Good grief!'

'Come back to our light!' called the captain, but she didn't answer. 'Maybe someone should look after her.' Hardcastle looked at McCormack and they both shrugged. Hardcastle went off to relieve himself in the shadows. 'I'll go,' said Lambestyo, standing self-consciously. 'I mean, it's best I go and find her.' He looked around, unsure which way to set off. Her lamp had vanished.

'I know where she is,' said Lenore. 'I will witness what she's doing. I'm bored anyways.'

The girl floated off after the botanist. Lambestyo sat down again. They heard a bird's call from the undergrowth so loud and sudden that they all jumped.

A dark and dreary fog was creeping in.

Hardcastle returned to the group with an object he'd found buried in the mud near the swamp. It was a sphere of brass and wood with several moving parts. 'Look,' he said, 'it's a child's puzzle.' He wiped away the mud as Carrofax appeared and said, 'He should not be playing with that. That isn't a happy toy.'

'Give that to me,' said Fabrigas, but the sailor said, 'Get your own toy!'

'If I may, sir,' said Carrofax, 'and without wishing to interfere in your . . . human things . . . I think it might be time to prepare for a quick departure.'

Roberto had walked a few feet away and was bouncing higher and higher in the flimsy gravity. He was bouncing so high that at times only his pale legs were visible. Higher into the darkness above, floating back like a leaf, until each time he left the ground he was gone for minutes.

Then he didn't come back at all.

For ten minutes the captain wandered around below, vainly calling up, until finally Roberto floated down and touched, crouched, paused, his hair thick with leaves and bugs. He put his hands flat upon the ground. Fabrigas noticed. 'What is it?' The boy's face was soaked in fear. He swung instinctively around to find Lenore, but she had already vanished from sight.

Now the dreadful fog had hidden even the darkness.

Then Roberto left the ground like a bullet, springing into the foggy heights, and was gone.

★

Miss Fritzacopple stood in a grove of luminescent ferns. 'There's enough here to make lanterns.' She looked over at Lenore, standing among the ferns, cast in an eerie light. 'You look like a young ghost!' she laughed. 'What is it?'

'There's something strange upon us,' said the girl, 'down up there,' and she was off. Miss Fritzacopple hurried to gather her things and follow. She saw the girl's shape, a whisper of light, vanishing and reappearing among the thickening trees, and she experienced a rapid beating of her heart. She heard, she thought, a child's laugh and stopped. But to her right she saw no lamplight, just her own – ending at a grove of thorns and skeletal trees that vanished into darkness. The girl had vanished, too.

She ran on, her boots coughed in the mud, the tip of her tongue dabbed at her teeth, until finally she entered a swampy grove where the green girl was standing, arms wide. The tree she stood beside was old, its ancient skin spun in jagged eddies, its broad, knuckled roots grasped the earth, its bare branches reached down, it seemed, to cradle the girl.

'You see now?'

The botanist went towards the ancient tree. 'Well I never.' She held up a jar with a piece of glowing fern in it and studied the patterns on the bark of the tree. 'In all my years,' she whispered. 'This reminds me of the old trees of the Timberlak tribe,' she said. 'They used them as signposts for the dead. So they could find their way home. But how would they get here?'

On the far side of the clearing was a thin creek spanned by a small wooden footbridge. The bridge was made of two halves joined at the centre by rusted hinges.

'Just look at that!'

'We should not cross it, my lady. We should not.' But the botanist ignored the girl, taking her by the hand and leading her up the bridge and down the other side.

'See? Not so bad. But I wonder who built it.'

'We did, of course,' said a child's voice. 'But you really ought not to have crossed it.'

*

'Roberto!' called Fabrigas. He knew what the boy had felt: vibrations, and kneeling himself he too could feel them.

'Look, the lovers are leaving,' said McCormack.

And it was true, the two horned beasts were trotting quickly off into the darkness.

'Something frightened them,' said the bosun.

'Let's form a defensive position on that hill,' Fabrigas said.

*

A boy and a girl stood together. Miss Fritzacopple and Lenore had jumped when the boy spoke. Lenore had jumped particularly high because she was not used to being snuck up on by anything. 'What's there?!' she cried. 'I can't smell you.'

'We didn't mean to startle you,' said the girl. 'We heard you from our camp and came to see.'

They were young, the boy around nine, the girl perhaps eleven. They both wore strange outfits: the boy a purple tunic, belted trousers and boots, and the girl a short dress with green stockings and boots. Although it was dark at the edge of the clearing, beyond the reach of the lamp and the jarred fern, this pair seemed to glow. 'We're glad you came. You're the first visitors we've had in ever such a long time.'

Lenore went to Fritzacopple's side and grasped her hand. 'Who are they, Miss Lady?' she hissed. 'I can't smell them. I can't smell them not at all!'

*

The drumming clicks had quickly grown from a soft rain of pins falling on glass to a sound like the rattle of bones in a sack. The party contracted to a tight group around the tree at the top of the hillock. Each had a blade in one hand and a pistol in the other, but as the drumming grew louder the two sailors, Hardcastle and McCormack, broke away and ran back towards the boat, screaming, 'Forgive us, please! We don't want to die today!' Soon they were pushing off from the beach and out into the fog.

'Cowards!' yelled the captain. He took his heavy flare pistol and aimed it into the heights. The pistol gave a throaty 'chonk' as it released its charge. There was a delay, then the charge lit, turning night into day. This was the first time they'd seen the full scope of the jungle valley they were in. The walls of a ravine rose miles on either side and curled over so that it looked as if it closed above them, and the vines fell, in some places, almost to the ground. There were groves of trees, hissing rivers flowing delicately over the contours of the land. And down the valley came another kind of river: thousands upon thousands of creatures were charging towards them. They were like great spiders with the armour and weapons of the crab. They came at them, their razor-sharp claws a-clacking, their eyes unblinking, and their call was like the squittle of a million rats.

*

'It's this way,' said the boy. 'Our ship is this way.' Miss Fritzacopple and Lenore followed the children down a narrow path through a copse of low-spreading thorns. The thorns grabbed at our dear friends' clothing, imploring them to stop. 'Don't go with these strange children!' the bushes seemed to say, but the women didn't listen. They felt compelled to follow.

'Miss Lady, why can my nose not see the children?'

'I don't know,' said the botanist, though she secretly thought she might.

'It's like they're not even there!'

'It's not much further. When our ship crashed we built a camp and we've been here ever since. It's not so bad when you get used to it.' They broke from the thorn grove and came into a clearing. In the clearing was an old saucer craft, rusted and broken. Its front landing gear had given way and plunged the disc's edge into the earth. A red fluid had oozed from the ground and dried around the rim. The whole ship was overgrown with weed and vines, and bugs crawled down its flanks and in and out of its shattered eyes. Next to the ship was a low table and chairs, the kind a family might take camping.

'Won't you sit for a while?' said the girl. 'Our parents won't be back for some time, I'm afraid, and our friends are out, too.'

'Miss Lady,' hissed Lenore, 'I hate this. Please let's go backwards.'

'In a minute,' replied the botanist. 'There might be something useful here.'

'Won't you sit with us?' said the children, in one voice. In the darkness somewhere Fritzacopple thought she heard another voice, an urgent voice calling out a single word, over and over and over.

'Of course, we'd be delighted,' said Miss Fritzacopple through a rigid smile. 'But would you mind if I took a look around your camp first? It's just that it seems so . . . lovely.'

The boy and girl looked at one another. 'Of course,' said the boy. 'But don't go far.' Then together: 'It's dangerous here.'

Miss Fritzacopple retreated into the darkness, lamp held at arm's length, never turning her back on the children, and Lenore clung tightly to her arm. 'I am a scared person.'

'I know.' They moved towards the voice, and soon the single repeating word resolved itself. Their lamp found the skeleton of an adult, face down, arm stretched out, then another skeleton. It looked as if they'd been trying to reach an amphibious vehicle which stood a few metres away. The vehicle's tracks were busted, and the bulbous plexiglas enclosure had wide splits in it – as if it had been taken to with an axe. Not far from the vehicle they found two small mounds of earth, and a third skeleton, curled into a foetal position nearby. The voice grew louder, heavy and monstrous. They pushed on through the darkness. Soon they came upon it. It was a machine, an automaton based loosely on the human form. It lay twisted on its back. Its legs were smashed, its arms lay metres away, torn off and cast aside, but its brain was still intact in its glass dome, and in its strange mechanical voice it spoke the same word, again, and again, and again . . .

DANGER!

DANGER!

DANGER!

DANGER!

DANGER!

DANGER!

DANGER!

DANGER!

DANGER!
DANGER!
DANGER!
DANGER!

*

'Hold your line!' yelled the captain as the first wave of spider crabs swept up the slope, their long legs singing like war-rattles as they lunged for the visitors' faces. It was not much of a defensive line: a boy, an old man and a giant. As fast as they killed a spider crab another one took its place, snapping at their faces with its claws, tearing at their clothes with its many barbed legs. Fabrigas produced numerous gadgets from his cloak: a high-powered air cannon, a gun that shot webs of electricity. The spider crabs squealed and died, their broken bodies formed a three-foot-high wall, but still they came, and when Fabrigas had used up all his tricks he too resorted to slashing at them with his blade. 'We need to retreat!' he said, but there was nowhere to run. The flare had faded, leaving them in a small, orange puddle of light. The captain flung three skewered crabs from his blade. The bosun had done away with his blade and was smashing crab after crab with his now-bloody fists.

That's when a strange thing happened. Strange, you say? When everything else that's happened up until now has been completely normal? Well, strangeness is a matter of perspective. Fabrigas would later say how natural it seemed when a young female voice, so close that it seemed to be coming from inside his head, said, 'Unlight your lamp.'

'Who said that?'

'Do it. Do it now.'

So he did. He grabbed lamp and pole and hurled them into a nearby puddle. There was a *hisssss* and they were plunged into darkness. 'What the holy mistress are you doing, wizard!' screamed the bosun.

For a second or two the assault continued, and they had to slash blindly in the air, but then the onslaught stopped. They could hear the stream flow past them and away, the legs clacking off into the distance. Then there was silence, the sound of heavy breathing. 'How did you know?' said the captain, kneeling to suck in bladders of air.

'Someone told me,' said Fabrigas. 'Perhaps a little bird.'

'Well, what do we do now? We're blind. The others won't be able to find us.' That's when they saw something new: a crowd of pale blue beacons coming down the valley.

★

DANGER!
DANGER!
DANGER!
DANGER!
DANGER!
DANGER!

Lenore and Fritzacopple, arms knotted, left the broken robot, the broken rover, the graves and the skeletons, and inched slowly, like a crippled crab, back to the saucer craft. The place was empty and silent. The children were nowhere to be found. 'Let's go please now, Miss Lady,' said Lenore.

'I want to check the ship first. There might be something useful in there.' They walked up the creaking gangplank and into the lightless ship.

It was a two-level craft. On the lower level were the atomic motors, the living quarters, the galley and the robot's compartment. On the upper level they found the control room, and the cryogenic 'suspended animation' tubes often used by primitive cultures for interstellar travel. In the chair at the main control desk was another figure, slumped.

'I don't like this, I don't like this, I don't like this –'

'Be brave.' She shook the girl off and walked quickly through the cabin, picking up objects and examining them as she went. She pocketed a map book, a journal. Resting inside the cover of the journal was a starfish. She looked up to the windows and saw the children standing hand in hand at the edge of the clearing, their eyes slashing the darkness.

'What are you doing?' they said. Their voices somehow penetrated the hull of the ship. They said, 'You don't go in there. Daddy will be very angry.' Fritzacopple shuddered and turned back to her work, ignoring the leathery and lifeless form, the long nails, the tufts of wiry hair, the pistol in his hand.

'What are you?' said the girl child.

'Isn't it obvious?' said the botanist. 'I'm a person.'

'Not you. We weren't talking to you. We meant her. What is she?'

'What am I? What means they what I am?'

'You aren't a normal person. You don't belong here.'

'You don't belong anywhere. Daddy is going to be *so* mad when he meets you.'

'Miss Lady? What do they mean?'

'Well, I'm sure Daddy will learn to live with us,' said the botanist as she stuffed some blueprints of the ship inside her leather jacket.

Then a man's voice said, 'Who are you?!' and Lenore screamed.

*

The scream blew the darkness away. It was so loud that the men, still gasping for breath on the pile of crab remains, stopped, and even the lights approaching in the distance halted momentarily. Fabrigas looked to his captain, then into the darkness. 'Roberto will reach her,' he said. 'We have to prepare for these new attackers, whoever they are.' The crowd of blue beacons was getting closer.

OTHERS

High above, Roberto swung blindly, reaching forward for the next vine, ignoring the slithering shapes that lurched all around him, ignoring the hideous bugs that splattered against his face, shrieking as they burst. There was nothing familiar here, he could not feel the familiar loving currents of electricity begging his fingertips to tame and enslave them. There was no information running up his arms, no swarms of bits tingling the base of his ancient young spine, just the faint, almost imperceptible electrical energy of the primordial plant life. All he could feel in his hands was the slimy blood of the vines mixing with the redder juice from the cuts on his own hands, and all that nagged at the base of his skull was a leaden, animal fear: the kind he had not felt since the day of the surge. Even in the murderous tunnels of Bespophus he'd felt no fear. All he'd had to do there was place his hands against a wall and know he had millions of volts at his disposal. Here in the jungle he was deaf (obviously) and blind in the dark, and swinging towards an unknown danger over which he had no power. Suddenly, the light he'd been moving towards disappeared. He stopped, hanging in the darkness, waiting for the lamp to reappear. It did not. Instead he *heard* the scream. It was the first thing he'd heard since the surge.

★

The man in the doorway was bearded, with sunken eyes. He towered over them. 'What are you doing aboard my ship?' Lenore retreated into the waiting arms of Miss Fritzacopple, but the botanist did not retreat.

'Don't worry,' said Fritzacopple. She could feel the small girl's heart beating faster than a sparrow's. 'He's not real.'

'Exactly what do you mean I'm not real?' said the captain. 'You'd better show some respect when you're on my ship!'

Outside, the children laughed brightly. 'We told you so,' they cried. 'You made him angry. You won't like him when he's angry.'

*

DANGER!
DANGER!
DANGER!
DANGER!
DANGER!
DANGER!

Roberto had swung towards the screaming voice, then got lost again. He was lost inside the canopy, and inside his own terrible silence. But now he could see red lights blinking faintly. He pushed off from the vine and drifted down. He drifted down through the darkness towards them.

*

'We just want to leave quietly now,' said Fritzacopple. 'We don't want trouble.'

'Well, you've got trouble, missy,' said the man. 'And plenty of it.' Then he strode from the room, ducking under the low door, slamming his hand on a big red button as he left. There was a sound of terrible gears, gears that hadn't moved for a long time, and the door rolled shut.

'You can't escape now!'

Miss Fritzacopple leaped for the door but it was too late.

'You horrible spy! You'll be trapped, trapped for ever!' The children were peering in the windows with their liquid eyes.

Fritzacopple felt the air in the cockpit tighten, felt her head lighten. 'He's draining the room,' said the botanist, as her body grew heavy. She heard Lenore say, 'Miss Lady, don't die! I don't want to be alone.' Tears filled the girl's dead eyes. Before she passed out Fritzacopple saw Lenore lift her snotty nose and sniff the air, smile and say, 'Roberto. He's coming.'

DANGER!

DANGER!

DANGER!

DANGER!

DANGER!

DANGER!

MELANCHOLY AND SADNESS

Space sickness, loneliness, melancholy, despair, cabin fever, paranoia, these are the diseases of the mind which affect, to some extent, every space traveller. It is not natural for a person to leave the familiar gravity of their home. And when they do, the things that happen to their minds are sometimes catastrophic. And if you think these are personal diseases, that they are non-contagious, then you're mistaken. These mind-fevers can be passed from person to person as easy as lice or plague. When plague starts to appear on his ship the captain knows they'll have a devil's job getting rid of it; but when space sickness starts to spread through her crew a captain knows she's probably doomed.

★

DANGER!
DANGER!
DANGER!
DANGER!
DANGER!
DANGER!
The door opened again with a terrible scream, widened, then changed its mind and began to close, then stopped halfway. A lawn chair was thrown into the gap. It buckled, but held, and soon the

iron gears ceased their anguished cries and fell into a low moan of acceptance. Fritzacopple woke from near asphyxiation to see Roberto's face in the doorway, caked in mud and dead insects.

★

The blue beacons grew large in the mist and, with them, silhouettes and low voices. Soon the lights of the approaching party illuminated a boy, a giant and an old man standing on an oozing, wriggling pile of spider crabs. A slender figure stepped forward.

SWAMP FOLK

She was a woman, or at least a kind of woman. Tall with pale, greenish, jelly-like skin suffused with glittery specks, and black saucer-eyes. Stepping out of the mist she addressed them in an unknown language, in a voice that sounded like water running over the eyes of a flute, and they stood patiently as she spoke. She made wide, grand gestures, and pointed to the distance – to the darkness. Her party was six: three women and three men. They almost looked like people. Almost. They wore strange clothes made from a shiny leather, and each had a long, three-pronged spear – like a fork for turning hay.

'How very odd they are,' said Fabrigas.

At this point, Roberto returned on foot with Lenore and Fritzacopple, throwing up his arms as he approached as if to say, 'Women! I ask you.' He was covered from head to foot in jungle filth.

'Why did you run off like that?' said Lambestyo to Fritzacopple. 'We were all worried to sickness.'

'You worry too much. I'm a big girl.'

'You are. I see you are. Which is why you should know better.'

The botanist rolled her eyes.

Soon Carrofax appeared. 'Sir, you'll be interested to hear about the place you're in. You could write a book.'

'Yes, yes, just tell me what this woman is saying.'

It turned out that the woman was saying a lot of things, and Carrofax translated as best he could, and Fabrigas conveyed his translation to the group. They were very lucky to be alive. The spider crabs were attracted to their lamplight. If they hadn't cast their lamps aside the deadly crabs would never have stopped, and the visitors would have found themselves slashing at the creatures from atop a pile of remains a mile high. They are nice in soup, the crabs. Several of the strangers stepped forward to put some into sacks.

And the spider crabs, it turned out, were one of the least deadly things that could have been attracted to their brassy, alien light. Giant hornets patrolled the area, as did schools of flying leeches. Poison-whiskered catfish hid in the mud. There were giant death-slugs that could swallow you, digest you, then emit you as a fine and fragrant powder. The woman bent and scooped up a handful of powder, let it run through her fingers. It sparkled in the lamplight.

'Also nice in soups,' said Carrofax. 'She's going to take us back to the compound.' Her limpid eyes restlessly roamed the darkness. Her name was Kandy.

'So what are we supposed to do, just trust them?' hissed the captain as he roughly wrapped a piece of rag around a deep wound in his arm.

'I'm sure we'll be fine,' said the old man. 'I think you worry too much.'

'Is that so?' said the captain. 'Well, maybe you worry too little. Maybe it's my job to worry, I have children to look after. We were only supposed to go out for supplies.'

Fabrigas frowned. 'Why are you so moody today?'

'I'm not moody. You are moody.' The old man went to put a friendly hand on his shoulders and the pilot said, 'Don't touch me.'

They trekked away through the darkness, the rescuers' sure-footed feet slapping slickly on the earth, the visitors stumbling and lurching out for vines that in some cases turned out to be snakes. 'They were a group on their way to a folk-music symposium when they lost their way and were pulled into the orbit of this world,' explained Carrofax as they were taken through a dense patch of jungle. 'They lost their navigation systems . . . solar storm . . . everything black . . . somehow ended up here . . . did the best with what they had . . . bug attacks . . . captain eaten by giant slug . . . mysterious stranger . . . it's all pretty routine really. But now look!' As they reached the top of a shallow rise a fort emerged from the mist, suspended, it seemed, in the palm of Kandy's hand. The fort comprised stepped palisades of sharpened logs with a shining silver dome in the centre. When they approached, silhouettes hurried out to pull the gates open, but not a word was exchanged; the place was quiet as a tomb. The other residents all looked like Kandy. Then the rescue group vanished and Kandy took them on through the compound.

They were taken into a bare barn with low benches and a fire pit in the centre. Soon, a group of youngsters scuttled in with wooden bowls and clumps of dried moss. They pulled up when they saw the strangers, but Kandy gave a few gruff blips and they began to shyly dab away at their guests' cuts and crab bites. All except one child, who could not be made to approach the hulking figure of the bosun. Kandy took the bowl and tended to his wounds herself, speaking as she did.

'She says they will look after all our weapons until we come to leave. They will be kept in a secure barn. They can't have heavily armed strangers wandering around their camp. I suggest you agree, as a gesture of goodwill, but keep your hidden weapons. You'll be given sleeping quarters for tonight. It's too dangerous to take you back to the ship right now. There is another tribe in the area who will have seen you arrive. They'll likely attack in great numbers . . .' Carrofax yawned. '. . . Excuse me. She says they are savage creatures . . . they move silently, like a pack of wild beasts, and if they should catch you they'll make you wish for death . . . etc. So there's that as well.'

Their quarters were clean and comfortable: a room of bunks each separated by a screen made from vines. 'Well, I suppose after all we've been through we deserve a short rest,' said Fabrigas as he tested his vine mattress.

'I still don't like it at all,' said Lambestyo, standing warily near the door. 'We need to get back to our ship. We shouldn't have followed them here. You're too impulsive sometimes. We should steal weapons and bust our way out. You've always been impulsive.'

'Nonsense,' said the old man as he lazily picked a piece of crab shell from his beard. 'You always say that. If anything you're too cautious. Now come and sort out your sleeping area – you'll be too tired to do it later.'

FEAST FIRST

It was a miraculous community these Marshians had built. With no way to generate electrical energy they'd had to be inventive. They used the constant rain to turn wheels. They harnessed luminous ferns for light. They used swamp gas for heat. They had domesticated a number of local creatures. Once a week they'd rub furry rats together to generate enough static charge to power up their distress beacon, which sent a stream of blips into the heavens in a vain request for deliverance.

They were taken to the feasting hall for, predictably, a feast. A hunting party had killed a slug. It was a sickening white flesh, a meat which had had all the colour and nutrients leeched out of it. The creatures, too, who sat at the tables, looked to have had their life force drained; their complexion resembled the sad old faces in portraits faded by the sun. They looked like once-grand splashes of life and colour dissolved into listless puddles of tinted water. There were bowls of green algae stew, rows of glistening marsh oysters and platters of steamed spider crabs. A special table had been set aside for the guests.

'But what I want to know,' said the old-beard to no one, 'is do they know where exactly they are?'

'Oh, I could tell you where you are if you wish, sir.' His butler was teasing him mercilessly.

Their hosts were shovelling food into their fishy mouths with great abandon; the noise was tremendous.

'I don't want you to tell me; I want to know if *they* know,' he said to the air.

'It hasn't come up yet. Please let me tell you.'

'No!' the old man shouted – apparently to an antlered skull hanging on the wall. He realised that their hosts had paused in their munchings to blink at him with their huge, sad eyes. Then they heard the sound of drums in the distance, deep and warlike, and the guests paused also. Kandy stood and raised both arms to soothe them. That's when Fabrigas looked up and noticed another figure at the leaders' table. It was so strange not to have noticed a man like this earlier – if indeed a man was what he was. He was not beguilingly aquatic like his brethren. He was more troll-like, dirty like an orphan, with an outsized head and tiny, twinkling, moleish eyes. He stood on scrawny legs below a potted stomach, never taking his eyes off the beautiful young Miss Fritzacopple, and he spoke to them in their own language.

'Don't be scared of the drums, humans. Those drums come from the other tribe. The Ubuntu are primitive, aggressive, but harmless so long as we're inside the compound. I am Skyorax. I am the keeper of this most modest society, and servant to our master, the colonel. He regrets to say he'll not be able to see you during your stay. He has many more important things to contend with. He sends his best regards, but urges you not to disrupt the lives of these kind and simple country people, to be impulsive, or to . . .' he turned his twinkling eyes on the captain, 'bust your way out.' His eyes skipped back once more to examine the botanist from head to boot. 'I think you will be very comfortable here. And now I must be getting back to the colonel. This is a very busy season for us. Yes. It is the breeding season.' He let his words hang in the air for an age before Lambestyo coughed into his hand and said, 'Well then.' Skyorax took one last lingering look across the group, nodded once, and walked slowly out of the hall.

'And then there's him,' said Carrofax.

'So they have a master? A god of some kind? Not this Calligulus we've been hearing about?'

'Oh no. The colonel is a man. You won't quite believe which man he is. If I told you who it was, you'd die of surprise. He lives in an underground bunker in the centre of the compound. He calls himself Colonel, although his own people call him the Worm. At least they do when Skyorax isn't near. Don't trust either of them.'

'You don't have to remind me not to trust people.'

A cloud of frightened yelps drifted in from the main compound. They heard a gurgling roar, like a bassoon full of water. They left their meals and hurried out into the compound where some of their hosts were tracking huge shapes moving up the side of the dome. Soon Kandy was approaching them, palms raised, burbling. 'She says it's just a minor slug attack,' said Carrofax, 'nothing to worry about. She says to go back to enjoying your meal.'

'I think we'll wait here, thank you,' said Fabrigas, and Kandy looked mystified. The two shapes were inching their way slowly up the dome, stopping to release shrill cries, the whole structure groaning under their weight. They were as big as elephants, and even in the gloom it was possible to see their lumpy hides, their horrible round mouths with rows of slender teeth. The hosts were firing spiked balls from slingshots through the shell of the dome, but the shiny stars were simply bouncing off the beasts' rough hide and falling back upon the heads of the villagers.

'The crown of the dome is the weakest point,' said Fabrigas. 'If they make it to the top it will break.' And as if on cue the dome let out a cracking sound. 'I think it's time to put an end to this,' said the bosun. He casually wandered over and picked up a three-pronged spear, weighing it carefully in his huge paw. He sized up the creature above him, and flung the spear casually into the darkness. It passed through the thin skin of the dome and out into the night. In the distance a bird cried out.

'That's fine spearmanship,' called the captain.

The bosun ignored him. He picked up another spear, tossed it three times in his hand, then flung the pole with all his strength. It hit the lower beast directly in the mouth-hole. The slug squirmed and gave a pulse of low booms.

'You made it angry,' said Lambestyo. 'Good work.'

Then they all leaped in the air as they heard a slug's shriek from right behind them, and when they spun round they were aghast to find that the cry had come not from another slug, but from their tiny, green friend. The two slugs paused in the heights, then cried out in unison, and Lenore replied again with a long shrill wail. Then the larger slug rolled back down the dome to earth, and shrugged away into the darkness. The other beast gave one more cry, then shuffled off after its mate.

No one really had a thing to say. Except Lenore.

'It is the breeding season, you know. They is a pair on their honeysmoon. They came here as this place looks to them just likes a gigantuan slug. I told them it was a house. It was a giant mistake, and they are sorry. Did they not mean to frighten you? Yes. And I said we was sorry for throwing sticks at them. What a day!'

Again, no one really had words. Lenore turned and walked off.

Kandy approached, muttering as she bustled them towards their sleeping barn. 'She says they're attracted to noise. With all the fuss since your arrival they must have become curious. That's why people around here don't speak much.' And then, as if to emphasise her point, she walked off.

*

Later that night, as he lay on his bed, on top of his covers, Fabrigas was assailed by noise. He heard, with his sublime earholes, the heavy hooting of some soon-to-be-mating birds, the beat of large wings flying over, the huff and snort of the honeymooning beasts wallowing in their bog a mile away, the titter of the rodents small enough to clamber through the holes in the huts, and in the distance, the ceaseless and hypnotic drumming, mingled with a million other sounds: bull cries, fearful shrieks, throaty rattles, sleepy toots and bleeps. But these comforting and terrifying sounds were almost impossible to concentrate on when he had a voice in each ear.

'Master, they keep pushing back the time to return us to our ship. Now it's after the so-called full-moon festival. If it's too dangerous for you to be out there then what of the others on the *Necronaut*? What desperate state must they be in? I could tell you if you like, because I know exactly what state they're in.'

And in his other ear, a less familiar voice . . .

'It's me, Judy. I'm from the saucer craft. I saved your life today. I whispered in your ear to tell you to put out your lamps.' The voice was like an echo carried on the wind. 'You need to leave here, it's very dangerous. I will help you, but you need to do something for me.' Fabrigas rolled onto his side and clamped his giant hands around his ears, but he could block out neither voice.

'Sir, are you listening? I'm concerned that if we wait too long we might lose the *Necronaut*. Then where would we be?'

'One of your people went into our ship and took my journal. I need you to destroy it. That plant lady took it. I don't trust her. A girl shouldn't read another girl's diary, don't you agree?'

'Sir, if we just *demand* to be returned to our ship they might listen. I could teach you the rudiments of their language.'

'And I need you to help put my family to rest. I know you can help, I just know you can. And I will help you.'

Until finally Fabrigas sat up and said, 'That's enough! I can only handle one imaginary person in my head!'

Even the calls from the swamps seemed to pause. A few seconds later the captain appeared around his screen. 'Are you having a scary dream?' he said. 'Do you need a night lamp?'

'I'm fine. It's nothing.' Fabrigas fell back on the bed and his captain shrugged and left, and once more he heard the orchestra of the night grind to life.

'Well, I hardly think I'm imaginary,' said Carrofax.

From the diary of Miss Maria Fritzacopple

This is the first opportunity I've had to write since I was forced to make the crossing with these people. We have been lost in a jungle of carnivorous plants, and now are trapped on a mysterious, low-gravity planet populated by dangerous beasts and swamp-ghosts. I have no explanation for the emanations I saw around the crashed saucer craft yesterday. The most likely explanation is that they are some kind of holographic security system. But that kind of technology would be far too advanced for the saucer craft we found. It makes no sense. But what does, lately? This trip is forcing me to reassess my ideas about almost everything.

And now we are prisoners in a village of primitive marsh folk. We haven't met their leader yet, but if his hideous troll-servant Skyorax is anything to go by we are in trouble.

The journal I found aboard the saucer craft is very interesting and casts a different light on the fate of the crew. It opens with a warning: 'Judy's Property. If you're reading this, and you aren't me, DON'T.'

The entries themselves are mostly the musings of a young woman: 'No one understands me, I hate X, I love Y, Daddy is so mean, the doctor is an ogre, little brothers are the worst.'

But then, on Day 1497:

'We've got so little food that Daddy says we might have to eat the starfishes!!! Eat them? They're my little friends! I'd rather starve.'

Then, Day 1511:

'Daddy just gets meaner every day. He frightens me some-times.'

Day 1519:

'They ate them! All of them! Except Gloria. They'll never find Gloria.'

The journal had a live starfish resting inside the cover – Gloria, I suppose. I have given it to Lenore to play with so she will stop asking silly questions, but perhaps I will show it to the old man.

Now I must go because I hear someone lurking around our barn. If it's that Skyorax I think I will die.

STARLIGHT TUBE

The night was a ghostly den of mist and shadows – much like the day – and the moon hung low and silver. They had spent another day confined, bored, to the compound. There had been another lavish feast that night – a lavish feast on top of a lavish lunch on top of a sumptuous breakfast – and now Roberto couldn't sleep because his belly was swollen. He poked it with one finger and it gurgled angrily. Little slugs. That's what they'd become if they carried on like this. A band of little slugs. He sat by the window, staring out into the darkness. If his ears worked he would have heard the night commanded by the bosun's epic snoring, and he would have heard that the drumming had stopped, briefly. They had all stood out by the cage and listened to the drums. Roberto had placed his hand on the wet earth and raised an eyebrow.

Something moved in the darkness. A shadow passed with quick and easy steps. It was her, he knew, the local girl who'd bathed his wounds the day before. She had brought him his food the first night and when he'd smiled she'd looked at four different spots on the ground. The previous day during the slug attack he'd approached her. She'd stood by one of the cabins, one webbed hand on the wall, looking frightened. While the bosun went about his business, Roberto had taken a silver coin from his pocket, held it before the girl's astonished face, and in a flash made it disappear. The girl had jumped. Then she gave a quick flurry of blinks and scuttled off. He knew that later she would find the coin in her pocket and, he hoped, be pleased. She wouldn't even realise that it was a coin from another universe. She wouldn't know, he mused, that the boy who'd given it to her was a powerful master-being whose head contained a universe of data. The coin trick was only in his brain because someone, somewhere, sometime, had sent an instructive illustration of it to a friend. Of course, Roberto couldn't have known, even with the spinning galaxies of information trapped inside his skull, that the flurry of blinks the girl had given him was a coded message: 'You and your friends must run away. Now. You don't know how much danger you're in.' He instead took his information from *Hazmatt's Guide to Romantic Etiquette* – a few chapters of which were lodged somewhere in the recesses of his brain – which told him that when a woman flutters her lashes at you it means she likes you.

Now she was walking quickly past their sleeping barn. It was a sign, he thought. She was giving him a message by walking past his barn – although, to be fair, *Hazmatt's* mentioned nothing about flirtatious walk-bys. To be sure he took his Magic Eighth from his pocket, shook it, and observed the quivering message. He stood for a few moments, flicking the gems in his pocket with the tips of his fingers. Then he saluted the moon, then leaped from the window and into the night.

*

Fabrigas was also puzzled by the presence of the moon, and troubled by his stomach, and bothered by the voices in each ear. He'd gone for a walk to soothe his system, but it hadn't worked, so he'd decided to go back to the sleeping barn and ask Miss Fritzacopple to hand over Judy's journal. Before he'd even arrived his powerful ears had picked up the nightmarish hiss of Skyorax. 'This is a very dangerous place. No one makes it out alive without our assistance. Our beloved leader grants favours, but they must be earned. Tell us about this girl, the one who talks to giant worms. Who is she? Where did she come from? Where is she going?'

'I don't know a thing about her. I can't help you. And I'm confident I can make it out of here alive without your help.'

'Who is she? Where did she come from? Where is she going?' Skyorax said more urgently.

'I told you, I have no idea.'

'My master begs to differ. The colonel thinks you very much know who this girl is. It is a mysterious group you have. But they could be useful to us. You should ensure that when the time comes you are positioned well.'

'Positioned well?'

'This is a community which needs women with your . . . fertile qualities. My master could make sure you were treated like a queen. You would be favoured above all others in his care.'

'I don't much care for his favour. Now if you'll excuse me, I was just getting ready to sleep.'

'To sleep, yes. But I would not close both eyes if I were you. We have been patient with you. But there's a price for delay. Every hour you refuse to cooperate you fall lower in his estimation. Delay too long and you'll be no better than worm-food.'

'It's time for you to leave. Don't make me ask again.'

'Or what? This is my camp. I am the keeper. I go where I like. You, however, are in a corner, yes?'

'This lady has asked very nicely if you would leave her to prepare for bed.' Fabrigas's monstrous frame cast a shadow over the troll-man.

'Ah, your knight is here to save you. I will leave you. But if I were you I'd look to your team. Your boy is about to go horribly astray.'

'Which boy?'

Skyorax smiled. 'Take your pick, old man.' He left. Miss Fritzacopple looked sheepishly at him. 'Thank you. I didn't know what he was capable of.'

'Did you not? And the journal you took from the saucer craft? Were you not going to show me that?' The botanist couldn't disguise her surprise. 'There's a young she-phantom who very much wants me to retrieve it for her. Please give it to me.' The botanist fetched the slim book from a hiding place under her bed. 'What is this place?' she said.

'I don't know. But I'm willing to bet it has a few more hidden surprises.' He flicked rapidly through the book. The botanist could not believe how fast he absorbed its contents. 'So they ate the starfish. How very intriguing.'

That's when Carrofax appeared and said, 'Your boy is in trouble, or near enough.'

'Which one?'

'Like the man said, take your pick.'

*

In the centre of the compound there was a large barn, like an aircraft hangar, and at the front was a hatch leading underground. The barn and the hatch were special, Roberto knew, because they were always under guard. Light oozed from the slits in the walls and the shuttered windows: the bluish light of the luminescent ferns they'd found around the swamps. But Roberto didn't know entering these build-ings was strictly forbidden, because he hadn't heard Kandy's speech, as translated by Carrofax, as recited by Fabrigas. He was thrice removed from that important piece of information. So when the girl tripped lightly down the steps and inside the basement room he'd ducked into the shadows, and when the guard stepped around the corner he'd made his move. The door to the basement was protected by a lock ripped from a starship. It had a government-level encryp-tion code. It took the boy four seconds to crack it.

Behind the door were steps leading down to a long passage with four doors on either side, one door at the far end. The girl had disappeared. He tried the first door and it opened into a small room. The lighting was dim and the fern lamps were coated in amber. On one table stood an array of medical equipment. On another was a row of tanks and in those tanks, suspended in fluid, was a collection of creatures. Some almost looked like people. Almost. Others were monsters who looked like spiders crossed with crabs. He touched a finger to one of the tanks and the creature inside snapped its claws.

The next room was stacked with disused navigation equipment from a ship, some busted, some stripped for parts, and in the next (and this was very surprising) was a full-grown apple tree growing under solar lamps rigged to a ship's battery. Roberto knew every object he saw by scanning images from the messages in his database – even though he'd never seen any of the real objects before. He'd come to know the whole universe from inside a pod the size of a taxi carriage. When the surge came, Roberto had been practising his coin tricks. The mechanics of routing could go on without him. He could sleep, or eat, or think about girls (which he was doing more and more often these days, though at that time he hadn't even met a real one). The images of girls and geese and a million other things all came through his brain. All the routing happened in his subconscious mind. It was something he could do, but not explain.

And that was why, as he pulled away a perfect red fruit and examined it, he knew exactly what he was looking at. 'Apple.' Or, 'leatherberry', as it was sometimes called. He took a bite and his mouth exploded, a cascade of flavour scattering stars of pleasure through his brain. He had never in his life eaten anything like it. 'You shouldn't eat this,' said a voice behind him in a broken version of his language, but he didn't jump, because he couldn't hear the voice. 'Them are the colonel's apples,' she said.

*

Fabrigas had wandered out to the edge of the compound in search of Roberto and had quickly become distracted by the moon. He took out his telescope and held it to his eye. But he really couldn't make sense of it. It was a round, silver blur. At that moment the truth of where they were and what that moon was hit him with the force of a punch. How could he have been so stupid? But he had no time to dwell on it, because right then he heard a voice in his ear say, 'You read it. You read my journal. How could you do this to me?'

'I needed to know what happened to your family. It's the only way I can help you. Now I know what needs to be done.'

'Destroy it. Burn the diary right now.'

'Here?'

'Yes.'

'Very well.' The old man took out the girl's journal, produced a small acetylene torch from his magical cloak, and in seconds had incinerated the book.

'Thank you. Now I will help you. The boy you're looking for is under the barn in the centre of the compound. It is extremely dangerous in there.' And then the voice vanished. Assuming that Roberto couldn't have gone down into the guarded basement, Fabrigas stalked around the barn above. It was large, dark, and had a set of wide doors like an airship hangar. The walls had a gap of a foot at the bottom. Fabrigas rolled under. Now he lay in the darkness, listening for movement, but he could only feel a large rat scurry past his ear. He felt for a small penlight he kept hidden, he turned it on, he gasped.

★

Roberto gasped too when he turned to find her standing in the corridor, but then the girl ran off, and when he put his head out he saw the last door closing.

DOOR 3: More things from a ship. Furniture, fittings, an old movie projector and screen. Inside the projector was a bright fern. There was a cavity with a small wheel in which a creature could run, and a little hook on which tempting food could be spiked. He gave the wheel a spin and saw, projected upon the wall, a man – a prince – walking proudly down the stairs from a ship. The prince was receiving a royal welcome. He shook hands with hosts in fine clothing. People cheered. He knew the prince's name. He knew from the messages in his brain.

DOOR 4: Some kind of war room. There was a table laid with a map of the area. Roberto recognised the fort, the swamp nearby. There was a spot marked with a large 'X' and next to it was the title 'NEW SHIP'. There was a large area, heavily marked, and beside it was the word 'UBUNTU'. He scanned his entire database, through all the trillions of bits of information stored in his head, but he could find no meaning for the word 'UBUNTU'. Some information, granted, might have been lost in the surge.

Back when the surge came Roberto had felt a white-hot pop inside his head, the smell of burning, and a terrible silence. His pod had quickly filled with smoke. He'd stumbled out into the hall, mad with terror, seen the smoke pouring out from under the doors of the other pods. Inside the first pod he'd found a small, limp body with lolling tongue and blood trickling from its nose. And in the next pod the same, and the next. He'd never seen any of these boys, but they were, he noticed, just like him. Alarm lights were winking at him through the smoke in the corridor and he could see the hammer blurring against the bell. It was at that moment he knew he was deaf. He also knew he had less than a minute. There were doors – these would be covered – and a fire hatch – this too would have a shock-trooper at the end – but there was one final way to the outside, a light-tube: a long tunnel roughly the width of his shoulders that carried starlight in from outside. He knew that to get inside this tube, where the pure, unfiltered starlight streamed, was suicide. He would be burned to a crisp in seconds. He could hear voices approaching.

In their pods they had a panel containing an emergency sack, and a flask of water. In the event of a 'sun-leak' they were instructed to crawl into these silver sacks and wait. This, of course, was pointless. A boy inside one of these sacks had probably four minutes at most until he was cooked, and it would take the fire team ten minutes to arrive. The 'cleaning' teams arrived much quicker. The shock troops would soon be there in their black suits and gas masks, their handcuffs and hoods, and there would be no bargaining. He could feel their boot-steps growing louder. They ran in sync.

Roberto had zipped the sack up to his neck and prised away the seals on the edge of the UV shield across the cover of the light-tube. He'd put the water flask under his chin and zipped the sack over his head. Then he'd slipped into the starlight tube. It wasn't easy to open the UV cover with his hands inside the sack, but he'd managed.

The heat was instantly unbearable, far worse than he'd imagined. He'd felt his hair singe and the sweat leave his body in mad fright.

Outside he'd felt the drum of boot-steps enter, searching the pods. Two minutes, he thought. That's if they didn't leave a guard behind.

He counted, 38, 39, 40. He felt the sweat sizzling under his legs. He was drenched in his own water. The sack was filling with steam, smoke and gases. He felt the beat of each pod slamming shut as it was searched, he marked the time. It might as well have been hours. He saw a burning sun, a tube descending, a ladder leading up, a heat so strong it pushed the tiniest pieces of him apart. He was a cloud, a vapour, a lovely rain, he was dying.

Soon he felt the boot-steps leave and the outer door slam shut. The whole place would be in lockdown. There was no escape.

He rolled out of the tube and hit the floor hard. He clawed away the silver skin and emerged like a newborn, slick and tearful, his face twisted into a horrible grimace.

When he'd mopped the sweat and tears from his eyes with his knuckles, he saw the trooper at the end of the corridor, in a black mask and holding a long club. He was far too short to be a guard.

The trooper said, 'Don't run. I'm here to help.' The voice seemed to come from inside his head. 'I work for a group called Dark Hand. We've come to rescue you.'

'We have a job for you,' they told him. 'We need you to help us stop a war,' they said. 'We need you to use the things inside your head to stop a war,' they said, 'and we will teach you how. This is a secret battle,' they told him. 'It is a battle to stop a war to end all wars. We need you to go to the Worlds' Fair. You will meet a girl there. Have you ever met a girl before?'

Roberto had not.

★

DOOR 5: Drawers filled with preserved butterflies and insects, anatomical drawings and instruments. Roberto pocketed a small scalpel; he hid it in his sock. A shadow flashed by in the corridor behind.

DOOR 6: Weapons of all kinds.

DOOR 7: Locked.

DOOR 8: A bare room with a stack of old books.

Roberto went back out into the corridor and considered the final door.

★

It was a ship. Fabrigas ran his light along its blonde flank, from its steam rudder to the tip of its bow, back to the name, shining in gold letters: the *Prince Albert*. 'Well I never,' he whispered. 'Well I never, ever.' It was a small galleon, the hull smooth and familiar. It had been seriously damaged, perhaps in a crash like the one they'd been in, and repaired crudely. The far side of the ship had been virtually melted away by sunlight. He climbed the ladder through the docking bay and walked the deck under the triple-reinforced glass roof. It was a miracle of engineering, the spaceship. Something which looked as delicate as a flower bulb, but which could withstand impacts from space-junk, cannon fire, and smashing into moons and planets at fantastic speed. He had often mused that the ships they used to sail the heavens were so strange and miraculous that they seemed like foreign objects, like devices gifted to their species by a mysterious alien culture.

He wandered the ship, a man in a waking dream. What madness was this? He went to the navigation room and was not surprised to find old tools, decades out of date. Much of the fittings and equipment had been stripped from the ship. In the living quarters he found personal items. A man owned this ship, and from the items he could tell he was of royal descent, and from the line of Queen Gargoylas. He found a repeating watch with the cipher of Gargoylas X, a ring with the cameo of a kneeling warrior, a garter badge and a dress sword.

On the desk he found a letter.

Dear friends and family,

By the time you read this I will be dead. As the youngest member of this most royal family I have come increasingly to feel as if I have no place. I feel that my views are never heeded, and I have come to tire of the duties I am expected to perform. For what, I ask, do we do these things? For what purpose are our feeble deeds in such a mad and violent universe? It is such a black and brutal place that I see no longer a point in dwelling on within it.

Thus have I schemed to pilot my favourite ship into a sun.

I wish you all well. Weep not for me, for I died long ago.

Junior

Fabrigas put down the letter and left the suite. This was as strange a thing as ever he'd witnessed. The privy beside the prince's suite was unlocked. He pushed open the door, but there was nothing in there that surprised him.

*

The door at the end of the corridor. Roberto touched the door and felt the crude latch submit. Even he was astonished by what he saw behind it.

A BURST OF VERMILION

Please remember, there is no limit to the number of times you can access your Little Page of Calmness (LPoC), page 620.

★

'Oh, hello,' said the man behind the last door. 'Is it seven already?' But Roberto couldn't hear his voice: genteel, boyish. His voice, the voice of someone who does all the talking, did not need to make itself sound interesting. 'Sugar,' the man said to the girl Roberto had followed here, 'get this boy a drink.' The girl, whose name was Lulabelle, obeyed. Roberto was in a room: soft cushions, a table covered with partly nibbled fruit, sofa seating ripped from the withdrawing room of a ship and thrown in the corners upon which several Marshian youngsters lounged. A wall hung with tapestries, all austere, yet wet with colour, a man in the centre of it all with sparkling eyes. He had full lips, impossibly smooth skin – but for visible sunlight burns on the left side of his face. He was a young man with longish hair and the makings of a fine beard. He wore an expensive leisure suit which showed signs of wear, and his shirt was open to the third button so his chest hair bloomed. He lay back upon a pile of cushions, one hand hanging limp, the other lightly gripping his lapel. He was not at all afraid to let the silence hang. It seemed an age before he took a sip from his glass and said, 'I have heard a lot about you. I am sure you've heard of me.' Lulabelle brought back a tray with two glasses of burning red liquid on it. The man reached up languidly to exchange his empty glass for a fresh one. He sipped, he savoured. 'Please, sit.' He gestured to a blood-red cushion. The boy, interpreting his gesture, shook his shaggy head. 'No? Will you at least have something to eat? Drink?' He gestured to a bowl beside him which seemed to be filled to the brim with red worms. They squirmed in the bowl. 'No? Suit yourself.' The man lifted a single worm from the bowl and let it dangle on his tongue before he chomped it. He took another sip and licked his upper lip. The Marshian youths were motionless. The red liquid shone. The wind outside was growing stronger, carrying from far away the sound of drums. Lulabelle stood to one side, green with fear. Or perhaps just green. Her skin sparkled. She was blinking madly at him. Roberto could see the tray she held shaking, and the bubbles in the glass dancing. The colonel squinted at Roberto, then turned to Lulabelle and said, 'Thank you, sugar heart, you have done well. You can leave now.' She left quickly.

Roberto couldn't hear what the man was saying, and his lip-reading abilities were minimal, but Carrofax was there, watching, invisible and helpless from the corner. The master's teeth moved up and down. Big, icy teeth.

'So.' The man adjusted his position on the cushions. 'You are the boy with fire in his fingers. The boy who brings trouble.' Roberto recognised the last word, 'bubble', and he observed the bubbles dancing in the bloodish liquid in the glass the man nursed. Roberto learned lip-reading from a manual which had flown into his mental database, but he wished now that he'd practised more when he'd had the chance. There was something about the way those red lips pulled back across his perfect white teeth that was frightening. The other youths who lay on the sofas and cushions looked stupefied. They were limp-limbed, dead-eyed, the breeze which found its way in through the gaps in the barn-room walls indolently flicked their hair and clothing. Roberto touched a finger to the scalpel hidden in his sock. It was there if he needed it.

*

Fabrigas examined the propulsion system and found a perfectly ordinary magnetic engine. So there was no conceivable way the ship could have, as it appeared to have done, drifted calmly through dimensions. There was obviously more to this ship than met the eye. Carrofax appeared beside him and said, 'Your boy is in trouble. Fetch that starfish and come on.'

'Starfish?' Fabrigas peered down into the vents. There was an alien object attached to the gears of the engine, down where the vacuum tubes gave way to the clockwork mess of cogs and wheels. 'A starfish on the inside of a ship?'

'Yes, yes, it's a starfish,' said Carrofax. 'Just take it and I'll explain later.'

Fabrigas peeled the sea creature from the engine. He shone his light on it, trying to make out the strange markings, but he couldn't. If only he had more light. Then, as if to answer his prayers, the ship's lights came on.

'So, you have found the colonel's ship,' said Skyorax. 'Ah well, it is nothing that he did not want you to see. All is just as he planned.'

*

The beating of the drums was louder now and it filled the air with long, lingering murmurs.

A wind was rushing through the valley, throaty and threatening, and with it came a low, bubbling moan.

'I've become good at spotting bad apples,' said the man. He slowly shut his eyes and spoke as if he needed to meditate carefully upon every word. 'You, my boy, are a bad apple. My own master would have picked you out right away, tossed you in the mud.' He opened his eyes. 'But the thing about this community is that we recycle everything, even our bruised fruit.' Roberto wasn't following any of it. He planned to run, as soon as this crazy man closed his eyes again. But the man seemed to sense this, and he fixed Roberto with a burning glare. 'Do you understand what is happening here? Do you know how important this project is?' Roberto had seen his face many times before. He'd seen his photo beside his name and his name attached to orders for terrible things. He knew what he was capable of. 'They tried to do away with me. But I survived. I'm building my army. Ready to return as conqueror.' Roberto backed slowly towards the door, just as it opened. He felt a hand upon his shoulder, and he wheeled round to find Fabrigas. The old man was flanked by two Marshians, and behind them lurked the menacing Skyorax. 'It all went just to plan, Lord,' he slithered.

'So it seems,' said Fabrigas. 'We can't stay long, Albert. I just came to tell you we were leaving.'

'Oh, but you've only just got here,' said Albert. 'Surely you can stay for one last meal.'

*

In the sleeping barn, the wind was ramming icy spikes through the gaps in the walls. Miss Fritzacopple woke and found Lenore staring out the window. Ghostly. The wife of the sailor lost at sea.

'What are you doing staring out the window? You can't even see. Go back to bed.'

'Something is happening,' replied the girl. 'Can feel it in my airs.'

'Oh, nonsense,' said the botanist. 'It's just the wind making you moody.' But then she saw Roberto's empty cot. 'Well. Perhaps he just got hungry in the night.' She placed her hand on her own swollen belly.

'Hungry. Yes,' said Lenore. 'But for what kind of dish does he hunger?'

INTO THE SUN

'So. You know who I am. Was.'

'Yes. You are Albert, heir and prince, colonel in the Royal Navy. You went mad and flew your ship into a sun. It seems, however, that you missed your target.'

'Colonel,' said Skyorax, 'I have done as you asked, I have lured them here. Give me the fancy woman – as a treat. Or just give me the boy!'

'Fool!' cried the colonel, and he flung his glass across the room at the man-troll. It smashed against the wall, leaving a burst of bloody vermilion, and Skyorax cowered in fright. 'I'm sorry, master, I'm sorry!'

'Get out of my sight, all of you.'

Skyorax slunk from the room, the guards followed, and the colonel turned his attention back to his prisoners. 'I apologise. Skyorax is criminally impertinent. I rescued him from the mud, taught him the names for things – in many ways he's still a savage. But unfortunately he's all I have since my master, the doctor, passed on.' He took a sip from his glass. 'You have deduced some of the facts, old man. I am Albert. I was the prince. But I never tried to take my own life. My ship was sabotaged. Apparently I've made some very powerful enemies.'

'They wanted you dead?'

'Silenced. They drugged me. They left a copy of my suicide note for me to find, just so I would know that I was about to die in disgrace. They are artists, I must give them that.'

'Why kill you?'

Albert smiled. 'Because I know a secret. I know a secret greater than any other. I know a secret that would destroy the royal line, bring down the Empire.'

'Tell me.'

'You first. Who is this boy, and where did you find him?'

'He found us. He is a Router, an escapee from the pods.'

'You stole a Router? And yet you live.'

'We didn't steal him. He stowed away aboard our ship.'

'This boy is a classified file. The agencies will have sent their deadliest operatives to track him. If you're wise you'll kill and bury him in the swamp, then get as far away as possible.'

'I'm not sure it's possible for us to flee much further than we have. Now you? Who's trying to kill you?'

'As I said, I've made some powerful enemies. Have you heard of the Thorn Table?'

'I have not.'

'They are a group of businessmen. They are more powerful than any other group in the Empire, more than all the royal lines combined. For now. They create governments, destroy kings and queens. Now they have their sights on universal domination. They want to smash through the Wall, reunite the empires, and rule the Sphere unchallenged. To achieve this they signed an alliance with a powerful entity. This entity will give them the means to win the final war between the empires of the universe. This entity has *real* power.'

'The Xo?'

Albert chuckled through his nose. 'Oh, my dear old man. You clearly have no idea.'

'Enlighten me.'

'I was approached by the Thorn Table and asked to be their contact inside the royal family. I was told that the group had made contact with a very powerful ruler from "outside" the universe. He has promised to give the Thorn Table power to rule unconditionally, and for all time. No more empires. No more wars. They said our royal line would be made sovereign rulers for life.'

'For a price.'

'For trivial favours. That we bring him the tiny green head of his enemy's daughter, for example. And yours. He is particularly hungry for yours.'

'Why mine?'

'Because you pretend to be a god. You believe you can circumvent the natural laws of time and space. At first I cooperated, but when I expressed moral doubts I was quickly disposed of.'

'You have morals?'

Albert smiled brightly. 'I dabble. Oh, I had no problem with slaughtering you and the girl. It's when they proposed doing away with my sister, the Queen, that I expressed alarm. I think they mean to abolish the dynasty, create a hyperpower of their own. My three treacherous cousins, I assume, have taken my duties. The Queen is oblivious, a puppet. My ship was sabotaged. When I woke from my wine stupor I was lost in a white foggy atmosphere. When the fog cleared I found myself crashed here. But so it goes. It was a glorious accident that it happened this way, because it has allowed me to build my perfect world. I was rescued by a doctor, the only survivor of a wrecked saucer craft. He had made camp here and begun a series of experiments in biological engineering. When my adoptive father passed away he left me this project and I continued to build on its greatness. I took a small group of frightened creatures huddling in the darkness and I made them great. We built our fortress. We built our defences.'

'You mean the crabs?'

'I'm impressed.'

'Don't be.'

'You strayed into our zone, triggering our automatic defences.

When you were able to save yourselves I deemed you worthy and sent a party out to welcome you.'

'You shouldn't have. And the phantom family my crewmates encountered? Were they part of your defences?'

Albert looked briefly confused. 'Phantoms? We have no phantoms.'

'And yet some of us experienced phantoms, visual and aural.'

'It was probably swamp gas.' The old man raised an eyebrow. 'If you breathe too much swamp gas you start to hallucinate. This is a mysterious place. But you'll come to love it with time. This is my new kingdom and I am shaping it as I please. It is a paradise.'

'A paradise?'

'Don't let appearances fool you. Everything we need is here. With you and the boy I can repair my ship and perfect my army. I can finally defeat the Ubuntu. Then I can return to the Empire to tell them all about the world I've built, and the plot against them.'

'My boy,' said Fabrigas with a gentle smile, 'where exactly do you think you are?'

Outside they heard the wind regather to carry towards them the low, steady heartbeat of the drums. The master began to rant, his lips were slick with spittle. 'I'd like to have a ceremony to officially welcome you into our family. Then we can start to move forward. With your brain and this boy's hands we can do anything. And I haven't even begun to talk about the girl! What do you say? Shall we toast our new alliance? Will you call me Lord?'

'Lord? From what I've heard your people call you the Worm.'

The Worm smiled even wider, his teeth sparkled, his gums were a burst of vermilion. 'I do not take it as an insult.' He reached over for the bowl of worms. He took a handful and shoved them in his mouth. His mighty teeth slashed them to pieces. 'To be called a worm is a compliment. The worm is the master. The worm is king. All life grows from decay and the worm lives among it. People look to the bear, the lion, the eagle. Does the bear survive when cut in two?' Bits of worm were stuck to the Worm's lips, and worm juice trickled down his chin. 'You don't think much of these parts. You think they are ugly and deadly. Let me tell you, I have sat on celestial thrones, I have dined with rulers, known pleasures you could never dream of. And yet there is no place I would rather be than here, because here I am king.'

'King of the worms.'

'Precisely. When I return as a conqueror it won't be under the banner of the dragon, it will be beneath the banner of the mud-snake.'

'Boy,' said the old man, 'I think you are two mud-snakes short of a feast.'

The Worm laughed, long and loud. 'Two mud-snakes short of a feast! That's very funny. You have no idea how *wrong* you are! Well, it's a shame, it really is. But if that's your decision.' He reached for a small bell.

'No!' cried Lulabelle, running forward from the shadows. 'He'll eat you!'

Fabrigas sighed and muttered, 'Great, just great.' Roberto couldn't have read Lulabelle's lips, since she didn't have lips as such. He didn't hear Prince Albert turn to her and say, 'So that's how you repay me for my gifts! Now you'll be eaten, too!' or the sound of the bell, and he didn't hear the guards enter the room again behind them.

CARNIVAL

The moon was high and bright, the drums loud, as the old man and the boy were led in vines through the vine huts to a vine cage at the back of the compound and shoved roughly inside. Kandy stood in the gloom, peering at Fabrigas with those huge black eyes. Then she spoke three words, but they were shocking, because she spoke, haltingly, but clearly, in their language. She said, 'I . . . am . . . regret.' Then she walked off quickly, her hands behind her back. Then the traitor Lulabelle was ushered gently in by two distraught-looking guards.

There was another man in their cage, a humanoid pilot. He wore a ragged military uniform. He had clearly become marooned on this world too, been rescued by the Marshians and then somehow transgressed their laws. He was also as crazy as a boat full of monkeys.

'The moon is full! Our time is done, oh yes, we are certainly done for!'

The ragged man cowered in the corner of the cage and Fabrigas could see the wide white of his left eye as he peered at the old man through a slit in his fingers.

'Nonsense, crazy man,' said Fabrigas. 'There's no need to mess your flight suit. We will get out of this if we keep our wits, though I fear yours might have fled already. What is the worst that could happen here? We die? So be it.'

The pilot laughed and dashed his gaunt and battered face against the light. 'Oh no, no, no!' he said. 'Dying is not the worst that could happen. Dying is not the worst that could happen at all!' He was babbling on. 'More meat for the larder!'

Their companions were brought to see them. 'What did you do?' said Lambestyo.

'I followed Roberto. Where have you been?'

'Snooping around. Not getting caught. And what did he do?'

'He followed a woman.'

Lambestyo let his eyes flick over the desolate Lulabelle, then shrugged. 'Well. There isn't much I can do right now. They have me under guard,' and he gestured with his thumb towards a team of Marshians with guns and spears sitting some distance away.

Lenore and Miss Fritzacopple stood stony by the cage. 'What a coopload of turkeys,' she muttered. Lenore said nothing. She sniffed the air. Roberto refused to look at her. He sat in the corner, turning his pet starfish in his fingers.

★

Later that day, Roberto felt himself shaken from a nap.

'Roberto. You need to escape from here and take a message to the *Necronaut*. You can slip through the gaps in the fence.' Fabrigas had scrawled a picture of their ship on a scrap of paper. He pointed to the picture . . . and to Roberto . . . 'You . . . *Necronaut* . . . You . . . *Necronaut.*'

Roberto got the message, but he didn't like it. He shook his head slowly while never taking his eyes from the old man's.

'Roberto!' He drew a crude cartoon: Roberto running to the *Necronaut*, then an arrow showing him returning with help, then everyone dancing for joy. 'It's the only way!'

Another stern shake of the head. 'Roberto!' and the old man drew another picture, this one of himself and the captain standing on either side of Lenore, both holding swords. 'Trust us, boy. We'll protect her. We can't all escape. They'd hunt us down in minutes.'

Roberto stared hard.

The old man pointed to the pocket where he knew the boy kept his precious talisman. 'Well. Why don't we let the Magic Eighth decide?'

Roberto huffed and turned away. He carefully took his Magic Eighth from his pocket, pressed it to his forehead, then shook the sphere hard six times. Then he took his hand slowly away from the readout panel and spent a long time staring at the hazy text. Fabrigas could not see what it said, but he saw the boy's shoulders drop.

Roberto looked out into the twilight, past the gently dozing guards, to the high palisades with gaps he knew he could so easily slip through, to the jungle beyond. He sighed heavily.

*

Roberto never looked back at the old man.

He cut the knots around his hands and ankles with the scalpel in his boot.

He passed through the compound as quick and soft as a midnight shadow.

Roberto climbed the palisades and slipped through a narrow gap.

He passed within three feet of a guard and didn't rouse him.

Roberto took a single great leap and floated silently over the final palisade, swinging his arms around in broad hoops, like a new bird taking its first flight, clearing the sharpened spikes by a few inches.

Roberto landed in the jungle, and his bearings caught up with him. He recognised the swamps.

Roberto sprang into the jungle and vanished.

Lenore sensed him leave. With her fine nose she followed him into the jungle. Soon he was gone, mingling with the trees, the mud, the beasts.

She lay back on her cot. 'He abandons me,' she said to no one.

ROBERTO AT THE WORLDS' FAIR
WITH DIAMONDS

We cannot know what Roberto had been expecting as he waited at the Worlds' Fair, near the South Marina, somewhere between the Helix of Progress and the Avenue of New Ages, dressed in his Imperial Postal Service jumpsuit, with a small bouquet of pungent flowers and a pocketful of diamonds. His date would arrive, he'd been told, sometime after the climax of the starlight charity celebrity dinner at the Elektrotek Ballroom to honour the winner of the 3,145th Beauty of the Universe Pageant. The Purple Corpse Blossom is her favourite flower, they'd told him, and though their smell is repellent to most humans, their stench would attract this particular guest from miles away. Literally, miles. The diamonds in his pocket were to bankroll their evening together, which, depending on their fortunes, could last anywhere from a few hours to a lifetime. He had been told to prepare himself for someone who was unique, perhaps more so than any other individual in the Cosmosphere. They did not even bother to describe her to him. 'You will know her when you see her,' they said. They also told him that his date would be instantly recognisable to every *other* person at the fair that evening. Furthermore, every law-enforcement unit, every secret agency, every public official, mercenary, bounty hunter and ambitious amateur thug in the Sphere would be hell-bent on intercepting her. And, of course, the Imperial Postal Service would be looking for her. This most feared of secret agencies saw everything, and not a stamp could be licked without them knowing about it. Nevertheless, they said, it was his – and only his – job to protect her, and to use the tools at his disposal – the data in his head, the diamonds in his pocket – to ensure her safety.

These two ran from insurmountable odds, you might say. The people who'd rescued him from his hub had described to him the complex computational simulations they'd been running to discover a strategy which would allow this small, blind – though not entirely helpless – girl to traverse the Sphere of Empires, to slip through the impenetrable net, and to escape this universe. In the end, they'd said, after lifetimes of running their simulations, on a computer-array more powerful than any known, they had discovered one single strategy which could give them a chance of success. A 12.5 per cent chance, to be exact. And that singular strategy, they'd explained to him, was Roberto.

Also, they'd said, there was an old man who could help them.

Reluctantly.

And so with that heavy weight set upon his young shoulders, it is hard to even fathom what Roberto thought as he stood at the fair with his reeking posy and his pocketful of diamonds, and waited.

He would not have heard the explosion, he would only have seen the silent, silky river of smoke burble and boil from the doors of Elektrotek Ballroom, people running out, eyes wide with fear, guards falling, choking from the doors, VIP guests – the kind used to seeing people grovelling under their feet – clawing their way over the dusty ground, and being trampled by the heavy boots of blind and frantic guards.

And then a figure walking serenely from the deadly mists, nose in the air, stepping carefully over the weeping dukes and semi-conscious beauty queens. There is another figure following just behind, a woman. She is wearing a gas mask. They stop at the edge of the cloud of smoke and dust which now has enveloped the Elektrotek Ballroom. The tiny figure turns and says something to the taller silhouette, curtsies politely. The woman removes her gas mask, nods, and they part.

The tiny figure approaches Roberto where he stands shivering in the cosmic night, and she says, if his lip-reading is accurate: 'Hello. I think I am your date. My name is Leno.' What a strange name for a girl, he thinks. And then he gives her the flowers, and she curtsies. Then he shows her his diamonds, letting her rub a few together in her small, green hands. She seems impressed so far. And then with nothing else to do, and with the rides at the Worlds' Fair closing for the night, they go down to the marina, and out into the wide, wide universe together, and vanish.

GLORY BE TO HER, OUR QUEEN,
FOR SHE WILL LIVE FOR EVER

When the Man in the Shadows stepped into the silver elevator car he heard a song and knew it from his childhood. 'Glory Be To Her, Our Queen, For She Will Live For Ever'. He had heard the ear-haunting melody as many times as he had pennies – and as you know the Man in the Shadows had many a penny. He knew that this time it was being played by a small, brass orchestra somewhere deep inside the palace. Day through night the four musicians played the song and their notes were channelled through the web of copper pipes to every corner of the grand city. If you arrived at the palace in the morning the song would sound bright and full of energy, but throughout the day, as the band played towards exhaustion, the song would wilt, so that if you rode the car down in the evening you'd hear a hymn full of agony and sadness. And if you happened to be wandering the gloomy palace at midnight, the time when the dirge stopped briefly so that the graveyard band could take its place, the dimly sparkling corridors would be filled, for a few seconds, with the rasping breaths and desperate sobs of the exhausted musicians.

Then the song would start afresh.

When the elevator door opened at the highest floor he saw three rigid shadows.

'How do, sisters?'

'Sir.'

'Please excuse this meeting place, sisters. The Queen, I think, suspects our plot.'

'Then let her suspect. It makes no difference. Would you care for some cactus julep?'

'No, thank you.'

'It is freshly smuggled from the fields of Zapotek. It's rather tart.'

'I'm sure. I have my own smugglers. To business.'

The first sister gave a sign and the deaf-mute servant pushed his drinks trolley away.

'If my intelligence is correct, sisters, Her Majesty does not know the ship survived. But she is suspicious about the Vangardik attack on our fleet. She wonders why they would want to start a long and bloody war. She is not completely slack-brained.'

'She is ugly and stupid. When we rule she will be flayed, and her octopus, too.'

They walked, and the ancient song walked with them.

'And what news from beyond? Is the Vengeance yet drained of all her blood? Can we send a pint to our master, Calligulus?'

'The plot thickens there, I'm afraid. My assassin has turned silent.'

'Assassin? You said there were six hunters.'

'Did I not say? All dead but one. Very strange. But I am confident he will kill the girl and erase the file. Meanwhile, our master's envoy, Lord Bosch, grows impatient. He asks after proof of the green girl's death. And the wizard's. I have told him he perished at the crossing. It was a necessary lie. Now we are truly in a corner.'

'We sigh. Must there always be bad news?'

'Sisters, do not give in to misgivings. Fortune goes always to the strongest, the most cunning. You do not see the worm striking fear into the heart of the crow. Be patient and we will conquer.'

'Who would have imagined that a plot to rule the universe could be so complicated?'

'It only becomes complicated if Calligulus finds out, sisters. He has strictly forbidden us from travelling to foreign dimensions. If he finds out you signed an order to send the Pope to the next universe he will have you dismembered, then tortured for all eternity. An eternity is a blink for him, but a very long time for the likes of us.'

'He is vicious.'

'He has given us much.'

'Things, sir, he gave us things. It is Final Power we crave. The Wall of Peace taunts us.'

They heard a noise down the corridor.

'I must bid you farewell, sisters. It is dangerous for me to stay too long. There has been an incident at my Hotel Empyrean which I must attend to.'

'That old dusty inn? Why bother with it?'

'We can't comprehend why you don't turn it in for scrap. It would be worth more.'

'You might be surprised, sisters. Not all treasures glitter brightly. That hotel has been in my family for more than a hundred generations. It is the only hotel with a view of the centre of the Sphere. It is a monument to the charms of the old empires, and I am rather fond of it. But now I must rush. All will be fixed soon. Our enemies are about to meet the ungodly power of the Pope.'

The Man in the Shadows left, just as the palace's clocks struck midnight and the halls were filled with the sound of bloody breaths through ragged throats. He vanished into the darkness.

'I believe,' said the first sister, 'that we were in the middle of a game of hide-and-seek.'

'Yes,' agreed the second, in a voice like the echo of the ghost of a raven. 'The first one to find the child who was late with our supper gets to smother him.'

DINNER BELL

'When the night becomes hungry we must give him food.'

These simple words were spoken as an explanation to the prisoners who stood on the platform at the edge of the compound, and it addressed the issue of why they were about to be eaten. The wooden stage backed onto the jungle. It was walled in on the sides and roof by batteries of sharpened bamboo spikes, and at the back by a huge carved face whose mouth was an entrance to a wooden slide wide enough for several people to pass through – and several soon would. The slide led down to a clearing before a dark jungle cave. The whole set-up looked like a fun-ride at a family-friendly amusement park. It was not. Our friends from the *Necronaut* were gathered in the centre of the platform. When given the choice of throwing in their lot with the Marshians, or joining Lulabelle and the old man for what seemed to be a fairly standard sacrificial death ritual, the other travellers – Bosun Quickhatch, Lenore, Lambestyo and Miss Fritzacopple – had chosen to die with their friends. So a round of slow applause for them.

'Well, this is a thing,' said the captain.

'Some sort of ritual sacrifice?' said Fabrigas, and his servant grinned.

'Some sort, my old friend,' he said, and a female voice in Fabrigas's left ear said, 'I told you. I tried to warn you. You should have destroyed my journal sooner. There's still time. Help is coming. Survive the slaughter for as long as you can. And don't go down the slide. Oh lord!'

On the unwalled end of the platform, opposite the idol's grimacing face, stood a group of Marshians dressed in ceremonial masks of leaves and feathers. They lingered near sacrificial tables upon which were laid out a selection of frightening tools. One Marshian beat a drum, another played a crude trumpet. Birds flitted around the diners, attracted by the plumage they wore, and the birds enjoyed the bugs in the air, and the whole spectacle was merry, even in the grismal half-light. (Grey and dismal: 'grismal' – it's a word, consult your dictionary!)

On a smaller balcony above the platform the Worm sat cross-legged, surrounded by some of his young acolytes. Skyorax lurked behind him like a foul shadow. The Worm wore Fabrigas's cloak, and the rest of the group's possessions, recovered from the sleeping barn, were laid out on a low table nearby. Fabrigas had been given a crudely made cloak which more than ever made him look like a wizard.

'Friends,' said Skyorax, 'when the moon comes we gather in the sacred place to offer sacrifice, and to consume the meat . . . of power!'

'That's us, I think,' said the captain. 'Well, they're in a for a treat because after years in space my skin is dry and far too salty.'

'Bring forth . . . the seasoning!'

Two young girls brought out an urn which looked like a giant salt shaker. Lulabelle was sobbing quietly, and the humanoid pilot who shared the stage with them was laughing, laughing! 'Now we're done! Now we're meat! They'll eat our hands! They'll eat our feet!'

'Quiet, fool!' said Miss Fritzacopple.

'Here comes the storm again,' said the captain. Yes, the wind came strongly now, sweeping and singing through the jungle. His mad fellow pilot moaned, 'I can feel the knife already. I can feel it sawing on my very bones!'

'Be brave, young lady,' said Fabrigas to Lulabelle, 'we won't let them eat you,' but the girl was somewhere else.

'You have a plan?' asked the captain.

'Of sorts,' said Fabrigas. 'I'm wandering upon it. And you?'

'I will make them regret trying to eat me.'

Finally, the Worm raised his hand, the drums ceased. It was a mad pretentious affair. 'Friends,' said the Worm, 'I have such great news. You are all to be released. You are free to go. You have a choice. You can go down the slide into the jungles, to commune with the Beast. Or you can stay here and enjoy our hospitality.' The Marshians by the tables each armed themselves with a cruel instrument of human gastronomy: some took long blades, some cleavers, some saws, some rib-cutters. They stood waiting.

'A fine set of choices,' said Fabrigas. 'We choose to leave.'

'Very well. Let the games begin!' The Worm picked up a hammer and hit a small gong. The sound shimmered through the night. Then, from the idol's maw, they heard the roar of a great beast. 'He always comes when we ring the dinner bell. You are free to change your minds at any point. Do you still wish to leave, or will you stay with us for dinner?'

'We still want to leave,' said Lambestyo, as he snapped off a bamboo stake like it was a stick of hard candy and brandished it. 'But I think we'll leave by the front door.'

'Very well!' The Worm gave a small gesture to a Marshian who stood beside an inconspicuous-looking wooden lever. The man pushed the lever forward and suddenly the entire lower platform tilted like a see-saw, sending the prisoners tumbling, all except Lambestyo, who merely shifted his balance, and the botanist, who rolled gracefully backwards and onto her feet again. 'I used to be a dancer,' she said to Lambestyo, who simply shrugged.

'Here we go! Here we go!' said the mad pilot as he fell towards the idol's mouth. 'Meat for the oven! A feast fit for a beast!' and he cried out in terrified joy as he slid down into the beast's domain.

CANNIBAL CULTS

Blood! Flesh! Sacrifice! You won't be surprised at all to know that there are many cannibal cults around. The Bones Simple, of the planet Little China, are big trouble. They are a secret society of movie stars who believe that eating the spleens of ordinary people will keep them young for ever. The Cannibotes of Pii believe the only way to keep the spirits of their slain enemies from seeking revenge is to eat every part of them. As you can imagine, the task becomes a nightmare after significant massacres, and sometimes, as in the case of the Battle of New Hebros, when nine Cannibotes defeated an enemy force of seven thousand soldiers, basically impossible. The Triste de Coeur steal hearts in the night and use them in fine-dining recipes for wealthy patrons. The Tremenon del Diablo are a sustainable cannibal cult from the jungle world near Bonidune. They take non-vital organs from their anaesthetised victims before returning the patients to their families. The Uvons travel their universe in spaceships shaped like saucers. They abduct their victims, remove their brains and replace them with those from monkeys.

There are many more.

The Burger Time burger chain operates in seven million locations around the universe and is best avoided.

THE BEAST WITHIN

Oh, the other one I forgot to mention was the Minionites, sometimes called Marshians because of their love of swamp-life: a small subgroup of an ordinarily non-cannibalistic tribe under the power of a charismatic human ex-prince which once every full moon gives sacrifice to a great beast in return for its protection, and draws power (or so they believe) from the consumption of human flesh.

When the stage tipped, Lenore and Lulabelle went tumbling back towards the idol's mouth, and the bosun, with a cry, rolled after them. The giant was not a dancer like Miss Fritzacopple, and the children slipped beyond his grasp and down the throat of the idol. As they vanished a great roar smashed the darkness. The beast's cry floated up through the mouth, and was so dreadful that every heart upon the platform stopped drumming, briefly, before hammering on faster than ever. But the call of the beast was nothing compared to the shrill, shredding screech of the green-skinned ladyling who had fallen into its lair. 'I'm coming!' cried the bosun as he threw himself down the idol-mouth.

Skyorax cried, 'Oh great one! For your protection we offer you the flesh of these mortal souls! But please don't take the beauty! Please leave her pretty flesh for me!'

'Quiet, fool!' cried the Worm.

Captain Lambestyo met the viciously armed Marshians who inched their way down the platform, hungry for people-flesh, and, armed only with a shard of bamboo, he began to make them regret their poor dietary choices. Miss Fritzacopple, unarmed, ducked around the swinging blades like an expert contortionist. In the flimsy gravity she darted, tumbling over the heads of the frustrated locals. 'Exactly what kind of dancing did you do?' said the captain.

'Modern!' she replied as she arched her back below a flying cleaver, which split a bamboo stake in two.

The battle continued. The Worm was enjoying it greatly from his perch, though it was hard to tell. He smiled, bemused, at the impending slaughter. His mouth watered. The botanist would be a tender morsel, true, though the old man was probably only good for stew. He nodded, impressed, as two of his best men cornered the hooded old man and moved in for the kill. He was rather surprised when, at that moment, he glanced to his left and saw Fabrigas sitting cross-legged beside him. 'Hello,' the old man said. 'Impressive set-up you have here.' Albert was dumbstruck. 'Oh, you thought you saw your butchers cleaver me to death?' said Fabrigas. 'Just a parlour trick. I also do a fine turn with trick knives. They're in my beloved cloak there, which I'll now be taking, along with those things belonging to my crew.'

'Skyorax!' Albert called. 'Kill this man immediately!'

'Oh no, master. Don't make me fight a wizard. Anything but that!'

'Coward!'

'Oh, Albert,' said Fabrigas, 'this will all be over soon. It can only play out one way. He who lives by the beast, as they say . . . '

At that moment they heard the beast roar louder than ever, but this time it was a cry of pain and anger. They heard the bosun's voice: 'These children are not your meal to take!' Another roar, louder, angrier, the whole jungle shook. The bosun clambered to the top of the idol's mouth, the two children tumbled from his shoulders to safety. And then a look of shock came across Bosun Quickhatch's mighty face. The creature had him by the ankle. Before it hauled the giant back into the depths the man paused, a look of tranquillity on his face, and said, 'It was ever so nice to know you

342

all.' Then he vanished. They heard him cry out – a cry of war – then the creature cried out – a cry of pitiless fury. The captain left a blade in a masked figure who had dared to step before him and cried out, 'Bosun!' There was no answer from below. Marshian reinforcements armed with guns and crossbows were now arriving at the platform. Things were hopeless. In one corner, Miss Fritzacopple was surrounded by attackers. Captain Lambestyo gathered himself and sprang to take Lenore in one strong arm. 'Roberto would kill me if we lost you,' he whispered.

'*Pfhh*,' said the girl. 'And he is where?'

But Lambestyo was not the only swiftly moving shadow that night. Black shapes fell from above, faster than the eye. They smashed easily through the flimsy bamboo roof. As the feasters raised their blades to end Miss Fritzacopple a shadow fell upon her, then sprang with her into the heights, leaving the Marshians standing with their blades quivering over an empty space. 'The Ubuntu!' cried the Worm. 'The savages have come to steal our meal!' More shadows fell upon the platform and took each of the prisoners flying up through the holes in the roof and into the darkness. It all happened so fast that no one had time to react. 'Well,' said Fabrigas, 'it looks like we have some new friends to bunk with. This has been fun, it really has.' He wore his beloved cloak now. He stood wearily, just as another hulking shadow fell from the jungle heights, took the old-timer in its strong arms, and sprang upwards.

'Stop them!' cried the Worm. A great angry cry came from the mouth of the idol. 'The beast is furious!' said the master. 'Run, children!' And they did, the surviving Marshians, leaping over each other to escape the black, clawed beast who now rose up through the darkness, smashing away the wooden idol face like it was paper. Even Albert fled. Or tried to. Before Fabrigas had left he'd found time to tie one end of a vine around the leg of a table, and the other around the leg of the Worm. As the old man was carried away into the darkness, he heard the mad Prince Albert's screams as he was munched by the beast he loved.

AND HOW DID YOU LIKE THAT?

Is your blood moving? Is your heart pumping fast? How do you think our friends felt as they found themselves flying through the jungle heights, through a cloud of bugs and giant insects, fat leaves and vines slapping them senseless, then back to their senses, then out again, the whole jungle seeming to assault them mercilessly for their carelessness? They heard heavy, steady breathing near their ears and felt strong arms wrapped around them. Then they were drifting down, down from the canopy and into the village of the Ubuntu.

UBUNTU

People came from the huts to see the visitors, and when I say 'people' . . .

The Ubuntu are muscular, ape-like creatures, their skin is perfectly black, their arms hang almost to their knees, allowing them to reach for vines, or run swiftly on all fours across the ground. In the dark they disappear, only their glowing blue eyes visible – so they keep those closed most of the time, moving through the jungle by smell, by instinct.

Fabrigas was the first to gather himself. 'Are we all present?' he said. 'Where is the girl?'

'I am over here,' said Lenore as she and the captain touched the earth. Lulabelle arrived soon after, tearful and bewildered.

'I have to go back for my bosun,' said Lambestyo, distraught. 'He is my friend!'

'He is lost,' said Fabrigas. 'Not even he could match that beast's strength.'

Everyone was silent. The only sounds were the soft calls of the jungle, and the cries of the beast still raging and hungry in the distance.

'We will perform our rites for the bosun later,' said Fabrigas, as their dusky and inquisitive rescuers drew closer. 'But in the meantime we need to find out who these people are and why they stole us.'

'I can answer that,' said a young voice. A tiny, pale figure stepped forward from the wall of dark skin. 'My name is Kimmy Persuivus. I'm ten years old. I think you need to get back to the ship rather urgently.'

ON/OFF

Kimmy Persuivus is a very small, very quiet girl. She is a girl that if you passed in a hall you might not even notice. If she tugged you on the sleeve and said, 'Excuse me,' you might think, 'Who's this, a talking hamster?' Kimmy Persuivus is not a hamster. She is three feet tall, plus change, with a round face and round glasses. She mostly likes to read. In the lunch room of the factory where she works you can usually find her at one of the tables, trying to support a tattered book in one hand, and a penlight in the other – because the work-house is a gloomy place, and her eyes aren't very good. At night you might see her small shape glowing faintly through the blankets. Her favourite stories are ones in which a small girl whom nobody thinks very much of goes off to have great adventures and perhaps marry someone very handsome – but also someone with a dependable income, because looks and daring aren't everything. 'Who needs to marry a dragon-slayer?' she often says to herself. 'What kind of career is *that*?' Her ultimate dream would be to marry a handsome adventurer who also has his own mail-order books service.

Kimmy Persuivus was only assigned to the *Necronaut* because of a typographical error. When she'd tried to explain, in her soft voice, that she was K. Persuivus, and that the person they were after was probably K. Persuavis, the confident and athletic older boy from the next dormitory, she'd been told to shut her hamster-hole. It was usually the way (although, to be fair, Kevin Persuavis had got a similar

347

reception when he'd asked why on earth he'd been assigned to catalogue books in the library).

And so, Kimmy Persuivus had reluctantly joined the crew of the
Necronaut, and, as it turned out, would become more vital to their
mission than almost anyone else.

When the bosun saw her clutching her copy of *Brenda the Dragon
Befriender* (a book about a young girl who negotiates for both parties
during the great dragon/human conflicts), he'd simply shaken his
head and walked off. But Kimmy Persuivus is a very hard worker,
and she did much more than her fair share around the ship. After
the first attack on the *Necronaut* she had dragged fire extinguishers
almost as big as herself, and fought the flames until her face was
black. The bosun had noticed, and as he strode past had given her
a gentle pat on the shoulder that almost knocked her down.

But to everyone else she had stayed invisible.

*

After landing in this swampy world, Kimmy had quietly watched
events develop.

No sooner had the food-gathering party left the ship than things
began to unravel. A giant slug had swum up and tried to mate with
the ship, but they had managed to prise it off with long poles. Then
the Ubuntu arrived. At first, a group of five appeared beside the
ship in a dugout boat, chattering and marvelling at the hulk.
Shatterhands suggested firing off a warning shot, but Descharge
overruled him, and bravely went to meet the visitors. Things went
well, although without a translator it was difficult. They were able
to get somewhere with crude drawings in the dirt, and a lot of
pointing at things. 'I think that if I wrestle his eldest daughter I can
have the hand of his strongest warrior,' he said, returning, and
Shatterhands had rolled his eyes.

The Ubuntu, it turns out, are a sweet, good-natured people with a wicked sense of humour. Descharge invited a group aboard for a modest feast. The Ubuntu brought strange and wonderful foods, and a bottle of their best spirit, which made Dr Sackwell's Rum seem like cordial. It was a grand evening and there was much dancing and singing. But not everyone was happy.

'These people are savages,' hissed the surgeon. 'Who knows what they're capable of.'

'And then there's the giant slugs,' said the cook, 'and Gods know what else.'

'The others are certainly dead by now,' said the poet. 'Gone, gone, gooooone!'

'There's no way they could have survived, not with a blind girl leading them. We must leave this beastly realm,' shrieked G. De Pantagruel, whose nerves had been ravaged by the trials of the past few days. His Gentrifact companions murmured in agreement.

'By my butcher knife, you're right,' said Huxbear the cook. 'If we were wise we'd push off now, while we still have our heads.'

The surgeon agreed, but urged caution.

Kimmy had overheard it all from her secret reading place, a small nook near the foredeck where she'd sneak away to read a book she'd stolen from the galley. No one noticed her there. At the end of the night, an Ubuntu chief, whose name was Chima, was attracted to her pretty penlight. Kimmy impressed him by turning it on and off – at least he appeared to be impressed. 'On, off,' she said, clicking the small brass button, and she taught him several other words: 'ship', 'dragon', 'castle'.

When the Ubuntu left, Shatterhands and the cook came on deck. Again, they thought they were alone, but they weren't. Sometimes it helps to be small and quiet. She turned off her reading light and listened.

Then the sailor, Hardcastle, showed up, dis-burbling about giant crabs, and a swamp girl who'd risen from the dark lagoon, holding a child's puzzle in her lifeless hand. When his friend McCormack had refused the swamp girl's gift she had taken him into the depths. Hardcastle had pushed his boat away in panic, circling the swamp for hours, weeping, until he'd accidentally stumbled upon the ship. 'They're dead!' he cried. 'Oh mercy, I have never seen such an abode of monsters!'

'This is just exactly what I expected,' said the surgeon. 'This is a cursed place and no one who wants to live would stay here.'

Late that night the ship had been woken by Hardcastle's screams. When they got to his bunk he was already dead. Wet footprints led out of the bunk room.

The next day the Ubuntu returned with more food and gifts, and in greater numbers. But they discovered a ship descending into anarchy. The repairs had been going well, certainly, and the vessel was all but space-worthy, but now most of the crew agreed that they should flee while they had the chance. Amorous slugs were showing up in increasing numbers and becoming harder to dislodge. It was clear, the surgeon argued once more, with support from his friends, that the others were dead. Descharge saw his allies dwindling. Even when Roberto showed up and frantically began to draw impressions of his friends' plight on the walls in chalk, Shatterhands was unmoved.

'The only conclusion we can draw from these sketches is that this boy is utterly mad.'

But the one thing Descharge had in his favour was the broken piston-rod which could not be repaired without a replacement part. He and the engineer had tried several makeshift options, but they'd all failed under tests.

'There's no flying without this,' said Descharge, as he held the broken rod before the surgeon's long, damp beak. One of their Ubuntu guests, though, had been watching, and he walked over to inspect the part. He gently took it and held it up to the light. 'What is he going to do?' said the surgeon with an evil sneer. 'Perform some kind of black magic on it?'

An hour later the same tribesman appeared, grinning, with a

replacement part in his big, hairy paw.

And so Descharge saw the writing on the wall. He had no excuse now. It wasn't the Ubuntu he feared; his own tribe was turning on him.

Kimmy Persuivus also saw the state of play. Late that evening she slipped quietly off the ship. No one saw her leave, because no one ever really saw her. No one saw her wade out into that deadly swamp and duck beneath some monster lilies. She wasn't frightened in the swamp, even when the swamp girl rose up from the waters in front of her. Kimmy helped her solve her puzzle. As she would explain years later in her best-selling book, *Swamp Girls Are People Too*, swamp girls are people too. The swamp girl led Kimmy safely through the bogs to the edge of the Ubuntu camp. The person she was looking for must have seen her light flashing in the darkness, because minutes later a tall figure appeared in front of her and said, 'On-off?'

*

Kimmy had drawn pictures in the dirt of a girl, a woman, a beardy man, a giant and a man with a scar on his face. The chief had pointed into the darkness with a dread look in his eyes. The Ubuntu knew all that happened in this jungle. The chief had assembled his best men for the lightning raid, and they had brought her friends back from the mouth of death. Now this tiny hero stood staring up at Fabrigas, and the old man stared down, bewildered at the girl, for although she'd clearly been aboard his ship, he swore he'd never seen her in his life.

'We have to get back to the ship,' she said. 'Something terrible is happening.'

*

Fabrigas and the captain raced through the jungle on the backs of two loping beasts and broke through a wall of vines beside the wide stretch of bog where the *Necronaut* was waiting.

Except that it wasn't.

There was nothing but a calm lagoon with flattened swamp trees. The Ubuntu stood around, smiling, pointing to the place where the ship had been. 'Dragon,' said one, helpfully. The captain stalked around the edge of the lagoon, throwing up his arms and saying, let's be honest, some bad words.

'Those ————, ————! I'll ———— their ———— when I get my hands on them!'

Fabrigas stood motionless. As he always said, you only have to imagine what lies ahead. There are no surprises.

'I am very surprised!' he said. 'This makes difficult things even more difficult.'

'You think?!' said our captain, and he went off on another blind rant, shaking his fists at the imaginary moon so that the Ubuntu laughed with delight.

'They must have repaired the ship,' said Fabrigas. 'I cannot believe that they would betray us.'

Back at the Ubuntu camp, the atmosphere was tense. Lenore sat on one end of a log, Lulabelle nearer the other end, and Miss Fritzacopple sat in the middle. And no one spoke.

Kimmy sat on a rock nearby, watching.

'Well . . . isn't it good to be out of danger again? Yes,' said Miss Fritzacopple.

Lenore was doing her best not to smell . . . *her*. The fishy girl. But it was difficult. Lenore was not yet a young woman, but she had started to have certain ideas about how a boy should behave – especially one who was supposed to be protecting her from harm on a deadly planet. They should definitely not go off protecting other girls. And they certainly shouldn't just vanish without a word. Not that he really had any words. The captain, now there was a man to depend on. She sniffed. 'It is getting much crowded on here. I believe I'll walk.'

'Don't go for a walk. Please,' said the botanist.

'I won't go a long ways,' said the girl. 'Not that some people would care how far I did.' It was a remark meant for absent ears.

*

'So our ship is gone. A hijack is possible, though it's more likely they fled. There were quite a few slug tracks around. I'm afraid, for the time being, we're stuck here. Also, have I mentioned that we're living in the belly of a giant beast?'

He had not.

Fabrigas had returned to the camp and now strode around behind the small fire, swimming and vanishing in the smoke and heat, oblivious, it seemed, to the blinking, uncomprehending eyes of his friends.

'You said you had *good* news!' said Miss Fritzacopple. 'How is being stuck inside a beast with no way to escape in any way good news?!'

'Well, the good news is that the Ubuntu have had a meeting. They have no chief, as such. But in this tribe everyone believes themselves to be the chief, and no one contradicts them. Isn't that wonderful?' No one said anything. 'But they decide everything by meeting, and they have decided that we can stay for as long as we like. So isn't that good news?!'

*

They had a service that night to remember the bosun. They gathered near the swamps to float lanterns. The captain said a few words. He said that their bosun was a courageous sailor, and a fearless human being. He said this even though he knew, from years spent in his company, that he was none of those things. The bosun was not brave, courageous or fearless.

353

The bosun, you may not have realised, was afraid. Deeply, *deeply* afraid in a way that you or I could not imagine. Now, you might think it strange that a man so afraid would choose to travel on ships which venture to the most dangerous parts, but the bosun did not think it was strange at all.

'The best way to deal with death is to keep him right beside you, where you can see him.' That was what the bosun used to say.

It is worth briefly describing the life of Jacob Quickhatch. He was born in an insignificant mountain town to a watchmaker and a schoolmistress. He was the largest baby anyone had ever seen: even the local farmers were impressed. They came from all around to measure him. He nearly ended his mother on his way into the world – for which she forgave him – and he grew a foot every year for his first six years. But despite his size Jacob had been a terrified child. His mother recalled him crying at the sound of a cricket on his sill. No grown-up could speak to him without him breaking into tears and running to bury his face in his mother's skirts. His father had had the idea – if you could call it an idea – to scare the fright right out of his bones. He prepared a set of wooden boards with scary demon faces on them. He rigged them with bed springs so that they leaped from the floor when the boy passed, and hung leering and bobbing before his hysterical face. The boy couldn't open a cupboard door or use an outhouse without meeting one of those grimacing faces. As a consequence he went to the privy half as often, but twice as much, if you get my meaning. The boy did not lose his fear of scary faces, but he did develop three brand-new fears: bed springs, boards, privies.

But Jacob was a clever child who did his family proud. By eight he'd taught his mother to read the Holy Books, and she was most happy. His father complained of rats in his workshop, so his son made snares and trapped them. Trapped all the rats. His father was so happy he made him a watch; he poured all his soul into making the finest watch he could for his only son. Jacob would make snares to catch the rabbits who ate their vegetables. He would bring them home for his father. 'Son! Are you not afraid?'

'No, Father, they are small.'

'Good boy!'

But when his father put a rabbit upon the butcher's block his son would cry out, 'Father, no!' His father had to release them all.

But the boy could make a snare in under eight seconds, and that was something.

Around the boy's tenth birthday, a local priest, a close friend of his mother, began to teach him the finer points of scripture. At twelve he made the decision to join the seminary. He travelled to the Black Mountains and spent four blissful years in peace and quiet, learning all about the universe he lived in. The brothers called him 'Gentle Giant'. One afternoon he and the other brothers were picking strawberries in the fields when they heard cries and saw a large wolf carrying a baby off into the forest. Without thinking, Jacob ran after it, covering the ground with astonishing speed and cornering the beast in a rocky crevice. The wolf dropped the child and leaped for Jacob. There was a furious battle. The two rolled around the glade, both barking and snarling, but when Jacob got to his feet again he had the wolf limp by the throat. Later, when asked by a senior brother to recall the experience, Jacob could not remember a thing, and when witnesses described to him what had happened the boy began to wail.

The baby was fine.

Word of Jacob's deed spread through the country and one day he got a visit from two papal guardsmen. The guardsmen are awful men: large, brutish, the worst kind of bullies. They told Jacob that because of his bravery he was to be enlisted as a guard in the Fleet of the Seven Churches (as it was called then). Jacob was distraught. He loved life in the monastery. He didn't want to go into space. He pleaded with the monsignor to send the men away, but there was nothing that could be done. 'If I defy a papal order, I'll be killed,' he said.

And so Jacob was led away and soon found himself in a galley with a hundred other recruits. It wasn't as bad as he'd first imagined. For most of the time they just floated around, waiting for trouble that never arrived. He got to see deep space, and that pleased him. He thought the stars and galaxies from a distance astonishingly beautiful. His faith, if anything, deepened and richened. Then one day he was told to prepare for battle, and he felt the blood stop under his skin. 'I'll surely die today,' he thought.

And he said that same thing every day of his life. Every morning when he woke in the darkness on one of the Pope's great ships. He said it when he was forced to embark on his first crusade. He said it on the day he came to escape the Pope's clutches, and on the day he got his first job aboard a freighter ship, and on the day he first looked into Lambestyo's eyes he said: 'I will *certainly* die today.'

He'd even said it the previous morning, when he woke to learn that his captain and the old man had been taken prisoner and were to be executed. And on that day he was right.

The bosun knew, as you and I perhaps do not, that there is a big difference between being afraid, and being a coward, between feeling horror creeping up your legs and ordering those legs to run. An attentive observer might have heard Jacob Quickhatch whisper as he stood on the deck of the *Necronaut* and heard his captain speak of certain death; and she might have observed a faint wobble in his knees as he turned to face the ravenous plants in the tunnels on Bespophus; and she might have even heard him say a faint 'Oh, Mummy' when the horde of death-crabs had descended. And even when he threw himself into the mouth of the idol, as he blinked within the ashy darkness and saw two great red eyes, each as big as portholes, he had not made his last words 'Don't hurt us, please', as he had desperately wanted to. He had said, in a voice that made even the fearsome creature take one small step back: 'These children are not your meal to take!'

And he was right.

'Our actions tell our story,' said Lambestyo, 'and when we die we leave our bootprints for everyone to see: bootprints that run towards, or away, from people less fortunate than us.'

The Ubuntu, sensing their unspeakable sorrow, abandoned their own moon-party and gathered to sing. Their song was low and mournful, part hymn, part wail, and it rose and died like a wave.

★

Lulabelle said goodbye to Roberto at the edge of the camp. Not to his person, because his person had vanished (along with the *Necronaut*), but to a vague picture she'd drawn in the dust. She couldn't explain to him, obviously, or to anyone there, her reasons for returning to her people, that they too would be mourning, and looking for a way to rebuild their broken lives – now that the strange tyranny of the master was over. She might have explained how her mother and sisters were probably already mourning her, thinking she was lost, and that she missed them. She couldn't explain any of that, so she simply pressed the coin Roberto had given her into Lenore's dirty palm, and walked off into the darkness.

Lenore sat for a long time, sifting through some of the more confusing questions a young and green girl can have. Why life was so painful and confusing, and why she even cared about a stupid boy. It was all stupid. Boys are stupid.

Soon, Fabrigas came and sat next to her and for a while they rested in silence, listening to the warm beat of the drums and gazing into the starless wall of black whose only light came from the portal which hung high above them, and which resembled, at least from a distance, a moon.

'I hates him,' said the girl.

'They'll come back to us,' said the old man.

'I hopes so,' said the girl.

SKELETON YARD

'There is one more thing I need to do before we leave,' announced Fabrigas the next morning.

'Do?' said Lenore.

'Leave?' said Miss Fritzacopple.

'Yes. It's time for us to leave,' said Fabrigas. 'I do not know how. I do not know to where. And I still don't know exactly for what reason. But I think you'll all agree that anywhere in the universe is better than inside this beast.'

'And what is the "one more thing" you need to do?' said Fritzacopple.

'I'll come to that.'

The Ubuntu were surprised to learn that their guests wanted to leave. It turned out that they knew a lot of important things about the land they lived in. They knew, for example, that the moon whose fullness they were currently celebrating in a week of feasting and singing wasn't really a moon. They called it 'the hole of fog and air', and they also knew that it was a portal to another world, because they'd been up to inspect it. 'It seems these people are fine navigators,' said Fabrigas, as he squinted at the illustrations the Ubuntu had carved for him in the dirt, 'and they have confirmed my theories about what this world really is. They say that travelling in these parts is challenging. They say that everything a person could want is right here: food, drink, man–bear wrestling. We may not have translated that last one right,' said Fabrigas. And it was true. It turned out that the Ubuntu are descendants of a tribe of great navigators. Their ancestors had been to every corner of their cornerless galaxy. But a few generations ago this tribe stopped their roamings of a sudden. This generation had been up to the great hole, peered out, and realised that they didn't even recognise the stars they saw. It was very strange. They also discovered that they were inside the belly of a giant beast. In the end they decided that leaving the beast to explore a whole new universe would be a lot of trouble, and that they had everything they needed right here. It was a dark, quiet and bountiful world. The problem was that it had turned out to be a bit more busy than they anticipated. Strangers were frequently crashing here, starting fights, forming flesh-eating cults, engineering horrible beasts and generally disturbing the peace.

'So how do we get to this portal?' said the captain. He had calmed down now that he was back in camp and receiving some of the Ubuntu's hospitality (and frankly, hospitality doesn't come much better).

'Well, that is the question. We could always go back and steal the *Prince Albert* from the cannibals. It is a fine ship,' said Fabrigas. But that idea was quickly thrown out. Whatever state you were in, it was wrong to steal another tribe's ship.

So Fabrigas, through Carrofax, asked the nearest chief if he had any ideas, and he was extremely surprised when the chief replied, 'Oh, we have spaceships.'

*

Ships. Ships upon ships upon ships. The guts of ships strewn on the ground, rusting skeletons, groaning bulks. There is a word for this in Ubuntu which roughly translates as 'skeleton yard'. When the Ubuntu arrived, this is where they dumped their old ships, and whenever a strange ship crashed here the Ubuntu would help the injured, bury the dead, and drag the broken vessels here. There were cargo ships, still with their containers of toys and tinned brains. That's what I said, tinned brains. There were racing ships, some still with a pair of skeleton hands wrapped desperately around the wheel. There were prison ships, pleasure ships and pirate vessels. 'Our botanist found a haunted saucer ship. Why wasn't that dragged here?' Fabrigas wondered. Carrofax replied: 'They're too scared to go near it.'

And that was exactly the 'one more thing' the old man had to do. 'To perform this duty I'll need your assistance,' he said to Lenore.

'Oh no, no, no. I don't want to there go back!'

'You can't possibly expect this child to go into the marshes again,' said the botanist.

'I guarantee no harm will come to her,' said the old man.

'And what exactly are you going to do there?' said Fritzacopple.

'We've had help from a stranger, and now we must return her favours. We are going to perform an exorcism.'

THE EXORCIST

This man, the hero of our story, was a man of science, a child of his universe(s). He did not believe in magic, or astrology, or ghosts, or poltergeists, or any supernatural phenomena that he was not able to see and test for himself. Yes, he had a phantom butler, but life is filled with contradictions. It is sometimes possible for a man or woman of science to observe the effect of the supernatural, and to apply to it his or her own principles.

That's how Lenore found herself standing in the centre of the familiar dead clearing, inside a set of symbols burned on the ground with petroleum distillate, surrounded by a circle of fine brass reeds pressed into the mud, while Fabrigas stood to one side with a small harp. The harp was brass with copper strings and, like many of the artefacts he kept hidden within his cloak, it was very, very old.

'And why are we here again?' said Lenore.

'I made a promise to one of these phantoms that I would free her and her family from this place.'

'Oh. And how does that involve me?'

'You seem to be a fine conduit for trans-temporal vibrations. Or, as many people crassly call them: ghosts.'

'Oh.'

'It is confounding the kind of junk which can collect over the years,' the old man said as he placed more of the brass reeds around the edge of the circle. 'This whole world would have been clean and fresh once. Then, a stray seed here, a lost spaceship there. Before you know it, jungles, peoples, the walking dead!'

'The walking deads?' The green-skinned girl glowed so brightly tonight that she seemed not to be part of this or any familiar world. She was from elsewhere, of elsewhere, belonging nowhere. 'I think you mentioned that they are not ghosts,' she said.

'They are not. They are echoes in the valleys of perception, they are counter-moving waves in the quantum seas, and they come as much from within our brains as without. Everything we perceive is created by our minds. Our minds collect this phantom noise and turn it into shapes we can understand, just as we see familiar objects in clouds. And then we take it one step further: we build stories around them. We call them ghosts because we like to think our loved ones haven't vanished for ever, you see?'

'I see.'

'It really is amazing where life can spring up, and how hard it is to vanquish it, even after death. But we must, or it hangs around and causes untold damage.'

Lenore gave a sharp yelp.

'What is it?'

'Our guests are arrived.' One of them had whispered right in her ear.

'You again,' it said. 'Don't you know you aren't welcome here?'

'They are saying that please we aren't welcomed here!'

'That's splendid, please keep them talking. We need the whole family to arrive.'

'You cannot see them? Miss Lady could see them.'

'I cannot, but they may not materialise until they feel under threat. Keep conversing with them.'

'So . . . how are you all? Everything is . . . well?'

Lenore heard a hissing from the darkness.

Fabrigas had finished setting up an array of amplifying speakers made from parts he had salvaged from the skeleton yard, and he had wired them up to his small harp. It looked as if he was about to perform a recital.

'Who is that man? We don't like him.'

'Oh, don't worry about he,' said Lenore. 'He is a crazy old thing.'

'The strange thing about the so-called spirit world is that it really is just a wave, after a fashion,' said the crazy old thing as he finished wiring his instrument. 'And every wave can be cancelled by another wave. Are they all present?'

'No. Still some to arrive.'

'I'm here,' said a girl's voice. 'I'm Judy.'

'Please to meets you, Judy.'

'Oh! You're wearing Gloria around your neck. I was wondering where she went.'

'Gloria?'

'My starfish. We've been lost here for so long. Though not as long as Gloria. She will be looking forward to travelling again.'

'Oh, Judy, your head is so full of strange ideas,' said a young man's voice, and now more voices entered, a cast of phantom players, their words overlapping and colliding like waves in a pool. 'Children, I told you not to play with strangers.'

'Oh, darling, this place is all strangers. Strangers upon strangers.'

'I want to take the rover out, I'm bored.'

'I'm bored too, can we get a monkey?'

'We don't want you here.'

'Go away.'

'We don't like you.'

'We don't like you at all, you frighten my children.'

'These voices are making my head hurt!'

'That's good, we are nearly set!' Fabrigas was hooking up his amplification array to a large ship's battery. Then he struck a chord on his electrified harp and suddenly the whole clearing was lit by sound. They heard it far off in the camp; the Ubuntu looked at each other and grinned.

'What is that noise! For the love of –'

'We hate that noise!'

'Make it stop!'

The burst of sound had illuminated the figures like a powerful lamp. Now they were clearly visible. The oozy figures of the ship-wrecked family were stumbling back, fingers stabbed into their ears as Fabrigas's chord shimmered mercilessly in the air like a rolling clap of thunder.

'Stop, you're hurting us!'

'What *is* that awful music!?'

'I think you are hurting them!'

'It's all as it should be, it's all for the best!'

The figures began to lose their shape, they warped like reflections on the surface of a pond.

'Please stop! If you don't stop, we'll hurt you, we'll take out your eyes!'

'I think it is working,' said the green girl. 'Or not!'

'It's working,' said the old man, 'just don't move from where you are.'

It was a good thing that Lenore could not see what was happening around her, because now the family's faces transformed, contorted into shocking grimaces, and they began to lash wildly at her.

Even Fabrigas could see the family now, and he said, 'Great ghosts, I can see them!' before he let rip with another ear-shredding chord. When the wave hit the family they were sent stumbling back, and their reflections began to burn and twist.

'You evil people!'

'We hate you!'

'What are you doing to us?!'

'I want to ride in the rover!'

'I made us cookies for a late snack!'

They came storming back again, their faces bent and demonic. They reared up beside Lenore and hissed, as one . . .

'He's coming! Calligulus is coming with his army! He's coming for you. The Vengeance! He laughs at your vengeance! The great one, destroyer of worlds, taker of souls, is coming to destroy you. He slaughtered your father, his enemy; he slaughtered your friends; he killed everyone you know. Soon he'll throw you into a pit of hell. You won't believe his power and his cruelty. You will suffer for eternity!'

'Well now,' said Lenore.

'We're sorry.' And then they began to dissolve like fine sand. 'We are so very sorry.' Until each figure was a galaxy of spinning grains. 'We didn't mean to frighten you.' And the last voice they heard was that of a young woman saying, 'I'm so sorry. Thank you. I won't forget this.'

But she would forget, because she was just a memory herself.

'Please take care of Gloria.'

And after that the clearing was very, very quiet.

★

'Calligulus,' said Fabrigas later. 'Does that mean anything to you? We've heard mention of him several times. Once in that mad botanist's lab, once during the exorcism. Albert mentioned a pact with a powerful being from outside the universe. Could it be him?'

'I've never heard of him,' said Carrofax. 'But he could well be from the ectoplasmic dimensions, or an even higher sphere. As you know, I cannot return while I serve you, but I have been to the borders. The Thresholders know nothing about him.'

'Could he be as dangerous as Albert said?'

'It depends. A non-mechanical can only manifest here by becoming "flesh" – by taking the burden of mortality – or by coming here as a relatively harmless spectre, as I have done. Unless . . .'

'Unless?'

'Unless someone invites him into the material world. But none of your people would be foolish enough to do that. Surely. In any event, one thing we've been able to establish for certain is that he wants your green girl dead. And you, for some reason. Perhaps because of your dimension-hopping abilities.'

'So you admit now that I can travel between dimensions?'

'It seems so. Although I would point out that you seem to have had help from unlikely quarters.'

'So you apologise for mocking me earlier?'

'I wouldn't go that far. But all this makes it even more vital to keep an eye on that green girl and get her home as soon as we can.'

Lenore was sitting alone at the edge of camp, a beacon in the twilight. She had wandered out there after the exorcism. She had a lot to think about now, it seemed.

*

Day became night, though of course it was hard to tell.

The men came back from the skeleton yard dragging a giant rocket and beaming. 'When you hear our plan,' Fabrigas said to Miss Fritzacopple, 'you will be sceptical. But please hear us out.'

The plan was as simple as it was mad. They had searched the skeleton yard from end to end but hadn't found a single working ship. None of them, not even Fabrigas, had the engineering skills to fabricate a ship from parts. It had looked hopeless, until they found a military hospital ship with an old-fashioned escape rocket.

'They outmoded these long ago,' said Fabrigas. 'They're just too dangerous. They were designed to go flying way out into space, away from the ship, and danger, but mechanical problems often caused them to go off when they weren't needed, or worse, when someone was cleaning them. Or when the captain was giving a royal tour. Also, they have no steering, meaning that whatever direction it was pointing, that's where it went. Even if that way was blocked by a spaceship, planet or space-cow.'

'I do not like where this story is pointed,' said Miss Fritzacopple.

'Now keep an open mind,' said Fabrigas. 'It is true that we are currently trapped in a haunted beast. But we can escape. What we're going to do is aim this rocket towards that blowhole up there.' He gestured vaguely towards the silver circle in the sky. 'The Ubuntu have assured us that if we can get through, there'll be friendly people with working spaceships.'

'So this is another one of your explosive exits?' said Lambestyo.

'It's perfectly safe. We should be fine.'

'Should?'

'I will calibrate the rocket precisely. It will be a controlled blast.'

Miss Fritzacopple walked away, leaving the old man to stand beaming beside his rocket.

*

Fabrigas and the captain were working through the night on the rocket, which had been dragged to a nearby clearing, stood upright and leaned towards the blowhole.

'We need much longer to prepare,' said Lambestyo.

'Nonsense,' said Fabrigas. 'We don't have longer. The Ubuntu say that the blowhole will be visible for one more day. Besides, we can't risk those marshy types reorganising and coming to attack us.'

'Do you think it will work?'

'I have calculated our trajectory as best I can from the information I have, which isn't much. But I am very confident of my mathematics. Fairly very confident.'

'I see. So we might not hit the hole.'

'The fuel is old. It might just explode on the ground. But it will be fun trying!'

'Well, I can't wait to leave this place, even if it is in a ball of fire.'

EJECT US

The day of the launch. Can you feel the excitement? The crew stood nervously around the scarred metal tube. The Ubuntu stood a long way away, looking nervous. They had packed their new friends a picnic of mushrooms, moss and honey grubs. The goodbyes had been tearful. Kimmy had found her friend and pressed her little torch into his giant hands. 'For you,' she said.

'On-off,' he replied sadly. Then he'd swept her effortlessly onto his shoulder with one arm and carried her out to the rocket. Now he was far, far away, with the rest of them.

The Ubuntu were lit from behind in fern light. Small children sat on shoulders for a better view. Carrofax said, 'I'll see you on the other side, wherever that is,' and the captain sealed the door and strapped himself in.

'Are we ready?' he said. No one replied. 'Very well,' he said, and he hit the big red button marked 'Ejectus'.

*

I'm not sure if any of you have been in a rocket. And if you haven't I'm not sure you can imagine what it's like to take off in one. It's like having your stomach smeared across your brain while your brain is swung around in a sock. The explosion from the rocket knocked the Ubuntu off their feet and turned the eternal night into furious daylight. Suddenly, every dark corner of the interior was illuminated. In the dome, the Marshians ran from their huts. There was light, even in the deepest depths where the beast called the Makatax had dragged the limp corpses of the bosun and Prince Albert deep into his cave, and tossed them on a pile of bones and rags, ready for the feast. Even beyond his lair, in the deep corridors of vines and thorns where light had never penetrated, and where the most terrifying creatures you can imagine live, it was suddenly twilight. As the rocket traced an arc towards its target it illuminated everything, even the small camp by the old tree, where the saucer craft stood, and where everything was still.

BOOK THREE

I am Calligulus!
Creator of empires,
Master of puppets,
Controller of the mortal worlds.
The dead and forsaken call my name.
The lost and broken cry out for my mercy.
The empty and forgotten dance before my idols,
Dance, dance, dance!
See this Empire I have built.
Is it not pretty?
I am Calligulus!
Son of Zep,
Son of Mat,
Child of the darkness of the bottomless abyss,
And the fires of the infinite sun.
Zep rules!

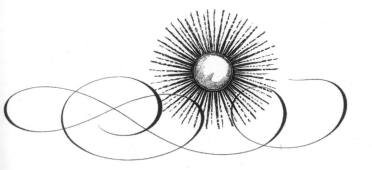

UP

In space there's no such place as 'up'. No up, no down, no sideways, no forwards, no backwards. When a rocket takes off, a rocket such as the one our friends are in, it's convenient to say that the rocket is travelling up, when really it isn't. The best we can say is that the rocket is travelling 'away'. Away from ground, away from friends, and into the unknown at a frightening speed. In another sense it can also be said to be travelling 'up' and 'away' from all other possible events. But this is a complex subject.

It has been weeks since I last sat down to write because I have been away getting the old man's mail. I went because I wanted to see if anyone else was trying to reach him in his mansion on this deserted moon beside the sea guarded by fearsome serpents. Sending mail here is no simple matter. We are countless billions of light-years from anywhere populated, and we have no electricity, so sending electronic messages is out of the question. The only thing that really works is telepathic monkeys. Ours is Fergus, a fine monkey who lives in a small hut on the far side of the moon, the side which gets the best signals from the outer worlds. You'd like him, you really would. How the system works is this: the individual who wants to send a letter dictates it to a mind monkey on their world. Then the mind monkey sends it telepathically to Fergus who writes it down. It isn't a perfect system. For a start, for it to work all the monkeys must have met. This is called 'entanglement', and it is vital to any psychic-monkey mail service. Also, the messages are never written down exactly as the sender intended. But no matter, it's a lot better than trans-dimensional homing squirrels. That system was very messy, and sometimes deadly, though *always* adorable.

The main problem with this system is that every time I want to get the mail I have to make a journey of several weeks following a narrow trail through a stony wilderness, along narrow ledges, skirting chasms of despair. At one point I have to sneak past a mud-dragon who has been sleeping for 700,000 years. In all that time he hasn't even twitched, they say, but there's a first time for all things.

When I finally reach Fergus's hut he'll come out and hand me whatever has been sent, and a tin of hot soup, for which I am very grateful. This time, all that was waiting for me was a note from a communications company saying, 'Are you currently happy with your mind-monkey coverage?' And underneath, Fergus had scrawled, 'Yes!!?? x.x.' He eyed me carefully as I read it. I guess I should have known that there wouldn't be any real mail. No one, after all, even knows the old man is alive. But I do like to get out once in a while.

EXIT WOUNDS

They seemed to travel 'up' for 'hours'.

Then there was a heavy sound, a cross between a thud and splat. It was a *thplat*, definitely, and it seemed to sound their end. Then the engine cut out and there was silence. Everyone opened their eyes and saw that their craft was falling over a bright terrain of crumbling mountains. The chute had opened. That was good. Below they saw an amazing sight: it was a creature, serpentine, fat and burning emerald green in the sunshine. The creature was so vast it defied belief, and so ugly it defied it a second time: it had folds of skin, red, orange, yellow, green, and great scarlet pustules all along its flanks, each as large as a volcano, each erupting with yellowy pus. Its eyes were black and cloudy; it had a row of spiny fins along its back. It had one back leg upon the side of a volcano, and one of its forelegs planted square in the middle of the remains of a mid-sized village. A deep canyon in the jungled earth showed where the dragon had made its slow, merciless progress, while ahead of it – just a few hundred miles on – was a madly gleaming city built around a set of mountain peaks. Just behind the creature's eyes was a blowhole – probably for breathing or expelling gases – and just behind the blowhole was another hole, red and frayed at the edges, a hole made by the rocket which had just punched through its tiny brain like a high-powered bullet.

'I knew it!' shouted Fabrigas. 'We were inside a beast the whole time!'

Below, the beast was writhing in its end. This brand-new hole would be terminal. It reached up into the sky and snapped at the empty air with its long, terrible teeth, before falling back and coming to rest with its head upon an active volcano; the plume of burning gas and rock began to scour the flesh away from its skull.

'It must have grabbed us in its jaws as we flew towards the planet from the moon. This would explain why there were so many crashed ships in there. At last, a solid reality to put our feet upon!' And then, as if to mock the man of reason, the whole scene below them vanished like a dream – the serpent, the city – and they found themselves drifting down towards a silvery forest.

'What madness is this?' said Fabrigas.

FORBIDDEN, FORGOTTEN

They landed with a soft bump because the land was covered in a layer of crimson moss. The trees were short conifers whose needles were silver, smooth and shiny as wire. The glade they landed in became a valley which channelled the moss down in a red river to a broad, scarlet plain under a sky as rough and grey as soldiers' coats, singed bright orange at the horizon. There was no animal life, it seemed; no birds or insects called to them. There was only the calm, eerie ring of a billion needles rubbing together. It was so strange and beautiful that they sat there for a full minute before the captain said, 'So. We missed the hole?'

He left the capsule cautiously, his heavy boots sank deep into the plush, red carpet. 'This bothers me,' he said to no one. He wandered to the edge of the clearing, put his hands on his hips, and peered down the long valley. The others waited with steepled fingers. He wandered out of sight and was gone for a full five minutes before he ambled back, paused, strolled to the hatch, frowned and said, 'We make camp.'

★

There was no food to gather, no critters, no mushrooms, no toadstools. There was nothing to make shelter with, and no need anyway, since the evening – if it was an evening – was warm and pleasant.

Fabrigas made coffee on his small stove. Miss Fritzacopple made soup with mushrooms the Ubuntu had given them and some herbs she had kept. Kimmy watched her stir the pot.

'This place is disturbingly uniform,' said Fabrigas. 'These needles are all exactly the same length. It's as if they've been made by machine. They remind me of the Festivus trees we had when I was a boy. We used to hang decorations on them, and on Festivus Eve Brother Love would come and leave presents for us.'

But no one had the energy to think about what Festivus was, or where they were, or what it meant. All they could do was let their tired bones sink into the soft earth and sigh.

*

Lenore woke to feel someone gently tickling her face, and she opened her nose to discover . . . What is that? . . . Butterflies!

A swarm of white butterflies had flown into the clearing; not just hundreds, or thousands, but *millions* of butterflies were floating up the valley in a shivery cloud. What a sight. Everyone ran around the glade, throwing up their arms and giggling. Except the captain. Soon they were lost in the cloud, not even knowing which way was which. They enjoyed themselves for almost an hour. Thousands of butterflies were soon spiked upon the ends of the conifer needles, so that in a few minutes the bare trees seemed to have sprouted exquisite foliage. Then, another sign of animal life: from nowhere, bright orange spiders ran down the needles and began to feast on the tender creatures. It was quite a slaughter.

The butterfly extravaganza continued for hours. The sun refused to set, the light remained soft and steady, the spiders grew fat. Everybody sat in silence and watched the never-ending drifts of snowy Lepidoptera. After a few hours the captain said, 'I hate these damned butterflies,' and no one bothered to disagree.

*

Then they were gone, as quickly as they'd arrived, and the clearing was once more deathly still and quiet.

'I feel like I could just lie here for ever,' said Kimmy. 'The ground is so soft, I feel like I could go on listening to the music of the trees for days. It's so beautiful.'

Fabrigas heard her and knew at once that she was right and that they should move on very quickly, without delay, right this second, let's go. But then somehow seconds later he was thinking of something else. He was staring up at the trees and marvelling at the way the geometry of the needle-straight spines caused circles to pulse through his eyes.

★

Circles, upon circles, upon circles.

★

Fabrigas looked up. He'd been writing in his journal, but all he'd written was page after page of nonsense. But he looked up now because standing on the far side of the clearing was a man.

★

Miss Fritzacopple, wandering among the trees, could not make sense of any of it. She had a specimen jar in her right hand but nothing really to put in it. She'd pulled up a clump of red moss and plopped it in a jar, noting, as she did, that the earth below was a fine, pale sand, dry and uniform. The music of the needles had become a deafening chorus to her now. It ruffled her consciousness and made her think, as she stared at her arms and hands, that they were ugly: that they belonged to an alien creature. When she'd walked to the other side of the clearing and looked back at the hole in the mossy ground it had looked like a terrified mouth screaming at her, so she'd put the divot back in its hole and patted it lightly into place. The bark of the trees was hard and white with calluses of black. When she pulled the bark away she found a raw, red wax. She pressed the bark back into place. Patted it lightly. She felt an urge to throw off all her clothes and wander like a child through this landscape, but she quickly checked herself.

She noticed something strange: the jar which had held the moss had a layer of golden goo in the bottom. She held it up, noted the tiny air bubbles. It looked so familiar. And then she did something so shocking that later, when she thought back on it, she'd shudder. She took her finger, dabbed it lightly in the goo and touched it to her tongue. She let out a cry of delight.

*

The stranger wore the remains of an expensive suit. It was the first thing that struck you. Despite the fact that both trouser legs had been shredded to the knees – as if by the claws of a wild beast – despite the fact that his jacket was stained and rumpled, and that one of the breast pockets was torn back so that a red nipple peeped out like a rising sun, you could tell that, originally, this had been his best suit. But now his long hair was slicked over with some kind of luminous goo, though without a mirror he'd created a parting as fiercely crooked as a lightning bolt. The stranger was mad-eyed and emaciated. The stranger had dead butterflies in his hair. The stranger said, 'You have to leave!'

'Who are you?' said Fabrigas, snapping out of his reverie. The others swooned awake. Lenore had been dreaming that she was being eaten, piece by piece, by butterflies while a madman read her stories.

'You have to leave! My God, you have no idea. If only you knew. If only you could grasp the situation – My word, my God, is that the DX9100?' and the man skipped alarmingly fast among them to where their capsule sat, embedded in the moss, its chute strung along the needles like drying laundry. Kimmy noticed that she had cocoons hanging from her nose, her earlobes, the captain too. She plucked one off and showed it to him. He wrinkled his nose, then scrabbled at his head with both hands. The stranger was poring over their capsule, running his hands up and down its surface. Then he tapped the fuselage with a bony knuckle and listened as it boomed. Then he kicked it, hard, and listened again.

'Hey!' said the captain. 'Would you mind not kicking our property? And who are you?'

The strange man's head swivelled slowly, like a carnival clown, and he stared wide-eyed at the captain. Then, slowly, he began to walk backwards, like a man retreating from a dangerous beast; he raised his palms and stepped, slowly, one foot over the other, until at last he was safe behind a tree.

The captain and Fabrigas looked at each other, expressionless.

'We can still see you!' said the captain.

The strange man pulled his spine straight and buttoned his jacket. 'What about now?'

'Yes,' said Kimmy. 'We can see you very clearly.'

'Right!' said the stranger as he purposefully clapped his hands together. 'I'll give you thirty thousand rupits for the DX9200. I don't have it on me,' slapping his breasts, 'but I'm good for it. I come from a fine family. Tin miners. Twenty thousand if I can take it now.'

'You said it was a DX9100.'

'I did?'

'Yes, when you first saw it you said, "Is that the DX9100?"'

'Yes, note the interrogative, my boy: *is* that the DX9100? On closer examination and extensive tests –' *tong!* – 'it turns out that it is, after all, the DX9200.'

'Really?'

'Yes.'

'Well, why does it say "DX9300" on the side?'

'Ah,' said the man, 'but that's just what they want you to think.'

FORBIDDEN ZONE

'Loneliness,' said Fabrigas, 'is harder on the mind than the fiercest opium. Strange things happen to the mind when you spend too long alone, and unlike other brain maladies it cannot be undone. The damage cannot be fixed.' He spoke as if he knew well, but none of the others noticed. They were all staring at the man.

'If you untie me,' said the stranger, 'I'll reduce my offer to twenty-five thousand.'

The captain had tackled the stranger and tied him up after it became clear that they'd get little sense out of him otherwise.

'I am sorry I tried to dance with you,' the man added, his head bouncing from side to side as he spoke, his restless eyes roaming the cloudless skies. 'It was unprofessional for a man of my standing, and I apologise for any offence my actions might have caused. Now if you'll only untie me I'll take my ship and be on my way.'

'We'll let you go soon,' said the captain. 'First, tell us why you called this the "Forbidden Zone".'

'Because it is!' cried the stranger.

'What makes it forbidden?'

'What doesn't?! There are dangers innumerable here.'

'Such as?'

'Oh,' said the man, dropping his voice to a whisper, 'some men have been driven mad by the butterflies, others have done themselves nasty injuries on those needles, look,' and though his hands were bound by his sides he was able to raise an index finger to show the tiny red puncture wound on the tip.

'Right.'

'The moss conceals deep pits!' the man continued.

'Right, and what is at the bottom of the pits?'

'More moss!'

'So, sharp trees and comfortable traps. That's the Forbidden Zone?'

'Yes. And bears.'

They had managed to get a small amount of information about the man. His name was Corpram Boniver; he had been a scientist of some note, apparently. He'd been a pioneer in the field of feline interreal zoology, the science of putting cats in boxes and then guessing what they're up to. Then, after an incident about which the man refused to speak, he had been banished, exiled into the Forbidden Zone, a sentence which held a great irony, for among Boniver's many significant achievements he had helped design and build the Forbidden Zone.

'You designed this whole dimension?' said Fabrigas, amazed.

'Yes! I built it with a man called Dray. Executions are barbaric, and prisons are pointless. We wanted prisoners to go to a place where they could confront their very nature. That's why we invented the Forbidden Zone: not as a prison for the body, but as a prison for the mind and soul. We who are prisoners here have committed a crime to which, given the opportunity, we will always return. And so we must be kept away from common reality.' As he spoke about his work the man's madness seemed to vanish; he spoke quietly, and his eyes stopped roaming the skies, and everyone watching caught a glimpse of what this madman used to be.

'The bears,' said Boniver, 'were just to keep things interesting.'

★

'He's clearly nuts,' said the captain.

'Clearly,' said Fabrigas as he cleaned a nail with a needle. 'But he's all we have to guide us out of here. At least half of what he says is true, I'm convinced of that. At least every second word.'

'But what if he leads us into a trap?'

'What trap? A spongy pit? A bear's picnic?'

'What if he's telling the truth about the bears?'

'We would have seen signs: droppings, paw-prints. Besides, there's nothing to eat around here.'

'Except us.'

'And that's a point. If we don't find a way out, we'll starve.'

'I smells animal,' said Lenore, from the far edge of the clearing, and that's when, from the distance, they heard Miss Fritzacopple scream.

'That'll be her shoes,' said Corpram.

'She's gone and got herself into trouble again,' said the captain as he stood lazily and ambled away among the trees.

★

Miss Fritzacopple, who was a sensible woman, but who had a strange habit of wandering off and getting into trouble, was up a tree. She was a long way up a tree. How she got up there was a mystery. The captain found her soon enough and pulled up on the edge of the glade, about ten yards from the tree. He stopped there mainly because below Miss Fritzacopple, swishing at her legs with his paws, was a largish bear.

'How did you get up that tree?' called the captain.

'I used to be a dancer!' she replied.

'Just stay where you are,' said the captain.

★

SOME USELESS THINGS PEOPLE SAY DURING BEAR
ATTACKS:
1. Just stay where you are!
2. He's more afraid of you!
3. Don't let him smell your fear!
4. Play dead!
5. Throw the ham away! He only wants your ham!

★

'What do we do?' said the captain.

'We need to create a distraction,' said the old man, who had caught up with him. 'I'll get his attention, you get her down.'

There was no one there, even the botanist, who didn't notice how pretty the bear looked. He was a golden bear with hazel eyes and a white muzzle. His pink nose and outsized paws said, 'Let's cuddle,' though his bared black claws and bright gums said, '. . . cuddle to the death!'

Fabrigas strode into the glade with his arms raised. 'Bear!' he shouted, and the creature turned its huge head; his eyes narrowed in a way that said, 'Have we met?' Then he turned back, extended to full height, and continued trying to paw the legs of the terrified botanist.

The captain heard a 'Hup. Hup. Hup' behind him. Looking over his shoulder he saw Boniver, still in ropes, hopping towards them.

'Hup. Hup. Hup.'

'Oh, great,' muttered Lambestyo.

'Tell her to throw her shoes away!' cried the man, breathless.

'Go away.'

'He only wants her shoes. Tell her to throw her shoes away as far as possible.'

'Don't be stupid.'

'If you want her to live, hup, you'll tell her to throw, hup, her shoes away as far as possible.' The man had now hupped his way to the captain's side. The captain sighed.

'Miss, listen carefully!' said Boniver. 'I want you to take both your boots off and throw them as far as you can!'

Miss Fritzacopple thought long and hard. She loved these boots. She'd seen them in a vintage store in a place called Melrose Heights. She'd spent a month's wages on them. She'd lived off noodles and bread so she could have them. They were pretty as well as comfortable, which is very, very rare, and important when you might be collecting samples in a jungle one minute, and meeting a high-ranking member of the scientific community the next. Was life worth living without them? She looked down at the bear, who was pushing on the trunk with a single paw now, seemingly testing its strength, perhaps wondering if it might be climbed, or brought down.

'Well? What the heck are you waiting for?'

With a heavy sigh, Miss Fritzacopple pulled the boots from her feet and threw them far into the trees. They made no sound.

The bear followed their trajectory with his big, brown eyes. Then he let out a marbly cry and huffed off after them, and no one, except Corpram Boniver, could quite believe it.

*

'These bears are very territorial,' said Boniver. 'You only find one in each region of the zone. Most of them like honey, or human flesh, but for reasons I can't even imagine, the bear who roams this region likes ladies' shoes.'

The group was silent. What could you say?

'Of course,' continued Boniver, 'it might just be that ladies' shoes generally have narrow heels and they push further into the root honey,' and he ripped up a clump of moss and squeezed, releasing a rain of golden liquid. 'It's honey!' he cried, his fingers smacking in his mouth. 'You should try some, it's really very good,' and though he was clearly mad, everyone had to admit that he was right about the shoes, and the honey.

★

They ate honey until they couldn't.

★

'I can't possibly lead you out of here,' said Boniver.

It was late, although you wouldn't notice any change in the light. The only way to tell it was night was that that was when the bears liked to feed. 'And how do the bears know it's night?' Fabrigas had asked.

'Because the butterflies wake them.'

'And how do –' but the old man stopped himself.

Kimmy and Lenore were sitting near the edge of the glade. Lenore had found a way, even in this pretty place, to look completely terrifying. 'I smell a coming,' she said softly. No one heard her. Miss Fritzacopple was sleeping off her terror.

'But I still don't understand *why* you can't lead us out,' said Fabrigas.

'Because there is no way out. If there was, don't you think I would have found it?'

'Is there a wall?'

'Better,' said Boniver.

'An electric field?'

'Better. I designed the Forbidden Zone to be a mini-universe. If you head in one direction for long enough you end up where you started. Anyway, it's all very complicated. I wouldn't expect any of you to understand.'

'Nonsense!' cried Fabrigas. 'Why would you say such a ridiculous thing? A child could understand this,' though in truth he was absolutely staggered.

'I smells bees now,' said Lenore.

'Rubbish,' said Corpram Boniver. 'There are no bees here. You are confused by all the honey. Go back to sleep, little girl.'

'So there's no way we can ever escape?' said the captain.

'No. This universe would have to expire first.'

'How horrible,' said Miss Fritzacopple as she roused herself from her nap.

'Bees. Definitely bees.'

'Though if you untie me, I'll show you some secrets.'

The captain sighed. 'I suppose we should. But you must promise not to touch our craft.'

'Wouldn't dream of it, my boy.'

There was a hum growing, low and angry. The captain felt it first. He stood and walked to the edge of the clearing.

'What *is* that?' said Miss Fritzacopple, whose hearing was acute.

'I tells you, it's *bees*.'

'Ball-cocks! There's no bees here. I should know, I invented here. Only butterflies and bears, in that order! Never have three Bs together, everyone knows that! You're talking crazy!'

Fabrigas noticed how easily the man had slipped back into being mad since they'd loosened his ropes.

'Definitely bees.'

'No bees, no bees!' But then Boniver stopped. He shrugged off his ropes and walked to the edge of the glade, stood next to the captain and quietly murmured: 'No bees.'

BEES

The bees came through the clearing like bullets. Fat, black, yard-long bees with terrible black eyes. 'Bees!' screamed Boniver. 'We're all done for, it's every man for himself!' And he ran, clearing the glade in a few short skips, stopping for a brief moment to lay his right index finger tenderly on the side of the escape rocket before fleeing, screaming and giggling, among the silver trees.

'Into the rocket!' cried Fabrigas, and they dived in as the glade began to fill with black buzzing nuggets. From inside they could see them circling, spiralling into the sky, swooping down in military formation, passing the windows of the rocket with inches to spare.

'I miss the butterflies!' shouted Miss Fritzacopple.

That's when they all noticed that Lambestyo hadn't moved from his spot at the edge of the glade. He was staring down the valley, one hand on his hip, as the bees swarmed around him.

'Where's our captains?' said Lenore.

'He's . . . he's fine,' said Fabrigas. 'He seems to be making friends.' Two big drones hung bobbing in front of Lambestyo's face like carnival balloons. From far off came the sound of drums, also trumpets. The bees ceased their swoopings.

★

First came the giant insects, stamping and clicking, sinking deep into the moss, each twice the size of a bull elephant, each bearing a

391

heavily armed soldier upon its armour-plated back. There were trumpet players followed by a regiment of young soldiers with white rifles. The convoy stopped in front of Lambestyo with a big right-foot stomp and the soldiers' rifles leaped from their left shoulders to the earth with a loud, collective crack, and the giant insects – who numbered at least a thousand – moved and rattled.

Nothing happened for a while. Then, a ripple in the ranks as a short, round man with a bright red sash grinning like a gash across his torso came tumbling through. He ignored our boy captain, scuttling past him up the mossy crimson carpet and up to the rocket with the tiny, precise steps of a tightrope walker. He peered into the porthole, and smiled broadly. Then he knocked politely, three times. Fabrigas opened the porthole and said, 'Yes?'

'On behalf of the Independent Constitutional Monarchy of Diemendääs, I would like to extend our *extreme* gratitude for your brave and wholly unsolicited assistance in ridding our hinterlands of the great worm who was threatening our lives and livelihood and laying waste to our beautiful countryside. We do not know how you fell into the Forbidden Zone, but on behalf of Their Majesties, the Emperor and Empress of Diemendääs, I would like to offer this royal escort from the zone to the city, where you will be afforded all the comforts and hospitalities that we can offer, for as long as they shall be needed. What say you?'

'We accept,' said the old man.

*

They were being assisted into a carriage on the back of a giant scorpion. It was taking a long time. 'We really do appreciate your efforts in killing the worm,' said the man. His name was Valkilma; he was youngish, perhaps only in his thirties, with limp jowls and lizardy black eyes. He was Diemendääs's Lord Mayor. 'Tell me, where did you get the idea to punch through his brain-pan with a rocket? So bold!' He leaned forward eagerly. 'And how were you able to target its tiny brain so precisely?'

'I would not want to bore you with the details,' said Fabrigas, and Miss Fritzacopple coughed politely.

Upon entering they saw that their sting-tailed taxi contained a small and slightly pudgy boy. He wore white britches and an embroidered silver-buttoned coat covered in medals. 'Is this going to take all day?' he said. 'I would have stayed in my room if I thought they would smell this bad.'

'Ah-ha-ha,' laughed the mayor, nervously as he took his own seat. 'This is His Majesty, Prince Panduke. He insisted on coming along today.' He spoke, as a dentriloquist does, through gritted teeth, '. . . Even though we explained how long it might ta-aaaaake.' In his nervousness he sang the last word. In the pristine carriage our friends suddenly became aware of their filth. Their clothes and faces were streaked with mud and sap and chunks of goo. Fabrigas's beard looked like a sparrow nursery. Lenore's face shone as if a team of snails had performed a dance routine upon it. 'I'm suddenly aware,' said Fabrigas, 'that we smell somewhat . . . gamey.'

'Not to worry,' said the mayor, 'we will disinfect you thoroughly before you enter the city.'

'What is that?' said the prince, pointing at Lenore. He looked terrified. 'She's *green*. I don't like it.'

'Am I green? I would never have known.'

'And why are that one's eyes made from glass?'

'Ah-ha-ha-ha,' laughed the mayor. 'So inquisitive!'

'They're my glasses,' said Kimmy, 'I need them to look at things.'

'Well, I hope you're not going to look at me,' said Prince Panduke.

'I wouldn't need glasses to see you,' replied Kimmy.

'Ah-ha-ha, wonderful!'

'I'm bored now. I hate this place. I only came to shoot a bear.' Then the train departed, leaving the clearing, the escape pod and the body-shaped indentations in the moss.

'It seems like a lot of fuss for little old us,' said Miss Fritzacopple.

'Nonsense!' said the mayor. 'You're all heroes now. It was rather uncanny that you landed right in the heart of our Forbidden Zone. It shouldn't actually be possible. Our best scientists are working on it. But we'll soon have you out, and that's the main thing.'

They came to a gate: a black iron structure whose posts were topped with laughing gargoyles and a sign cast in black steel which read 'This Is Not A Gate'. 'A gate!' exclaimed Fabrigas. 'I thought there was no way out.'

'As you can see from the sign it is *not* a gate,' said Valkilma. 'We use a gate to send the prisoners in. This is the first time we've ever had to make a retrieval. You are going to love our city. It is quite magnificent.'

Miss Fritzacopple stared forlornly at her feet. 'I hope that bear enjoys my boots.'

'I despise bears,' said the prince. 'I think they should all be shot.' Kimmy clicked her tongue. 'I keep owls,' he continued.

'Of course you do,' said Kimmy.

'Now you might find the scene beyond the gate slightly shocking,' said the mayor. 'Rest assured that it is not representative of our great city and the experiences you will surely have there.'

And as they passed through the portal the Forbidden Zone vanished, and they found themselves on the burning edge of a battlefield.

THE EMPEROR KARN KARN-ZHENG

Karn Karn-Zheng was a great emperor. He ruled the state of Qin (formerly of the Xo) for thirty years. He was intelligent, clever, capable, and strong in battle. People called him Daffodil, because when his aides were speaking to him his head would bob continuously, like a flower in a gentle breeze. When he took over as ruler his state was on the brink of chaos. Zheng not only saved his state from destruction, but he reunited it with several neighbouring states, expanding his empire considerably. He called himself Zheng Shi (First Zheng). He divided his state into prefectures. He unified the weights and measures. He standardised the money. He fixed the axle-length of wagons, the height of masts, the length of skirts. He developed a new writing language. He built an impenetrable wall around his city. He built himself a citadel shaped like a daffodil head. He made all the men wear hats. He shut himself inside his citadel, never leaving. He collected his urine in jars and arranged the jars on the floor of his bedroom suite in the shape of a pentagram. He had everyone in the capital city lose one finger in his honour. Finally, he sent his entire standing army to lay siege to a city called Diemendääs so that he could capture the most beautiful woman in the universe (whose face he'd never seen). Then, when his citizens were nearly in revolt because they'd suddenly lost their supply of honey, he declared that his army should only attack the western wall of the city.

The path to greatness has not gates.
A thousand roads lead to it.
When one passes through this gateless gate
He walks freely between heaven and earth.

DIEMENDÄÄS

The great army was throwing itself against a wall a mile high and thick along the top with defenders. Bees poured from the fortifications to tip cauldrons of boiling honey on the invaders, while the invaders attacked the wall with iron siege machines. Behind, a line of trebuchets threw spiked explosive devices. Some smashed into the battlements, raining fire on their own men, and some sailed high over the wall. Behind the siege machines were legions of soldiers waiting for a breach in the fortifications.

'Emperor Karn Karn-Zheng has been attacking our wall for decades. His army has come for our own Empress, don't you know!' The mayor laughed nervously and put his hands to his face.

'The Empress?' said Miss Fritzacopple. A siege machine groaned and crumpled in the distance; the troops on the battlements cheered.

'Of course. The Empress is the most beautiful woman in the universe. Any ruler would give his manly parts for her. If you saw her, you'd understand. But you'll never.' He pointed a finger to the ground; it was unclear why. 'Fortunately they are limiting their attack to our western wall. Unfortunately, this is where the gate to the Forbidden Zone is located.'

'I thought you said there was no gate.'

'There is not.'

'But why attack just the western wall?' said Fabrigas. 'With their numbers they could easily surround the whole city.'

'Oh,' said the mayor as he studied a nail, 'we've signed a treaty that they'll only attack from the west. They are one of our biggest honey traders after all.'

The old man's shoulders rose and slumped. In the distance, another siege machine crumbled, arms flailing, like a stricken giant, and the troops along the battlement cheered again, but soon another had been wheeled forward to take its place.

'Look at that,' said the mayor. 'It's been going on like this since I was a boy.' On the horizon above the battlefield and nearly three hands at arm's length wide was a black moon. 'Is that Bespophus?' said Fabrigas as he raised a bony finger.

'Oh, you know of Bespophus? Yes. It comes six feet-inches closer every year. Eventually it'll smash into us. If we aren't killed instantly we'll have those plants to deal with. Honestly, will our troubles ever cease?'

Valkilma excused himself and went over to an official-looking tent. He was gone for fifteen minutes. When he returned he said, 'I have contacted our enemy's diplomatic office. We should be given passage through soon. Fingers crossed!'

And soon enough a trumpet call was sounded and the battle stopped. 'Forward easy,' said the mayor, and their caravan moved forward through the field of tents, through the lines of weary enemy soldiers, through the idle siege machines. They saw piles of burned and broken corpses. They heard wounded soldiers crying out, they heard the wind moving banners and signal flags. And when they approached the massive city gate – and this truly was a gate; don't get me started – it opened. The enemy troops stood patiently by their steam-powered battering ram, just feet away from the soldiers on the other side. The convoy passed through the gate and they heard it close behind them with a stroke of thunder. Then they heard the battle stagger to its feet again.

'I sense our deaths here,' said Lambestyo, and Fritzacopple nudged him.

'I just don't understand how all this can be about a woman,' the botanist said.

The mayor laughed. 'My dear, it's *always* about a woman.'

BLACK CITY

Towers, miles high, stabbing at the misty sky. Countless forbidding towers the colour of dark honey: liquid-skinned towers caught, it seemed, in the act of melting. Supporting the towers from below were black-eyed monoliths carved with coiling serpents and gargoylish beasts from a disturbed imagination. All about the towers was a shifting haze of dots like the imperfections in an old film, a grain to every surface moving with the faint jungle breezes. Bees. Like a black rain, like notes cascading from the pages of the music of the universe. And from the towers came a hum. Not a low, peaceful hum, not the sound of a field in summer – assuming you have experienced such a thing – not the sound of a hive, not even the sound of a field of hives, but something much, much greater. It was a music which made you feel as if the individual grains of your body were shaking loose and dancing you to joyful oblivion.

'This city is . . .' Miss Fritzacopple had not the word to hand. She leaned from their carriage to hear the buzz. The air in Diemendääs is like a spider's web; it tickles the skin. She saw a row of temples carved with dancing dipping demons, their mouths wide and fanged, some weighed down by powerful phalluses. The demons challenged every visitor to the great city, and they seemed to turn to watch these strangers as they came down a boulevard thick with carriages hauled by giant creatures. She saw their scorpion's claws rasping at the pristine paving stones. She breathed out so hard that she forgot to breathe in again.

'I know this place!' cried Fabrigas, and then to undermine his exclamation: 'Do I know this place?' He was leaning out of the other window like an old wolf. 'I travelled here on one of my earliest adventures, I think. I drank tea with a mystic. He showed me how to vanish my own reflection from the shiny back of a spoon. I rode a raft down rapids into an almost bottomless cavern. I . . .' For a second his great brain seemed to break its banks and his eyes fluttered.

The old man is recounting all of this to me, he remembers each event precisely. Each moment is stored like an ancient artefact in the great palace of his memory. And yet he yells at me now, in the darkness of the basement of the mansion on the moon: 'How could I not remember I had been there before?!'

'But you clearly have not been to here,' Lenore huffed from her seat in the carriage upon the scorpion's back.

'No,' the old man replied heavily. 'This is obviously a different city, in a different universe. Though not everything is different.'

From the journal of M. Francisco Fabrigas

With all that has happened I have had little time to write. We crossed over from our universe, despite it being technically impossible to do so, and despite me sabotaging my own engine, and despite a fleet of our own ships trying to destroy us. We wound up on a man-eating moon. It is a tantalising outcome, for it proves substantively the existence of alternate realities, and thus the possibility that somewhere in the Infiniverse is a moon upon which my father and my nanny, Danni, still live. Such a place inevitably exists.

In any case, we are now in a city called Diemendääs. This Gothic city sits at the foot of seven sleeping volcanoes. It is frightening to behold. And yet its nature compels the visitor to keep his eyes wide open. Its name in the traditional local language cannot be translated, but it loosely equates to . . . 'Glory passes', or perhaps 'Flesh is brief', or perhaps 'Rest in peace'. It rises up in broad plateaux to battlements containing inner suburbs of exquisite geometry, before becoming a series of spires and castles (known locally as the Royal Lily-pad – the home of government and the ruling family), then terminating, finally, at sheer mountain cliffs into which are carved its very ancient monasteries. Inside this labyrinth live ten thousand monks who, our host tells us, expend their lives excavating the catacombs. They work like moles, running through the caves with lamps attached to their foreheads. They are piecing together evidence from their city's past so that they might learn the precise date on which their city, perhaps their universe, will end.

We have arrived, by fair wind, or not, at the precise hour of the beginning of their most sacred month, the Festival of the Dead.

That is all I know so far.

I must accompany my suit and cloak for decontamination.

Tonight there will be a banquet in our honour.

THE EMPEROR

Our friends were taken to a decontamination centre, then to their suites where they bathed and rested. Their clothes were kept for further decontamination. At 500 local time the guests were taken by boat to the royal banquet hall for a feast in their honour. Perfume River was six miles wide and thick with pleasure boats, carnival ships, multi-storey steamers, many as high as six levels; their paddles flashed in the foggy air and from one bank you could not see the other.

At 535 local time they arrived at the banquet hall, a mile-long open-sided hall placed in the middle of the river. The hall was filled with Diemendääs's greatest citizens: artists, poets, leaders, generals, the conspicuously wealthy; they all stood to applaud our friends, their jewels and medals tinkling merrily. The people of Diemendääs applaud in time, did you know? They were escorted to the far end, to a raised platform below a throne some eight feet high and carved with serpents. At 548 local time Lenore complained of a fever. 'Miss Lady, I don't feel good. This place is all too much. There's a beating in my head.'

'It's just the heat. Drink some water.'

At 549 local time Lenore drank some water.

At 600 l.t. the royal barge came through the mist like a river monster, and the assembled guests rose, a gangplank fell, a figure emerged, a tall shadow in a long coat who spasmed in the hot and hazy air. The figure lingered along the gangplank and spent a minute staring down the river, and Miss Fritzacopple would observe later (at around 2213 l.t.) that he seemed lonely, and the captain would observe (at roughly the same time) that he seemed 'stupid', and Fabrigas would comment that he didn't seem to be the man he remembered.

'That's him?' said Fabrigas.

'If you mean the Emperor,' said the mayor, 'then yes.'

'I've met him. I think. I do not remember him ever looking so . . . imperious.'

'Our beloved ruler has many things on his mind,' said the mayor. 'With the giant worm, the armies camped at his western wall, the terrible virus that recently struck our bee community, the outbreaks of dancing sickness, the monks who every day proclaim the coming end – even our own moon wants to destroy us. The stress has begun to show . . . And of course there's the deaths.'

Yes, a series of mysterious deaths in the steamy jungle city.

At 616 local time, with several thousand heavily armed guards surrounding the venue, with 'frog-men' in the river, and snipers with blow-dart tubes hidden in the eaves and on the roofs, and several thousand guests each holding a fluteful of wine and a lungful of foggy air, the Emperor turned and walked briskly to his throne. He was followed by three boy-servants, one carrying a ceremonial bowl, one carrying a golden egg and one carrying a lamp with lighted wick. The Emperor ascended his throne and sat stern, motionless. The pudgy Prince Panduke arrived, stood by his seat at the lower table and frowned. 'So it's you people again.'

'Yes, hello, I will have a brandy or strong wine,' said Lambestyo, and the prince snapped, 'I'm not a wait-boy, insolent fool!' Kimmy and Miss Fritzacopple smiled behind their hands. There was no sign of the Empress. It was 618 local time.

'Honoured guests,' said a young crier, 'you bless the royal family with your presence. You have destroyed a creature which could have ridden across the city's walls as if they were made of chalk, smothered us all beneath its blubbered belly. But you killed it with a manned bullet through the brain-pan, and for that they are royally grateful.'

'Who? Us?'

'Shhhh.' The botanist glared at the captain. 'Put down your fork.'

The captain put down the fork and turned his chair, slung one arm across the back. He did not enjoy long speeches.

'. . . Our city is suffering a tide of misfortune. The worm, the outbreaks of the initially hilarious, but now tragic, dancing fever; the invaders massed upon our western wall, though fortunately not our eastern!'

A shudder of agreement passed through the crowd.

'Oh, oh yes,' the captain gestured with a steak knife, 'not the eastern!'

'Shhhhhh,' said Fritzacopple. 'If you don't behave I'll send you home.'

'You aren't the boss of me.' But he put down his knife.

'And of course,' continued the crier, 'there are the recent misfortunes, those which have made us all afraid to leave our apartments, mansions and bungalows.'

Killings. He could have said 'killings' and heard no less a desperate wind pass through the room. A plague of brutal and mysterious deaths had beset this city. The city's elite had begun to dispatch themselves in increasingly bizarre ways. Only a few days before, Krugg Micentrappen, acclaimed for his adorable photographs of babies dressed as vampires, was found suffocated to death, his mouth stuffed with several cubic feet of purple velvet, though there was no sign of forced entry to his apartment.

And late the previous morning, just as our guests were punching through the skin of the great beast, Gustvavas Kambert, a hat-maker famous for his outrageous fashion statements, was found beaten to death with a steam iron. Mysteriously, he was found still clutching the iron, lying in a room locked from within. What could have compelled him to do such a thing?

The Emperor remained motionless, emotionless, as the speech

went on. Just the week before, the poet Deltiminy – a good friend of the Emperor and twice awarded Diemendääs's annual 'Strangest Attired' award – was killed by consumption of a poisoned pudding. What was most bizarre was that only the victim's fingerprints were on the poison jar. Also that, according to the post-mortem specialists, he seemed to have continued eating even as the poison took hold.

'. . . And so we bring to you this humble banquet in your honour, for we are humble people.'

'They're what now?'

'Shhhhh!'

MENU

*For the enjoyment of the Emperor and his
honoured guests at his banquet table on this,
the 1st day of the Festival of the Dead.*

Aperitif

Bitter essence of mountain cave-slug
on a bed of snake-blood ice

Starter

7-times-cooked blood-sucking fire ants
scorched in 400-year-old tortoise
liqueur and served on a paradise of
giant mountain-sloth's ear-fungus
with a drizzle of salty dove tears

Entrée

A bird's beak of cold were-weevil flesh
soup smoked with giant cave-bat wings
and graced with a lattice crown of bees' web
and preserved jungle-leeches

Main

Cutlet of giant western fighting crab
(from the Sea of Sadness) embalmed in
Royal Jelly from Their Majesties' hives
and served with 10,000-year-old falcon eggs
on a tapestry of uncooked pheasant eyes

King's Plate

Live Northern Black Widow butterfly
held in a droplet of gorilla snot

BANQUET

At 630 local time the first course was served.

'So it's you again,' said Prince Panduke.

'So it is,' said Kimmy. The prince was at the second to last place at the table, and the last place was empty.

'Who sits there?' said Miss Fritzacopple.

'That's Mother's place,' said the prince. 'She never comes to these events, but we always leave a place.'

'How sad. Is she ill?'

'She is . . .' said the mayor, interjecting quickly, '. . . shy.'

At precisely 800 local time the King's Plate was served, centrepiece of the entire feast, a signature delicacy chosen by His Majesty the Emperor to dazzle his guests.

'. . . Butterflies?'

Butterflies.

'It is so. These are from the Emperor's private nursery. Each was raised by hand and they have a flavour I think you will find . . . quite unlike anything you've tasted.'

'I'm sure,' said the captain.

Each plate set before them had a single butterfly, and each butterfly was held to the plate at one leg with a dot of amber snot.

'I like my butterflies . . . done,' said the captain as he held his shaking specimen up to the light. Each butterfly was a work of art in its own right.

'Sweet mercifuls,' said Lenore. 'Even the smell of them is ferocious.'

Miss Fritzacopple said nothing. Her butterfly was deepest black with pale violet circles on her wings, and she quietly pulsed upon her silver platter. Fritzacopple became aware of the freakish crunching of butterflies between teeth. The people were eating them. Not admiring the exquisite markings on their wings. These people . . . they were *eating* them.

'Is everything quite all right?' said the mayor.

Would you eat a painting? Would you eat a song? Of course you wouldn't. How absurd.

'Everything is fine,' said the botanist. 'This food is . . . not what I'm used to.' Her butterfly was still. The time was 816.

By 824 a diplomatic incident was pending. Every other guest in the room had finished their King's Plate, even Lenore and Kimmy. Several servants were now standing by the botanist, even the Emperor was gazing down from his throne at her stiff little figure.

'My Lady,' said the mayor beneath a whisper, 'I do not want to press you, but to not eat the King's Plate is considered a tremendous insult.'

'He shouldn't treat it that way,' she said.

'If you close your eyes it can be gone very quickly,' offered Fabrigas. He had not eaten his butterfly either. But he had had the quick wit to hide it in his robe before the attention turned to him. Now it was gently tickling his bosom.

'And when you eat it you get a warm feeling, like a short glass of brandy,' said the captain. 'They have brandy, do you think?'

The butterfly was still, the botanist was stiller, but at 827, the Emperor, who had been all but motionless himself throughout the whole event, stood suddenly and floated down from his throne. The room fizzed, his porters were thrown into confusion. The ruler came to stand before the startled botanist – and her butterfly.

'Does this delicacy make you uncomfortable?' He spoke a regal version of the Internomicon.

'It does, yes.'

'And why? Because it lives?' he snapped.

Her eyes were still fixed upon her plate. 'This is the Northern Black Widow. It is an extremely rare specimen who mates but once in its life. We have them where I'm from. You can tell when it is about to mate because it develops these violet patches here.' And she still did not meet the Emperor's eyes, but she extended a single finger to the butterfly's wing. 'She would have mated tonight.'

The Emperor smiled faintly. It would be reported in the city newspapers the next day that he smiled faintly. It would be reported that he then ordered his porters to take the butterfly away and release it back into the butterfly garden, and that his porters did so in a panic of arms and legs.

'Your compassion is . . . an admirable quality,' said the Emperor, and he smiled again (faintly). The papers would report the next day that he smiled faintly and that the botanist raised her chin and smiled faintly too.

Then the Emperor bowed and left, drifted back down the gangplank of his barge and vanished, and soon the barge too vanished in the mist.

After the dinner the children of Diemendääs (not all of them) arrived in national costume to perform a short play about the history of their great doomed city.

THE LEGEND OF THE FOUNDING
OF OUR GREAT CITY

[As told by the children of Diemendääs.]

Once a noble family was forced to flee their planet by a war. They were shipwrecked on a strange world. It was a wild wilderness with fierce jungle beasts. Their bodyguard was killed by wolves and the family underwent many hardships. They barely survived the first winter.

One day, foraging for tree-sap in the forest, the father found a giant bee trapped in a spider's web and he cut it free. The next morning, the mother found a hollowed-out nut filled with honey on the step of their cabin. Every day they found a new delivery of honey and so were able to survive and have a daughter.

One day the father decided to travel deep into the wilderness to find the source of the honey. His wife said don't, but he was firm. 'Yes, I will travel. Bring me my questing hat.' His journey was difficult, and he came close to death too many times, but eventually he found the Bee Kingdom. The man paid honour to the bees and befriended them. The bees had a parasite on their back that was slowly killing them, but the man was able to take a burning stick and scorch the mites from the back of the bees.

The man spent many weeks learning the bees' dance – for this was how they communicated. The bees' dance told him their oldest stories, and of villages on the far side of the mountain. The man suggested they go into business together, selling honey to the villages.

By cooperating, the humans and the bees were able to build a thriving town. The man and his family grew rich from the honey, and the man was able to help the bees defend themselves against the wasps and other predators.

The man's daughter, meanwhile, grew into a beautiful young woman, and she fell in love with a boy whose family had come to live in the town. The boy was very handsome and brave. But the King of the bees had also fallen for the daughter, such was her beauty, and one night he stole her away. The village boy went to take her back from the King. There was a terrible fight in which the King bee was killed. The boy returned home with the woman and they married.

Soon after, the girl found a tribute of honey left by Queen bee. 'See,' said the girl, 'all is forgiven between man and bee.' The couple ate the tribute and fell deathly ill. The boy died, but the girl, by some miracle, survived. The Queen's tribute not only spared her, it made her immortal, and she lives to this day in the great city built by human and bee, blessed to see each passing year, but cursed to see each husband, child and friend pass on and leave her.

The end.

To Miss Maria Fritzacopple
Perfume River Suites

From His Royal Majesty the Emperor

My Lady,

    I admire anyone who loves the natural kingdoms as I do. But on our world the Northern Black Widow is not rare. Her ardour in this generous tropical climate goes unchecked and makes her abundant. The males, with their showy wings, cannot hide from her love. I have many thousand in my garden, and I tend to them personally. At night, during mating season, the sound of their pulsing wings collectively is like a breath. This is why I chose to present some as my King's Plate. This week while you are our guests I will personally take you and the children to the Museum of Natural Monsters. There you can see all the butterfly specimens we have. And the honey factories, if there's time.

    This is one rare honour which you are not entitled to decline.

    In kindness,

    H.

THE DEAD OF THE NIGHT

As promised, the Emperor took them to the Museum of Natural Monsters. The Emperor walked ahead of his party as they toured the rows of specimens in the prehistoric wing. He wore a finely embroidered coat. A trained eye would have been able to tell it had been stitched that morning. They traced the course of history – not the fleeting history of human battles and discoveries, but the long, bright trail of life. They walked past dishes of microscopic uniplasm, past tower-eyed trilobites, mammoths, borenyxs, woolly rhinos, glyptodons as big as houses.

'And tell me, please,' said Lenore, 'what is this?' She stood beside a large display whose salty aroma had stopped her short.

'Ah, the voodoo crab is a troublesome creature,' said the Emperor. 'Once you've bonded with it, anything that becomes of it becomes of you. A scientist can discover one in a rock pool, they can go their separate ways, he to his house, the crab to her burrow. They can live for years, decades, oblivious. Then one day the crab gets eaten by a giant eel and the scientist drops dead where he stands.'

'My word,' said the botanist.

The Emperor, proud to be able to astonish his beautiful guest, smiled, turned shortly and went on: 'These I think you'll very much admire . . .' They passed by brightly ornamented sea lilies, limpets, algae, antlered laughing fleas. Lenore tried to keep her head within the storm of smells. Young Prince Panduke lagged, nose in the air, and he never stopped talking to Kimmy, though he couldn't stop himself from glancing at Lenore. 'I know a lot about animals. I keep owls.'

'You said that already. Owls are stupid birds.'

'They're not, they're surprisingly clever. I've trained mine to take messages to people. They can track their smell.'

'I see. They should have no trouble finding you then.'

'When my parents die all this will be mine, though Mother won't die for a long, long, long time. And I'll make it bigger and better. For a start I'll build robots to do most of the work. And I'll find a way to make the honey without those stupid bees. And I'll send my armies to make people buy our honey. And I'll be rich!'

'Well. Enjoy that,' said Kimmy.

'Who is that girl? Why is she with you?'

'She's my friend.'

'Is she a devil?'

'Yes, she's a devil and she steals people's breath when they're asleep.'

'She does not.'

'She does. She said she planned to steal yours tonight.'

'She can't, I'm a prince.'

'She doesn't care. She's stolen the breath from kings and emperors. She said she likes princes' breath best of all.'

The prince was silent as the party walked into a large room whose only exhibit was a towering glass box. The glass was two feet thick and held in place by bolted planks of steel. In the centre of the enclosure, on a plinth, was a small jar of yellowish ooze.

'The zombie-moss spores,' said the Emperor. 'There were almost riots in the streets at the mere suggestion of bringing them here. The case is bomb-proof, earthquake-proof, and the spores have been killed with intense bursts of radiation. There are motion-sensing and heat-detecting lamps around to detect even the faintest signs of life, and in the event of a containment breach the entire enclosure will be injected with a fire hotter than the core of our planet, then liquid nitrogen, before rockets fire the entire case through the domed roof and into space. And yet some nights I still wonder.'

'I'm speechless,' said Miss Fritzacopple.

They wandered the rows of glass-fronted cabinets with their ranks of omni-legged soldiers, the thin, white Emperor bending to peer into a display now and then, but listening still as best he could to the endless questions from Lenore.

'Tell me, what is this creature?'

And the Emperor broke away to tell them about the deadly fossil squid, who sinks itself into the mud and pretends to be a fossil, waits to be dug up, then kills and eats the discoverer. 'We lost two good geologists to the creature,' said the Emperor.

'I am speechless,' said the botanist, without looking at the case.

Again, the Emperor smiled.

*

'But how is it possible,' said M. F. Fabrigas, scientist, explorer, 'for me to have memories of this place if I've never been here?'

'Well, that is hard to say,' said Dr Dray. The lab technician who the day before had overseen the decontamination of the old man's treasured suit and cloak was a delightfully cheerful man who spoke about matters of high science with the disarming manner of a plumber talking about his pipes. 'The memory is a slippery fish. I sometimes wonder if all memory is not just an elaborate and freaky act of storytelling, yes? When we recall something – right? – do we, or do we not, reimagine it? If you catch my shift?' And it was true, the old man knew. The memories he was trying to discover and polish were almost a thousand years old, and so had become little better than folk legends.

'But I've been here. At least a part of me has visited a part of this. If that makes sense.'

The kindly lab rat shrugged his nostrils. 'I find it's wise to forget what you don't know and focus on what you do, petal. You left your home to travel to the far edge of your galaxy, along the way you lost a fleet but gained two children. One's a human computer, the other . . . a strange fruit.'

'She is.'

'I'd love to meet her.'

'You will. If there's time before we leave.'

'You have somewhere to be, rosebud?'

'Of course. We have to find our ship.'

'And where is your ship?'

'We are not sure. But we must also help this girl get to where she's going.'

'Which is where?'

'We don't know that either.'

'And why does she need to go there?'

'Those reasons are also . . . foggy.'

'I see.'

'But the boy! Ah! He is the real concern. He might have details in his head of a plot to take over the universe.'

'Well, that does sound interesting, poppet. Where is he?'

'We . . . mislaid him.'

'So, my old spoon, you need to help a strange girl you've just met, and a small boy you don't have, get somewhere you don't know . . . for reasons uncertain . . . on a ship you no longer possess, and which our observation stations have tracked leaving this planet and heading out into an empty region of space? That is the oddest mission I ever heard of, sparrow. And I once accompanied an emperor on a voyage to retrieve his stolen private parts.'

'Yes. Well, I suppose it is odd. But it is the mission I have been given.'

'And who gave you this mission?'

'That is uncertain.'

'I see. I see. And do you have any idea at all where your ship could possibly have been flying off to?'

'I have absolutely no idea whatsoever. But it is possible they are trying to go home.'

EXECUTIVE DECISION

When Roberto had arrived back at the *Necronaut* he'd grabbed a piece of chalk, snapped it in two, and scribbled an elaborate mural across the ship's deck with both hands. His mural was meant to explain his friend's predicament.

Everyone on the ship gathered. 'I cannot fathom this boy's art,' said G. De Pantagruel. 'Is it abstract?'

'It is obvious,' said Descharge. 'Our shipmates have been captured and taken to some kind of giant mushroom. We must stall our departure and mount a rescue party immediately.'

'Ah,' said Shatterhands, 'but let us not rush *too* hastily into a confrontation with the natives.' The surgeon wore a rubbery smile. 'It is hard from this crude drawing to know exactly what is in store for us. Though if the poor sailor who returned was to be believed there are innumerable horrors out there.' He pressed his long fingers together. 'Better to rest, then move at dawn.'

'At dawn? Have you not looked around you? There is no dawn,' said Descharge. 'Only a perpetual twilight. With every minute we wait our shipmates move closer to death!'

'Of course, of course. I want to aid them as much as you do. But let's not act impulsively. Let's take a few hours to nut out a strategy.' Those around him murmured in agreement. But the salty old Descharge smelled his thoughts, wet and ugly: 'All dead. That mystic. That Devil Girl. That trousered whore. That morbid pup and his man-giant. Sunk in bloody water. Pulled to their depths by dark hands. The giant rats have gnawed away their lips already. And that madman Descharge wants to take us out there again. We will pay tongue service to him, then tie him down. We can pilot off this moon without him. Then we'll force the boy to use his magic fingers to take us back to our own universe. We'll be heroes there. I'll be made a Knight's Surgeon.'

When the boy tried to leave the ship he was knocked out with chloroform and thrown in the brig. 'We cannot allow someone with his mechanical expertise to leave again,' said the surgeon. 'Now get a bucket of water and clean away that chalk.'

The mutineers pounced that night, moving quietly through the quarters with a rag soaked in more of the surgeon's chloroform. Descharge, a canny sailor, was waiting behind his door. He fought bravely and killed two sailors, but was struck on the back of the head with a lead bust of the Queen. He was thrown in the brig with Roberto and several loyal sailors. The prisoners felt the ship lift away. As Descharge woke, groggy, he heard laughing, cheering. He heard G. Scatolletto shout, 'I still have two bottles of Effervesco in my cabin!' Descharge's head had been severely dented. His ribs had been busted by the sailor's boots. He heard the popping of corks on deck and knew they were doomed. 'I never thought they'd get the ship working,' he said. 'I underestimated them.'

It only took an hour for the first argument to break out on deck. Oh yes, it doesn't take long when no one is clearly in command. Shatterhands's voice came through the loudest. 'It isn't that way, it's this way! You're holding the compass upside down! Am I to be always surrounded by idiots? Give it to me!'

Then the unmistakable sound of a compass smashing on the deck. 'You fool! Now look what you've done!'

Then came panic. They heard screams. 'It's a creature! We're inside a creature! Oh, the teeth!' There was a tremendous groan as the craft beached upon a slimy molar.

'Well I never,' said Descharge drily. There was much more yelling, then somehow they seemed to break free and for a while there was quiet. Then another fight. 'We cannot land at the city!' yelled Shatterhands. 'They'll ask to see our manifest. They'll ask too many questions.' A child, Peter Braika, came below decks for a barrel of water and said, 'They don't know what they're doing. The cook is holding his sextant backwards. They want to make the jump home to our universe.'

Descharge shook his head. 'Roberto is the only one who can make the old man's engine work. And it would take most of our power. We would be stuck without engines, and God knows where.' In any case he knew Roberto wouldn't cooperate. The boy sat on the wooden floor, facing straight ahead, his eyes burning holes through the wall opposite. His adversaries had had the sense to put him in a non-electrified cabin in the guts of the ship, in a cage normally used to hold livestock. They had taped rubber gloves to his hands and tied his arms behind his back.

Descharge weighed his options. He wasn't dead or badly crippled. His cage had a lock he could pop in seconds if he had to. He'd been trained to survive at sea with few or no rations. His one ally was a boy who doubled as a quantum super-computer, and who had blue-prints for most technology in his head, and who, if given the oppor-tunity, could raise havoc with his hands.

It wasn't long before they came for the boy. They came slowly down the stairs like monks: the surgeon, the cook and several of the larger sailors. Shatterhands approached the cage. 'Now that we are in open space we wish to make the jump back to our own universe. You know it is the only correct decision.'

'If I live to see my Empire,' said Descharge, 'you'll hang.'

'You won't live to see your Empire,' said Shatterhands. 'Of that I'm certain. Tell the boy we want him to jump us home.'

'He won't do it.'

'Just ask him.' The surgeon tossed a piece of chalk into the cage.

Descharge grabbed the chalk and scrawled 'RIPS?' on the floor. The boy hocked noisily and laid a hunk of phlegm upon the letters.

'He says "No".'

'I thought he might be obstructive,' said Shatterhands. 'Bring the slavey.'

Her name was Mikalla Lott; she was nine. She had a round face and round eyes which always made her look astonished. One of the sailors brought her shivering forward. Shatterhands took the girl by the shoulders and turned her to face Roberto. He bent at the waist to kiss her head, and whispered, 'This will soon be over.' He took an instrument from his pocket – a special tool used by anatomy lecturers to peel skin away from the muscle of a cadaver. He held the instrument up so that Roberto could see it. He did not need to tell Roberto what the instrument was. He did not even need to show the boy pictures of what the instrument could do. The pictures were all in his head. 'These are desperate times, boy. Tell him these are desperate times.'

★

Around fourteen hours after the mutiny (by Descharge's estimate) they made the jump.

Miss Lenore
Perfume River Suites

From an Admirer

My Dear,

So here you are at last. You thought you could flee to another universe to escape me, but there is nowhere you can go I wouldn't find you. I can't tell you what I had to go through to get here. I won't bore you. I have been waiting for you in this city for, it seems, an age. I've been keeping myself busy by cleansing the city of a few of its less well-presented citizens. It is a service I provide free of charge. This letter, for example, was kindly written for me by one of the palace guards just before he threw himself from the walls. I do find the guards' uniforms so, what's the word? Garish.

In any event, you are here now. You have finished with those lesser monsters: the flesh-eating plants, the mountain-sized worms, and now you are ready for the ultimate beast. Me. We will meet soon. In the meantime I am having ever so much fun. The human mind is a jaunty fairground which I never tire from playing in.

Do take care.

W.D.M.

[Letter written in blood and found slipped beneath the door of the recipient's suite.]

DAYS OF THE DEAD

Lenore returned to her suite exhausted, bewildered. They had only been here three days and she already wanted to leave. It was the month of the Festival of the Dead, when the gates to hell are opened to allow spirits to return to the earth; when the souls rise and walk again among the living, allegedly. The city was hung with flowers and painted skeletons, and the people sent a constant stream of floating lanterns into the burning sky.

They had been ushered back to their residence when word arrived that there had been another strange self-killing. Jonselm Valder, great-nephew of the Emperor and designer of the controversial new City Police uniform, had fallen to his death from a restaurant viewing platform, plunging down through the cloud of red lanterns, meeting the stone pavement with a smack which woke the sleeping guards. Though there were at least fifty other diners present, no one claimed to have seen a thing. What had compelled him to leap from the platform? How was it that none of the other diners, even his fiancée, Claratte, had seen a thing?

Lenore at least saw these seemingly random killings for what they were: the entrée to a banquet of blood and death. She saw the black ships descending through the clouds, lit by the broad moon behind them. She saw fire raining from the skies, the pristine streets below torn open in fiery gashes. She saw . . . snow? Could that be right? She saw snow in the steamy jungle. She saw an elegantly dressed stranger, the Lord of Death. She saw it all.

She commanded these thoughts to leave. 'Go off, dark thinkings!' she said. Lenore smelled a clean wooden floor in a huge bathroom filled with marble and glass. Lenore ignored the bloody smell of the bloody note lying on the desk in the next room, even though its scarlet letters clawed at the door of the bathroom like a mad hound. The note slipped under the door – a note which, of course, she could not read – was written in a web of bloody swirling curlicues of the kind favoured by the lunatic poet or the egotistical vampire. She blocked it out. She sank into the fragrant water and imagined she was in a universe all her own making, a universe she commanded.

Something was awakening in Lenore. She returned to her room, to her old clothes, now clean and folded – although not entirely free of mud and worm, but close enough. It would fade.

And then a frightening moment . . .

'Who is here? I'm not ready as yet.'

She heard a woman's voice say, 'He cannot hurt you.'

Then, as quickly as the sensation came – the presence of a woman with wild thorns tied in her hair and black ash upon her lips – it left, it took the letter too, it erased the smell of the victim's blood even, and nothing lingered.

NEEDLE IN THE HAY

He had tracked her all across the galaxy to Akropolis. Certain minds gave off very strong signals, and her signal was stronger than any he'd seen. It was strong enough to follow from billions of miles away, through countless trillion other dreaming consciousnesses. He now knew exactly what ship she was on, what small room she was in even. What tiny winged mammals shared that small space. He knew she had the file with her. When he arrived he found nothing. No ship. No bounty. Just the wreck of a civilisation dressed in still-smoking flotsam of a ruined fleet, its death-smoke pulled into fantastical curls by the force of a nearby nebula. Failure. He was just a few days too late by the sense of things. She was gone, and the file with her.

He went below to his withdrawing room, sat down in his leather chair, and was still for several hours. As savagely still as a predator floating on the surface of a swamp. That still. His eyes were open and inscrutable. At last he stood promptly and smoothed his perfectly tailored trousers. Then he viciously smashed several of his most treasured possessions. And that was it: fury disposed. She was gone and he had lost her. There was nothing left to do but go back to his employers and explain that he had failed. Yes. And yet he waited. Days passed in silent meditation. His ship's magnetic systems kept him still against the frightening currents of the midnight seas. He waited. Why was he waiting? Because he felt something coming through the night. He felt a great monster moving towards him through the tumbling reaches. Something vast and merciless was rising from the deep to greet him. So he waited. Days became weeks. A kind of madness began to gnaw his arm. His left arm, below the shoulder. It started as a dull nagging feeling. No person could stand to sit in a silent capsule for so many days without beginning to feel a sickness spreading from their arm, across their shoulder, and down towards their heart. True, if any mind could withstand the pulsing grip of space-madness it was this one. And yet here he was: silently succumbing. He lost hours. He would go to sit down with a book and come to his senses standing in his dining compartment with a smashed hourglass and pockets full of sand. He passed the limits most could stand and went beyond. His own mind was torturing him. Oh, the irony.

But something was coming, he could feel it. And one day he opened his eyes and there it was: an imperfection in the blackness which began to resolve itself into a city. A *kind* of city. It was a mess of floating palaces whose black edges caught the sunlight from the nebula and cast a dwarfing shadow across the ruins of Akropolis.

'Of course,' said the Well Dressed Man as he removed the intricately folded newspaper crown from his head. 'The Pope. Why wouldn't he be here?'

★

'What is this place?' said the Pope. He stood on the flight deck in his red jumpsuit with white stripes down the side, a silver cap upon his head. He called it his 'action suit'.

'It is the remains of the battle, Holiness. And beyond is the ruins of Akropolis,' said Cardinal Mothersbaugh, the Pope's long-suffering aide. 'It is the most ancient set of ruins in the known –'

'I don't like it. Spooky.'

'It is, Holiness. If you will return to your seat –'

'Command chair.'

'If you'll return to your *command chair* we can activate the Ring and clear away the debris before our crossing.'

'Yes, clear away all this,' said the Pope as he flicked a chubby finger across the ancient ruins of Akropolis.

'As you wish, Holiness.'

The Pope's fleet was surrounded by a ring of powerful force generators called, imaginatively, the Ring of Truth. The Ring of Truth was designed to send out a powerful shock wave to clear the district of all debris. It was specifically meant to smash away broken ships from a battlefield, thus revealing active enemy vessels, or those simply playing dead. The Pope's engineers had realised that it could also be used to sweep debris from the jump-zone before they made the crossing to the next universe. Not that they believed in such things.

In his ship, the Well Dressed Man saw a bright blue bubble expand from the Pope's ships, blowing away the remains of Akropolis, of the great exploratory fleet.

'Fudge monkeys,' he said. Or let's pretend that was the curse he chose. The shock wave slammed into his craft, knocking him across the room into a bookshelf, and leaving him unconscious. But the powerful magnetic engines quickly righted his vessel, and when the seas calmed the observation crew aboard the Pope's palace was astonished to see the small, elegant craft sitting in the middle of that spotless stretch of space.

★

When he first came to consciousness he could not work out where he was. He had suffered serious head injuries. His vision was blurred. He could see vague black shapes in front of him. The shapes were yelling things at him. The shapes were *doing* things to him, a part of his brain was telling him, and those things they were doing were causing him incredible pain. He became aware that he was hanging by his arms; he was stripped to the waist. Then he fell into darkness again, waking occasionally to find that he was already screaming, and that he was in more pain than he ever imagined was possible.

There is no counting how many times across those days of pain he woke up, and fell back. But eventually he woke up for keeps. He found that his vision had cleared somewhat. He could see that he was in a cell. The cell had racks with torture devices of such startling imaginative brutality that the Well Dressed Man was almost impressed. He was still strung up by his arms. All but naked. But there was no one there to cause him pain. There was someone just outside the room, in the corridor. He could sense him.

He summoned him.

The door groaned open, and a fat, vicious-looking man in black leather trousers and a black leather waistcoat entered. 'So,' said the man, 'you are finally ready to talk, I think?'

'I am,' said the Well Dressed Man. 'But I think not to you.'

'You think not?' The fat man waddled over to his rack of treats and took down a device of hooks and screws whose function no one unfamiliar with the darkest art would be able to guess. The fat man knew what the instrument did. 'Let's just see if you're ready to talk to me.'

'I have a better idea,' said the Well Dressed Man. 'Why don't you go and see the Pope? Tell him God is here to speak with him.'

'The Pope.' There was no question in his voice.

'Yes. I want you to deliver something to him.'

'You want me to deliver something. To the Pope.'

'Yes. I would like you to take him your eyeballs.'

'My eyeballs.'

'But first why don't you release my arms? Oh, and go and get some of your friends. The ones who helped to torture me. We're all going to have *so* much fun together.'

*

431

As I have made very clear, the Pope does not abide other universes. 'I abide them not!' he said once, probably.

The Pope had long ago set up a 'Special Papal Inquiry' into the question of multiple universes, but this had essentially involved visiting leading scientists, threatening them, bullying them into 'confessing' that it was all a load of nonsense, and, if necessary, sticking hot things in places where hot things are unwelcome. But the Pope had been forced, by circumstance, to soften his stance on Cosmic Abominations and allow technicians working for the Man in the Shadows to install RIPS engines on the holy palaces of the Fleet of the Nine Churches.

And so, here he was: somewhere. 'Why is it so foggy?' said the Pope as he stared into the whiteness of the Ghastly Blank. 'I hate fog. Make it stop.'

'It is normal for it to be . . . foggy . . . when you travel to another . . . place,' said Cardinal Mothersbaugh. 'But it will clear soon, I'm sure.'

'It had better. And why are all these butterflies here?'

'Oh, these are gifts sent by well-wishers to cheer you up.'

'I don't like butterflies. Poison them. And let's fire the cannons now, see who is out there in the fog.'

'Let's save that excellent suggestion for later today, Your Holiness. Look, that butterfly is the colour of your hat.'

The Pope frowned. 'And when will we find these people we are here to kill? When will our crusade begin?'

'The spy aboard has left a trail. It should not be difficult to find them.'

'Holiness,' said a messenger entering the room, 'I'm sorry to interrupt you, but it is urgent. One of your prisoners wishes to speak with you.'

'Prisoner? I do not speak to prisoners. Go away.'

'He says to tell you he is God.'

'God? Which god?' For the first time the Pope turned towards the messenger and beheld with horror the hollow cavities in his face, the tray he held, the pyramid of glistening, peeping spheres.

'He says he is the God who sees all things.'

A NEW DAY

'We must leave!' Lenore said to a startled Fritzacopple who was brushing the knots from the girl's hair as they rode to the honey factory to meet the Emperor. 'There's a man here who is going to make us do the worst *things* to each other. There is a fleet of death arriving! I see a snowy death for everyone if we stay!'

'A snowy death? What kind of nonsense is that? It's thirty-eight degrees. You had another bad dream. Keep still now.'

Lenore had suffered many bloody dreams in the week since they'd arrived – even while awake. She dreamed 456651: The One with the Thumb; 456669: The One with the Evil Orthodontist; and 466612: The One with the Girl from Poughkeepsie. In that, the sky was raining blood and fire. She had met Roberto in a city in flames.

'Why are you still in that city? Don't you know there are people there who want to kill you?' Roberto had swatted angrily at the coils of smoke.

'We have not a ship! You went off in it! I thought you could not speak.'

'In my dreams I can speak and hear. You're endangering our mission.' It was a beautiful day and Lenore let her hand drag through the cones of ash upon the ground where she sat. It was good to see. Even though she had a magic nose it was still nothing like seeing things in full, radiant colour. People ran screaming, a man in black ran past on fire, the snowflakes laughed sweetly in the air.

'What mission? You took me from the fair. Now I don't know where I am.'

'I rescued you. You were a prisoner, and now I'm helping you home. It's what they asked me to do. They said the life of every living thing depends on us, and you could help by not getting yourself killed.'

'Well, *that's* a funny thing because the Dark Hands told *me* to protect *you*. And you are not helping much as far as I can see. Running off with that froggy-looking girl. I don't know why they'd send a deaf boy to protect me anyway. Surely the boy who hears is better.'

'They chose me for my skills. They said that if I couldn't hear people I wouldn't be able to listen to cowards and grown-ups telling me what's good for me. Now the bad doctor and his friends have taken the ship. They've flown us into death. We have no wind or food. I think they might try to eat me.'

'You? But you are not even a mouthful, Roberto.'

'Just try to stay out of trouble until I get back. It won't be long.'

'No, *you* try to stay out of trouble until we find *you*. I'm supposed to protect *you*.'

'No, *I'm* supposed to protect *you*!'

'Why did you leave me, Roberto?'

'Because the Ball told me to.'

'You should not listen to balls.'

'I have to go now. If that man comes into your dreams, don't tell him where I am.'

'I don't *know* where you are!'

And then he was gone, and Lenore was left standing in the burning sunshine, in the burning city, listening to the fires whisper.

'And that's when I a-wakes!' She'd told Miss Fritzacopple about it. At length. That was the last time she'd spoken to Roberto. He no longer appeared in her dreams. It was as if he'd vanished completely.

'Well, there's nothing we can do about all that,' said the botanist.

'We don't know where to look for our ship. We can't afford to purchase another.'

'If Roberto was here we could use some of his diamonds to buy a ship.'

'Well, until then we should enjoy the comfort and protection of this great city. Now, be still, we're nearly at the factory. The Emperor is a fine man, don't you think?'

*

'So. This is . . . this was . . . your Sweety?'

'If you want to use its layman's name, sure,' said Dray. He and Fabrigas were looking at stunning cine-images of the great serpent taken with cameras attached to high-altitude balloons. The worm's width had been calculated at 14 miles, and its length, 785 miles. Roughly.

'Such a massive creature.'

'What, this old thing? Pupa.'

'Pupa? No, no, no.' Fabrigas smiled pretentiously and shook his beard.

'Pupa. Been with us for centuries, moving across the surface, devouring whole jungle tribes, snatching ships who strayed outside the shipping channels, and generally thwarting our efforts to destroy it. You know how it is.'

'I . . .'

'Without a mate, as you undoubtedly know, the polycraebianatic supermorphic embryo will never leave the larval stage, fortunately. If it did, it could grow much bigger than our planet, or even our suns.'

'Impossible. No. A creature so big could not find enough nutrition.'

'Ordinarily. His quantum acetabula allow him – or her –'

'Uh-huh.'

'– to draw nutrition from multiple dimensions. He can vacuum

436

up the vast clouds of sugar around stars in many universes at once. He, or she, is an omnivore in the truest possible sense. Just like your friend here.' He held up the starfish Fabrigas had plucked from the engine of mad Prince Albert's ship. 'This little beauty is almost as old as the universe, and it has tiny nodes on its underside which seem to allow it to exist in all universes at once. I bet you've noticed some strange activity wherever one of these has showed up.'

'That is an understatement.'

'Well, again, we want to thank you for bringing this treasure out of the worm.' He placed the starfish on the steel table. 'What we'd love to know is how you were able to target the creature's brain so precisely using a primitive rocket. We can't recreate your experiments in our advanced labs.'

'Well, I wouldn't want to bore you with details –'

'Go on.'

'You'd have to understand conflatory interstertial-plasma vectors –'

'I do.'

'Even with enough hours to explain, I confess my calculations were tempered with instinct.'

'I see. In any event, the great mystery is how you then vanished into the Forbidden Zone.'

'About that I confess I have no idea.'

'. . . Well, at the end of the day it's a good thing you did, hamster. Your trajectory otherwise would have put you right in the middle of the battlefield and certain death at the hands of our enemies. You silly puppets.'

'Certain death, you say?'

'Yes. Almost seems as if someone did it intentionally to save your life, chipmunk. Almost.' He held the starfish up to the light again.

'I still don't entirely understand exactly what the Forbidden Zone is, and I have the most powerful brain of anyone I've met in my universe.'

'Well, this is a whole new universe, lovebird. The Forbidden Zone is a finite dimension. We keep it in a box. And for obvious reasons we keep that box in a high-security facility.'

Fabrigas was speechless. He slapped himself on the forehead and left a pink mark.

'Careful now. Yes, it's all very exciting,' said Dray. 'Now we're starting to worry that the boundaries to our artificial universe might be becoming unstable. Thanks to certain entities.'

The starfish twinkled in the light of the laboratory lamps.

'We've learned a lot about the universe by building one. We've managed to strip away illusions of space, time and matter, and reveal the Omniverse as it is: a continuum in which everything is one, all is connected, and death does not exist. So we have that, poppet.'

'This confirms all my theories,' said Fabrigas, breathless. 'This universe could almost precisely mirror our own!'

'Yes, pumpkin. A universe could be an entirely new sphere, or it could differ by as little as one teaspoon, or a single, lonely starfish.'

*

The others, minus Captain Lambestyo, had been on a whirlwind trip to the honey factories, the hydro-subway, the Museum of Alternate Histories. Now the party took high tea in the dining rooms floating above the barracks of the Royal Armoured Insect Division. There was a lot of activity today because the monks had announced that they were about to declare a date for the end of the world. And yet there was no panic among the people. The citizens of Diemendääs had been told to prepare for the end days many times before. They were presently too busy with the Festival of the Dead to worry about the monks' dire proclamations.

A woman and her young daughter were having cakes at one of the small tables nearby. The girl had a bee in her lap and she absent-mindedly stroked its black, fuzzy belly while the bee cooed and wriggled with pleasure. The mother wore a skeleton tiara and a black

438

dress. Kimmy was transfixed by the girl and her bee. 'I could get you one if you like,' said Prince Panduke. And for once Kimmy didn't have a smart reply. Lenore had a seemingly inexhaustible reservoir of questions for the Emperor.

'And what is that down there?' she said, pointing vaguely out the window.

The tea platter tinkled as it was set down.

'That is the barracks of the Royal Armoured Insect Division.'

'I see. And those insects work for you?'

'They do.'

'And what do you pay them?'

'We pay them with food and shelter.'

'And the bees? What pays you them?'

'Our bees have no use for money, of course. They are content to make honey.'

'I see. So they are slave bees.'

'Lenore!' said the botanist.

'It's no insult. I would be surprised beyond words if they saw it that way. They spin their webs and make honey in them – they would do it if we were here or not. But we help them to sell their honey and the profits are used to protect them from invasion and disease.'

'I see. And where is Our Lady this day?' she said. 'Will she be not adjoining us?'

The Emperor arranged himself. 'Not today. Perhaps you will meet her before you leave.'

'Mother would not want to meet the likes of her,' said Panduke.

Lenore ignored him. 'And then tell me, why does she wear thorns up in her hair?'

The Emperor, who had been gazing out the window, turned and looked down at the girl with, Miss Fritzacopple observed, a look of surprise. 'You do have a lot of questions.'

'She doesn't mean any offence,' said the botanist.

'Of course. Tell me, young lady,' said the Emperor, as he topped his tea with milk, 'do you have memories of your younger years? Of your home, your family?'

'I don't remember very much. My dreams tell me my family was killed when I was tiny. But dreams aren't always to be trusted.' Then the girl added, brightly, 'I can sometimes see the future!'

The Emperor smiled somewhat smugly. 'Is that so? And can you see my future?'

'I can.'

'And?'

'I see . . . only grand things.'

Again the Emperor smiled. 'Perhaps lying is one talent you don't have. If you're anything like my wife you see fire and death ahead. As you know, our people are obsessed with the end times. Last year the monks had me evacuate the entire population to the mountains to wait for an asteroid called Big Lance. It never came.'

'End . . . times,' the girl mouthed, before adding, 'Also! I know who is your murderer.'

'Murderer? There are no murders here. We have had some assisted killings at best.'

'As you wish. There is a very powerful man inside your city. He can make people do what he wants. He is the Emperor of Minds. Will you give us fools a ship so we can flee?'

'Lenore!' said Fritzacopple. 'I'm very sorry, Your Highness.'

'It is quite all right. My girl, after what you and your friends did for us, I'll certainly give you a ship. I'll let you know as soon as one becomes available. Though I don't see why you'd want to leave just yet. We haven't even heard the bee orchestra. In the meantime, if there are any dangerous operators at work in the city, our Secret Police will find them. They are experts. Just last month they caught a pair of spies. Imagine that, spies, right under your nose.'

Miss Fritzacopple was looking at the Emperor's worried face, its deep lines and sunken eyes. She could tell from the lines around those eyes that he loved to laugh. He was staring at a spot in the middle distance. And so they sat, the prince gazing at Kimmy, who was gazing at a girl with a bee, who was transfixed by the lustrous and unruly hair of Miss Fritzacopple, who was staring at the Emperor, who was staring at a fading memory of a fleeting moment of happiness.

226413: THE ONE WHERE THEY'RE UP ALL NIGHT

'Hello there.'

  'Who's there?'

'Are you sleeping well this night?'

'I am not. This city is too hot.'

'Isn't it, though? I am happy that we are finally in the same great city. I trust you got my letter?'

'It was an horrible letter.'

'Oh? I'm sorry about that. You see, I have a dark side to my personality. But you must understand that what I'm doing is for the best. It might seem cruel to you, but it's part of a bigger picture. I need you to understand that. I'm actually a big fan. I've followed you all the way to the city at the end of the universe. I had no magical engine. I had to hitch a ride through with a pope. Imagine that. I have been waiting for you to come out of the worm. Killing time.'

  '. . . Killing people.'

'I confess, I have been indulging my dark half. But only on the ignorant and poorly dressed.'

'It's wrong to kill people.'

'Really? But you killed your bosun?'

'. . . I did not.'

'You did. You saw what was coming and did nothing. You let him come for you, then you ran away. You let the beast have at him.'

'I didn't have the power to help him.'

'Power is a state of mind. You've brought doom to this city just by visiting. The whole city will burn because of you. I get the feeling you think you're the hero of this story.'

'I do.'

'Are you sure? Are you certain you're not the monster?'

'I don't think I am.'

'Your captain thinks you're a monster.'

'I do not think he does.'

'He does, I know his mind.'

'What do you want with us?'

'I've been sent to kill you. Not immediately, though. Where is your friend? The boy.'

'_____'

'Oh. He ran off and left you. The cad! Never mind. He'll come back. Probably. When he sees what I mean to do to you he'll surely come back. He won't want to let you die. Not the way you let the bosun die.'

'My captain will protect me from you. He is strong and clever.'

'Oh really?'

'Yes.'

'When you meet them tomorrow, observe their hair or beards. Then tell me they are worthy protectors.'

'Please leave my dreams now.'

'As you wish. Sleep well, my little monster.'

★

The next day, when the old man arrived for breakfast he had a pretty pink bow in his beard. 'Fabrigas!' exclaimed Fritzacopple. 'Why do you have a pretty pink bow in your beard?'

'I do?' said the old man. He could not remember putting a pretty pink bow in his beard.

Soon, the captain stumbled in, drunk. 'Why do you have a lovely bow in your beard, old fool?!' said the captain as he slumped upon a chair and slopped coffee in a cup.

'I'll answer that if you tell me why you have a silky purple bow in *your* hair!'

But neither man was able to remember or explain why they had decided to tie pretty, silky bows into their hair and beard, or why each bow held a slip of paper with a fortune on it:

'You will soon meet a handsome stranger.'

IN MOTION

At breakfast they had a meeting. They had been in the city almost two weeks and still had no plan for the next stage of their mission. The Emperor had laid on traditional local pastry treats, as well as an invigorating breakfast tonic called 'Gangdara'. Fabrigas chaired the meeting. Miss Fritzacopple took the minutes. As he was the only other grown-up left from this ship of fools, Captain Lambestyo, aka the Necronaut, aka Snatch Masters (long story), was forced to attend. Lenore had smelled them waking and would not be excluded.

MOTION: That immediate steps be made to procure a new ship and able crew to use to go in search of our own ship, the *Necronaut*. Proposed: M.F.F. Seconded: Miss M.F. Motion carried.

MOTION: That should no ship be available to them, or should be made unavailable by cost, the Emperor would be implored for assistance. Proposed: M.F.F. Seconded: Miss M.F. Motion carried.

MOTION: That meetings are boring and stupid. Proposed: C.G. Lambestyo. Seconded: Miss Lenore. Motion split.

MOTION: That children are to be excluded from voting in meetings. Proposed: M.F.F. Seconded: Miss M.F. Motion split.

MOTION: That beards are stupid. Proposed: C.G. Lambestyo. Seconded: Miss Lenore. Motion carried.

MOTION: That someone needs a bath. Proposed: M.F.F. Seconded: Miss M.F. Motion carried.

Meeting adjourned.

The Emperor, who had sat at the back of the room during the at times chaotic meeting, was sympathetic on a number of counts: 'I realise that my city owes you a lot. I just ask that you be patient while we find you a ship.'

'But you have thousands of ships,' said Fabrigas. 'Surely it can't be that difficult to loan us one. A coal-ship, a junk-barge, anything. Obviously not *literally* a junk-barge.'

'I understand your frustrations, but there are difficulties: some agitators in government are making trouble. They are saying that we can't just go handing out ships to people we don't know. You might be pirates.'

'Pirates?'

'Well, obviously *I* don't think you're pirates. But these agitators are claiming that you created an ecological disaster zone when you killed that worm.'

'I beg your pardon?'

'Some are even saying criminal charges should be brought against you.'

'Criminal charges?!'

'Obviously it is nonsense. This is just a vocal minority in Parliament. But we must be patient. We will continue to offer you the finest hospitality. In the meantime I have an invitation from the Empress.'

'The Empress! At last we shall meet this famous beauty.'

'It is not for you, I'm afraid. Just the girl.'

'Lenore?'

'Yes. My wife is very curious to meet her.'

SUPPER

Lenore was taken by carriage through the quiet streets to the royal residence. She was taken through corridors lined with heavily varnished wood and marble. She toyed with the gift she'd brought for the Empress. The Emperor had made it very clear that she should bring a gift, but, having few possessions, she realised she would be forced to give the only thing she had. She was led by two servants. She was brought to a set of doors whose handles burned with traces of a man whose hands had held a brandy glass just minutes before. An ancient odour crawled out from beneath the door.

'Do I knock?' But she realised the servants had left.

'The door is open,' said a voice from the other side.

*

The room had tall windows, heavy curtains, the odour of a stagnant lake. The only furniture in the room was a table with a small armchair, and a bed set on heavy velvet paws. The voice spoke softly. 'Come in, mouse, your supper is ready.'

Soup. A small glass of wine. She sat before the soup and breathed deeply. She couldn't sense her host. It was as if only her voice had come to supper.

'I hope you don't mind eating late.' The voice was so soft you could hardly hear it, like a sigh. 'I always eat late because I sleep poorly otherwise.'

'I know that you do,' said the girl.

'The girl that knows too much. Let's drink a toast to you becoming a woman then. In Diemendääs the older children are allowed a bee's-nose full of wine with dinner. Here's to you and all you'll soon become.'

'They say bad things will happen when I become a mature woman. I hear them talking.'

'Never mind about that. I too had a troublesome adolescence. We become what we become. Drink.'

Lenore took a sip and suddenly she was no longer in the room. The ways seemed to part, the heavy flesh vanished, and she found herself inside a humming cloud where for a brief second she could see the colours dancing. The sensation vanished in the flick of a wing.

'Isn't it wonderful? In human tradition wine is drunk to escape life. In our tradition it is a sacred thing, a revealer of life and truth. In reality we are so much more than the cages we live in.'

Lenore felt as if she'd just been told a great secret. 'I have brought you a gift. They said I should.' She produced the starfish from her pocket. For a few seconds, as she held it up, she thought her host had left the room. A vacuum seemed to tear open in the air.

'Where did you get this?'

'Oh, we have found them along our way. They arrive where we are.'

'Girl, this is one gift I cannot accept. She is your guardian, a living thing.'

'She is *my* guardian?'

'Yes, and you cannot give your friends as gifts. You will need her where you're going. She is bringing you home. You are about to go on an adventure that will make everything you've been through so far seem mundane. But to get there you have to be prepared to face a terrible enemy, and to lose the people you love.'

'I don't want to do either of these things.'

448

'But you have to.'

'He's a man. A man in a suit. He takes people's minds.'

'Very good, yes. Destroying him will be a big test.'

'I'm too frightened to face him.'

'You don't need to be frightened. I can protect you. I can show you a secret you can use against him. He won't be prepared for your power. But you'll need to give me something in return.'

'I don't have anything to give you.'

'Yes you do. You just don't know it yet. You must make a choice: do you want to give me a small gift, something you won't miss, or to die?'

'It depends. What is the small gift I won't miss?'

'I don't know yet.'

'I don't want to die.'

'Then it's decided. As a reward for your good work so far I'm willing to let you ask me three questions. But choose very carefully.'

'I dreamed my captain left us. Will he leave us? I loves him.'

The voice, deep yet light as air, made a sound as if to laugh but checked itself.

'And you say you have nothing to lose. You don't know love yet. Love is pain, not fulfilment. You need to get used to losing friends, because you're going to lose many. Forget about the captain.'

'I'll not forget him.'

This time the voice did laugh. 'You've already wasted one question on a boy. That should be your first lesson.'

'Who am I?'

'You are Lenore. There's no one like you.'

'That's not what I meant.'

'I can't tell you what you are. It's something you have to discover.'

'Then what good are you?'

'Be careful.'

'I'm sorry. That was not one of the questions.'

'I will grant you that. You are a genetic aberration, a glitch in the great and ancient code. Much like the starry creature you wear around your neck. That is why people want to destroy you. You are like a beacon in the blackness, drawing moths of destiny towards you.'

'I am, I am the talisman.'

'I suppose that's another way to put it.'

'And you are what?'

Again the voice laughed. 'I am a lonely woman. A lonely woman and a prisoner in my own city.'

'You have powers.'

'Sometimes power is a weakness. You'll learn that soon. And I am just a whiff of what you'll be one day.'

Lenore felt the world rushing away and she felt very alone.

'Don't be sad. You're going to see things that no one else can dream of. Just be brave. And remember, there's no such thing as death. And now the secret I promised to tell you.'

Her secret, sacred words enveloped Lenore like a fog. She felt as if she was leaving her body, and then a face began to show itself, dimly, a face so luminous and beautiful that Lenore forgot to breathe. The face vanished.

'You must tell no one what I've shown you.'

But later, Lenore could not even remember, and she had no idea what price she'd agreed to pay for the secret she'd been given.

CAPTAIN

Hadley's People's Almanac has several Carlos Góngora Lambestyos, among them one who fits the basic story of the man we've come to know. A bastard baby born to a young prostitute via a prominent naval officer. The baby was left at the Royal Naval Hospital for the officer shortly after he returned from a campaign against the Vangardik hinterlands near Bohemia. To cover up the scandal, he paid the woman off, enrolled the boy in a secret and elite naval school. The mother returned the money, along with a note, shortly before she leaped from a bridge. The baby received state-of-the-art naval mods, and a first-rate education from the day he turned one. He flew his first mission aged ten, and was a decorated Black Ops pilot by the age of fourteen. At fifteen he was lost during a top-secret mission. No attempt was made to recover his remains. Details from here are sketchy at best.

There was little to see of the young hero in the captain these days. The city had taken the life from him. The noise of the bees had become an infuriating fuzz inside his skull, like the static from a modern radiogram. All he cared about was drinking in the Land's End, the old tavern by the space docks.

Fabrigas had gone to find him the previous day, but he wasn't in the reeking den. He had waited as patient as a toad as the hours passed, observing the grimy sailors come and go. He would never admit it, but it made him happy to sit in such a place and watch the comings and goings.

It was almost four hours into his meditations when he looked up to discover a boy at his table. And what a face this boy had, such a face you've never seen. When the old man addressed him he raised a pair of glassy eyes. It was as if he did not even remember sitting at the old man's table just a few seconds ago.

'I'm becoming sadder by the hour. I no longer sleep. I feel like my spirit is being drained from me. I lose whole days. Where do they go? I can't tell you.'

This tavern did not have jasmine tea. Fabrigas took a pot of gingered beer and listened to the boy as he talked endlessly. It was necessary, he thought, with all this boy had been through, with all he'd seen, to be constantly in motion. A person might describe this feeling as 'wanderlust' – if that person was an idiot. Wanderlust is the feeling that if you don't take a trip you might start knocking people's hats off. What this boy had was the feeling that if he didn't move soon, he would die.

'Everyone is very worried about you. We are like a family now.'

'Don't talk to me about family. You abandoned me. You gave me poison soup. You were going to leave me in space.'

'I know. There are some things I need to work on.'

'There is barely any love in the universe. And where there is it is an evil magic. It is a superstition of the heart, yes? You told me this. So don't talk to me about family. You abandoned me and you'll do it again. That botanist does not care about anyone but herself. The girl is a monster. Everyone else is gone. Even the man who swore to hang me has abandoned me.' He laughed. 'But it's not the first time he's done that. I forgive him. I forgive him for everything. Let's drink some more and forget. Let's let the booze delight our minds with forgetfulness. Let's become like old men.'

'It won't be long, boy. They'll give us a ship. And then we'll find the boy.'

'That boy! What's his name?'

'Roberto?'

'Yes! The crazy boy. Whatever happened to him?'

'. . . If you remember . . . he vanished with our ship.'

'Why are we waiting here, then? This city is eating our days. It is stealing our minds!'

'For now, we have no choice. We must be patient. The Emperor is attempting to arrange a ship for us. We could try another meeting.'

'No more meetings! He is Emperor, he should be able to conjure a ship like this!' He tried to snap his fingers. He could not snap his fingers.

Fabrigas went back to the others and expressed concern. 'A boy like that can't stay still for long. A boy like that needs to stay in motion or he'll drown in his own black waters. A boy like that is like a shark!'

'Yes,' said Fritzacopple, 'a shark.' The others nodded, then returned to their activities.

Late at night, when the innkeeper finally kicked him out, the shark would drift back home through the halls and outer palaces, dunking his head in the fountains and snorting at the ostentatious royal portraits that hung along the marble warrens. Tonight was particularly quiet; his boot-falls boomed along the passages, and the warm air swooned and wobbled. There was one painting he always stopped to see and never snorted at. She stood in leaves, a white gown falling over her like seawater. Behind her was a forest; blood-red limbs enfolded her. She seemed to be about to step from the frame into the real world, but also to be retreating, falling away. The strangest thing about the painting was that every time he looked at it he saw something new. Last night he'd noticed that on the lake in the distance was a small rowing boat with a man in it. His face was just a smear of paint. Tonight he noticed a second man, a twin; he held a knife to the first man's throat. Captain Lambestyo felt a predatory breath upon his neck, then looked round to find nothing.

What preys upon a shark? That is an excellent question. You really do ask very good questions.

SOUND AND VISION

A week became two, then three. Strange and awful things had begun to happen in the city of Diemendääs. Or perhaps that should be *stranger* and *awfuller*. As if the mysterious self-killings had not been enough to keep the populace terrified, the remains of a palace guardsman – half eaten, as if by a beast – were found in one of the courtyards. People reported bizarre distortions of their familiar realities: doors that appeared from nowhere, that opened into forests, or caves, or other people's living rooms. One night it rained green crickets, and someone even reported seeing a large, shaggy creature with a pretty muzzle. The city's Secret Police had finally acknowledged the fact that malevolent forces were involved in the recent self-killings, self-mutilations and auto-decapitations which had scythed through the city's wealthy classes, and they decreed that until the killer was caught, every citizen should be home by a certain hour.

There was still no sign of their old ship, or word of a new one from the Emperor. Fabrigas took an apartment overlooking the river and began to fill it with books and things as if he never planned to leave. The city's great minds arrived like moths, drawn to the light and heat of scientific speculation. They spent the nights sucking coffee through their teeth and flitting from one grand subject to another.

When Fabrigas wasn't holding court at his bachelor pad he could be found in Dray's laboratory. Lenore had started coming along too, since Miss Fritzacopple had begun to exclude her from her field trips with the Emperor. 'It is far too dangerous now to take the children to public places.' The Emperor agreed.

'Running across the place with the older man of marriage,' said Lenore. 'Is that how the woman behaves?'

The two men ignored her. 'My experiments have determined that the membrane between our universe and the Forbidden Zone has weakened significantly,' said Dray. 'That might explain why you cherubs were able to enter the zone without any advanced equipment. Very troubling, tortoise, yes. We can't just have any old thing entering the zone.'

Fabrigas nodded gravely.

'And look what I found when I checked my equipment today: another starfish!'

Dray handed Fabrigas another silvery star. 'Well I never.' The old man held the creature up to the light and examined the fine old markings on its surface.

'Anyhow, we'd better get you kittens home, the curfew is nearly here!' He reached for his coat.

'What in the black hole sun is that?!' Fabrigas exclaimed. He had a bony finger pointed at a large gun on a wooden tripod pointing at a black cloth screen.

'Oh, now that *is* special,' said Dray as he hung his coat on a chair again. He had been trying for more than an hour to get his visitors out the door. 'That's a new remote viewing system I've pioneered.' He pulled a switch and a set of lamps came on with a heavy *chank*, throwing the room into brightness. 'This machine here,' he said, patting the gun instrument, 'is an image-capturing device. Keep your eye on that vision unit.' Fabrigas peered at the glass-fronted wooden box. It was black and empty behind the glass, yet when Dr Dray walked in front of the capture gun he appeared instantly behind the glass, a tiny version of himself, waving.

'Sweet-smelling stars above!' the old man shouted. 'You're in two places at once!'

'Don't be silly, chook,' said Dray. 'That's only a facsimile image of me in the box. My image can be transmitted to another location, or recorded for later.'

'How does it work? Magnetically charged ethers?'

Dray snorted. 'This invention is going to revolutionise the way we communicate. No more telegraphic messages, no more hyper-space pigeons, just instant audio-visual contact.'

'Audio-visual,' whispered Fabrigas breathlessly, and he reached out to tap his finger on the glass screen.

'We're putting those boxes into thirty thousand homes across the city, duckling. Think of the possibilities. The Emperor will be able to personally address his people. We can stage dramas and readings for the citizenry. It will be useful to have something to help people forget about all this "end-time" nonsense. Soon, everyone in the universe will be talking about Omnivision™.'

'Omnivision™,' whispered Fabrigas.

'I'm right now getting it ready for a trial run at the Ring of Iron next week. Tell you what, sugar-pips, why don't you perform a dramatic reading from your journals – as a warm-up act?'

'I am not much of an orator,' said Fabrigas, 'and it's unlikely we'll be around for much longer. As you know we have a rather pressing mission.'

'Ah yes, the girl. Astonishing specimen. Potentially quite dangerous.'

'I'm right here in the room,' said the girl.

'So you are.'

★

It only took a few more minutes to persuade Fabrigas to appear on Dr Dray's Omnivision™ to perform a dramatic reading of their plight at the hands of the cannibal cult.

'Thom! The drum sounded. The Marshians raised their blades. Bright they gleamed and silvery as a moon's dreadful edge, despite the greenish sickly light. How bright the single star that hung upon their deadly tips. How dread the *thom!* which rang twelve times the dismal hour of our deaths!'

As you can well see, the old man has an artful prose style. Though, in my opinion, a tad overcooked. But the whole city tuned in to watch his reading. Those who didn't yet have Omnivision™ sets crowded into neighbours' houses, and thousands packed theatres whose proscenium stages had been adapted to support screens. Our friends watched from the Emperor's own private viewing room and were amazed. Even the Emperor seemed to enjoy himself. In fact, they had all noticed a remarkable transformation in the man during the time he'd spent with the children and their attendant botanist.

Fabrigas capped off his appearance with a short magic show, even persuading Miss Fritzacopple to be his beautiful assistant. (And she was a particularly beautiful assistant, people remarked.) He performed, for the people of Diemendääs, feats of showmanship, suggestion and misdirection. He performed the trick of vanishing, the trick of levitation and, most dramatically, the trick of pretending to stab Miss Fritzacopple through the heart with a real dagger.

'But how do you know that you've pulled the trick dagger from your robe?' his very lovely assistant asked later.

'Trick dagger? My dear, there's no "trick dagger".'

The botanist was aghast.

Fabrigas became an instant celebrity. He couldn't walk the streets without being mobbed by autograph hunters, a problem he solved by taking his morning walks while waving his cane in front of him and yelling, 'Get back! Get back!' But he seemed to be secretly enjoying himself.

'What is happening to us?' said Lenore. 'It seems as if everyone is breaking apart. Did we not have a mission? Are we not supposed to be finding our ship, finding Roberto?'

'Are we not indeed,' said Fritzacopple, from somewhere far away.

★

Prince Panduke showed Kimmy his owls. He even let her name one of the chicks. She named him Vince. Then Panduke snuck her in to see his iron man. It was a great automaton, a hundred feet high, with hands that could bend steel. The machine had been unearthed, along with many other strange artefacts, during the first excavations of the mountains centuries ago. It belonged to a culture long forgotten. Dr Dray had found him gathering dust in an old warehouse and had fixed him up for employment as an industrial tool, but the machine – which could snap a steel beam like a toothpick between its thumb and forefinger – had been deemed too dangerous for public use, and so he was given to the prince as a birthday gift – with strict instructions that he was not to touch him until his eighteenth birthday. And so the giant was left asleep in his hangar.

'What good is a birthday gift that can't be used until another birthday?'

'He certainly is handsome,' said Kimmy. 'Tall, too.'

'I can show you where the keys are hidden if you like,' said the prince.

*

These were the days of their lives: all missions set aside for lazy, civilised fun, for museum trips and magic shows. Throughout this whole time, throughout the many days of the Festival of the Dead, the Empress – the supposedly most beautiful woman in the universe, the woman whose face launched a hundred thousand ships, some tanks and an array of siege machines – was never seen in public. She remained the shadow of a rumour, passing from lip to lip in darkened cafes, as frail and weary as huffed smoke.

And then she made an announcement which turned the city upside down.

THE RING OF IRON

Every year, at the height of the Festival of the Dead, at the darkest hour, in the dimmest place, Diemendääs commemorated the glory of the fallen with a cage-combat event called the Ring of Iron. All around the city fireworks flared, ship bells rang mournfully, airships trailed banners a mile long.

Fritzacopple had decided that the captain would enter the Ring of Iron. 'It will be good for you,' she said. 'Put some fire back in your belly.'

'I don't need fire in my belly. If you don't leave me alone I'll set a fire in your hair.'

But she put his name on the register anyway. Every year the Empress would choose her own champion, someone who would battle on her behalf. It was the highest honour, and the winner of the event would receive the keys to the city, and a ball in their honour the following evening. So the city was sent into a lipothymy when the Empress announced that her champion for this year would be a foreigner, one Captain Carlos Góngora Lambestyo. The captain was sleeping off a hard night and had to be woken. He angrily told the servants to leave him alone – one got a blackened eye – but when he was informed that to be chosen was the highest honour possible, and that refusal would most likely lead to his execution, he reluctantly agreed.

Lenore was furious. 'So this is her game. She takes *my* captain and makes him the champion of her. She knows that I have fondnesses.

Well, if she wishes to play this game then I am ready to play. Yes.'

'I don't know what you're talking about,' drawled Fritzacopple. 'Frankly, dear, you are not nearly old enough to have "fondnesses", or play games, and you are *definitely* not old enough to play games of fondness with the likes of him.'

'We'll see.'

And so the captain stumbled, cursing, into the iron arena – a vast black cage of iron ribs lined with sharp spikes. The cage was surrounded by ranks of the Emperor's Insect Legion. When the royal referees asked Lambestyo to state his fighting manifesto he said, 'This is stupid.' And so the referees hastily stitched him a flag with 'This is Stupid' on it. Then he was stripped to the waist, and the crowd in the Omnivision™ Arena gasped. The spectators in their homes and in the theatres gasped too as Dray's cameras, bolted to a grid above the ring, zoomed in upon the snake-nest of scars which ran across his lean and muscled torso. The boy turned his burning gaze towards a tiny chamber high above: an aperture covered in gauze from which the Empress was rumoured to watch. He saluted the empty heights. Miss Fritzacopple personally ensured that he was greased down, limbered up, then she pushed him into the arena to face a man who called himself 'Ulrich'. Ulrich had just arrived in port and was said to be one of the best freestyle wrestlers around. He was a hulking sailor with tattoos featuring hideous acts of violence. The captain performed just one act of violence before picking him up and throwing him out of the cage.

His next opponent was also a large man with a fearsome reputation, but Lambestyo had little trouble dispatching him. 'They're trying to throw these fights.'

'I know,' said Fritzacopple as she surreptitiously dabbed fake blood on her fighter's eye. 'No one wants to win. The defending champion must be a monster.'

'Well, then why do I want to win?'

'Because if you can get close to the Empress you might be able to get her to help us leave. Here, let the next guy hit you and bite down on this blood capsule. Then at least the people will be happy.'

'How did you get a blood capsule?'

'I used to be a dancer. Try to make him look good.'

But this was harder than it appeared. The opponents seemed to be getting weaker with every round. When the Necronaut strode towards him his opponent crawled up the side of the cage, squealing.

'Don't run,' hissed Lambestyo. 'Just come down and I'll let you hit me.' But there was no coaxing his opponent, Hetfield, from the cage heights. Not until the fight was called off.

Then the referee announced that the captain had now earned the right to face last year's champion. A hush fell over the stadium as his opponent entered.

'A girl?' said the captain as he caught his breath. Shona entered the arena and glared at her opponent. They met in the centre and the captain said, 'Our mothers taught us not to hit girls.'

'I spit on your mothers,' said Shona, and she spat right on his boot.

'OK then,' said the captain.

The bell sounded and before Lambestyo could even raise his fists Shona cracked him across the jaw with a brass chain, sending the blood capsule pinging off the bars like a bullet.

'She has a chain!' called Fritzacopple unhelpfully. The captain wobbled for a second and before he knew it he was on his back, Shona's face an angry inch from his, and her chain was wrapped around his throat.

'I would just like to say I am sorry for my earlier comments about not hitting girls,' rasped the captain. His face was turning purple. 'I can see now you are a strong and capable young woman.'

'Try not to let her strangle you!' yelled his coach.

If the captain had talked to anyone before the event he would have learned the reason this competition was a little soft. It was soft because most of the men in this city did not want to be humiliated into a bloody pulp by Shona. She had won three years running, and all the men she'd beaten were broken men.

'Take this, Renaldo!' she said as she rammed the captain's head repeatedly against the iron floor of the ring. His head ran thick with sparks. 'Renaldo?' he gasped.

Again, if he had bothered to speak to any of the locals before the event he would have learned that Renaldo was the name of a man who had, some three years ago, broken up with Shona so that he could run off with her best friend. She had decided that if she couldn't exact her revenge on Renaldo, she would instead exact it on all Renaldo-kind. Any Renaldo who stepped into her ring had received the same bloody treatment. Now, as he lay on his back under a barrage of astonishingly brutal blows, he realised that his stance on striking a woman had been logically flawed. 'Perhaps,' he thought, 'if women are truly to take their place in society as equal partners with men, we need to stop treating them as precious objects. Certainly,' the captain thought, as Shona put him in a choker hold, to the cheers of the assembled, and began to pound the back of his head with her chained fist, 'I would never strike a woman in anger. But if, for example, a woman had me in a choker grip and was pounding the back of my skull with her chained fist while squeezing my eyeball with her spare thumb and screaming, 'You like that, Renaldo! You like that!' then I would be within my rights to fight back. Yes. I do not think this is unreasonable at all. OK then.' And with that he flipped Shona over his shoulder with one single casual motion, and the crowd went *absolutely ballistic*.

★

Later, as Miss Fritzacopple dabbed his blackened eye with a cotton ball, he tried to explain his position. 'She was crazy! She thought I was called Renaldo!'

'She was smaller than you,' said Miss Fritzacopple. 'You should be ashamed.'

'What was I supposed to do? Lie there and let her beat me to death?'

'Oh, you're being overdramatic. She would never have beaten you to *death*.'

'But what about equality?!' cried the captain. 'Isn't that what you want?'

'The rules are simple,' said Miss Fritzacopple. 'We want equality, but you must not hit us, and if the ship is on fire we get the lifeboats.'

The captain tried to throw his arms up in disgust, but it hurt too much.

'How do you think that poor girl feels right now?'

'She feels fine,' he replied. 'We're meeting later to drink a bottle of rum.'

★

Lambestyo was declared the Knight of the Night of the Ring of Iron. He was told a ball would be held the next evening in his honour. He was told he must attend on pain of death. After the contest he had been ordered to climb a ladder into the heights in order to pay his respects to the chamber where the Empress was rumoured to sit. He found himself on a narrow ledge before a diaphanous screen. He never saw her face; she was just a quivering silhouette, a voice, calm yet dreadful. Later, he wouldn't say what the Empress had said, but in his journal he wrote, over and over: 'A shark, a shark, the life of a shark . . .'

★

The curfew had been suspended for the Night of the Ring of Iron. Maxwheel Struff, theatre director, dilettante, gourmand, author, raconteur and chairman of the Grand Ball Committee, was stumbling home in the witches' hour in his pink top hat and gold-leaf-encrusted britches when he felt the inexplicable. He felt compelled to take the small, bone-handled butterfly knife from his left boot – 'Because walking at night with all those creeps and jealous former lovers about – always bring protection, I say!' – and to calmly open a vein in his wrist, and then to smear five words in foot-high letters. The words were on the temple walls the next day when people began to arrive for prayers:

'SEE YOU AT THE BALL'.

AT THE BALL

In calling for the lady invited, the gentleman should be punctual in arriving at the hour agreed in writing or telegram prior to the event. If the gentleman is of enough substance to have ordered a carriage, he sends her in first to sit facing forward, then sits opposite the stinger end of the carriage – unless the lady requests him to sit somewhere else. In leaving the carriage the man goes first and helps the lady descend, being careful not to drop her or become caught in her skirts, and being careful to protect her hair or fascinator from snagging on the stinger. He then escorts her to the ladies' dressing rooms where he leaves her in the charge of the matron, while he goes to the gentlemen's apartment to divest himself of coat and boots.

Diemendääs by Night: A Guide to Common Etiquettes and Courtesies for Debutantes, Maxwheel Struff

THE NIGHT, THE SHARK

The Ball of the Knight of the Night of the Ring of Iron was the event of the year. To cancel it because its chairman had killed himself and scrawled a dire message on a temple in his own blood? Unthinkable. The city elite turned out to the event. Lenore stopped traffic with her dress, her make-up and her hair woven with a knot of black thorns. Miss Fritzacopple had carried out her orders with a set of faint *tsks*: dark around the eyes, dark upon the lips, no colour on the cheeks.

'Do you think our captain will be well to attend us this night, supposing?'

'I have no idea. I believe he is recovering from his date with a fighting lady and a gallon of rum.'

'I think he'll come. I want him to view upon me in my finest.'

'Do you and all?'

'I do.'

'You want him to see you looking like you've been woken from the grave?'

'I *was* woken from a grave, remember? A coffin of ice. I wonder if he will notice.'

'I don't believe our captain notices much any more. And you're too young to be noticing the likes of him.'

'I'm too young to notice things?'

'Too young to crush on things.'

466

'And how old were you when you first crushed on a thing?'

Miss Fritzacopple staunched a lovely memory of the friend of an older brother. 'That's hardly the issue. And I don't think any age is old enough for his like.'

'That Empress is plenty old enough. I'll show that old woman.' Then brightening: 'I need a protector, you know. The man of my dreams is to be attending, remember?'

'Honestly, Lenore, there's more guards than guests here tonight.'

The room stood still as they entered. The Emperor, dressed in his most lavish outfit yet – a dazzling scarlet saloon coat with silver thread stockings – looked alarmed when he saw Lenore. 'This look is . . . new for you,' he observed.

'But not for you, I fancy. Am I not just a chicken off the old block?'

The Emperor turned quickly to the botanist. 'And where is our man Fabrigas tonight? Fashionably late?'

'Off with Dray, no doubt,' said the botanist. 'They are a pair.'

'They are. And Our Lady's champion?'

'He is arriving now. I smell him,' said Lenore, somewhat breathlessly, and sure enough the murmurs rose upon the stairs, and then came busting through the main door, and there he stood at the top in a fine coat and a pair of shining boots. The Emperor had sent his best tailors to his suite with orders that he was not to bar them entry – on pain of death. The Emperor had learned that if he wanted the captain to do anything he had to add '. . . on pain of death'. The captain's hair was still wet and rough as waves, and his coat was rebelliously unbuttoned. He carried a bottle in his left hand, and the women all swooned upon the stairs as he came lazily down to meet his friends.

'I'm here!' he announced.

'We are glad,' said the botanist. 'Aren't we, Lenore?'

'I suppose we are to that,' the girl replied.

'Lenore has put a lot of time into her look this evening.'

'I can see. And . . . what is this all about?' He circled his head lazily with his finger.

'If you remember,' said the Emperor patiently, 'it is a grand ball in your honour.'

'Ahhhhhh, jess.' He ruffled his own hair and took a swig from his bottle. 'Keep up the good work.'

Then the captain was off to the bar, the seas parted. Later in the night they saw him near the dance floor, surrounded by some of Diemendääs's most beautiful women. They saw him once more, alone upon the balcony, staring out into the night with his black eyes. And then he vanished.

'What is to become of him? And us?' said Fritzacopple.

The Emperor, who had been spending a scandalous amount of time with the botanist that evening, seemed about to answer when an aide appeared, breathing heavily. 'Your Majesty, I'm afraid there's been . . . an incident.'

A young man, a visiting explorer, had been caught canoodling with a general's wife and had fled the ball, pursued by officers. He had vanished into the night.

'Our Lady's champion, Lambestyo, no doubt.'

'Not him, Your Highness.'

*

'He's leaving us,' said Lenore. 'I can feel it. He didn't even let me have a single dance.'

'He was off talking to women his own age. You can't expect him to hang around us.'

On the dance floor, couples floated madly by, ghastly grins upon their faces. Shrieks came from the balcony as an admiral tried to lift a lady's skirts. There was a mania settling over the room.

'One day I'll make him dance with me,' said the green-skinned girl. The grimness with which this was said alarmed the botanist. But then a shadow rolled across her. The music and all the voices in the Grand Ballroom stopped abruptly.

'Hello, little monster,' said the botanist, in a voice that was both hers and not. 'I wonder if *I* might have the next dance.'

'Miss Fritzacopples?'

'She'll be back before you know it. I'm just borrowing her mind for a few minutes. I wanted to talk to you in person. At last. Are you well? You look well. Are you enjoying your voyage?'

'It isn't the kind of voyage which you enjoy. But well enough.'

'And where are your friends? The old wizard?'

'Elsewhere. Who is for the asking?'

'And your dear captain?'

'Also absent. Who will I say is calling?'

'You know who I am. You know what has to happen.'

'You're going to kill me.'

'It has to be.'

The botanist's voice was calm and measured, but with a raw edge, the sound of a good pair of scissors cutting cloth.

'The men you said would protect you. *Vanished*. No one here to stop me killing you.'

'Please leave My Ladies' body. You don't belong in there.'

'I won't stay long. And your little boyfriend? Where has your friend gone to?'

'I have not any idea. He is *not* my boyfriend. And I have given you more words than a lady should for a stranger.'

'Quite. But then everyone you know is a stranger, isn't that so? You don't have a person in the universe you could say you knew for sure.'

'I have my friend, My Ladies.'

The botanist's laugh filled Lenore with dread. The band had stopped. There was near silence in the Grand Ballroom. Some of the guests were snoring faintly.

'You . . . put everyone to sleep?'

'I did.'

'That's the finest trick.'

'A simple parlour trick, like your wizard's gag with the fake knives. I could teach you if you like. I know many tricks.'

'I have some for my own.'

'Indeed you do. And plenty of time to practise. It must be hard to feel as alone as you.'

'I don't feel so alonesome.'

'Do you not? Are you sure?'

'I'm sure.'

'Really? You have countless billions of miles to travel and no one to travel with. The most powerful beings in the Infiniverse want you dead. And even if you did manage, *somehow*, to escape me, someone else would come along to kill you. You fled the universe and we found you. Does that not make you feel desperately alone? You want to get home, but where is home? You have no place, no family. You know this in your heart. You are an alien creature. You don't belong here. The best thing you could do would be to end it all now.'

'Is that a fact?'

There was a pause in the conversation. 'My word,' she heard the hijacked botanist say, 'you do have a strong mind. Slow claps for you,' and at once all the sleeping citizens in the Grand Ballroom began to clap in time, a resounding clap for every second, like the report from a line of rifles at a funeral.

The clock in the Grand Ballroom struck eleven and the pair waited for its chimes to fade.

'You simply have no idea, Lenore, of the power you have.'

'I don't?'

'No. But how could you? You have *real* power.'

'More than you?'

'More than I and all these sleepyheads combined. But unfortunately even you can't stop what's coming.'

'Well, why do you not just kill me now?'

'I will. But first I'd like to peel open that skull of yours. Take a look at that miraculous little brain.'

'And you are waiting for something else. The file. You must have the file.'

'Very good. You are very good.'

'I don't know of any file.'

'Of course you don't. Don't worry your pretty head about that. Once I have it I can kill you.'

'I'm not afraid of dying.'

'That's because you don't know what it'll be like, Lenore. When people die, they sleep. When you die you won't sleep. Even when I've killed you you'll lie beneath the heavy soil, rotting all the while to bloody jelly, the fat worms coiling through your ribs, maggots seething in your soggy abdomen. But your mind will live on. Your ice prison was a few millennia. Imagine an eternity. Now tell me that doesn't frighten you.'

Lenore was alarmed to hear the clapping cease as the clock struck twelve, though but a few seconds had passed since eleven bells. She heard Miss Fritzacopple say, 'Gosh, the ice in my glass has melted.'

The band swelled into life again: 'Our Lady Lives On'.

THE NECRONAUT

The captain had left his ball hours earlier. He had seen a fuss around the carriage park as teams of guards set off in pursuit of the explorer who had kissed a general's wife without asking. He drifted through the darkened halls, whispering darkly in his wiry head, stroking his scars and incanting magic spells of misery. His black eyes roamed the stone arcades, scanned the shimmering shadows for movement, drifted up to the dreaming spires where the evening bells tolled softly, to the dark mountains above, to the stars beyond, and his dry lips parted for a moment. He had felt her watching him home on many an evening. But tonight was different. Tonight she walked with him, her soft arm through his. He found himself in a corridor where statues of half-angel creatures rose and spread their wings, as stiff and ready as vultures. In the windows of the arcade the curtains filled like sails and released, it seemed, with heavy sighs. The captain thought he could hear an ocean. He found himself in a doorway where a woman's voice said, 'At last. My champion. I was calling. Did you not hear? Why did you not come when I called you?'

He found himself saying, 'Because I'm afraid.' He found icy hands touching his face. A single frozen finger ran the length of the scar on his cheek. Icy blue hands touched his and brought him forward. The next thing he felt was the sun.

463171: THE ONE WHERE NO ONE'S READY

That night Fabrigas had the strangest and most vivid dream. It was perhaps the *most* strange and *most* vivid dream he'd had since all those centuries ago when he'd survived the cannon and dreamed that there were infinite universes, all singing together like voices in a choir, that life was a continuum of possibilities, that the separation between objects was an illusion, that reality itself was one great glorious game.

'Hello.'

'Hello there.'

'Who are you?'

'My name is Carl.'

Carl sat on a rock and considered the waves. He looked handsome in his polo-neck sweater.

'Pleased to meet you, Carl. Have we met?'

'No. I am a friend.'

'Oh. And why am I standing on a beach?'

'Because you are dreaming.'

'Oh. And what are all those starfish doing?'

'Very little. They are your friends, too. We're all your friends.'

'Oh. That's pleasant.'

'It is. We've finally found a way that we can talk to you directly. Having our friends at Dark Hand send you all those letters was very difficult. And you don't sleep much.'

'I never have.'

'We wanted to encourage you. We need to tell you how important it is that you keep trying, and that you don't get sick-hearted. Things are about to get strange and tragic, but it is vital that you stick to your mission and bring these kids home to the beginning of time. Or as close as you can. That boy has a lot of important information in his scruffy little head. But it's encrypted with a quasi-infinite prime-number key. With an infinity in front of us we should have just enough time to extract the information and prepare for the great battle.'

'But you always taught me time was irrelevant.'

'Ha! You clever thing. Time is like a river to an ocean.'

'Because it flows?'

'No, because it makes us think.'

'I lost Roberto. It's my fault.'

'Don't beat yourself up. He's a clever kid. Maybe the cleverest. He'll find his way back. Right now he's in another dimension helping an advanced civilisation fight a giant monster.'

'Is he now?'

'Oh yes. Like I said, he's a smart one. But the code in his head reveals, among many things, the hidden structure of a universe. And we can't have that just roaming around.'

'We can't?'

'No. But there isn't time to explain why just now. It would take at least a dozen of your lifetimes. Your enemies from your old universe have sent some fearsome adversaries to kill you all. You can't defeat them with weapons, or by running. Sometimes to keep your mind you have to let the monster in.'

'I'm very, very tired.'

'We know you are. But we're confident you can find your old spark. You just need to remember what set you sailing through this great expanse in the first place. For small creatures like us the vastness is bearable only through love. Well, we should probably let you go. It looks like there's someone at your door.'

Fabrigas woke to hear a heavy and persistent banging on his door. 'Things are about to get messy again,' said Carrofax.

'You're back! Did you find our ship?' said Fabrigas.

'No,' said the demon, 'I did not. But I can tell you that the *Necronaut* does not sail in this dimension.'

'I already know this.'

The banging on the door grew louder.

'It gets worse. Some fools from your old universe have signed a pact with a monster.'

'I know this too!'

'In any event, you have more immediate dangers to worry about right now. Is your beard on tight?'

CELL

The cells in Diemendääs are bright and sunny. They have comfortable furnishings and paintings on the walls. One painting is of a brave soldier holding a child at arm's length, but that isn't important right now. Brave Captain Lambestyo leaned against the wall – he still wore his evening coat and boots – and mused upon a picture which was much less rousing than the ones he'd seen at night during the past weeks. This one was of a pompous-looking sailor holding a sextant as he gazed towards the stars. The captain smiled. He was happy. Though he was now a prisoner he was happy for the first time in a long, long time. He had tasted paradise. It was as if he were lost in a beautiful waking dream.

He could hear his lawyer talking to Fabrigas. 'I'm afraid this is very serious,' explained the lawyer, an earnest young woman called Solman. 'He was caught in Our Lady's quarters, though thankfully she was elsewhere at the time.' The captain smiled. 'But the family are very distressed, especially the Emperor. For him to make his way through nine heavily bolted doors and past countless guards shows someone who desperately wanted to get to the Empress.'

'But how, *how*,' said Fabrigas, 'could he have managed to get past all that security? The guards saw and heard nothing. He would have needed inside help.'

'Doors don't seem to stop this man. He's already broken out of his cell once: if only to make himself some tea.' Solman began to put away her papers. 'And it does not change the fact that he is charged with the most serious crime possible of any in this city.'

Captain Lambestyo smiled again and shook his head. He could still hear her voice, faintly. 'Champion, my champion. You belong only to me.'

*

The captain's trial took place in a private hall away from the public. It was a fair trial, conducted well, but the crime of consorting, or attempting to consort, with Our Lady was a crime which carried heavy punishment: expulsion from this reality into a compartmental auxiliary punitive dimension, otherwise known as the Forbidden Zone.

'I am aware that at the time you were in a fragile state,' said the judge, 'but I have no room for leniency in this instance.'

The captain by this time had cast off his spell, and the full weight of what he'd done bore down on his head and shoulders.

Fabrigas had gone to the judge, the prosecutors, even the Emperor to try to win the captain's freedom. He pleaded with Dr Dray to tell him the 'cheat code' for the Forbidden Zone. 'If we can sneak him out a back door we can be gone and no one will be the wiser!'

'I wish I could help you, froglet,' said Dray. 'But they would find out, and I would be tried as a traitor. I'm afraid I can't bring myself to sacrifice my life for your friend.'

'And I would not expect you to.'

Given a rare few moments alone with his captain, Fabrigas had whispered, urgently: 'So this is a tight spot. In a high-security prison and about to be cast into the Forbidden Zone. What is your plan for escape?'

'For escape?'

'Yes. It is a difficult challenge, but if you need WD40-X I think I can make you some.'

'I cannot escape from here.'

'Come now. I've seen you get out of much worse than this.'

'Jess. Let me put it some other way. I *will* not escape from here.'

Fabrigas blinked rapidly at him.

'Even if I escape from this prison, I still cannot escape from her. I am her prisoner. Even if I go a billion light-years away I'll always come back. It's just the way it is. She's just one of those women.'

Miss Fritzacopple, too, pleaded with the Emperor, but she couldn't get him to grant the captain clemency. 'Once a person falls under the spell of Our Lady there is no hope.'

'Then let us leave! We'll fly to another place, we'll leave for ever!'

'He would return. My dear, we've been here a thousand times. Why do you think we have a Forbidden Zone? Why do you think we put men there? Why do you think there's an army at our western wall?'

★

And in the Lotus Garden, Prince Panduke told Kimmy that when he was finally Emperor he'd destroy the Forbidden Zone and free her friend. Kimmy let him hold her hand for exactly one minute.

★

Our friends farewelled their captain at the gate-which-wasn't-a-gate and they wept. Even the great army of the Emperor Karn Karn-Zheng ceased their assault on the western wall and stood by to watch a ritual they had seen hundreds of times: the banishment of the mortal fool.

'Farewell, friend,' said Fabrigas. 'We'll rescue you when we can. I almost guarantee it.'

'I don't want to go into the Forbidden Zone,' said the boy. 'It's boring.'

'I know. But the bears will make life interesting.'

'I have something to tell you,' said the boy. 'I tried to tell you on the ship, but I fell asleep. I'm not really the Necronaut. I was his cabin boy. He died while we were at sea. I didn't throw him overboard like I said. He went of natural causes. Too much rum. So I took his life. Apparently he had once done it to another man called the Necronaut. Only the bosun knew.'

'I knew.'

'I was an army pilot, though. And I did get this scar from a woman.'

'With you it's always a woman. But you're a fine captain. You have done well and should be proud.'

'So you aren't angry?'

'Of course I'm not.'

'And my fee?'

'We'll discuss that later.'

'Please tell Commander Descharge that I'm sorry he's missed his chance to hang me. I'm sorry to disappoint him again.'

Lenore threw her arms around him and whispered, 'I'll not forget.' Then she pressed a star-shaped object into his hand. 'It's to protect you,' she said. 'I was told not to give Gloria to anyone. But I am the boss of me.' Even the stoic Maria Fritzacopple approached him to say goodbye. She put her hands on his shoulders and said, 'You are a maddening fool.' Then she smashed her mouth against his with a passionate intensity which made them all shield their eyes. Lenore said, 'I smell odd things. What's happening?'

'What was that for?' said Lambestyo.

'So you'll forget about that woman and start acting like a man again.'

Captain Lambestyo felt his heart crack open like an egg, the oozy lava crawling from his chest, up his neck, into his brain. He had had no inkling that any of his shipmates loved him. He would always remember the feeling as he walked through the gate to his death. It was the first time he'd felt as though he wanted to be alive. He also found that the Empress had vanished from his mind.

When the captain too had vanished, Lenore turned slowly to the Emperor, who stood to one side, and said, 'Do you know how long your goodly wife has been alive, sir?'

It was a strange question, and the Emperor took his time to say, 'She has been living for . . . some thousands of years.'

'Good,' said the girl. 'Because one way, or another way, I will make her suffer for many times longer.'

465671: THE ONE WITH THE
SEVEN SAD MOUNTAINS

A day passed in which our friends did not eat, or leave their rooms, or receive visitors. It was such a cloud that hung above that even Carrofax began to feel the drag of the human heart. 'You must shake off this grief!' he said, but Fabrigas wouldn't even reply.

Lenore would not come out of her room. Anyone who approached the door felt their hair rise up as if by electrical force. A servant who touched the latch was thrown back across the hall with a powerful jolt. He was admitted to hospital.

The girl remained in a trance: a waking dream-state in which she drifted through a sea of lucid visions: 465254: The One with the Metaphorical Tunnel; 465273: The One with the Ultimate Fighting Champion. Finally she found her mortal enemy, somewhere beneath the Seven Sad Mountains.

'You took my captain, woman. Now we are enemies.'

'I didn't take him, dearest. Blame the bee, not the honey. Your captain is a man. You, on the other hand, have a way to travel.'

'I am older than you.'

'That is technically true.'

'You tricked me and betrayed me. You said you'd help me, then you took the only thing I cared about.'

'It was our deal. You asked me for protection. In return you had to give me something you won't miss. And you won't. Eventually.

We are even now.'

'We are not even. You will pay a price. I've come to bring destruction on your city. I've come to bring snow and fire.'

The Empress laughed. 'That's not how this story plays out. You are handed over to the Pope. He does with you what he will. He throws you into a black hole. He leaves. That is your story.'

'You said we wouldn't be killed!'

'No, I said *you* wouldn't. And you won't. You'll survive the black hole. But all your friends will die. The problem is you think this is a fairy tale, but it isn't. It's life. Just look at me. I'm a cursed woman whose only solace is to feed on love. I can see how it all ends. Would it help you to know that some day someone will open the box containing the Forbidden Zone? The lovers inside will swarm upon the palace and tear me to pieces.'

'That's bad.'

'Isn't it, though?'

'Things can change. You know I can change things.'

'Oh, Lenore. You are in for some real surprises. Remember what I taught you. It's not always wise to run from a beast. Sometimes to kill a beast you must let him get close. So close you want to scream with terror.'

The whole palace woke to the sound of the girl's scream. A few minutes later the door opened and she appeared, looking more than ever like a terrible young monster, and said, 'The time has come to face our enemies. And bring me a glass of milk.'

DEARLY DEPARTED

There had been another death. That night at the Domus, the city's largest temple. A socialite well known for his flamboyant sense of dress had been compelled to kill his wife, then himself, but not before he'd scrawled six words across the side of the temple in his wife's blood:

'TODAY IS THE DAY, LITTLE GIRL'.

There wasn't a person in the city who didn't know which little girl he was referring to. People painted their own banners. 'GIVE HIM WHAT HE WANTS!' and 'ONE GIRL FOR OUR LIVES SEEMS A FAIR PRICE'.

The little girl was not anxious. 'He is right. Today is the day. Let him come. I am ready.' She sipped her lemon tea.

The Emperor arrived and told them that he was putting them in protective custody. He wore a particularly elegant purple hunting jacket with gold stitching, white gloves, white boots and an ornamental bronze 'crotch-piece'. He had prepared a cave annexe high on the mountain where they would be safe. He appeared unusually upbeat about it all. He took them quickly through the corridors, his shoes clacking on the hardwood floor. 'I have prepared a great breakfast for you. You will want for nothing.' Miss Fritzacopple couldn't help noticing that he wouldn't meet her eyes.

'Ah yes,' Lenore said. 'Breakfast in the caves. Cannot see anything wrong with this.' The Emperor glanced quickly at her. 'Where's that other girl? Kimmy?' He scanned the group.

'Kimmy will not be here for breakfast,' said Miss Fritzacopple. 'She's gone to see your son.'

The Emperor showed a brief expression of panic that neither Fabrigas nor Fritzacopple could fail to notice. Then he sped on again, saying, 'Can't be helped, can't be helped.'

'What do you mean it can't be helped?' said Miss Fritzacopple. She nudged Fabrigas firmly in the arm. The old man was squinting at the Emperor.

*

Soon they were riding up the mountain in one of the antique cable carriages. The carriage rocked and cried above the crags. Lenore was conspicuously quiet. The Emperor said, 'You are quiet this morning, Miss Lenore. Did you sleep badly?'

'Not at all. I slept like a baby log. Everything is just as it should be.'

'I will stay for a quick breakfast,' said Fabrigas. 'I have a coffee date with Dray, and then antique shopping.'

'So you keep saying,' said Fritzacopple.

But the old man continued. 'I was going to sketch the birds as they hatch outside my window this morning. They are ripe any day now.'

'It would really be wise if you stayed in the annexe I've prepared. It is much safer there.'

'Nonsense. Coffee, shopping, sketching birds. This is my day.'

Their host said nothing more as they docked and left their car. The annexe was even more impressive than Fabrigas imagined. A web of tunnels and arcades had been drilled through the dormant volcano. Some of the tunnels were wide enough to drive a carriage down, others were hardly big enough for a single person to squeeze through, and all were carved with mysterious cyphers. Some led to ancient digs, others to dead ends, others to lonesome mystics, others to cascading waterfalls and lush mountain-top grottos. It was a work in progress. As they walked the ancient stone tunnel towards the hall where they would hide from their pursuer they found they almost had to run to keep up with the Emperor, ordinarily a rambler. A pair of robed monks, headlamps lit, leaped to get out of his path.

Carrofax, who had been spending most of his time lately vainly searching for the *Necronaut*, appeared and said, 'I don't like this. This is all bad. Turn back,' just as the hall doors flung themselves open to reveal the long table set with coffee, pastries, soup.

Sitting at one end of the table was a pudgy, smiling man in a white leisure suit and a white, pointed cap. 'Good morning, friends!' beamed the Pope. 'Do you know me? I am the Pope!'

POPE

'So, you are the people causing all the troubles!' The Pope had greasy pastry freckles on his face. With every word he said flecks fell like snow upon the table. He wore a white leisure suit with gold stripes and a gold monogram on the right breast. The year was embroidered in gold on the left breast. The limited-edition leisure suit had been designed to commemorate the Great Crusade. 'His fleet arrived some days ago,' said the Emperor. 'They have the planet surrounded on all sides. They said they would destroy my city if I didn't cooperate. I had no choice.' They all sat, solemn and silent, as the Pope sent morsels in after the morsels already in his horrid purple mouth. The Pope's guardsmen, great hulking men dressed in black, had barred the room's only exit.

'Do you say your prayers every morning?' said the Pope. 'Do you recite the Plasms? Do you read stories from the Holy Neon Bible? Are you good children?'

'Do you plan to keep us against our will?' Fabrigas spoke and the Pope froze, mouth in mid-chew on a load of snowy-white moosh, and stared at the old man with an expression of a child who has just seen a stranger pull a pencil from his ear. He put his pastry down directly on the shiny surface of the table and smoothed the crumbs from his leisure suit with his two fat hands.

'I have declared a crusade. I have come to find the people who ran off from our universe in defiance of the laws.'

'Which laws?'

'The laws of nature!' The Pope slammed his open palm upon the table, leaving a greasy print. 'This group of rebels has something that belongs to the Queen.' And while his head remained perfectly still, his eyes, squinting, made a slow, slow journey to Lenore. 'Hello, little girl.'

'Hello.'

'I hear that you have a nose much like a dog, more or less.'

'Better.'

'Better?'

'Yes.'

The most feared and powerful man in the universe, in any universe, drew a love heart with his finger in a sheet of icing sugar.

'Your devil-nose can tell what I had for breakfast this morning?'

'It can tell you what you were having for breakfast *yesterday* morning. Half of a dead chicken and a bowl of sausages. With a jug of wine.'

The most powerful man in the universe, in any universe, was still looking at her sideways, and now his squint was so profound that his eyes became two gleaming slits.

'I am allowed to eat what I would like for breakfast. I am the Pope.'

'So you are.'

The girl could not see the Pope begin to turn, by minute shades, to a kind of purple found only in the berry kingdom, and she could not see the perfectly manicured fingers of his left hand draw back, slowly, into a fist, leaving long claw-marks through the icing-sugar heart. Then the Emperor spoke calmly.

'Holiness. Please forgive the girl for her impertinence. They have had a long and difficult journey. I hope that we can remain civil, and that any business we need to conduct can be done in a –'

'You are a king?'

'I . . . no, an emperor. We met yesterd—'

487

'What do you eat for breakfast?' The Pope looked towards the Emperor.

'. . . Toast.'

'*Pphht*. What on it?'

'. . . Honey.'

'Pah. That is no breakfast. Honey is devil juice. Little buzzy devils with their busy, buzzy devil-dancing,' as he made a pair of tiny wings with his hands and rocked from side to side. 'I am the Pope!' He stood – though it was hard to tell, he was so short. 'And you had better all start showing me respect! Because let me tell you one thing: people who don't show me respect, they vanish! *Poof!*' And he rose to full height. 'The people who cross *meeeeee*, who think they can take advantage of *myyyyyy* generos—'

'Pope! Enough!'

The voice seemed to come from the very air. The Pope froze, one finger pointing to the heavens, and the others, looking around the room for, it seemed, the first time, found a man in the corner. The man was sitting, one leg across the other, in a plush leather chair and reading from a small, leather-bound book. He was *exceptionally* well dressed, and immaculately groomed, but for some fading bruises on his face. He did not look up as he said, 'Please forgive our Pope. With great power comes a great lack of manners. I think it is time we got to know each other.' The Well Dressed Man stood now, placed the book carefully inside his jacket pocket, turned towards the group and touched a finger to his cuffs.

A WELL DRESSED GENTLEMAN

'So you are the great Fabrigas, the magician who made the universe disappear?' The Well Dressed Man had taken the Pope's seat at the head of the table. He had taken a perfect white kerchief from his breast pocket and wiped the top clean of pastry crumbs.

The Pope was sitting, upright, in the leather chair, looking for all the world like a young boy waiting for his mother. The Well Dressed Man held the kerchief in front of Fabrigas, snapped it firmly, and the thing disappeared. The old man shrugged.

'I am Fabrigas, yes. And you are . . . a travelling entertainer?'

The Well Dressed Man found a minute crumb on the sleeve of his perfect jacket. 'Oh, but I thought you loved magic shows. I saw your prank with the trick knives. You almost had me fooled.'

'There are no trick knives. I made that very clear.'

'Really? Fascinating. Would you like to see one of my tricks? Pope! Kneel!' The Pope fell from his chair into a kneeling position.

'Pope! Pray!' The most powerful man in the universe raised his eyes and hands and fell into a babble of silent murmurs.

'Pope! Slap!' The Pope struck himself hard across his face, immediately leaving a perfect pink handprint on his baby-smooth cheek. The sound was so loud they all jumped. All except the Well Dressed Man.

'Again!' Slap! This time on the other cheek. 'Again!' And now two huge black shapes passed by, and the murmuring Pope was joined

489

by two of his hulking guards, in their high-necked black sweaters and silver ear studs, who waltzed merrily in each other's arms.

'This is the Pope, in case you didn't know. He is the most feared and powerful person in the universe. His fleet can make whole cities vanish. And he works for me. You will soon learn that I am no entertainer.' The Well Dressed Man frowned, sniffed the air twice and sneered. 'Empathy gas? You are trying to disable me with an empathy gas? You can't beat me with gases, or fake knives, or any tired parlour tricks.' Now Fabrigas felt his right arm begin to move, slowly, from where it rested. He fought hard to stop it, but it was as if that arm no longer existed. His arm rose and floated to an inch from one of the heavy candles that sat along the table. Fabrigas felt the heat.

'It is a queer sensation, isn't it? You can feel the pain but not the arm, and you can't do a thing about it. It's almost as if you don't want to do a thing about it.' Fabrigas looked down at his hand. He saw the hand glowing orange. He felt the pain growing. He closed his eyes and breathed deeply. He tried to imagine a universe in which he really had no arm. Then he tried to imagine a universe where he had no mind. Then he tried to imagine a universe where there wasn't a well-dressed man sitting across from him. Slowly, the universe vanished. When he opened his eyes he saw that he had been able to move his hand an inch away from the flame.

'Very good!' said the Well Dressed Man. 'I've met stronger minds, but certainly I've met weaker.' He let the old man's hand flop back upon the tabletop. 'Emperor. You may go. We thank you for your assistance. You can rest assured that the killings will stop . . .' he turned his eyes back to his new prisoners, '. . . soon.' He smiled. 'And as we agreed I will compel the Pope to vanquish the armies from your wall.'

The Emperor rose and left quickly.

The Well Dressed Man rose and moved around the table towards Lenore. Fritzacopple stood to bar his way. 'And what do we have here? If it isn't the legendary assassin, Penny Dreadful. I was sure I'd killed you. Had I not? They said you fell from a bridge in a hail of poison darts.'

Miss Maria Fritzacopple – botanist, beauty – seemed to shrink a foot. But she held the man's eyes. Fabrigas turned towards his friend with a look of amusement, but when he saw her face he suddenly knew that it was true.

'It was no great thing,' said the botanist. 'I spent years building up a resistance to the most common poisons. And I was never afraid of a little fall.'

The Well Dressed Man smiled. 'Well, then get ready, my dearest.'

'An assassin?' said Lenore. 'What is this crazy man talking about now?'

'You knew, surely, Master Fabrigas, that bad people would be hunting you. But for one to infiltrate your ship! My word. You must be stunned.' He was. The old one stood and let his mouth fall open.

'This is a ridiculous. My Lady would not be an assassin. She's us!' The little girl's face was bright and urgent.

'It must be so difficult to learn you've been betrayed by someone you thought was your friend. Myself, I never keep friends. Sit, woman,' said the Well Dressed Man, and Penny Dreadful did. 'Good girl. Hello, little monster. So good to see you again, too.'

'You have met?' said Fabrigas.

'Oh, we chatted briefly at the ball. Pope! Stop muttering!' The Pope stopped muttering. 'Now what tricks can you do, little monster?'

'I'm not your puppy,' replied Lenore.

'Ah, the young. So impertinent. Why don't you sing us all a song? Something . . . jaunty.'

'Why don't you fold it twice and sit upon it?'

The faint and ever-present smile vanished from the Well Dressed Man's face. He bent his tall frame towards the tiny girl.

'Oh, but I'm sure you know a song you'd love to share with us. Something . . . *jaunty*? Perhaps a nice shanty.' He stared hard into the girl's tranquil face.

'I couldn't possibly know whatever you were talking about. What is "jaunty"?'

'Hmmmm,' said the Well Dressed Man. 'You still won't dance with me. Never mind!' He broke away brightly from Lenore. 'It's clear someone has been teaching you tricks, but I have never met a nut I couldn't crack.'

'But there's one more consciousness here. Yes. Not human. Not visible. Yes.'

'Just try it,' said Carrofax. 'Just try to enter my mind and see what happens to you.'

'A phantom friend! How extraordinary. This has been a day of surprises. Of course, you're of no use when you're forbidden from interfering in this universe, are you?'

'Direct assaults are a different matter. Just try entering my mind. I beg you to. Just give me an excuse.'

The Well Dressed Man laughed. 'Oh, I can tell we're going to have some fun here. The stage is set for a fantastic battle! But for now I think we all need some rest. I feel like this young girl is going to soak up a great deal of my . . . concentration.'

'I'm the Pope!' said the Pope.

'Yes, yes,' said the Well Dressed Man. 'Of course you are.'

BLACK WIDOW

Things began to move very fast. 'At least let us say goodbye,' said the botanist.

'Oh, my dear Penny, you have gone sentimental. You have forty-five seconds to say goodbye,' said the Well Dressed Man, and Miss Fritzacopple took Lenore in her arms. 'I will come for you,' she said. 'I promise.'

'Everything will turn out how it will,' the girl replied.

Fabrigas knelt before her and pressed a familiar object into her palm. 'Be brave,' he said. Then the girl was taken away by two towering guards.

'Old fool,' said the Well Dressed Man, 'I sense no fight in you. You may return to your apartment. A guard will be placed outside, purely for your safety.' He reached into his breast pocket, took out a straight-edge razor and unfolded it. 'And what would you like me to do with your assassin? I am happy to dispose of her.' He handed the blade to the botanist who raised it to her own throat. 'The choice is yours.'

The old man's face betrayed nothing. 'Tell me who you are.'

'I am Maria Fritzacopple.'

'Lies!' said the Well Dressed Man. The blade left a thin mark on the side of her throat.

'I have many names,' she said. And this was true. 'As you are the Queen's star explorer, I was once her top spy. My code name was the Black Widow. I escaped the Queen's service and became a private assassin. I assumed the name Penny Dreadful. Like this man, I was hired to track and kill you. As I became aware of the scale and brutality of the plot against you, I switched allegiances.'

'Why should I believe you?' said Fabrigas.

'Because if it wasn't true, you'd all be dead.'

'To be fair, that's probably fact,' said the Well Dressed Man.

'Since we made the crossing I have dedicated myself to protecting you and the children. You are not aware of the times that I have saved your lives.'

'Like I said, she's gone soft.'

'You had a good side once, Daniel.'

'That,' said the Well Dressed Man, 'is just a rumour spread by people I've killed. Well, old man? Shall we get this over with? Step off that antique carpet, will you, there's a good girl.' Penny Dreadful, aka the Black Widow, stepped off the carpet.

Fabrigas turned to the Well Dressed Man. 'Put her in a cell. A cold and dark one.'

'Seriously? Has everyone here gone soft? All right. As you wish. It will be very cold, and very dark.' The Well Dressed Man took back his blade and it vanished into his jacket.

Before she was taken away the Black Widow said, 'I will prove myself to you.'

'You already have, woman,' Fabrigas replied bitterly.

She was taken to a cell at the army barracks. It was indeed very dark, and very cold, and had just a small skylight in the roof. The rectangle of light at the end of the corridor shrank to a thin line and she was left in blackness with only the ghosts of her past for company.

RETIREMENT

'Sir?'

Carrofax had stayed silent through most of the night, unable to cope, as always, with the inky depths of human feelings. He could understand their violence. He could almost understand their lust. But their sadness, misery, the way they seemed to make every decision in their lives from within a cyclone of feelings, these were depths the phenomenal spirit could not fathom.

'I only wanted to go away to a moon. To find my father and my nanny. Was that too much to ask? To live in peace?'

'Sir, I just wanted to let you know that the girl is safe.'

'I don't care about the girl. I don't care about anything now.'

'I still have not found the ship, or Roberto. Though I have found out who this Calligulus –'

'I don't care about them any more, Carrofax.'

'No?'

'I am done with it all.'

'You are . . . done with it?'

'Yes, the ship, the boy, the girl, the spies, the giant slugs. I'm done with it. I wash my hands. I am retiring.'

'I beg your pardon?'

'I am officially retiring. I have had a true revelation in the past few weeks, a revelation which goes far beyond discovering the secret to travelling between dimensions, or proving that you exist. I have discovered that none of this matters.'

'It doesn't?'

'No. If all possibilities exist simultaneously in a continuum, and my experience of this continuum is but a subjective dream, then there is little point in concerning myself with the outcome of those experiences. I am not a hero in some action cine film or 8-bit novel. I am a real person.'

'I see.'

'The Emperor has offered me a dukedom here. Once the Pope leaves he will lift my house arrest and I can have my apartment, live out my final years in peace. There are more miracles here in this city than I have found in all my travels combined. Could I ask for any more?'

His spectral manservant could never remember being speechless before.

'The Pope will extract his toll here before he leaves.'

'Then let him. When the Pope and all his ships have gone I'll stay here, in peace. I'll die, go to heaven, end of story.'

'To . . . heaven?'

'So.'

'But . . .' how exactly to word this sentence? '. . . there is no heaven for you, master. I can tell you that for a fact.'

'Well, the *beyond* then! Wherever.'

'Humans do not travel to the beyond. Why would they?'

'Because . . . well . . . humans possess an immortal . . . thing, it . . .'

'Why would you presume such a thing?' His demon spoke gently.

'I . . . I don't know, I just . . .' and he didn't know why.

'Why would you assume that a frail creature such as you would be given not only the precious gift of life, but the ultimate gift, also – the gift of immortality? Even we spectral beasts aren't immortal. We live, we die.'

'Enough! You are free, Carrofax. I release you now. Go back to wherever it is you came from.'

'You . . . release me?'

'Yes. Was I not clear? I no longer need your assistance. I thank you for your services and I hereby release you to return to . . . the wherever.'

'I see. If that is your decision. Once you say it a third time nothing can be done.'

'It is my decision.'

'Sir. I have known you since you were a small boy. If you only knew how close you are to finding –'

'Carrofax, I don't care! A man can search for a thousand years and be no closer to the truth. I just want to be left in peace.'

'Well then. If there's nothing else I can do.'

'You can go and help the girl. She is partly your own kind after all.'

'Actually, she is not . . .' Carrofax decided to leave it aside. 'You know I can only do so much.'

'Do what you can.'

'I will. It has been an honour to serve you. A third time, then.'

'Yes.' He turned to face his servant. 'Carrofax. I release you.'

It was strange, but at that moment Carrofax experienced a sensation that he thought might be close to a real human feeling. But perhaps not.

Fabrigas stood most of the night on his balcony. His apartment overlooked the courtyard of the royal barracks. There was a small nest with four eggs near his window. Each egg shone like a moon. He went in and dozed fitfully until sometime before dawn when his dreams were invaded by the sound of a prisoner being brought in across the way. The man was shouting in a voice that could have been coming from the old man's own skull.

'This is an outrage! The general's wife and I had simply gone into the storeroom so we could have a moment's quiet to discuss the concept of gravity. Her girdle was unhooked because she was desperately hot. This is an insult of the highest magnitude!'

So, they had finally caught the man who had canoodled with the general's wife. He must have been a clever man to stay at large for so long. The man blustered all the way to his cell and then was silent.

THE MESMERIST AND THE MIND

The Well Dressed Man knew what a young girl's mind should look like and this was not it. A young girl's mind was a sweetly confusing place. Nothing was solid. Everything was constantly in flux, sliding and subsiding like an ice floe of pinkish consciousness. He had woken at dawn, excited to begin work on breaking into Lenore's giggly mind-palace, and had instead found a kingdom with a solid and precise architecture. This labyrinth had been here for, it seemed, countless millennia. Its walls were old and caked in moss, and there were carvings along the way that told the story of her life, the people she'd met, loved and lost. The newest part, of course, was still under construction, and the children in bright yellow hard-hats looked up briefly from their work as the Well Dressed Man passed by. He could travel at will through this girl's mind, as with any person. It was like a game to him, a simulation. But unlike other young girls' minds he couldn't change anything here. If he moved to pick up an object, a stone or a hammer, the object would vanish and reappear somewhere else, or he'd receive a sharp slap on the hand from a baby-builder, or a swift bite from a sleeping snake, or the object would burst into flames. It was extremely vexing. But worse than any of this, when he travelled back through the maze, back through the years, he eventually came to a great wall of ice. He couldn't break through, and the wall was limitless in every direction. He'd spent hours flying out at speed in each direction, but the wall had flown with him, on, and on, and on. He'd conjured fire to melt a deep hole in the ice, but it had taken all the strength he had, and at the end all he'd achieved was a crater a few feet deep which had frozen over in seconds when he'd stopped.

But it wasn't time to give up yet. It was important that he broke through this wall, because behind it was the secret to her power, and if there was one thing the Well Dressed Man liked more than killing, it was power. As his mentor always said, 'You can learn a lot from your prey before you kill it.' And with this girl his words were never truer.

'When you're finished playing inside of my head I would like to taste water.'

Lenore sat upright in her chair. The Well Dressed Man sat opposite, leaning forward, his elbow on his knee and his hand on his chin. He had removed his jacket, rolled up his sleeves.

'I'll give you a glass of water if you tell me who you are and where you came from.'

'That does not sound like a good deal. And I hardly know.'

The material of his trousers – a blend of the finest imported baby mountain goat wool and spider silk – swished as he changed position. 'Then tell me, where is your friend, the boy?'

'Roberto?'

'Roberto. Yes.'

'I have no ideas. He abandoned me.'

'Cad. Did he say anything before he left?'

'Such as what?'

'Such as where he might be going?'

'He might. Why would you want to know about Roberto? He is just a stupid boy.'

'Don't get me started. I was just making idle chit-chat.'

'That's fine,' said the small girl. 'We have all the time in the universe.'

As the Well Dressed Man stared into the hideously beautiful abyss that shimmered in the small skull on the slender shoulders upon the wooden chair opposite, he began to wonder for the first time who was really being kept against their will.

'Lenore.'

'It is me.'

'I know what it's like to be alone. To be unique. We could rule, you and I. The power we'd have together. If we could *blend* our talents there is no limit to what we could do. That Pope, with all his war machines, is nothing compared to you and me. I could be the father you lost. We could bring your friend Roberto back. We could retrieve your captain from the Forbidden Zone.' For the first time, a quiver. He felt her mind vibrate slightly. Love. The weakness of her human hemisphere.

'And wouldn't you like to have Roberto back again? If you tell me where he is I can help to bring him back.'

'Why are you so interested in Roberto all of a sudden?'

There was less assertiveness in her voice now. She was melting. He ventured in cautiously. He saw that she had carved two words in the hard white wall.

'I had no idea a girl your age knew such filthy words,' said the Well Dressed Man.

'I'm a very fast learner.'

*

But she wasn't the only one.

Diemendääs woke to a strange tyranny. Most were already aware that the city was now surrounded by battle stations. They blackened the sky, they upstaged the silvery sphere Bespophus. The end had finally arrived. Even the besiegers camped at the western wall halted their attack and sat around on their siege machines, staring up in wonder at the shapes which blotted the suns. But worse, as the locals awoke, they knew instantly that their minds had also been blotted. There was no panic. People went about their business. Or, to be precise, they went about *his* business. The Well Dressed Man ran the city like a puppet show. He instituted new laws with a flip of his mind: such that every citizen now found themselves skipping to work, and yelling 'Chicken!' before they entered a room. It was a strange spectacle.

Even the Well Dressed Man was surprised. He'd always been able to control the minds of small groups of people. And usually that was all he needed. To control an army, after all, you only had to enchant its leaders. But since he'd ventured inside Lenore's phantasmal mind his powers had multiplied. Now he could control an entire city. He did it effortlessly, while reading, or talking to the Emperor. He made legions of citizens perform complex recitals from his favourite operas – complete with choreography. And he *loved* it.

To make things even more bizarre, the Pope had made it snow. He had announced that it was the week of Festivus, and added that there was no such thing as a Festivus without snow. The Emperor had protested, pointing out that his people had never even seen snow before: 'They won't know what to do!' But the Pope was firm. And so his great snow-makers had descended from the clear, tropical skies, and they had covered the city and its mountain in a layer of feathery druff. The people came, stunned, to their windows, they pressed their noses to the glass, then they ran from their houses, pausing only briefly at their doors to exclaim, 'Chicken!'

'We won't be troubling you for long, Emperor,' said the Well Dressed Man. They stood on the Emperor's balcony admiring the fat white flakes which fluttered from above. 'Soon I'll have what I want and the Pope and I will leave.'

'The deal was you'd leave when I handed over the wizard and the children. My wife and I have done what you asked.'

'Yes, child-*ren*. I need the boy to come back. Was that not clear?'

'No. It was not.'

'Well, I'm sorry. It shouldn't take long. That girl in the cave up there will share her secrets soon, I'm sure. When I've got what I want I'll hand her to the Pope and he'll leave. That boy will come back, I just know it. This saga could hardly end without him.'

'Chicken!' A page entered and placed a bundle of correspondence on the Emperor's in-tray. 'Chicken!' and he left.

THE *NECRONAUT*

They returned Roberto to his cage. After the jump, everything was silence. Silence beyond all possible silence. And then, from above, there was a scream: low at first, then rising to a pitch only possible from someone under insufferable pain, or insufferable fear. Soon the entire crew was joining in – a choir of unspeakable terror. Then, silence again, for a breathless minute, and then Descharge heard the creaking of the stairs. Slowly, one step at a time, the stairs muttered like a toad. A figure was descending slowly, and soon a pair of red legs came into view. When the figure reached the bottom of the stairs Descharge beheld a sight so terrifying that his heart spasmed, and his cry caught like a bone in his throat. It was a tall, muscular figure, a man of pure flesh, only this man's outer flesh had been stripped from off his body, leaving only his red, raw muscles. He had nails punched through various points in his body – points which seemed to plot a web of satanic meridians – and on his shoulders were the raw, bony stumps of severed wings. Despite his state, the man – if indeed he was one – showed no signs of pain. He moved languidly from the stairs, leaving a pattern of bloody footprints across the room, until he stood before the cage. Then he turned his sad eyes on Descharge.

'Why have you made this crossing?'

It seemed like a simple question, but Descharge was unable to speak. He turned to Roberto, who sat staring, his face frozen like a boy who has perished of fright.

'I ask again: you are the commanding officer of this vessel. Why have you made this crossing? This crossing was not supposed to happen. This boy has endangered the entire operation. The Infiniverse is now in more chaos than it ever was.'

The flayed man's voice was not particularly menacing. It was calm, well mannered.

'We had no choice. They were going to skin a girl.'

'His actions have meant you'll all die. The whole of reality will descend into chaos. Is this better?'

'I acted out of conscience.'

'Your conscience is of no value. You need to undo what you've done. When you regain control of your ship, set a course nine clicks below the artificial meridian: 77.7 degrees magnetic Norde. This will give you the slimmest chance of success. Do you understand what I'm telling you?'

Descharge nodded. The visitor turned towards Roberto and fixed eyes with him. Slowly, the look of terror on the boy's face subsided. He nodded twice. Then the flayed man left. The screaming resumed above, then died.

Descharge slept fitfully. Roberto slept not at all. Descharge woke to find a curious scene: Roberto had his arm extended towards the far wall by the stairs. The wall had a small transformer box bolted to it. The clever boy had managed to remove his bonds and the rubber gloves – his hand sparkled blue, and there was a faint electrical haze extending from his fingers to the box on the wall. He sat frozen like that for minutes, brow wrought in concentration, until finally he dropped his arm, exhausted, and groaned in sheer frustration. Then, after a few minutes' rest, he raised his arm and started again.

Nothing had been heard from above for a long while, but then they heard the poet's shrieking voice. 'We are lost! Lost! Lost! You have doomed us all!' Then there was a scuffle, boots could be heard scraping across the deck. Then Braika, the boy who brought them food, came down again and said, 'The surgeon tried to stab the poet but stabbed the cook instead. He should recover, unfortunately.'

'They'll soon kill each other,' said Descharge. 'I just hope they don't kill us all.'

It continued like this for roughly a week: hours of deathly silence followed by cataclysmic arguments. Roberto kept at his electrical meditations, and now the haze of energy around his hand was so bright it was hard to look at. Occasionally the food boy would come below to deliver news. 'Nobody is talking. It's very grim.' Descharge knew that they were becalmed. He knew by the tilt of the ship and the tension in the hull that there wasn't a breath of sunlight to shift them. He knew that the magnetic propellers were still broken. He knew by the fact that their meals had been cut to one per day that supplies were running low. 'They must have been eating like pigs.'

One night the cook, the poet and the surgeon floated down the stairs. They were gaunt, exhausted, and in the dim blue light of the gas lamps shining through the hatch they looked like spirits. 'Would you be willing to glance at the charts and tell us where we are?' said the surgeon delicately.

'It's useless,' replied Descharge. 'We don't have charts for every universe.' Idiots.

'But perhaps if you were to look at the features around us you might recognise something. It would be in your interest. We're about to ration food to a few bites per day.'

'I can tell from down here that there are no features. We are not within sunlight, and so we can't move. Besides, if the ship comes under my power I'll simply take us back to rescue the others.'

'There'll be none of that,' said the surgeon. 'You'll be the first to be eaten if we need to.'

'If you take a step inside my cell I'll kill you,' and he took his hands from behind his back to show that they were no longer bound.

'We can wait.'

'No you can't.'

Later that night the cook entered and asked if he would be willing to join with him in overthrowing the surgeon. 'I have the surviving seamen in hand, and all the children.'

'Let us out and we'll consider it.'

He did not let them out. Later, Descharge heard a hoarse shouting on deck, then a weak scuffle, then silence. Knowing that the time had come to make his move, he woke Roberto. Roberto nodded. He raised his small hand and summoned a flossy streak of energy from the transformer on the wall as if it were the most natural thing in the world. When he touched a glowing finger to the magnetic latch it popped without protest. They crept upstairs. On the engineering level Roberto put his hand to the wall, and Descharge felt the ship sigh as all its non-essential functions were instantly shut down. 'Good boy,' he said.

The scene they found on deck was so bloody, so frightening, that I can hardly bring myself to describe it to you. Roberto was sick into an empty water barrel. A number of seamen lay dead. G. De Pantagruel and G. Scatolletto lay in a twisted heap. As they lay dying, the pair had become entangled in a deadly *soixante-neuf*, with each continuing to try to eat the other's leg. The poet lay bleeding in a sluice-gutter. Only a faint sobbing came from his hip. The surgeon was almost dead. He looked up at Descharge, smiled, and said, 'Onward,' before passing on himself. The children were cowering, weak, in the galley. Descharge went first to the engine room where he broke open the reserve refrigeration condenser and drained the water. He was able to fill four buckets with the precious liquid, which he put through the ship's filter. Then he and Roberto went around the children and surviving seamen and gave them each a mouthful of water. Following his instincts, Descharge made a thorough search of the surgeon's cabin and found a small cache of food. Then he went to the private cabin he'd been given aboard the *Necronaut*. It had been searched, though not well, and he recovered his secret supply of chocolate – a present from his mother – and he gave each of the children a small square. Then he went on deck and gave the cook a spoonful of water. 'Oh, thank you, boy, thank you,' said the cook.

'You'll be kept alive so you can be hanged,' said Descharge. Then he went to the galley and placed all the supplies on the table and said, 'This is what we have to survive. Anyone who tries to take food will be hanged. I want the flesh and organs of the dead cured with salt and placed in the refrigeration area. They are a last resort. Anyone caught eating raw human meat will be hanged. You have one hour to get this ship back in shape and then you'll get another piece of chocolate.' And that's how Descharge retrieved the very last crumb of his unconquerable fleet.

★

Descharge loved to sail. His father had taught him how to navigate by the stars; he showed him how to sit in the bow of his boat and steer with the weight of his body, so that even a rudderless craft could make it home. Descharge didn't know where they were. All he had was an obscure coordinate given to him by a fleshless angel of death. But it was better than nothing. He knew that Roberto could take them back to the others – if they could somehow find a place to replenish their ship's fuel. They had no energy left to run the ship's magnetic engines, they would have to make do with the sails. He took a magnetic reading and picked up the weakest signal from a shipping channel. He picked up a faint energy from a group of old stars and tacked along it, and slowly, as happens in a friction-less environment, they picked up speed. He threw every piece of surplus equipment overboard to lighten their load. He ordered all the dead's machine parts to be 'buried' in space, except for the batteries for their pacemakers, which he kept, cleaned and stored away. He rigged a gravity pump, normally used for heating, to give them thrust. Descharge stood in the wheelhouse, read the almost undetectable shifts in light, and watched the stars in the distance grow brighter. Somewhere among those stars, he hoped, was a society who could give them food, give them water, give them the energy to power up their RIPS so that they could return to their shipmates. Weeks passed. The poor children wasted away.

But none died, and the sense of relief when they saw a ship in the distance was like a volcano going off. The children, who had hardly been able to lift an arm before, were now dancing on decks. But soon they saw that the ship was not a ship at all, it was a sign, many miles high, and the sign was flashing words, and when they drew closer they could make out the glowing green text.

'Patush'

'Kushir'

'-=-==-='

'Silenci'

'Silence'

MASTER OF THE MIND

The Well Dressed Man felt tremendous. He had set up base camp at the foot of the ice wall in the unfathomable lantern dreamscape of Lenore's mind. Not that this was a dream, or a simulation. This was real. When the Well Dressed Man entered Lenore's mind he put himself in true danger, so he needed his full concentration. If she set a trap for him he could be stuck inside her mind until he starved to death. He had brought in equipment: two huge iron furnaces with steam-powered bellows and iron spouts to blow hell-fire directly at it. He had them working in tandem, and already there was an impressive-looking crater, ten foot wide and at least as deep. The surface had vitrified. He was beginning to see black forms hiding in the glassy waste. Secrets were floating to the surface. What he had learned so far had increased his power a hundredfold. Soon he would be unstoppable. Armies would cower before him.

'You may as well give up,' he said. 'You can't possibly hold me out for ever.' He turned back to tend his furnaces, expecting the silence he was used to. But this time . . .

'I don't have to do it for ever though, do I?'

The Well Dressed Man stiffened. The girl's voice had come from inside his own head. He opened his eyes. On the chair opposite him the small figure was faintly dressed in a shimmering green light.

'I only have to last for as long as you're alive. You're only a mortal, after all. Some days you will slip, then I will hurt you.'

The Well Dressed Man quickly composed himself. Smiled. Closed his eyes again. For all the inconvenience this girl was causing, he had to admire her style.

'Yes, I am learning quickly,' the girl continued. 'Watch this.' And the Well Dressed Man was stunned to see his lovely furnaces begin to spew a torrent of ice.

'Stop that!' The Well Dressed Man swept his hand and the jets of fire resumed. 'I could kill you in a blink. A blink!'

'So why do you not, Mr Powerful? Because you need something first. You know I have mind-treasures. And also you are waiting for something. For Roberto? Roberto has the file. You can't end me until he comes back. You need to destroy the file. That's why you've been asking so much questions about him.'

'You don't know as much as you think.'

'Ha!' Her laugh was like a gunshot in his head. 'You didn't know that I could read your thoughts.'

'I could kill your friends.'

'Then you know I'd kill myself. I'm the chicken who lays gold eggs, and if I die . . . no more omelettes.'

More laughter. It was a demonic laugh.

'You know,' said the Well Dressed Man, addressing this new voice, 'you *really* don't have to be here.'

'Oh, but I want to be here,' said Carrofax. 'I'm enjoying myself. And I need to keep an eye on this one.'

'You can't meddle in matter.'

'I can still be useful.'

'Doesn't it gall you to be a slave to a human? Isn't it demeaning for a demon to have to bend to the will of a man?'

'I am not a demon, flesh-monkey. Isn't it demeaning for a man to be foiled by the mind of a little girl?'

This time Lenore laughed loudly. It was a bell's laugh, as bright as summer, and it made the Well Dressed Man bloom white-hot with rage.

★

There were times, people noticed, when the fog of mental enslavement, if not the snow of papal dominion, would lift. The citizens of Diemendääs would be skipping about their business, shovelling slush, or delivering pies, when all of a sudden they realised they were walking again. Fabrigas noticed it first. He theorised that these rare moments of mental freedom were coming when the Well Dressed Man was concentrating fully on breaking the mind of Lenore, aka the Vengeance. He could only control so much at once, this master mesmerist. The hours he spent each day in her cell were the hours when life on the surface returned almost to normal.

Fabrigas woke at dawn to the sound of the prisoner being taken out. 'Am I not to even get a trial?' cried the prisoner. The timbre of the voice made Fabrigas sit straight up in his bed. There was something terribly familiar about it.

And then another voice: 'I will not be troubling the courts with your sorry lies.'

'That's outrageous! If the Emperor finds out –'

'He will not.' The other voice, too, was oddly familiar.

'That's utterly reprehensible!'

'So is kissing my wife!'

The second voice, Fabrigas thought – no, *knew* – was a general's. He even knew the general's name. Fabrigas sat breathless on his bed, hands shaking in his lap. Reality was crumbling around him, and the walls of his belief were being smashed apart; the floorboards of his knowledge were being torn up, to be replaced by the carpet of incomprehension. He rushed to the window just as the prisoner was being stood against the far wall. The pieces of cannon were brought out by the guards. The first pale light had appeared in the skies, the new birds were singing in the nest beside his window, last night's snow had melted leaving the ground and every surface wet and shiny. As the newly assembled gun was wheeled into place, the sun was peeking over the horizon. In the distance, the market cries were beginning. By the time the cannon had been aligned and the prisoner blindfolded, the birds were ravenous, but the mother bird was nowhere.

It was a bright and hazy morning. The Black Widow slept fitfully in her cell in the city near the army barracks. The Emperor was having his breakfast. Lenore was dozing on the chair in the room the Well Dressed Man had prepared for her in a cave in the mountain high above. The market was soon in full swing and the sun was blazing into the courtyard. Time seemed to be moving on at an incredible speed, and Fabrigas felt as if he might tumble. 'Load the cannon!' The general cocked about, and Fabrigas saw the prisoner straighten. The red rag was like a smear of blood across his face, and his brow was wet and glistening with sweat as the old him gripped the bars around his balcony. As the ball was set and nudged along the barrel he cried out, 'Listen!' and below he thought he saw the shoulders of the prisoner – his own proud shoulders – stiffen.

THE ARROW OF TIME

Looking back now, with the benefit of hindsight, Master M. Francisco Fabrigas is able to explain what happened, but not to accept it. It is simply beyond the boundaries of comprehension and mathematics. It used to jolt him awake in the night, and I for one have heard him scream.

'Listen!'

He watched events unfold again exactly as he remembered, but from a new perspective. The ball placed down the barrel stops and he can hear, even from up high, even above the merciless buzzing of the bees, that the cannon has been loaded incorrectly. It was as if a voice whispered in his ear. He can't hear exactly what the figure in the red blindfold says, because now the morning breeze has built enough to carry off his words, and the birds are chirping brightly right beside him, and the market is in full swing. But he knows what the prisoner is about to say. He sees him wriggle from his rag. He sees the prisoner straighten like a soldier and speak. The prisoner says, 'Gentlemen. There is no space. There is no time.' These are his final words: 'All reality is a continuum of every possible event. This is the immutable truth available to us: that all that was, and all that will be, exist at once in a magnificent spectrum of possibility. Life. Death. These do not factor. Our experience of reality is simply a hero's quest to preserve the idea of our Self in a sea of selflessness, and in our quest deny the truth: that reality knows no Self, that we are simply part of a great and everlasting instant. It might be possible to use this knowledge to build a machine which circumvents the constraints of time and space. But this is not certain. Knowing this, I do not see any reason for wishing to preserve my Self. But that cannon is loaded incorrectly and will explode.' He sees the general raise his monocle and lever at the waist to inspect the gun. Then straighten, frigid with alarm, then wheel, astonished, to face the guilty figure. There is a pause before the general says, 'Reload!'

Reload. The word clatters around the old man's head like a bearing in a drum. Reload? Reload! The general takes his hat and slaps the boy who fouled the priming. This is happening. The rag is hauled again across the prisoner's gleaming eyes. Once more the blood-red slash across the pale wall. Once more the ball rolled down the barrel. Once more the general's voice rings out, 'Aim!' And then. And then . . .

★

As the Emperor sat on his balcony with his breakfast he heard the shot tear a hole through the morning, and he saw the birds collected rise like bubbles in a flute; he felt a shift, the feeling that a new machine had just been set in motion, a machine that couldn't be stopped. The birds and bees dazzled the sky.

Miss Maria Fritzacopple, aka the Black Widow, aka Penny Dreadful, was taken from her waking nightmares by the cannon. She stood and went to the window of her cell before she remembered that her cell had no window – just one small aperture in the ceiling to let in light, snow and sometimes birds.

When he heard a cannon-shot from the city below, the Well Dressed Man opened his eyes briefly to consider it, then shrugged and returned to his work. Things were under control on the streets of Diemendääs. The Pope's ground troops stood guard among the mindless legions. He and his prisoner were in a well-fortified cave high up on the mountain. He'd been surprised, admittedly, when he'd gone outside for air and found it snowing, but you can't predict everything.

Fabrigas meanwhile fell back against the bed and let out a noiseless cry, like a trumpet blown through without a note, and he would have stayed there with that limp, ragged picture in his mind, splattered across his brain like blood upon a courtyard wall, if some sensation had not reached him from the yard below, an entanglement beyond space and time which made him stand, turn his face towards the rising sun, and the bright, red chirrups of the birds, then go to the window and cry, 'My friend! I am here!'

Sweet mercies, I can hardly hold this story together! The old man has simply turned on the faucet of his memory and aimed the hose-end at my face. He recounts his life not in the way a skilled storyteller would: in an orderly progression from calm beginning, via an increasingly turbulent middle, to a storm-wrecked climax, before finally easing into the calm lagoon of resolution. The old-beard at the table will be racing along upon a story, on a collision course with a cataclysmic incident, when of a sudden he'll fly off a thousand years or more to tell an incident from boyhood which has nothing to add to the story at hand, leaving the tale flapping like a flag as he talks of a treasured toy, or a lost friend, or simply recites over and over: 'Keep a good ship. Yes, keep a good ship.' And there'll be nothing I can do to snap him from his trance. He'll go into the abyss, and I will stagger upstairs to the room I'm occupying, to sit bewildered with my stack of notes written in a very specific kind of shorthand I invented to record the words of a lunatic.

And yes, I know full well what the notices will say about this book: 'Volcannon makes excuses for the fact that his ambitions far exceed his talents!' 'Too many characters! Too many threads!' 'Two thumbs downwards!' But I ask you: what is the artist supposed to do here? These are the confessions of M. Francisco Fabrigas: scientist, explorer, dreamer, liar, traitor, fool. This is the tale which came tumbling from the old man's mouth, and I have altered it hardly a bit. At least every second word is true, and that is more than most books. He casts his memories the way an aristocrat casts garments, and I, like a servant, scurry to collect them. So I say this to you, reviewers professional and amateur: save your rancorous reviews and scarlet epigrams – you who take a few coins for skimming the first hundred pages of a book with one eye closed, and another on the betting forms. Put your poison pen back in the tray, for it stings less than the spiny harpoons fate sent me when it made me a pathetic novelist, when it tossed me on this orphan moon with this great bearded lunatic.

Or perhaps grant me this: prove to me at least that you have read this far, that you are '. . . on this ship until the end'. To do that will only take a slip of the pen. Let me propose that if you happen to be writing a notice, that you include in it, somewhere, a secret word. Let us say, for argument, the word 'homunculus'. Include this word somewhere in your notice and we will all know, regardless of the quality of your analysis, that you have at least done us all the most basic courtesy: that of actually finishing the book. Likewise, any review appearing without the word 'homunculus' will reveal that the reviewer felt it unnecessary to read the *entire* book, but instead felt it was acceptable to read but a portion of a work that I have spent a lifetime on.

So it is decided. 'Homunculus.'

And now, back to the action.

HOMUNCULUS

It takes forty-seven people to bathe the Pope. It takes a small team to run his bath, another to prepare his lotions. Still another team readies the Pope for his bath, getting him into his robe and warming his towels, and there are two men in charge of the steam jets, and two large men whose only job is to lift the Holy Father into the tub. Then there is the lift-out team, the drying and powdering squad, and the clean-up crew. He also has a man to look after his battle-toys.

The Pope was steaming in his steam bath, in his star palace, high above the surface of the conquered city. But the bubbles, the star palace, the conquest brought no joy. Below was a city *begging* to be crushed, and he wasn't able to do a thing. Every time the thought to act arrived in his mind, it vanished. What good was being Pope of the universe if he couldn't make people love and fear him? He had been sent to bring this Devil Girl to justice, and where was she? Somewhere else. And where was he? In his pool. Hopeless. Even the snow falling on the city below brought him little joy. And he thought he'd seen the men in his bathing crew looking at him funny, mocking him. Did they think he was weak? He put a finger on the top of one of his boats and pushed it beneath the bubbling water. That's what he'd do to people who mocked him. He would show them all. Suddenly, an idea began to form in his mind. And it stuck, finally, like a pure flake upon a frozen pane. Ideas took a long time to form in the Pope's mind, and when they did they took a lot of polishing, but in the end they were always as hard and bright and cold as diamonds. Yes, this was a good idea. Yes. This is what he'd do. And 'Yes!' he said as he splashed the bubbles with his palms: 'Yes! Yes! Yes!'

Then he rose from his bath and cried, 'Get me a taxi-ship to the surface!'

*

The Well Dressed Man could feel the girl withering under his assault. With six iron blast-cannons firing heat at the wall, the ice was beginning to fall away in chunks, and he could see, what was that? The corner of a frame, a gantry, perhaps, an iron skeleton wound with chains and steel ropes as thick as an arm. Excellent. And then he heard her voice. 'It won't do you any good.' Joy! Her voice sounded tired, uncertain. He had kept her awake all night. He had built noise-makers in her head, and when he'd had to sleep he'd instructed the guards to make noise outside her cell. Then he'd got her up before dawn. And now she would be so, *so* tired. He could feel it. And what was this? As a huge slab of ice fell away he saw a book! Oh yes, now things were moving. The momentum was his. Must be careful not to set the book on fire.

'Lenore.'

That pesky demon.

'You're not allowed to interfere!'

'I can speak to whom I choose.'

'Carrofax?'

'Yes.'

The roar of the furnaces was so loud that it was hard to be heard.

'You're Fabrigas's friend.'

'I'm his friend and servant. He wants you to be very strong.'

'But I am so very tired.'

'Yes. She's tired, I can feel her strength failing. You can talk all you like but there's nothing you can do to help.'

'Lenore, I need you to listen carefully. I need you to know something.'

'What is it?' She sounded sleepy, like a drugged patient.

'You're not the one he's really hunting.'

'Silence, demon!'

'I know. Yes. Roberto has the file.'

'He doesn't have the file. Roberto *is* the file. He has been sent to kill Roberto. He's using you to lure –'

'Silence!' Lenore's head was filled with a crash of thunder so loud that even the demon was briefly startled.

'You almost did it,' said Carrofax. 'You almost came into my domain. Just do it. I'll make you cry for an eternity.'

'You think you're powerful,' said the Well Dressed Man, 'but when Calligulus comes you'll be the one crying.'

'If Calligulus comes then so will you.'

★

Fabrigas leaned across the unconscious figure of the man and marvelled. It was a younger him, there was no doubt. There was nothing in the universe he was truly certain of any more, but he knew his own face. His beard was sparser, but there was no mistaking those eyes. No one else in the universe had those eyes. Usually.

It turns out that a Gunsworth gas-powered shot-cannon is not quite as terrifying a weapon as it appears. The weapon was designed for duels. The pack of shot it carries has a low velocity and a wide spread. In fact, the Gunsworth brand gas-powered shot-cannon is really only dangerous when it is loaded incorrectly. Then it becomes truly terrifying. Nevertheless, the shot had made a mess of the patient's shoulder; he'd had to play dead by slowing his heart to just a few beats per minute – a useful trick he'd learned from a bandit while he was a prisoner on . . . Well, that's a long story in itself. The general had found no pulse and had declared him dead. When the men had come to take him away the general had demanded that they leave him for the vultures. Fabrigas the elder had unbolted the bars from his balcony, *quietly*, so that the hefty papal guards outside his front door wouldn't hear. He had fashioned a rope from his bed sheets and slung it over his balcony. He'd found his younger self still lying beneath the wall where he fell, and when he'd said, 'Wake! I've come to rescue you,' this young self had slowly raised his head and said, 'I must be dead, then.' It had begun to snow again.

Fabrigas sent an urgent memogram to Dr Dray and asked him to come to his apartment, discreetly, and bring medical equipment. Dray had told the guards that he was there because the old man was having heart palpitations. Which technically wasn't a lie. Fabrigas was beside himself. Literally. The two men had worked tirelessly through the night, to stabilise their patient and to stop his wounds from oozing blood. 'He needs a hospital, old crow,' whispered Dray, 'or he'll die.'

'Not possible. If the general found out he'd arrest him again.'

'And your stance is that this is a young you?'

'It's not a stance. I know it.'

'And why do you always twist yourself into the most impossible positions, parrot?'

'Because the most impossible things are often true.'

Dray left in the small hours of the next morning saying he would return soon with morphine and blood, and as the sun rose again the younger finally opened his eyes, turned towards his older self and said, 'Do you know the odds against this event occurring?'

'I do. The number opposing it is so large that it may as well be infinite.'

'Yes. Bring me a glass of water, would you? There's a good boy.'

★

'I'm getting sleepy, Mr Carrofax.'

'I know. But if you can just hold out for a while longer.'

'A while longer?'

'You can hold out, Lenore. I know you can. I know what you have in you,' said the demon.

The Well Dressed Man smiled. His eyes shone like frozen steel. This was his moment.

'You are correct,' said the small girl. Suddenly her voice did not sound quite so ragged. 'Things are going in motion now. That old woman says you cannot change the future, but I believe I've kept him busy long enough. Almost. Perhaps. Do you, phantom friend?'

'I do,' said Carrofax. 'She did not add me to her equation. I am part of this story now. A new sequence has begun.'

The steely smile vanished from that immaculate face. The perfectly groomed eyebrows sank. Why would this stupid demon want the girl to keep him busy? Now something was tickling at the back of the Well Dressed Man's skull. He leaned closer, risking his face against the roar of furnaces to peer in at the title of the book.

A Distraction for a Well Dressed Fool.

The well-dressed fool sat up straight, blinked twice. Now he knew. Something was happening in the city below. Something very, very bad.

He heard the demon laugh.

★

'So, what is your strategy?'

'My . . . strategy?'

'Yes, yes, your strategy, your escape plan, your grand idea?' Fabrigas the younger had regained his strength so quickly that it had alarmed his older self. Now he was even out of bed, stumbling around the room, left arm slung, impatiently picking up objects in the old man's apartment and glaring at them. 'You say you've been given the task

523

of protecting a mysterious child by a shady entity called Dark Hand. Now the child is being held captive in the mountain by a madman, the planet is surrounded, your ship is gone, your captain vanquished, your phantom butler has been dispensed with, you are a prisoner in your own apartment, the door is guarded by the Pope's goons, and the only other person who could help you is your enemy's assassin. Certainly a major challenge. So, what's your plan of attack?'

'Well,' said Fabrigas the elder as he stroked his beard, 'I . . . rented this apartment.'

Fabrigas the younger didn't blink. He turned and stared for a long time, trying to work out if his older self was joking. He put down the tribal mask he had been holding. It was hard for him, now that he had regained his senses, to believe that this old man was him. He looked worn out, beaten down, strung out, done in – the fire had gone out in his eyes, it seemed. Could this really be himself in the future? If it was, he wished the cannon had finished him. He gently tested his fragile shoulder. 'Well, I suppose I owe my life to this . . .' he glanced around him, 'apartment, but we'll need a much better plan if we're to break out, rescue the girl, escape the cordon and find our ship, eh? Shall we cook some WD40-X and blast our way out?' He turned again, expecting to find his older self invigorated by his speech. Instead, the old man would not even lift his eyes from the vase of posies which he patted with his outsized hand.

'Perhaps,' ventured the elder, 'an explosive plan is not what is called for here. Perhaps what is needed is a more gentle touch, something which will ensure our peace of mind and provide for a stable and fulfilling future. We have this neat pad. We have escaped the cruellest blows of fate. Perhaps we should just count our blessings.'

His younger self looked at him with total incomprehension. 'What in the holy heckins are you talking about?!' he cried.

'Well, it's just . . . nothing. I suppose I am talking about nothing at the end of it all. I am just very, very tired, I suppose. I'm tired of being rescued from my quiet life by fate. Tired and in need of rest.

I just . . .' He didn't finish.

'Old man. I don't know what has happened to you that has made you forget your purpose. But all life needs a plan. It's how we block out the fact that life is meaningless.'

'Well, then how about this?!' The old man turned towards him, suddenly full of passion. 'Let's break out of here, you and me. Let's run away from all this. Let's set our minds to our old goal. Let's work together to find the orphan moon where our father lives. In this universe you are still a young man, so there is a chance he still lives. And Danni, too!'

For a second he could see his younger self pause, his face soften as he considered the idea. But then he shook his head angrily. 'Old fool, there's no hiding from a destiny. You are part of a grand machine. If you try to escape, the machine will find you. Unless you have a plan, the universe will make one for you.'

Fabrigas the elder turned away and shook his head. He was about to tell his younger self how foolish the things he was saying were. He was about to tell him how words like 'fate' and 'destiny' were false and pointless, fit only for use by crooked astrologers, or as first names for royal children. He was about to adjust a crooked picture on the wall of his new apartment when the picture began to vibrate of its own accord. Then the whole apartment began to shake, and then the wall of his prison was smashed away by a great iron hand. The sound was tremendous. When the dust evaporated the twins saw, shadowed against the morning light, in the space where the wall of the apartment had been, in the courtyard where the attempted execution had taken place, a shining iron giant a hundred feet high. The giant spoke in an amplified metallic voice. The giant said, 'Doctor Fabrigas, it's me, Kimmy. I've come to rescue you.'

CYCLOPS!

The Well Dressed Man stepped out of the cable carriage into the streets of Diemendääs and found uncontrolled madness. And uncontrolled madness was something he could not abide. How he hated chaos. His was a world of order, his powers worked best when people were behaving in a predictable way. He smelled the noxious gas of free will in the air. Instead of skipping, and 'Chicken!' shouted at maximum volume, he heard sirens and heavy gunfire. What in the world had been going on here? Then he saw it: a towering figure of iron rising over the snow-covered buildings. It looked as he imagined a god would look: tall and shiny. Confident. Able to command a room. It rose into the sky, lifting its mighty arms to smash a passing papal patrol ship from the sky. The craft split open like a fruit, disgorging smoke and fire and chunks of sparking metal. Then the giant paused, turned and strode in his direction.

'OK then,' said the Well Dressed Man.

*

For some reason no one had bothered to ask the small, bespectacled girl what she was doing around the warehouses. She had walked right past two papal guards to enter one of the larger stores, and they barely glanced at her. But they certainly noticed a few minutes later when Cyclops! (for that is the name Dr Dray had given his iron giant) burst through the roof of the building, casually flicked away the reinforced wall and strode off across the city. A team of papal fighter-copters scrambled to intercept her, but she smashed them to pieces with her mighty iron knuckles.

'My girl,' said Fabrigas as he gazed down at the guards fleeing the rolling shadow of the giant, 'have I told you lately that you are a truly astonishing child?'

'I don't think so,' said Kimmy as she grabbed a Pope-tank by its gun and flung it a mile away. This Cyclops! made the GGPTBCE look like a child's toy. Another tank sent a shell whistling past the giant's head. Kimmy turned her beast and kicked the tank away as if it were a tin can. 'I sent a message about my plan to Miss Fritzacopple. I gave one of the prince's homing owls a sniff of her perfume and he went right to her. She sent a reply saying to rescue Lenore. When Miss Fritzacopple escapes she will meet us at the royal launch bays by the space-port.'

'Who is this Miss Fritzacopple?' said Fabrigas the younger. He sat behind them, nursing his heavily bandaged shoulder.

'She is a traitor and a dangerous assassin!' said Fabrigas the elder.

'Oh. But is she attractive?'

'Oh, please,' said Kimmy.

They were making steady progress up the craggy face of Mount Diemendääs, but the Pope's forces were massing around them. 'We're getting too much attention.' Machine-gun fire pinged off the skull of the giant. 'But I am having so much fun.' Kimmy picked up an airborne rocket-launcher and flung it into the swarm of attack ships.

'Just get us as close to the entrance as you can.'

And that's when the battle palaces floating above the city opened wide their terrible rocket-tubes, and the bombardment of Diemendääs began.

THE BLACK ARTS

The Black Widow, aka Penny Dreadful, aka Miss Maria Fritzacopple, aka La Pantera Plata, heard the rising chaos from her cell and knew that Kimmy had made her move. The guards would be distracted by the commotion. If her cell had had a window, she would have seen the iron giant moving up the side of the mountain, hand over hand, stopping to swat at the attack ships which buzzed around its head like flying insects. And now the Emperor's insect legions had risen up too. Giant scorpions, armoured spiders, combat hornets and legions of beetles as big as houses were rolling silently across the earth towards the mountain to attack the Pope's forces. And the bees were gathering above, a black tornado miles high; they fell wave on wave upon the papal guards, hitting each with the force of a cannon-ball, and each hulking man went tumbling over. Stingers pierced hearts and eyes. Meanwhile, rockets and artillery fire rained down from the Pope's fleet in space, slicing channels through the falling snow, smashing into the ancient towers and temples of Diemendääs, and the people of Diemendääs, who had always anticipated the end of days, put down their snowballs, put on their gas masks and wandered, dejected, towards the city's bunkers.

'Well, this is it, I suppose,' said some.

'Yes, I very well suppose it is,' others replied.

Fritzacopple closed her eyes, took a series of deep breaths, focused her mind on what would almost certainly be her death-mission. No matter. She had been trained to see her own death as an incidental event. There was a higher mission at stake, although it was no longer the mission she'd been sent on. This mission was to prove herself again to the people she now adored.

A minute passed in silent meditation.

She opened her eyes and they were steel. The door to her cell was no challenge, it took her seconds to finesse the lock. The sound of the door brought footsteps from the outer room. The spy swung herself up into the ceiling of the corridor, and when the two papal guards entered they walked right beneath her, and when the heels of her new boots touched the sides of their heads they dropped like dummies.

Dummies.

When she left her cell block she met four more guards with knives and clubs. She closed the first man's jaw with a deft uppercut just as he was about to challenge her, the second with a kick to the chin, the third with an elbow to the temple. It felt good to test her arms and legs after months of pretending to be a fragile former dancer. The fourth guard turned and ran. No more pretending to be afraid of ghosts and bears. She felt good. The spy picked up a truncheon from the courtyard dust, weighed it in her fine pale hand, took aim, and dropped the fleeing man from a dozen paces. Then she brushed the dust from the legs of her skintight riding pants and set off for the Emperor's residence.

★

'She's not here! Where is she if she's not here?!'

'Well, obviously I have no idea, old man. Perhaps she went for a stroll.'

Our friends had arrived at the top of the mountain to find that the chamber where Lenore was being kept was empty. There was a leather armchair beside a table stacked with books. Beside the armchair was a pair of slippers. Directly opposite was a wooden chair. This chair was ringed by strange symbols drawn in chalk on the stone floor. Fabrigas the elder knelt to examine the symbols. He knew them well.

Fabrigas Two, the younger, inspected the slippers. 'It is odd,' he said, 'that after several million years of human civilisation, slippers are still the only garment you can put on without using your hands.' Kimmy shrugged.

'There's only one explanation for all this,' the old man said, standing quickly. 'The Pope has somehow stolen her and taken her above.'

'How do you come to such a conclusion?' said Fabrigas the younger. Fabrigas the elder pointed to a line scrawled among the chalk symbols: 'Have taken the Devil Gurl prisoner. U R a bumface. Pope.'

'OK then. We need a rescue plan. We must get to the launch bays so we can steal a ship and go into space. We should probably hurry.' They had used Cyclops! to block the entrance to the cave complex, but now they heard the sound of the Pope's men attempting to haul it aside.

'This is where I have to leave you,' said Kimmy.

'What? Don't be foolish, you'll be killed!' said Fabrigas Number One, the elder.

'I'll be fine. I need to find my prince.'

'The prince? That little snotface?'

'Oh, he's not so bad when you get to know him. And it really is hard to find a good man. In any universe. You two look after each other. Here, Dr Dray said to give you this,' and she handed the old man a star-shaped object. It was silvery, rough-backed, with a salty sea smell, and it immediately moulded itself into the old-beard's great palm. 'He said he found it in his lab this morning.'

'This is getting ridiculous,' said Fabrigas. He peeled it off his palm and slipped it into his cloak.

'All the best,' said the girl.

All the best. As if she was signing off a friendly note.

'She seems a rather unique person,' said Fabrigas One as he watched her walk off down the tunnels and into the darkness.

*

As it turns out, Lenore had indeed gone for a stroll. She was wandering the streets of Diemendääs, the once peaceful streets now torn open in wide, smoking gashes. She seemed oblivious to the destruction, but the man walking behind her, the man who had brought all this destruction, was not. The Pope bobbed and winced as his own bombs fell from above and towers crumbled all around them. The Pope had made up his mind the night before that he would wait for the Well Dressed Man to leave his mountain cave, then seize the prisoner, no questions. He didn't know exactly what had put the thought inside his mind, or how he'd got free of the Well Dressed Man's enslavement.

The Devil Girl walked a few paces ahead. She was his prisoner, he had been ordered to bring her to justice, and no one would talk him out of it. Not this time anyway. 'Walk somewhat faster, if you please,' said his prisoner. 'We have not much time.' Above, a rocket punched through a snow machine, and it came spinning down, sending out streams of white like a Catherine wheel before it smashed into the side of the mountain.

When he'd gone to the Well Dressed Man's mountain chamber the Pope had found it empty. Empty except for the child in her tiny cell. Her cell wasn't even a cage: just some markings on the floor – markings to keep devils in, he knew. He'd wandered, bemused, around the chamber, the table stacked with leather-bound books. 'Pah!' he'd said. He'd taken up a large volume on modern philosophy and leafed through it, perplexed. Then he'd lifted a heavy fountain pen from the stand on the antique table, and after the phrase 'Language is the mother of all thought', he'd written, '. . . and you smell.' Then he'd scuffed away a few of the symbols on the floor with his shoe. His sleeping prisoner had opened her eyes suddenly, smiled a terrible

531

smile, and said, 'Hello there. I see you got my mind-message.'

A few minutes later the bombardment from space had started. The Pope had a simple standing order in place: 'If they give us any trouble, bomb them to hell.' His standing order did not take into account his spontaneously and secretly travelling to the city. Battle Command had no idea the Holy Father had gone down to the surface, so had no hesitation in commencing the bombardment when they got word that an iron giant was creating havoc. 'Little girl,' the Pope said, 'I think it is very dangerous for us to be down here.' His own men, picking themselves up bloody from the rubble, or locked in the claws of giant insects, looked with disbelieving eyes as the pair passed by and vanished into the smoke.

'What mean you, sir? This is all just a minor fuss, for sure, no?'

'A minor fuss?' The Pope looked up just in time to see one of his bombs slam into a temple, sending a gargoyle head spinning down the avenue, gouging a canyon in the paved street before skidding to a stop; its ancient eyes locked with theirs.

'I would like to leave now very much!'

'We will leave soon,' said the girl. 'You will have your trial. We just have to make one stop first.'

*

The Black Widow had not expected this. She was behaving like a fool. A damned fool. But she felt she had no choice. She'd willed her limbs to take her on to the docking bays to meet the explorer, but instead she found herself scrambling up the vines that clung to the side of the Emperor's residence, dropping lightly onto the patio. The bright explosions from the city lit her from behind.

'Hello, Heronmus.'

'Maria. I knew you'd come.'

'Did you?'

'Yes.'

'Well then.'

'Indeed.'

In fiction, the dialogue is very dramatic. It flows wonderfully and is full of ardour, as if the poets themselves were whispering in the ears of the participants. But in real life, words spoken are stilted, awkward. The Emperor stood on the balcony, in his morning suit.

'Why are you not helping your people? They are dying.'

'I can do nothing to help them. I'm powerless. The insect legions have risen up of their own accord. I do not sanction their revolt.'

'Well, I only have a few moments. I just wanted to stop by to tell you that I hate you.'

'You hate me?'

They had to shout above the sound of the bombardment.

'Yes. I hate you with a burning passion. You are arrogant, aloof. I hate that you betrayed us. I hate that you betrayed your city. I hate that you act as if you have all the problems in the world when in fact you have everything a man could wish for. Don't speak!' The Emperor closed his mouth. Behind them the aerial battle was filling the sky with white-hot fire, but neither had eyes for it. 'I hate everything that's possible to hate about you. Most of all I hate the way you make me forget myself. You make me forget who I am and what I'm supposed to be doing. And I hate that. I guess that's everything.'

'Well then.'

'Well then indeed.' She realised she'd been clutching a handful of vine leaves this whole time, clutching them so hard that their juice ran between her fingers. She released them over the edge of the balcony and watched them flutter away like moths. A doomed fighter streaked by, leaving a coil of smoke. She heard the Emperor move closer behind her, but not too close. He stood a few feet away. 'I really hate you,' she said.

'I know,' replied the Emperor. 'I hate you too.'

FORBIDDEN ZONE

'Someone's coming,' said the Black Widow.

'I hear nothing,' said the Emperor, but a second later he heard the footsteps in the corridor outside his suite. The Black Widow wound her long hair back up behind her head in a single deft twist and checked herself once in the mirror. 'Tell me where the box with the Forbidden Zone is kept.'

'It's in a security complex beside the Museum of Doomsday Devices, but I urge you not to go. The place is filled with deadly traps.' They heard the footsteps stop outside. The Emperor went to the door, put his hand to the latch and said, 'It's him. You'll need to hide,' but when he turned round she was gone.

*

The Black Widow made short work of the guards outside the complex, disabled the sentinel automatons by blowing fountain water into their workings through a bamboo reed, charmed the warning-crickets and prevented them from crying out by imitating their mating call, scaled the outer walls, cracked the exploding locks on the upper levels, scattered fine dust to reveal the sonic beams whose breaking would send a signal to the guardhouse, slowed her heartbeat so that its rhythm wouldn't register on the sensitive seismographs placed within, went in silently by crawling along on her belly like a snake, then dropped as gently as a butterfly into the main enclosure – all as she'd been taught to do in her first year of spy school.

In the centre of the room was a plinth upon which sat a black box, roughly the dimensions of a jewellery box, only slightly larger, and a slightly different shape, and of course without any visible joins or hinges, and in fact, on reflection, not much like a jewellery box at all. Also, it contained not jewels, but a universe.

Inside, somewhere, was their captain, possibly dead, possibly cuddling a bear for warmth, but almost certainly sulking.

There would be a final trap, of course. But what? Poison darts that made her sing for the guards? A snare of some kind? She lifted the box and found a note underneath:

Dearest plums,

I couldn't let you steal our Forbidden Zone. You are breathing a nerve toxin which will kill you within an hour. The antidote is held at the royal surgery. This building is surrounded by a small army. If you surrender to them they'll escort you to the antidote.

All the best!
Dray

The Black Widow said a word under her breath.

*

'I am very disappointed,' said the visitor. 'Very.' Before adding, 'Very.' And then, 'Disappointed.' This visitor had spent the last few days locked in a battle of minds and was not in a good mood.

'I know you are,' said the Emperor, 'but things were beyond my control. You have no –'

'Enough,' said the well-dressed stranger, whose eyelids flickered and whose lip was a thin blue chalk mark on a green wall. 'Where is my captain? I want him.'

'He is in a box held in a high-security annexe near the Museum of Doomsday Devices. It wasn't my fault. There was nothing I could do.'

'Of course, of course.' She steepled her fingers over her lips and crossed her legs, leaned back in the Emperor's big leather chair. It was terrifyingly uncanny to the Emperor the way this small girl had adopted the mannerisms, even the speech patterns, of her well-dressed interrogator. It was a pleasant morning and the breeze moved the curtains in the Emperor's study. 'I perhaps spoke harshly. Is it not terribly vexing to manage a city? Probably. So many *jaunty* problems.' The words wiggled from her mouth like bright snakes. 'I've only been here for a short time and already I'm finding it . . . stressful.'

'I suppose it is,' said the Emperor. It seemed like he knew it for the first time.

The stranger, in her elegantly trimmed hunting coat and boots, had learned much from the man she had met in the past few days, much about how to control the many feelings of the animal mind, much about how to control her own animal feelings, much about power, passion, revenge.

'So much stress. So many problems, so many difficult questions. And your lovely wife's . . . conditions. It would weigh upon a man. All the things that *jump* out at you on a daily basis. A man who's reached your *heights* must be afraid of *falling*.'

'Yes. It's a long way to fall from the top.'

'Yes. But when you fall it's over. No pressures. No disasters. No armies upon your gate. You can rest. This is the way, yes. Kings go marching up up up, they fall down down down, again and again and again.'

The Emperor looked towards the open window, the gently huffing curtains, the sky, the towers crumbling in the distance, the explosions ripping through the morning air. So warm, so pretty, so inviting.

'Yes,' he said. 'Yes.'

And then he was gone.

'I said you would pay,' said Lenore to the waving curtains, the vacant chair behind the desk, to the empty air. She went to the door and found the Pope waiting like a loyal dog in the hallway.

'And now we can go, yes?' said the Pope.

Lenore walked to the balcony. She carefully sniffed the air and smiled. 'Roberto. He is coming soon. We must go and rescue my captain.'

'OK then.'

When the small girl and her befuddled Pope arrived at the high-security installation they found it surrounded by troops. 'The Pope commands you tell him what happened here,' said Lenore to a bewildered soldier.

'There was a break-in,' said the soldier. 'Some crazy woman stole the box with the Forbidden Zone.'

'You let her escape?'

'Nothing we could do. She took off from the roof on a stolen set of rocket wings. Silly cow.'

Lenore's eyes narrowed. She made a small gesture towards the young soldier who slapped himself in the face – hard. She closed her eyes and concentrated for a second. 'Yes. She'll follow that wizard man into space. He has gone up to rescue me. And I'm down here. And the whole darned thing is topsy-turvy.' Then she turned to the Pope, who looked more than ever like a child of the universe, laid before him both her slender wrists and said, 'I am your prisoner now. Let us go up into space and have your trial.'

OH, AND THE CAPTAIN

Elsewhere, in the space between space, in a zone neither within nor without this universe, Captain Lambestyo sat completely unaware of the eventuating chaos. He didn't know that the universe he was in was actually inside a box, and that that box had just been stolen from a high-security facility by a sultry assassin and was now stuffed inside her top as she flew high above the city. All he knew was that, despite the odd things happening all around him, he was still unbelievably bored. Odd things, yes. For a start, the bear population had exploded. They were everywhere now, and he'd had to start locking himself in their old rocket – which still sat in its place in the glade. He'd uprooted a large circle of moss and dragged it inside. It was a comfortable enough mattress, but the rocket was very small and he had to sleep with his legs in the air. Odd things. People had started to appear and disappear: startled children, whole families. The day before an entire army had wandered through, lost, bewildered. That morning he'd come across a door. No walls, just a door. When he'd opened the door he'd found himself standing in a wide room with stone walls and another pair of large doors at the far end. An extremely well-dressed man sat in a leather armchair and nursed a glass of brandy. He looked depressed. Opposite the man, silhouetted by the light streaming in from the entrance way, was a small figure on a wooden chair. She appeared to be sleeping.

'What on earth are you doing in here?' said the Well Dressed Man.

'I don't know,' replied the captain.

'Well, hadn't you better leave?'

And he had. He'd gone back through the door and found himself once more standing in a glade of red moss. When he turned round, the door had vanished. 'Why didn't I leave through those other doors?' thought the captain, as he contemplated yet another night in paradise.

Just an hour before he'd seen a figure he could swear was the Emperor himself wandering among the trees, as if in a dream. He'd called out, but the figure had kept walking.

The captain lifted his bear's-head hat and mopped the sweat from his brow with a grubby sleeve. The other thing that was happening was that it was getting much, much warmer.

THE RACE FOR SPACE

What a place we find ourselves in now. What a mad and dangerous universe of possibility.

The Black Widow had stolen a set of rocket wings from a papal guardsman and was now flying over the city towards the royal launch bays where she hoped to find her former friend M. Francisco Fabrigas and give him the box containing a universe containing a world containing the captain of a ship from the next universe – all before the poison she had inhaled killed her. Meanwhile, that former friend had met his younger self and the two were currently arguing over who would get to fly the ship they'd stolen for a mission into space to rescue a small girl from the clutches of the Pope of the universe.

The Well Dressed Man had finally regained consciousness and crawled out from the rubble the Cyclops! had nudged upon him. He stood slowly and looked with disgust upon the state of his suit. It was covered in dust and the shoulder of his jacket was torn at the seam. Something would have to be done about this. All around him was dust and fire and patches of melting snow. The papal troops were regrouping. The towers were in flames. A web of silky rocket trails led down from the black ships above.

The Well Dressed Man was still trying to take back the situation with his powerful mind, but failing. He was exhausted from his efforts to subdue the mind of a small girl. The girl. He had almost forgotten about her. Never mind, she was safe in a holding cell inside the mountain. He let his mind run up the mountainside, felt his way back through the tunnels to where his small prisoner was . . . gone. The Well Dressed Man felt his heart flutter. He almost cried out. No one knew she was there. No one except . . . 'Dear Gods: the Pope!' It had to be the Pope. The Well Dressed Man strode towards the cable car. All the way up the mountain he stood perfectly still. At the top he left the cable car, walked past the discarded Cyclops! and into the cave complex. He emerged a minute later, stood by the fountain at the entrance, one finger on his lips, coldly surveying the continuing carnage in the city below. He saw a figure near the edge. The figure had a large lensed instrument on a tripod and he was using it to slowly scan the city below.

The Well Dressed Man called out, 'Good day, Dr Dray!' The figure turned, paused and bowed neatly. The Well Dressed Man smiled. 'Recording events for posterity?' Dray nodded politely. The Well Dressed Man made a faint gesture to a passing fighter craft. The ship swung round and came to land beside him. The pilot got out, walked to the fountain, and jumped in.

SPACE ATTACK

'Let the trial begin!' said the Pope. There was not a person in the room, the Pope included, who thought a trial was necessary. Everyone knew what the outcome would be. The girl in the dock would be found guilty of conspiring against the Church and the Queen, and being a Devil-child. She would be taken to a place of execution (it was almost always a black hole), and thrown in. The Pope had a machine capable of creating a smallish – but very powerful – black hole, if one was not available. He loved using his Glory Hole machine even more than he loved using his space-clearing Ring device.

But there would certainly be a trial first, because that was how things were done, and because the Pope also loved a trial. He'd arrived back at his palace as excited as a small boy on Festivus Day. His aides, who had been frantically searching for him, were astonished to see him step out of his small taxi-craft with the Devil Girl he'd vowed to kill. And now here they were. The courtroom was packed. Lenore stood in the dock. The Pope was in his jet-bath. 'Do you deny before this court that you are not guilty of blasphemy, treason, gluttony, simony, parsimony, rosemary, thyme and other mortal sins?' The judge was just making sins up. He knew that at least some of these sins were kitchen herbs, but his job was to put on a show. 'Do you not admit this isn't so?'

'Um. Yes?' said Lenore. The court exploded into shouts and jeers.

'So you admit it! Do you, or do you not, admit you just admitted it?'

'Um. No.' The court erupted again. Hats were thrown. Spittle sparkled in the air. Outside, beyond the broad glass dome, the sprinkled stars above the smoking ruins of Diemendääs appeared to laugh.

'Do you know,' said the judge, 'that to admit to such a crime means certain death? But to deny your guilt will also lead to death?'

'Well, then what is the point of saying anything?'

This time the clamour was deafening and joyous. A shoe hit the step below the witness stand. 'To death!' they cried. 'To death with the Devil Girl! Out into space with her! Out, out, out, out, out, out, out, out!'

'Yes, yes. Can we please hurry this all up? Roberto will be arriving soon. He is waiting behind the moon with all the naughty shrubs.'

The jeers abated as an aide ran into the room and smashed a gong. 'Excellency!' he said. 'Forgive me for gonging, but it's a matter of utmost urgency.'

'Can't you see we're having the trial?' said the Pope as he adjusted the position of a nozzle on his jet-bath.

'Your Holiness, we are under attack.' The Pope stood up suddenly and all in court averted their eyes.

'A space attack? How big is their army?'

'Extremely small, Holiness . . . One ship.' Laughter in the court.

'How big is this ship? Vast?'

'It is rather small, Excellency,' said the aide, again trying not to look.

The Pope looked confused. 'One ship?'

'Yes, Holiness. A stealth ship.'

'A stealth ship? How did we see it on our radars?'

'We did not, Holiness. The men on board left their radio on and we could hear them arguing. They appear to be on their way to rescue this girl.'

VENGEANCE

It was astonishingly ironic that two of the most powerful minds of their species had come up with arguably the worst rescue plan ever conceived.

'Attack formation!' cried Fabrigas Two – the younger. They had argued about which ship to steal. F1 had favoured the fastest ship available – a short-range courier craft, as fast as a mid-range fighter – while F2 had wanted the strongest craft – an armoured diplomatic carrier, as slow as a domestic rhinoceros. In the end they compromised and went for invisibility – discovering in a disused bay a small naval stealth craft designed to sneak up on smugglers. They had been fighting for control of the helm since leaving the docks. Both men put their case. F2 had argued that he was younger and therefore the more able pilot. F1 had responded that he had much more piloting experience, and that F2 had recently been shot with a small cannon. So F2 had capitulated, though he was still barking orders. 'Attack formation?' said F1. 'What do you mean attack formation? We're only one ship! Just let me fly for goodness' sake. We'll head for the main space palaces and trust they don't notice us. That's where the girl will be.' They were approaching the outer defences of the Pope's great fleet when their radio crackled into life and they heard a voice say, 'This is Commander Murial of the Fleet of the Nine Churches. We can hear you arguing. Change heading and leave this sector immediately or you will be destroyed.'

*

The court assembled to try Lenore for her crimes had watched through the great windows as a tiny ship approached the first ring of defence. It hadn't gone well. Soon the craft was streaking off, trailing smoke, pursued by a thousand fighters. It was unclear who was piloting the ship on this suicide mission, but it was clear that they were as mad as a bucketful of kittens. Now several dozen grappling ships were in pursuit. Their long steel ropes terminated in hooks which swung in wide and deadly circles. It wouldn't be long before one of them sank its hooks into the fleeing ship and pulled it in.

But Roberto would soon be here. Yes, Lenore could feel it. Soon the fun would begin.

*

Prince Panduke caught up with Kimmy in the Dedals within the mountain. He had seen the great iron giant wreaking hell and had immediately gone to get his jet-packs. 'You stole my iron giant!' was the first thing he said.

'It's good to see you too,' said Kimmy, as she pushed her glasses up her nose. 'We left her safely by the entrance.'

'You left *him* by the entrance. We have to get you into hiding,' said the prince.

'No, we have to get *you* into hiding,' said Kimmy. 'They'll be out to arrest you.'

'No, we have to get *you* into hiding. I'm here to rescue *you*.'

No one quite knew who had built the Dedals and why. But they had been used at various times to smuggle people in and out of the city, to act as refuges during aerial bombardment – such as the one they could hear below – to conduct secret meetings, rites and rituals. The tunnels appeared to travel down towards the core of the mountain under which the city stood, holding here and there a door or drain, and now and then becoming tiny black rooms or wide, spooky arcades.

Now Panduke and Kimmy were deeper than they'd ever been, and the tunnels had shrunk to hardly the girth of a person, and there were no doors to be found. 'Where are we?'

'I don't know,' said Panduke. 'These are the secret tunnels.'

'So we're lost?'

'No, we are in Diemendääs.' He put his hand against the mossy stone. 'And right now I'd rather be lost than found.'

'Shhhh,' said Kimmy. 'Listen.' They were so deep now that they could hardly hear the explosions. They had turned a corner into a narrow corridor that stretched to vanishing. There was a point of light in the blackness; looking down the tunnel was like staring into a great eye. Far away they heard a soft shuffle, like someone jogging on sand, and then a foggy shape materialised at the far end, moving quickly towards them.

'Run!'

The prince had already left. They ran as fast as their short legs could manage, driven on by fear, but the figure in pursuit was fast and gaining on them with every stride. Panduke stumbled and fell, Kimmy tumbled over him, and suddenly the footsteps were upon them. They scrabbled onto their backs but the corridor behind was empty. 'A ghost!' hissed Panduke.

'Don't be ridiculous,' said Kimmy. They stood and turned in the direction they'd been running. They both let out girlish screams. The man who stood before them was extremely short and very muscular. He had a tremendous head of bright red hair, well oiled, and a well-lubricated moustache. He wore a red-and-white-striped leotard – the kind worn by circus strongmen – and a pair of strange rubber shoes. He was not at all out of breath, despite having run the better part of a mile in less than three minutes.

'Sir!' barked the man. 'I greet you with all humbleness! On behalf of His Majesty's Secret Service, it is my duty to inform you that His Highness, the Emperor, is missing, presumed dead. I have no time to explain further developments. Please follow me.'

★

It was hopeless, their rescue attempt had been a disaster. They could outrun the smaller fighters, but the pursuit craft were closing. 'They mean to board us then,' said F2. 'Well, they'll get a fight.'

'Yes. A fight,' said F1. He could see the craft closing fast, the grappling chains leaving silver hoops in the blackness. He knew that once they were boarded it would come down to a hand-to-hand fight, and an old man and a one-armed youngster were no match for the bear-like guardsmen. 'We might have a chance if we head for that small moon,' said F2.

F1 laughed loudly. 'The moon, yes, what a grand idea!' Bespophus, with its armies of ravenous dinophytes, shone brightly in the distance.

They felt the whole craft groan as the first of the grapples punctured their outer shell. 'Prepare to fight to the death!' cried F2 as he pulled a hooked cargo-staff from the wall.

'You're halfway there already,' muttered F1, but there was no time for another argument. They heard the docking port being wrenched away. The hatch to the bay above fell open and two heavy shapes dropped into the cabin. One said, 'On behalf of the Pope, surrender or die.'

'We won't go without a fight,' said F2. 'Good heavens, what's that out there?'

A black shape approached fast from the left, its wings spread like a bat as it dived towards them. Rocket wings, incidentally, are not meant to be used in space. Only a mad person would try it. The Black Widow spiralled into the open docking bay. She threw off her rocket wings and took a few heavy breaths.

BATTLE STATIONS

On the bridge the Pope was hopping mad. 'Get them! I want them alive so I can kill them!' He leaped around the bridge and pulled at levers that did nothing but let out pre-assigned noises. The crew had been forced to put these in after the Pope had almost steered the palace into a sun. The levers gave the Holy Father the illusion of piloting his palace without giving everyone else the constant fear of dying.

'Yes, Your Holiness.'

They had now pulled back far enough from the planet to be able to activate their Glory Hole: the artificial black hole into which their prisoner would be cast. Making a Glory Hole is unbelievably complex. At the heart of a purpose-built battle station is a chamber containing a small glass bead filled with isotopes. At the given hour powerful lasers are fired at the bead, instantly creating a tiny artificial star. This miraculous baby star is then forced into collapse, tearing an orifice in space and time, and creating a miniature black hole. The subsequent black hole will grow quickly to envelop the battle station, so the entire engineering crew must be fired away in powerful escape pods. What remains when the rubble clears is a relatively small, but not unterrifying, vortex. It is a fantastically difficult, dangerous and expensive process, but the Pope would have it no other way.

On the giant screen above the navigator's station they could now observe the silvery whorl of their new Glory Hole. On the far side the bombardment division was still clustered around the planet, while between the planet and the Glory Hole (a minimum safe distance away from both) was a cluster of green dots – the main fleet of battle palaces. And curling away from that like a swarm of angry hornets was a stream of smaller dots, the pursuit fleet – they had moved to intercept a single tiny dot.

'We'll throw them into the Glory Hole, too!'

'Of course, Your Excellency. Our men are boarding their craft as we speak.'

★

'Come to Papa, gorgeous,' said the first priest. They were an intimidating sight in their black turtleneck sweaters and shiny black stomper boots.

'You come to us, handsome!' said F2 as he twirled the cargo-staff in his hand. 'That's if you can take it.'

'Oh, we can take it, sweetie-pie,' said the second priest as he smashed his clenched fist into his palm. 'We can take it good.'

'Well, if you want us, come and *gnn—*'

F2 swallowed his sentence as a pair of long legs came through the hatch above, coiled around the thick necks of the two papal guards, and gently smashed their skulls together, thus mercifully concluding a slightly weird exchange. The Black Widow had been trained by the very best teachers to dispatch her victims with whatever she had at her disposal: a candlestick, a loaf of bread, her shapely legs. Her own shiny boots gleamed as she dropped to the floor beside the two unconscious guards and scanned the ship's bewildered occupants. 'Could you have made more of a mess of a simple rescue mission?' she said.

It took a few seconds for the Fabrigases to even register what was happening.

'What in heck is happening?!' said F1.

'We don't have much time. We'll take my rocket wings,' said the Black Widow. 'This ship is about to fall apart.'

'Take your rocket wings? To where?!' said F1.

'To their command station. To Lenore. And we have to hurry. I am . . . short on time.' She glanced at her Lasiotek Magnesium Chronograph wristwatch.

'I'm staying here,' said F2. 'I'll try to draw those fighters away.'

'That's suicide!' said F1.

'As opposed to your mission?'

'Fair point,' said F1. 'Well, goodbye, young me.'

'Yes, goodbye, old me. It was surprising to meet you.'

'Ah, to be young again. When you reach my age almost nothing will surprise you. Oh, I could tell you some stories.'

'If we're both alive in forty-five minutes,' said the Black Widow, 'you can tell me as many boring stories as you like.'

*

Panduke and Kimmy had been guided through the catacombs of Diemendääs by their moustachioed stalker – whose name was Lamont, and whose full name was Special Agent Jerman James Lamont. Special Agent Jerman James Lamont had jogged off ahead of them, keeping a measured gait, his spine rod-straight, his body perfectly balanced, and when they came to an open culvert in the floor he would leap into the vaulted ceiling, sometimes hanging with just a finger in a crevice, and with his free hand he'd grab each child and fling them lightly over the creek before springing down to resume his gentle jog, and everything he did he did with a 'Hup! Hooo . . . Hup!' When they came to a stream where a small punt waited he helped them in, 'Hup! Hooo!' then pushed off from the stone jetty with an oar and began to row them down the black river in long, easy strokes, his oars gently cutting the steamy water, 'Hut . . . hut . . . hut . . .'

Soon they sailed out of the tunnels and into a bunker filled with countless ships of war.

'So this is where Daddy keeps his fleet,' said Panduke. 'I always wondered.' A group of generals waited on the shore, medals gleaming in the artificial light, and each of them bowed to the prince, and to Kimmy. Lamont helped the children out, then stood by the boat, stretching. A general stepped forward. He had so many medals on his chest that when he bowed they tinkled like a wind chime. 'Your Highness,' said General Spatz, 'we salute your bravery and cunning. In the mysterious absence of His Royal Highness the Emperor the Royal Air Fleet now places its warships at your executive command, as per our city's constitution. You may now give your orders, either to surrender unconditionally to the Pope, or to attack.'

Prince Panduke had looked from the general to the ships, their mighty cannons, the racks of ammunition stacked beside them. Then he'd looked at Kimmy and whispered . . . '*Awesome*.'

And so here they were, on the command deck of the Diemendääs fleet as it tumbled from the surface in a hopeless assault against the Pope's forces. The prince could see his city below – now a flaming glow upon the surface of the planet – and he could see that their fleet, the one which had looked so fearsome when stacked in bunkers underground, looked trivial when set against the black hulks of the Fleet of the Nine Churches, and the music in his skull was the timpanic drumming of his blood, topped with shrill, discordant notes of fear. Kimmy was there, and she was dressed in a naval jumpsuit that made her look fierce. 'Highness, we are in position. Your order?' said General Spatz.

The prince looked at Kimmy, then back at the general.

'Hit them with everything you've got,' he said.

★

'It is the city's war fleet, Holiness,' said Cardinal Mothersbaugh, as the first wave of fire hit their forward defences. 'They are small but heavily armed. They have destroyed the bombardment division.'

'Crush them,' said the Pope. 'Wipe them all out, and then destroy the rest of the city. Turn the parts we haven't bombed to ruins. And then destroy the ruins! And then throw that girl into the Glory Hole! I don't like her. She has funny skin!'

'We are in a tactically weak position, Holiness. We outnumber them ten thousand guns to one, but we have our backs against the Glory Hole. We will suffer losses. We could perhaps move to –'

'We must perform the execution! That's why we've been sent all the way here. What did you think this was, a holiday?'

Mothersbaugh did not think this had been a holiday, although he had been on holidays that were far worse. 'They are positioning their heavy guns to fire on our palaces.'

'Then get us behind the laundry palace! They can't hit us if we're behind a laundry palace!' And Mothersbaugh had to admit it was a pretty good idea.

*

'I'm not going on those,' said Fabrigas when he saw the Black Widow's rocket wings.

'Why not?'

'Because they are not meant to be used in space. Because they have no life-support equipment and they tend to blow up when struck by space debris. And because I don't want to.'

'Nonsense. Why are you sulking?'

'I'm not sulking. Why would you want to know? I'd only *bore* you.'

'Oh for the love of . . . Here, you can sulk all you like inside this,' she said as she handed the old man a crash helmet with a visor and oxygen mask. Then she slipped her own mask on, slung the rocket wings on her back, and threw a harness around Fabrigas's waist. 'Try to stay limp,' she whispered in his ear. Fabrigas hardly had time to gather himself before the Black Widow stepped backwards out of the hatch, and then they were tumbling end over end in space. Fabrigas saw their ship retreating quickly into the distance. Then the Black Widow hit ignition, and suddenly he saw their pursuers racing towards them at an unbelievable speed, their steel hooks slicing the air.

Then into the heart of the storm. The Black Widow took them on a sickening hell-journey, dipping and diving through the swinging hooks. The pilots, startled, began to flail and found their cables tangling, and there was a series of mighty explosions as grapple ships were swung against each other. 'Geeeeeeeeaaaaaaaaahhhhhhhhhh!' admitted Fabrigas.

Ahead, the palaces emerged through the smoke and fire. They could see the Diemendääs ships throwing themselves against the Pope's defences only to be forced back by the unbelievable firepower of the death-fleet. And the Black Widow flew them straight into it, straight into the cloud of dust, fire and debris.

'Sheeeeeeeeoooooooaaaaaaaaahhhhhhhhhh!' Fabrigas suggested.

The Black Widow sent them rocketing towards the docking bay of the largest papal command palace, where she assumed they'd find Lenore, and gave her jet wings one last burst of throttle.

★

Fabrigas the younger, meanwhile, was taking a few seconds to ponder the infinite strangeness of the universe. Just a year ago he was a junior monk at the Dark Friars' Academy. He'd left to join the Academy's Exploratory Unit. He had signed up as a science officer on a deep space expedition, had narrowly avoided death on fourteen separate occasions, before finally finding safe port in a city on the outer reaches of his universe. Once there he'd got into trouble after snogging a general's wife at a ball. He was placed before a firing squad and shot. He survived, miraculously, was rescued by an older version of himself and was caught up in some kind of transdimensional war.

It was a lot to fit into a single year. He had now eased his stricken craft expertly into the gravity of the moon. The grappling craft pursuing him would not dare to fly so close to Bespophus. They would have to take the long way round. He was, he had to admit, a damned good pilot, even with just one arm. He observed the peaceful jungles of the moon below, and for a second considered setting his craft down there and hiding in the undergrowth. But something told him that was not a good idea.

Then, as he came round the moon's dark half he saw a quite incredible sight. It was a fleet, massive and heavily armed – it had been tucked quietly behind the moon. The lead craft hailed him.

'This is Fleet Commander Descharge of the *Necronaut*. Please identify yourself.'

Fabrigas cleared his throat, switched on his ship's communicator. 'This is . . . Master M. Francisco Fabrigas . . . of the vessel . . . whatever the heck this ship is called. I didn't really have time to check.'

There was silence on the other end of the line.

THE SILENT ONES

A good voyage depends upon a good ship. A good ship sees many terrible things, in battle and in peace, but always remains a good ship. The *Necronaut* had proved itself, despite appearances, to be a very good ship. It had carried its present crew through several dimensions, a number of skirmishes and one major space battle, before it had brought them before a massive sign in space: 'Silence'.

This, briefly, is what had happened.

(Oh, I know, I know: the Pope, the battle, our friends. This really won't take long.)

In that lonely patch of empty space they'd sat until they saw a vast ship emerging from the darkness. The ship was painted black and what windows it had were dimly lit. Descharge could do nothing as the ship pulled up beside them and a wide hatch opened to reveal a softly lit bay. The bay was lined with deep, cushioned material. The *Necronaut* touched softly down and listed over in the plush upholstery. Four figures in hazard suits came through a small door and walked along the side of the *Necronaut*, studied its markings. They had a short conversation in sign language. One of the men punched some keys on an electronic sign he was holding and held it up. The sign read: 'If you please, have silence. Danger. Open hatch?'

They had no choice. The strangers entered the *Necronaut*. Two carried a large box. Black. About the size of a shoebox. Only slightly larger. It's not important. Descharge stepped forward, but when he took a breath to speak, the men began waving their arms frantically. The two put their box down, *carefully*, and from the box they unpacked sets of padded slippers and distributed them to the survivors. Then the two leaders beckoned Descharge to follow them, *quietly*. They took him from the ship and down a corridor to a padded room. The two hosts sank into soft chairs behind the desk and gestured that Descharge should sit opposite. The silence was maddening. They took off their hats and Descharge observed gaunt, weary faces, the faces of people who have trouble sleeping. Then one of the hosts, the one Descharge thought might be a man, leaned forward and said, in a whisper so soft it was hardly audible, 'Forgive us. We must . . . have total silence. We have . . . a *Sweety*.'

*

It takes some time to tell a long story in a whisper. It turns out that when the *Necronaut* had made the desperate jump from the previous universe (leaving behind their friends, the giant worm, the cannibal cult), it had landed in the outer regions of a doomed cluster of planets called Klaxonia. Klaxonia was once a prosperous and peaceful mini-empire. Then one year the Pope of their galaxy had paid an official visit and brought with him two slug-like creatures, each just a few feet long, which he said were a recent gift from a visiting explorer. Within a few days the creatures had doubled in size, then trebled, then trebled again. The Pope left quickly. A few days later the creatures had doubled in size yet again. By the time the experts gave their recommendation – that the pair be exterminated with all haste – the creatures had grown beyond the point where this would have been easy, and by the time a military force could be scrambled they were each as big as a mid-sized town, and the mid-sized town they had been sitting on was dust.

As we have seen from the experiences of the people of Diemendääs, a Sweety, even in the larval stage, can be terrifyingly destructive.

Within a year this breeding pair had taken over the Klaxon's entire home-world, and the survivors had fled to other nearby worlds. Calm took over, with the two species living as cautious neighbours. The two creatures, it seemed, were very happy together. They transformed, grew long, tentacle-like arms. They were observed sitting arm in arm on their new world, gazing out at the galaxy they now technically commanded.

And it would have continued like this, but for a still unexplained happening. No one knows how, or why, but one day the lady Sweety disappeared. Vanished. When Mr Sweety woke from his nap to find her gone his cries subdued the heavens. The Sweety began to search space with his long tentacles, and where his tentacles reached he left devastation. The Sweety, as I have mentioned, is attracted to the faintest vibration, the sound of a ship's horn, or the hum of an engine, or even an old man breaking wind, and when he hears it his instinct is to reach out for it. Overnight, the Klaxon Empire was devastated.

But it is amazing how life carries on. The Klaxons made adjustments. They took off their shoes, they spoke in whispers, they hand-sewed giant muffling gloves so that they could do simple tasks like open a tin can, or letter, or light a cigar, without making noise. Everything from pulling a cord on a lamp, to filling a water jug, creates a sound. And what happens when you have to fix a roof, or repair a road, or make a baby, or do any other noisy thing? And what about the things a person can't control? What about a hungry child, or a man who talks in his sleep? It was not uncommon in the early years for sleep-talking men to bring destruction on their city. And then there were the suiciders: those who were so utterly fed up with themselves, and society, that they would simply walk into a town square and yell, 'Take me now!' The Sweety always did. And what about absolutely unavoidable phenomena, such as rain hitting a roof, or a boulder rolling down a mountain pass? Well, unbelievable as it is, the Klaxons found solutions to all these problems, and many, many more. They created, in a few generations, from the ruins of their old, noisy society, an utterly silent one. They developed the galaxy's most sophisticated sign language (a language which incorporated not just their hands but every part of their body, even eyelashes). Their technicians invented silent drills and hammers, face-mufflers for toddlers and sleep-disorder sufferers, silent beds for the amorous. In fact, the birth rate climbed for the first few years. Danger, it turns out, is a powerful aphrodisiac.

After centuries of this, the Klaxons came to face the ultimate question: fight or flight? Now that they had managed to engineer powerful silent ships, should they evacuate their people to safer worlds, or stage an all-out war against the Sweety? An evacuation of all 789 billion citizens in their world-cluster would be unimaginably difficult and dangerous. And even if they could leave the district, where would they go? The planets in the region could not possibly accommodate the mass migration of their entire population. What if their migration caused a conflict of some kind? The noise from that could kill them all.

On the other hand, they would only get one chance to terminate the monster. And if they failed . . . well. They were a peaceful people, the Klaxons, and most had come to accept, even love, the Sweety, in all his slimy glory. He was representative of everything that was ugly and tragic about life. There were even protests in the streets of the capital of Klaxonia at the idea of attempting to destroy him. Silent ones.

But in the end it was accepted that a battle was the only way.

And so, the next few decades of Klaxon life were spent with two supreme goals in mind: 1. Assemble the most ferocious arsenal the galaxy has known. 2. Do it quietly.

The most powerful battle fleet ever seen was assembled around the edge of their territory, not far from the planet on which the Sweety lived. 276,000 heavily armed battleships waited for the order to initiate Operation: Deadly – Though Necessary, You Understand – Kill.

And that was when the *Necronaut* showed up.

*

This was the story as outlined (though in shorter form) for Descharge. He eased carefully back in his chair and put his fingers to his lips – his hosts winced. Then he sat forward again and whispered, 'I think I might have . . . another option.'

What Descharge suggested was delightful in its simplicity. 'We have at our disposal,' he whispered, 'a technology that allows a ship, or group of ships, to leave a universe silently, and to appear elsewhere. What we also have,' he said, 'is a walking boy-computer. He has the maps and secrets of the universes in his head. Granted, the technology isn't perfect, and it carries certain risks, but it would allow you to transport a large number of people with almost no risk of waking the Sweety. Our boy can operate the technology. And we would be happy to provide you with it, if you would be willing to give us the energy to power our engine, and to help us recover our shipmates from the belly of a giant worm.'

I do not want you to think that the rest was easy. It took some hours to explain the situation to Roberto (even with the rather elegant picture-talking machine the Klaxons had invented). It certainly took some time to convince him to take the pile of clattering diamonds from his pocket and put them in a soundproof packet. And it took some days to get a workable plan together, and it took some weeks to do the engineering work necessary to prepare an entire fleet for transport to another universe. But it was an opportunity for the crew to fatten themselves up again, and for Klaxon technicians to repair the *Necronaut* to a specification its crew could not have imagined. It was decided that a large and heavily armed exploratory fleet would make the jump, establish a base camp on a habitable world, with an aim to eventually bring the rest of their people through. The Sweety would be left behind to live in peace. It was such a wonderful plan that there were silent celebrations in the silent streets. When they made the jump to their new universe they found their quiet and near-invisible ships a great advantage. They sat silently until the Hex cleared. Then they slid silently behind the gleaming moon. Then they saw a small, crippled ship being pursued by fighters whose flanks bore the unmistakable insignia of the Pope.

STEAM

'You stupid woman! You nearly killed us!'

'But I did not! Now quickly.'

The Black Widow had flown them into the docking bay at high speed and into a pile of laundry. 'If it wasn't for that giant pile of man-knickers we'd have been killed and you know it.'

'Nonsense. You're being overdramatic.' She plucked a pair of man-knickers from the back of the old man's head and cast them aside. 'Now hurry, we haven't much time to save the girl.'

Or herself, she neglected to mention.

'I don't understand why you've suddenly changed sides, woman!'

'You old fool! How many times do I have to save your life before you realise I changed sides weeks ago?'

They ran on through dim, empty corridors lit only by emergency lighting. The evacuation of non-essential staff had been sounded and the bells still rang around the ship. The Black Widow led them through the narrow labyrinth without even pausing to check the way.

'How on earth do you know where you're going?'

'I don't know. I have the strangest sense of déjà vu. I feel as if I've been here before. The command centre will be this way, I'm sure.' Then, from the distance they heard a growing roar, like the sound of a waterfall. And then they heard a tremendous noise – *Kissssssss-Shoooommmmm!* – like the thunder of a giant tribal drum. As they turned into a long corridor they heard the noise again . . .

Kisssssss-Shoooommmmm!

. . . and they felt their bodies vibrate. 'I think perhaps this isn't the way we should be heading.'

'Nonsense!'

At the end of the corridor they went beneath an open iron fire door, burst through a set of chain-mail curtains, hit a wall of thick steam. It took them a few seconds to process what was happening. They found themselves pulling up inside a dim canyon – half a mile high, walled on one side by windows, and on the other by catwalks along which were spaced row upon row of thundering vacuum tubes, each big enough to take a large bundle of laundry. Down the centre of the room – which stretched to vanishing point – were twin rows of presses, each wide enough that you could lay a bed sheet across, and they all rose together in unison, like a gang of iron butterflies, and they fell together . . .

Kisssssss-Shoooommmmm!

. . . shaking the entire room and sending up heaping clouds of hellish steam.

'You foolish woman! This isn't the Pope's palace. You've landed us in the laundry ship!'

'But that's impossible. I was sure I –'

'I should have suspected with the man-knickers!' They heard the fire door slam shut behind them. 'We have been led like rats into the trap!'

Then through the silky mist a figure swam, tall and lean, like a ghost: a ghostly pale figure at an ironing board, tiny in the vast room, but giant, it seemed, in the eye. The figure led the iron smoothly around the contours of a perfectly white shirt.

'The thing about controlling the human mind,' said the figure, 'is it's a lot like ironing a shirt. First, the temperature has to be just right. Too hot and the material burns; too cold and there's no effect. You have to see the object not as a whole, but as a series of small parts which work together.'

Kisssssssss-Shoooommmmm!

'If you work across each part, smoothing out the wrinkles of perception, unfurrowing the fabric of experience, then you will be left with something truly beautiful. Something as blank and perfect as the formless void which exists at the birth of a universe, a new canvas on which you can paint your will.'

'It's that man again,' said Fabrigas.

The figure put down his iron and held the immaculately pressed shirt to the strange blue light of battle which sputtered in through the windows. 'But I could just iron for ever, you know? I could iron a thousand shirts and not grow tired of it. It does not seem like a mundane task to me, for such are the subtle differences in each shirt that each has its own nature. Sleep, woman!' The Black Widow slumped to the ground. 'She came here to try to kill me. Some people never learn. This is not exactly how I imagined things playing out,' said the figure, 'but one must adapt to circumstances.'

'What have you done with Lenore?' said the old man.

'What have *I* done with her? Old man, that girl has been sailing under her own steam. But she's safe for now.' The wall of small, square windows on one side of the great laundry room had become a flickering grid as the skirmishes at the edges of the Pope's fleet continued.

The Well Dressed Man put the shirt over his vested torso and buttoned it carefully. Then he tied his black silk tie and slipped the knot around his throat. Then he took an elegant, two-button jacket from a rack nearby, slithered into it, and stepped at last into the light. 'You know,' he said, 'in all my years as an assassin I have never killed a well-dressed person. Your cloak, if you please.'

I AM THE LORD OF CHAOS
& DESTRUCTION

The green-skinned demon-girl whose eyes were blue as gun metal and who smelled of roses (the thorns, not the petals) had arrived in a strange universe, on a small ship, frozen inside a block of ice, and now leaned calmly and attentively towards the voice who read her final judgement. She stood at the edge of the execution platform. The platform was separated from space by a thin bubble of life-giving gas, and from the death-bringing black hole by just a few million miles. Or thereabouts. Her features flickered madly in the pulsing light of battle, while the abyss itself was an invisible entity, perceivable only by the hazy coils of superheated gas which circled it as water gathers around a plughole. Pieces of debris were passing by at fantastic speeds, barely perceivable at the rate they moved. In fact, it was getting very dangerous to be out in the open. The judge, a portly man in golden cloak and silver wig, knew it, and he was hurrying through his proclamation. 'Child, you have been found guilty of . . . various things which I won't bother to elaborate on.' He flinched as the wing of a fighter craft sliced through the air bubble with a *pop* and whizzed above their heads. Seven huge men had been sent to guard her – heaven knows why – and they stood nearby. When the heavies arrived Lenore had caught a familiar scent and had barely stopped herself from crying out, 'It's you!'

'Don't worry, child,' said one of the hulks. It won't be long now.

You'll be down with the Dark Lord before you know it.'

'I'm not worried,' said Lenore. 'It should be you that's worried.'

A guard chuckled. 'And why exactly should we be worried?'

'Because,' said the green-skinned girl, 'I can smell your future.'

★

'You've already won,' said Fabrigas. 'You've got the girl. You got what you came all this way to find.'

The Well Dressed Man laughed drily. 'My dear idiot, she's not the one I've been hunting. How absurd.' He studied a nail.

'She isn't?'

'My dear, sweet fool, no. She was just a minor diversion. It's the boy. The *boy* is the file I was sent to delete. Oh, of course they want her dead as well, but the Router with the code to the Infiniverse in his head, he's the big deal. Not some green mini-goth with an unco-operative brain.'

'You never broke her.'

'And I never could. Not if I tried for a thousand years. But I got a taste of what's inside her mind, and that's enough. Now no one will be ready for my power. Especially not Electro the Wonder Boy. He'll be here soon, drawn like a moth to a beacon, and I'm sure his entrance will be *just* adorable. How about we kill a little time while we wait?' The Well Dressed Man led him back into the main room and over to a low table on which was draped a cloak, and in front of the cloak was laid the entire collection of the old man's instruments.

'I feel privileged to be one of the few to see the mysteries within the cloak of the mighty Fabrigas.' The Well Dressed Man touched a long finger to a brass reed.

Fabrigas stepped forward. 'Those things aren't for tampering with. Some of them are very dangerous.'

The Well Dressed Man let his eyelids flutter contemptuously.

'Frankly I'm disappointed. These seem like crude tools: a compass, a joy-buzzer, a starfish? Are you conquering the universe or putting on a magic show for children? My own mother used to say never trust a man who carries a starfish.'

'Did she?'

'She might have.'

'And just where is your mother?'

'Dead.'

'You may as well let us go. We still have time to escape this ship before it gets blown up.'

'Our Pope seems to be managing. And I have plenty of time to leave the ship. Well, enough chat. To business. I have been inconvenienced, and when I'm inconvenienced I get very . . . *killy*. Woman! Wake!' The Black Widow rose and stood on wobbling legs. 'Even with all your training you can't hide from me. Now, the wizard here is going to murder you. I've disabled the parts of your mind which tell you how to fight, but not the parts which tell you how to run. And scream. You have two minutes. You'll need every second. Off you pop.' The Black Widow looked to Fabrigas, who nodded twice, and when she saw the look in his eyes she turned and ran into the mist; they heard her boots on the ladder running up to the catwalks above.

While the Black Widow's two minutes elapsed the Well Dressed Man took Fabrigas over to the windows. From here they could see the battle unfolding in all its horrible magnificence. The Diemendääs fleet, thanks to the element of surprise, had done great damage to the Pope's outer defences. But the Pope had rallied, and the Fleet of the Nine Churches was raining heaven's-fire upon them, while preparing to outflank them with its mobile fleet. The Glory Hole lit the carnage from behind.

'No surprises here,' said the Well Dressed Man. 'These people aren't the first to underestimate the Pope's power. They'll wear themselves out on his forward defences. Then he'll send in the Wreckers and it'll all be over. And down there, look . . .' Beside them was the Pope's command palace, and from the palace stretched a long, narrow walkway, and at the end of the walkway was a platform in the middle of which stood a small girl surrounded by priests. 'If they miraculously manage to penetrate the Pope's defences she'll be destroyed. If not she'll be thrown into the black hole. That's that big swirly thing over there. I have to say, this is all working out near-perfectly. For me. From the very beginning all I wanted was . . . Old thing, are you quite all right?'

Fabrigas had turned a shade of green. His knees shuddered and he slumped, then rose again. 'I am . . . quite fine enough, thank you well for asking.'

'Why are you talking like that? Are you having a stroke?'

'What? This is just my natural voice. Absolutely.'

'Hmmmm. Well, that's two minutes anyway. Time for death. Try to stall yours till after hers if possible.' The Well Dressed Man strolled back to Fabrigas's possessions and swept his thin right hand along the row of instruments on the table. 'I'm sure you have enough to work with here.' There was a dart-gun whose poison-tipped needles could seek the body heat of their victim. There was a nerve-gas grenade, and a lovely set of knives. 'I like nothing more than a clean, fresh knife.' The Well Dressed Man held a blade to the light and admired the way the beads of steam water gathered along its deadly edge. 'Magic. Of course we'll need to eliminate the fake one. Which is . . . ?'

'There is no fake knife,' snapped Fabrigas. But his face grimaced as he strained to stop his hand from moving across, his long index finger extending to point at the knife upon the table. 'Good, then we won't be needing that.' The Well Dressed Man tossed the fake over his shoulder and tested the knife he'd been holding against his palm before handing it to Fabrigas. 'You need to work harder on your misdirection, old man. Not to worry. Show must go on.' He turned back to the misty room and said, 'Dray! Turn on your lamps, prepare to roll camera.'

Fabrigas heard a familiar *chank* and suddenly the dazzling blaze outside was overcome by the hard, steady light of Dray's cine lamps shining from the catwalks above. Fabrigas shielded his eyes against the glare and saw the unmistakable silhouette through the mist. 'Dr Dray! What are you doing up there?' Dray gave no reply, but the Well Dressed Man said, 'Oh, I found him below and couldn't resist inviting him along. We just *had* to record this night for posterity. What good is a grand finale if nobody gets to see it?'

Kisssssssss-Shoooommmmm!

'Now. Why don't you put on your magical, murderous cloak and we'll do some hunting?'

SOUNDS OF SILENCE

It is a fact of human life, if not *the* fact of human life, that things seem hopeless until they're not.

'Prince Panduke,' said General Spatz, 'the Pope has regained the upper hand. Our advanced attack has been routed. We should consider falling back to a defensive position.' From the bridge of the command ship the Pope's firepower seemed close enough to boil the liquid from their eyes.

'We can't allow them a tactical position above the city again!' said Panduke, who everyone agreed had grown several feet that day, even while his city had lost a few hundred. 'Prepare to regroup!'

'It is hopeless, Your Highness. He will crush us in minutes. We should negotiate a surrender. The Pope may still show us some mercy.'

'No chance,' said Kimmy. 'That man is a nutcase.'

'Sir,' said the radar operator, 'there's something new on our scope. Something rather big.'

And it was. Something unbelievably huge and swift was drifting silently across their scopes. From behind the ravenous moon of Bespophus, where the mighty jungle gnashed, came a stream of black shapes, barely visible until they passed across the whorl of dying light around the new black hole, and then their features came to light, their smooth, black hulls, their many, many guns. They covered the distance to the battle at a breathtaking speed, and fanned out behind the Diemendääs ships.

'Friends or enemies?' cried the heavy-fleet commander.

As if in answer, the mystery fleet released a silent stream of fire. It passed over the startled heads of the Diemendääs pilots, casually parted the Pope's forward defences, and smashed into the ranks of the papal fleet, setting off a chain of sun-bright explosions.

'I think . . .' ventured Panduke, '. . . friends?'

*

The Klaxons, during their time in silent exile, had built some frightening and fascinating weapons. They had managed to build (ironically) a sonic weapon which sends rippling beams of sound to shake the enemy to pieces. Also, a fear-seeking rocket which is inversely attracted to a ship according to the bravery of the crew. They had worked feverishly to prepare their arsenal for the Sweety, but now that a substitute enemy had been presented – a Pope, no less, and heavens knew they despised their own Pope – they were able to throw the full weight of their fury against it, and the effect was stunning. Almost immediately, the Pope's forward lines crumbled and he was forced to fall back even further towards the Glory Hole. Now the giant engines of the palaces were working frantically to keep them from sliding into oblivion. 'Where did those new people come from?' the Pope said. He was back in his bath now, observing the frantic activity on the bridge through slitted eyes.

'We don't know, but they are very powerful,' said Mothersbaugh.

'Well, they will learn not to mess with me. Did you send in the wreckers?'

'Yes, I sent in the wreckers. Now, if you don't mind, Holiness, I am *slightly* busy.'

He'd never raised his voice to the Pope. No one had. He took a quick glance over his shoulder to where the Pope, with a large red ship in his right hand, wore his upper lip behind his lower. 'I'm the Pope,' he said.

'Yes,' said Mothersbaugh. 'Yes, you are.'

The wreckers are a fearsome sight: unspeakably massive spheres of blackened steel with spinning blades around their circumference. When they spin, the diamond-coated blades become a blur of destruction. The effect is like being attacked by a gang of angry young moons. Whole fleets had been sliced to pieces by these weapons. But Descharge, standing on the operations deck beside the Klaxon commander, felt that the Pope's command had made a tactical blunder.

'They've had to stand down their forward guard to make room for the wreckers. Send your compact fighters through the gaps between the blades.'

The *Necronaut* was already ahead of all of them. Descharge had removed himself to the bridge of the Klaxon command ship where he could be of most use. Now he saw the small, familiar shape of his old ship streak towards the enemy lines. 'What is that fool boy doing?!' But he already knew exactly what the *Necronaut*'s new pilot, Roberto, was doing. He was going to rescue his friend.

Stupid boy.

★

'I wish you would not be so impulsive, boy!' said Fabrigas Two. When he had ditched his crippled craft and climbed aboard the *Necronaut* he was surprised to find it being piloted by a lone boy. The remaining sailors and slaveys had all opted to abandon it for the comfort and safety of the Klaxon cruisers. Only Roberto had refused to leave, and now he sent the craft skidding over the frightening blue disc of a wrecker. But where to find his friend in all this mayhem? As he flung the ship through a gap between the spinning balls and left the wreckers behind he found a zone of calm filled with smoking remnants. He had travelled through dimensions to find his friend, and now he didn't know where to go. He had the map to the entire

Omniverse inside his head, but there was nothing in his head to tell him exactly where his little green companion was. He closed his eyes, searching the darkness for a clue – just as Dark Hand had taught him to do. He searched his subconscious for details of the papal fleet, their prisoner management systems, their justice and execution protocols. He cut the whole fleet down to just a few possible places she could be. Then he saw her. In his mind he saw Lenore standing in space, but not *in* space. He saw her standing on the platform, and when he opened his eyes, there it was. He saw a palace, and from the palace stretched a slender thread, and at the end of the thread was a platform. She stood like a bright chunk of flesh on the end of a hook. Roberto pressed his hands against the windows of the *Necronaut* and cried out; it was a cry straight from his soul. 'Don't fear, boy,' cried F2. 'We'll rescue your little friend,' but when he turned again the boy was gone.

*

Lenore was running out of time.

'And now, by the power invested in me by – gah!' A fuel tank bounced off the platform deck with a ringing *tong-ong-ong*, then flew off in the direction of the hole, and the judge suddenly forgot what he was doing. 'I pronounce you ready to die. You may now kiss the . . . sky.' There was a rocket's roar as another piece of debris punched through the bubble, only this one didn't hurtle on towards the abyss, this one pulled up and landed in a cloud of purple steam. Lenore caught the scent and cried, 'Roberto!' Roberto shrugged off the emergency jet packs, looked around the deck at the gang of heavily muscled papal goons, then held up a hand, shrouded in blue energy, and spoke, in a voice he hadn't used in years. It was a breathy, husky slip of a voice, from a small, scruffy slip of a boy. He said, 'I am Roberto, and I am here to kill you all.'

The guards roared.

'It's kill or be killed here,' laughed the judge as a large gas cylinder caromed off the deck. 'Right then. I'm off.' He straightened his wig. 'Throw them in the black hole. But butcher them with your knives as well, will you? Can't be too careful.' And he trotted back down the catwalk on his fat little legs.

'Oh, we will,' called a guard. 'It'll be our pleasure.' They each drew a long knife from their cassocks.

'Well, Roberto, even though you can't hear me, I'm happy you came back to rescue me. I wish you could only buy me a few minutes. I'm trying to speak with someone. With my *mind*.'

As the guards came grinning towards him Roberto raised his hand, arcing blue, and sent a bolt of energy into the chest of the nearest guard who went skidding back with a grunt. As two more guards rushed him the boy thrust his free hand into his pocket, removed a small packet, and sent a haze of silver sparks across the shiny deck. When the guards trod on the diamonds with their heavy boots they found their legs flying out from beneath them.

'Good work, Roberto,' said Lenore. 'Just another minute, please.' But more guards were circling and the boy was almost out of tricks. That's when the children each felt a giant hand upon their shoulders. Roberto spun round, ready to deliver a blue bolt of death, and froze in amazement.

'Welcome back, my friend,' said Lenore.

The possessor of the giant hands leaned down and whispered in her ear, 'Hello, little peach. You'll have all the time you need. At least if I'm to have a say.'

MY MASTER THE MONSTER

Of course, you know that when a person is close to death – as so many of our friends are right now – the events of their life flash through their mind at a phenomenal speed. It happens as their mind scans its database for information, playing their life back like a high-speed cine play, searching among the flickering moments for an experience that might offer a way out of their predicament. Can you imagine what that's like for Roberto, whose mind was filled with a universe of information? Or for Bosun Quickhatch, whose memories from birth to death were mostly, though not entirely, terrifying?

Jacob Quickhatch had been grabbed around the legs by the Makatax and tossed against the cave wall like a broken puppet. He'd woken on his back in the monster's den, astonished to find he'd not yet been eaten. He'd watched red shadows sway drunkenly on the walls. He'd quickly pieced together the events of the past few hours: the cannibals, the slide, the all-too-brief encounter with the Makatax. He'd known he didn't have much time; monsters seldom leave their den for long. He'd heard a voice: 'Go back. Go back on the pile. There's a good thing. Back on the pile. With the bones and worms. My Master Makatax will soon return.' Bones, worms, he'd felt them wriggling under his back, the fat, maggoty worms. The smell was fierce, the kind so bad that you can taste it. 'It's a miracle you survived.' The voice, high-pitched and dull. 'No one has ever survived his attention. But you're hurt badly.' The red glow-worms hung in clumps, they shone like coals. He had tried to lift his head. Pain. Nearby he'd seen Albert the Worm lying, eyes open, neck at a whimsical angle. Jacob had struggled to all fours, wobbled, heard a laugh from the shadows. 'Don't try to move or I'll call my master the monster. He comes when I call.'

So that was who the voice belonged to: the monster's servant. Helping the beast in return for treasures pilfered from victims, perhaps. 'If you help me escape I'll give you a treasure,' said the bosun. It hurt to speak. 'It's true silver.'

'I am sure it is!' said the voice in the shadows. Quickhatch saw a gleaming moon swinging in the dimness. 'I stole your watch while you were sleeping. You have nothing to bargain with, giant.'

'That is not the treasure I was speaking of, devil. That is the watch my father gave me. It is more precious to me than anything in the universe, but worthless to you. It isn't even true silver.' The bosun dangled a sacred silver circle on its chain in his bloody, trembling fingers. 'But this is.'

'What is that?' the voice had said. 'What have you hid from me?'

'It's a Holy Circle, given me by the Pope the day I joined his guards. It's silver from the Church's mines – the purest there is.' A circle: because in life all paths lead back to the Pope. 'This object, and anyone who has it, is blessed.'

'You are a priest?'

'I was drafted. But I escaped.'

'Lie! No one escapes the Pope's mercies.'

'I did, after they went to pillage my home. They burned our villages, killed many of my old friends. So I escaped. I escaped and went off into space alone. And the Pope, you'll find, has no mercy.'

Silence. The bosun waited. He could see two glinting eyes in the darkness, moving back and forward in time with the swinging silver circle.

'Give it me then,' said the voice.

'I'll swap it for the watch and the way out. It's a good trade. The watch has only sentimental value. Show me the way out and I'll give it you.'

'But my master will be angry. He is already furious you stole those children from him. That is why he's gone away to brood.' The voice was moving around the clearing, thinking, pondering. 'I could take the circle.'

'Come close and see if you can take it.'

'I can wait for the master to kill you.'

'I'll swallow it, the beast swallows me, the circle is vanished.'

Silence.

'Show me the path. Then the circle is yours. You can have the prize and your master's love.'

'He loves no one. Except inside his belly.'

'It's true, but what can you do? We serve who we serve.'

Silence for a while. Then, 'Even if I show you the way out of my master's caves you'll still be in too deep. This whole world is a monster. I know it! I came from the outside. And the Makatax is just a gnat compared to the worm we live within. There's no hope for you. Foolish giant!'

'There's always hope.' By now Jacob's eyes had adjusted, and his accomplice had come shyly from out of the shadows. He could see that he was a very small man who spoke with a fine voice – or an average-sized girl who spoke with a normal voice, perhaps. Yes. She had a slender shape, doleful eyes. 'The way out is impossible, giant. You're better off here. Perhaps I can look after you, my enormous friend. Yes.' The eyes of this creature were big, black, imploring.

'Show me a way out and I'll give you the circle.'

The eyes blinked twice, retreated into the shadows.

*

Jacob Quickhatch fashioned himself a crude crutch from a branch. He felt his brain clouding with the smell of rotting flesh, and every crutch-step the pain grew worse. But he never minded pain. What disturbed him was the raw, intestinal darkness he was walking into as he set off through the caves of the Makatax, searching for the way out. 'Wait, where are you going, giant? You'll be lost if you go that way.' The monster's servant was following behind. 'You're doing it all wrong.'

'Then show me the way and you'll get your treasure.'

'It's this way, fool, you're going to hell that way.'

'Don't try to trick me. I smell fresher air this way. This is the way I came in.'

'Yes, the way you came in, but ho! What! You want to go back to the cannibals, the giant slugs? To get out from the great worm you must go deeper. You can only escape through the back passage. Come, I will do it for your silver circle, and perhaps . . . a kiss.' Jacob hesitated. In the dimness he saw now that his companion wore a white apron, of sorts, a little like a surgeon or a butcher, and it was stained with blood, and she had furry skin, and floppy ears like a rabbit – could that be right? His mind could be playing tricks.

'What? Are you afraid? Come, come!' said the creature. She stood trembling at the junction of the tunnel leading back into the domain of the Makatax. Over the apron she wore coat-tails – surely – and she skipped away, saying, 'Come on, come on, you're not dreaming this, the Makatax is coming.'

On cue, they heard the monster. His throaty roar came barrelling down the tunnels and made Jacob's eyeballs tremble.

'He is returning! Too soon! We must hurry! The back passage isn't far.'

Hobbling and hopping after his tiny guide, Jacob swallowed his fear and reasoned that this strange nightmare could only end in death or waking. 'You're getting weak, giant. Give me the circle now – for keeping!'

'No!' Jacob's throat was raw. He needed water, medicine, rest; he felt blood oozing at his side. 'How much further?'

'Right here. The back passage. It is the passage which leads to the world outside. Now give me your circle.'

'You've led me to a trap.'

'No, no, use your brain. Feel that new air rushing up. That is the outside. You only need to crawl towards the light. It is risky. You might drown in the waste fluids, or be crushed by the walls of the beast's bowels. And it won't be an easy landing when you get outside, but it's better than in here, no? The treasure?'

'My watch.'

'No watch. You can't have the watch. Your life is plenty. The circle, or I'll cry out. And, perhaps, my kiss.' The beast roared, closer. 'Hurry now.'

'I will put the circle upon the end of my crutch. Then pass it to you.' The bosun began to fuss about his stick.

'What's taking you so long? Just hang it from the end. Can't you hear my husband coming?!'

Husband?

'It is slimy with blood – the talisman won't stay,' the bosun said as he rushed to fashion the snare from the reed he'd pulled from the ground, leaning over his work so the creature wouldn't see. 'Here, it's done.' He held out the stick with the talisman hanging from the end, saw her hesitate.

'It's a trick. You're trying to make me grab it, then you'll have me.'

'No trick. Don't you want the silver?' He saw the rabbit grind her teeth, then lunge forward to make the grab, then howl, 'I'm caught! I'm caught! Husband, help!' The beast roared from back down the tunnels. He was just a few bends away now. Jacob drew his prey close, took her by the throat. 'You are caught in a snare. The more you struggle the tighter it gets. See?' He raised the creature's skinny wrist towards her button nose to show the trick. He had one hand around her neck. 'Let's not have any more yelling. My watch.'

'Here, here, take the watch, just please release me!'

'Why certainly.' The giant broke the snare with a finger. Then he put another finger beneath her chin and lifted her to eye level, so close their lips were almost touching, and her whiskers, twitching madly with fear, were tickling at his face. 'I could snap your neck now. But I won't. It's clear you're already in hell.' Then Jacob Quickhatch kissed her softly; her whiskers slackened. Then he snatched his watch up sharply in his fingers and hobbled away.

'Your talisman, giant!' The circle lay on the ground by the creature's feet.

'You keep it. It means nothing to me,' said the bosun as he flung his battered frame into the oozy passage.

★

Jacob Quickhatch had fallen down through the passage, been nearly crushed by the muscled walls which pressed together tight in places, nearly drowned swimming through bladders filled with rancid liquids, finally come out the end of the giant worm's slimy back passage in a slurry of half-decomposed matter and into a jungle flattened beneath the beast's bulk. He'd been stunned by the sudden brightness of this new world. He'd watched in amazement as the monster rode on towards a gleaming city near some mountains in the distance. The rabbit lady had been right: the Makatax was a gnat compared to this monster. He'd lain there, unable to move, for half a day. He was stumbled over by a jungle tribe hunting smaller serpents drawn to the surface by the vibrations of the giant worm. (The hunters were surprised to see him. They thought he was a baby god laid by the worm.) They'd taken him to their village, nursed him, tended to his injuries, tested their medicine by making him fight their strongest warrior. Then, convinced that he was at least a quarter god, they'd agreed to guide him to the city. Once at the battlements, Jacob had disguised himself as a washerwoman and entered the city of Diemendääs through the eastern gate. He had witnessed the occupation of the city, the plight of his friends. He'd knocked out a papal guard, stolen his clothes, made his way aboard the ships he had worked so hard to escape. If you could talk to Jacob Quickhatch – and sadly you cannot – he'd tell you kindly, but firmly, that there is not an ounce of bravery in standing up for the weak. He'd stood among the beasts he hated most – far more than any flesh-eating plants, or worm-loving ogre – as they boasted about how they would slit and gut this small green girl and her mute friend as though they were fishies in the sea. Then, when the time was right, he'd stepped forward and raised his great fists for his friends, and for true good.

GIANT

'Come on then!' said the bosun. 'Let's see if your gods are home!'

The priests fell upon him, black arms swinging. 'Is that all you have?' cried the bosun as he took a punch from a priest. 'You punch like a small girl. No offence, little one.'

Lenore said nothing. She was lost in a kind of trance. She had managed to reach a friend, one who had something which belonged to her. She was running through the dark corridors, through clouds of acrid steam. The bosun threw off a pair of priests and hit the third with a single blow that sent him skidding over the deck. 'Give me everything you've got! Can none of you fight?'

'Fight?' said another priest as he picked up a length of steel from the deck. 'Well, see how you fight with your skull spli—' *Klang!* The priest was collected by the flaming engine of a fighter craft and taken spinning into the Glory Hole. Two more guards crabbed forward. Cautiously.

'How goes it, little one?' said the bosun as he smashed a priest with each of his fists.

He took a quick glance up at the girl, and quickly stole another. Lenore was now enveloped in a sparkling blue electric haze. The bosun saw a chunk of metal glance off it. He traced the source of the energy from the haze, down a thin tendril, to Roberto. The boy was over at a maintenance panel on the deck of the platform. He was trying to divert enough power to the engines to stop the palace

581

from sliding into the black hole while also keeping magnetic bubbles around himself and his friend. A guard raised a steel bar and brought it down on Roberto's bubble, but it bounced off as if it were made of rubber and the guard went stumbling back.

A great fist struck Jacob in the jaw. A steel bar landed on his broad shoulders and dropped him to all fours, then a rain of kicks and punches fell upon him.

Lenore caught a whiff of his blood and terror, woke briefly from her trance to say: 'Bosun! What is happening? Are you hurt?'

'Not me, lovely,' said the bosun before the breath was kicked from his lungs. His arms quaked as he drew breath. 'This is a Sunday walk for me, my sweet, my pretty green treat.'

'So you side with devils instead of us,' said a guard. 'You'll answer for that in hell.'

Jacob took another steely blow across his back, fell to the floor and felt the blood trickle from his nose.

The terrible blows continued before finally the Pope's goons, thinking the watchmaker's son finally dead, stepped back and threw away their steel bars, clapped each other on the shoulder and roared with laughter. 'Let's kill the children and be done,' said one. 'I have me a powerful thirst.'

They were most surprised when their opponent shook the stars from his head, and lifted his giant frame to its feet. 'Now, if we've finished play-fighting,' said the watchmaker's son, 'I'll show you how a real man conducts himself.'

HUNTER

It would be fair to say that the Black Widow had not met many adversaries as worthy as Fabrigas. She had faced a pantheon of great assassins: the Eel, a contortionist who could twist his way down narrow pipes and attack his victims while they sat on the toilet; the Meccanaught, who had an encyclopedic knowledge of every martial art devised, even the silly ones. She'd killed them all. But Fabrigas understood, from his observations of the natural world, that timing was the art of hunting. He had the patience of a super-alligator, the eyes of a night-hawk, the ears of a Sweety. He trod the iron planks, eyes gleaming in the misty gloom. Beside him, the powerful vacuum tubes roared, and his beard rose and sank as he passed each one. By day the catwalks would have been full of stooped figures hurling bails of linen into the tubes. *Swish – Klang!* An iron bar used for poking stubborn bails flashed lazily past the old man's nose and hit the iron railing; sparks flew. Laughter floated up from below: 'Careful, she has a pole!' The Black Widow had ditched her boots so she could move in silence. The old man saw her shadow quiver across the iron rails and he raised the dart tube to his lips, aiming a few yards in front of her. They heard a yelp from the darkness. 'A singing dart, how *very* dull. If you really want to know where she is I can tell you.' And from the darkness above, Fabrigas heard the slap of a hand upon a cheek, followed by a thin yelp.

'Now find her, kill her, make me proud!'

As the dart's weird toxin took effect they heard her sing, involuntarily, in a high clear voice,

'Bridegroom, dear to my heart,
Goodly is your beauty, honeysweet.

Lion, dear to my heart,
Goodly is your beauty, honeysweet.'

Fabrigas found her in a bay for linen carts; he picked up her song, then her scent: a mix of expensive hand cream, manly shampoo and leather. He saw her wide eyes shining like ponds in the darkness where she cradled her song, and when she sprang for the edge of the platform the old man shot out an arm, caught her hair and dragged her back to the deck. There she lay, quivering like a sparrow, saying, 'No, my friend, no, no, no. Please, you don't want to.' Laughter drifted from the darkness below; the Well Dressed Man rose slowly up on a laundry lift, Dray and his camera beside him. 'Yes, yes, he does want to. He wants to murder you, O beautiful assistant,' said the assassin. 'What good is a magic show without the mortal blow?' Then in the glare of the cine lamps, within the rolling volleys of fiery light through the windows, the old man took her by the throat and raised her effortlessly to face him.

'Oh no, friend. You can't . . . you don't . . .' She spoke in a strangled voice.

'You do, old man. Remember how she betrayed you. Remember how you trusted her.'

Outside, the void was a whirlpool of fire and debris.

'Kill her,' said the Well Dressed Man. 'Give the dagger to her heart.'

Fabrigas held the Black Widow in one great hand. She hung like a rat in the talons of a weary old eagle. He had the knife in his left hand. The real knife. Do not think it could be any other way. Don't

584

let your mind consider any other possibility. Outside, the battle was coming to a terrible climax. There was a bright flash as a battle station flared and crumbled. The old man's eyes flared too, and his brow split and twisted like the bark of an old, old tree. And then, as another great ship gave way outside, crumpled like a paper lantern and soaked the features of our fighting figures in terminal light, outshining for a second even the hard glow of cine lamps, he said a word that could not be heard by anyone and plunged the knife into the Black Widow's chest.

'Fabrigas!' The Black Widow sighed as the tears bubbled in the cauldron of her eyes, and were drawn across her cheek by the vacuum force of the laundry tubes, and, 'Fabrigas,' she whispered one last time, the word catching like a dry leaf in her throat, and, 'No,' she said with her final, trembling breath. The old man, expressionless, withdrew the knife and let it fall to the ground with a ka-sklatter, leaned down towards her, his face dwarfing hers, then he let her fall too. She crumpled upon the iron floor.

Outside, the Fleet of the Nine Churches announced its counter-attack with a subsonic blast from its horns so powerful that some of the damaged ships fell clean to pieces; the Diemendääs commanders gasped as the steel parts slowly separated like a handful of leaves dumped upon the black still surface of a pond.

On the platform by the Glory Hole the fighting stopped briefly, and all the people on it raised their eyes to the skies.

'Oh dear,' said the Well Dressed Man from the shadows, 'that sounds like the siren of death for you and your friends. Such a pity.'

Then, from the depths came a response. Initially it seemed to be an echo of the Pope's siren call bouncing and returning from the planet, but it soon grew much louder, and much, *much* deeper, and when the pressure wave arrived it was a wall of power and fury, popping sails, extinguishing fires, taking the air from lungs, stopping the entire battle in its track.

The galaxies seemed to hold their breath.

'What . . . in the Holy Sea . . . was that?' said the Pope in his bath, and as if to answer him a curling black shape came from the depths, a tentacle uncoiled from the darkness, passing over the Klaxon fleet, lightly brushing aside the wall of wreckers as it slammed into the battle station from which the papal siren call had come, smashing it apart like a piñata, reducing it in a few seconds to a merrily twinkling cloud of rubble. The explosion was so huge, so bright, that every pilot turned away. Only the Pope kept his eyes wide open and fixed upon the merrily disintegrating castle.

There was a pause of a good minute before the Klaxon commander turned to Descharge, wrinkled his nose and whispered, 'I think the Sweety might have followed us through.'

I AM, I AM THE TALISMAN

Fabrigas stood enchanted as he watched the vanishing cloud of dust and debris that used to be the battle station. There was a shape emerging from the darkness now, dwarfing the planet, the moon and the assembled fleets. The creature swam towards them, a greenish blob with hazy edges. Its cry shook the heavens.

The Well Dressed Man, too, emerged from the shadows, alarmed to no longer be the most terrifying monster in the universe. 'Well, there is something I didn't expect. Time to go, I think. That was certainly quite a show, though.' The explorer turned to face him and the assassin took a small step back, suddenly alarmed by the way the old explorer towered over him, the calm fire in his eyes. 'OK. Give me the knife now, handle first, there's a good man.' Fabrigas stooped to pick the blade up from the floor. He held it up to the light and the Well Dressed Man squinted. 'No blood. Well, how on earth could . . . ? Impossible!'

Fabrigas pressed his finger to the tip of the knife and said, 'Not unpossible, sir, quite possible indeed, in fact.' There was a mousy squeak as the blade descended. The Well Dressed Man let his disbelieving eyes move slowly from the tip of the knife to the old man's face. Then he said a single word. It was the worst insult he could possibly have thought to call the old explorer, but this time the ancient face showed no signs of anger.

'You should not call him a wizard,' said Fabrigas. 'My friend the master does not like it when people say that word to him. Just as Carrofax does not like it when you call him demon. And I do not like it when you call me Little Monster.'

'You!' cried the Well Dressed Man.

The old man laughed girlishly, and curtsied. 'Yes, I have taken this old fool's mind so I could stop your plan. For I am rather fond of him. You have taught me very well, I think. And for that, I and him are most grateful.'

'But then where is the real . . .' The assassin felt the force of the blade passing between his ribs and gently tickling his heart. He stared into the old man's eyes with unguarded amazement as the Black Widow appeared behind him, kissed his cheek and said, 'I have it, Daniel.'

'I don't understand how –'

'Did you really think your parley games would work upon him?' the old man said. 'He is Fabrigas. He is my friend. He has the biggest brain the universe has made. Also, these two have the box with my captain in it. And I want him to bring it to me. Now be a sweetie and die.'

It is a truth that when the pale man can turn no paler he turns blue. The Well Dressed Man turned blue, then purple. He walked serenely away and leaned upon the catwalk rail. He looked out through the windows to where the greatest space battle the universe, perhaps any universe, had ever seen was reaching its dramatic climax. He saw a long, lean tentacle reach from the blackness and flick away a battle station as though it was a piece of dust on the arm of a fine coat. He let out a heavy breath.

The beautiful assistant turned to face her magician and said, 'Is it really you in there, Lenore?'

'Of course,' the magician replied. 'Now I think you have something which belongs to me. I need it very badly.'

'I'm worried what might happen if I give this to you.'

'You do not need to think about that. That isn't your concern. I need to feel like I have something in the universe. You know how it is.'

The beautiful assistant nodded. She took the small black box from her top and handed it to him.

'Thank you. I forgive you for kissing his face.'

The Black Widow looked at her Lasiotek Magnesium Chronograph wristwatch. 'I only have a few minutes left,' she said. 'Please tell this old fool that I'll miss him. And I'm sorry I said his stories were boring.'

'I will.'

The Black Widow nodded once, then threw herself into the black hole of the nearest laundry tube. The vacuum force took her flying away.

The old man woke from his dream to see the Well Dressed Man leaning on the rail, staring out at the battle. A red blossom had been left for him on the back of the Well Dressed Man's well-pressed shirt. He looked down at the discarded knives on the floor, furiously trying to piece together the past few minutes.

'Yes, she is a wonder,' said the Well Dressed Man. 'She pulled a veil over my eyes. Made me think I'd thrown away the fake knife when I'd really thrown away . . . well, who knows what it was.'

'It was a silver spoon,' said Dray from the shadows.

'Ah yes. You know, I was only doing the thing I love, the thing I was born to do. Some make shoes, some bake pies, I control minds. Could I do any different?'

'No,' said Fabrigas as he turned the black box over in his hands. 'We all do what we're made to do.'

Outside the windows and far away the tiny girl was still enveloped in a bubble of blue light. The Well Dressed Man turned and smiled. 'Old man,' he said, 'despite what I've been compelled to do, I have to say, it was the highest privilege to meet you.' Then he turned back to the fire. There could have been a glass of brandy in his hand. His pale face was caught perfectly in the flames of the burning warships. 'Do get her home, won't you?'

'I'll do my best.'

And with that the immaculately dressed assassin fell gently over the rail, his buttons clinking on the iron. Fabrigas never heard his body hit the flattened steel. *Kisssssssss-Shoooommmmm!*

Dray stepped from the shadows. 'Well, I don't know about "biggest brain in the universe",' he said, 'but well done anyway. How did you do it? Special earplugs? Foil hat?'

'To be perfectly honest,' said Fabrigas, 'I'm not entirely sure. I think I might have been temporarily possessed.'

'Typical,' muttered Dray. 'Anyway, old cock, I should probably get back down to the city and find my wife. Nice to meet you. Mind how you go.'

And off he wandered into the mist.

'Yes, I must head off too,' said Fabrigas as he looked over the rail to the steam press below. 'I'm rather . . . pressed . . . for time.' And he was sad that there was no one there to hear him.

*

'Get them! Kill them!' screamed the Pope. He screamed those words towards the closing doors of the command centre as he was led quickly, by Cardinal Mothersbaugh, towards his evacuation ship.

'I want them all dead, and their monster too!'

'Yes, of course,' said Mothersbaugh, 'but we really must get you to your escape ship, Holiness, before the monster strikes again.'

Outside, the Sweety *had* struck again. He'd sent another tentacle smashing through the heart of a planet-sized storage ship. Now the papal fleet had turned all its guns upon the furious beast, but the blows were as mosquito bites upon the haunch of an elephant. Meanwhile, the Klaxon fleet continued to surge like blood through the gaping holes in the Pope's defences, and the Diemendääs fleet received the order to fall back to safety – wherever that was. The eternal night of space was lit so brightly now that it seemed as if a